I0750208

LIBBY TANNER

Bigger than Versace

Bigger than Versace

FALLING IN LOVE NEVER GOES OUT OF STYLE

LIBBY TANNER

CITY OWL
PRESS

This book is a work of fiction. Names, characters, places, and incidents either are products of the author's imagination or are used fictitiously. Any resemblance to actual events or locales or persons, living or dead, is entirely coincidental and not intended by the author.

BIGGER THAN VERSACE
Falling in Love Never Goes Out of Style

CITY OWL PRESS
www.cityowlpress.com

All rights reserved. Except as permitted under the U.S. Copyright Act of 1976 and applicable international copyright laws, no part of this publication may be reproduced, distributed, transmitted, displayed, stored, scraped, mined, or otherwise used in any form or by any means, whether now known or hereafter devised, including for the training or operation of artificial intelligence or machine learning systems, without the prior written permission of the publisher.

Copyright © 2026 by Libby Tanner.

Cover Design by MiblArt. All stock photos licensed appropriately.

Edited by Tee Tate.

For information on subsidiary rights, please contact the publisher at info@cityowlpress.com.

Print Edition ISBN: 978-1-64898-548-5

Digital Edition ISBN: 978-1-64898-549-2

To Christie Tanner -- thanks for that time you birthed me, and for every moment of love and encouragement since. Your support feels bigger than Versace. And those guys are huge.

Chapter One

This is the worst.

The autumn breeze has gone from pleasant to annoying and carries the sharp scent of car exhaust and wet dirt. Tiny cars rattle past like wind-up toys as I stare at the building in front of me.

Marco Rossi, 36 Via Marmocchi Apt 3C, Milan, Italy.

The address on my phone matches the large black letters by the door. Just like every other building here, it's old. Tall trees with rust-colored leaves block most of the sun's feeble rays, their branches casting crooked shadows over the uneven cobblestones.

Of all the stupid things I've been forced to do, including taking family pictures dressed in matching plaids, I hate this the most.

I fish my lipstick out of my purse and apply a healthy dose of Dior's Red Royalty, then snap my compact shut with a clap. There's not a lot to do at this point, so I march over to the glass door of the apartment building and hit the buzzer for 3C.

Static crackles through the speaker, followed by a muffled, *"Pronto,"* like someone speaking through a mouthful of cotton.

"*Ciao,* this is Lydia St. Clair, your new nanny."

Just saying the words out loud sounds wrong. It's like saying Danny DeVito, the new *Vogue* cover model.

"*Ciao,* Lydia!" an excited voice responds. "We're so glad you're here! Do you need help with your luggage?"

"No, thank you. I'll be right up."

There's a buzz and a green light, and I push through the heavy door into the lobby. The heels of my Jimmy Choo boots tap against the white marble floor as I head to the elevator. Marco offered to pick me up at the airport, like I was a child, but I told him I could find the apartment just fine.

The ridiculously small elevator groans as it hauls me and my Louis Vuitton carry-on upward. Scratched gold mirrors line the walls, and the young woman staring back at me, while objectively gorgeous, looks furious.

I take a breath and school my expression into something less homicidal. The metal floor vibrates under my heels as the elevator pauses and gasps like an old man climbing stairs. The smell of someone's last cigarette lingers.

When I come to a shuddering halt on the third floor, the door to 3C is already open and a man, woman, and child stand in the doorway.

The woman is exquisite, with perfect olive skin and sleek brown hair that gleams in the dim hallway light. If I'm not mistaken, she's wearing a vintage Chanel blazer—cream with black piping. The man is short and chubby. His wildly curly hair and flushed cheeks make him look like a clown with a drinking problem.

Clearly, his wife didn't marry him for his looks. Or, judging by this solidly middle-class apartment building, his money.

Maybe she lost a bet?

The kid looks like a kid.

"Buongiorno! Benvenuta," they call.

As soon as I step out of the elevator, there are kisses and greetings and questions about the smoothness of my trip. My training from five years as a senator's daughter kicks in. So even though I'd rather walk back to Connecticut in four-inch stilettos than be their nanny, I tell them how delighted I am to be here.

"Your hair!" the child says gazing at my head with huge eyes. "It's gorgeous."

"*Grazie.* I get it from my mom." It's not true. My mom's hair is the same shade of chestnut, but it doesn't have the length and volume of a Disney princess the way mine does. People want an explanation for the phenomenon that is my hair, and genetics is an easy one to give.

The child reaches out a small hand and touches a lock that curls gently by my ribs. I resist the urge to smack her hand away. People have been touching my hair since I was a teenager, and I don't like it any better now than I did then.

"Let's get you inside," Marco says, leading the way into the apartment.

I follow him inside and immediately feel claustrophobic.

Yellow curtains hang limp in a small living room, like they've given up trying to brighten the space. The room opposite is the size of a bathroom, but the fridge, stove, and table crammed inside make me think it must be the kitchen. A faint smell of espresso clings to everything, mixed with garlic.

There's a short hallway, but no staircase. I turn in a slow circle, looking for the rest of the apartment. I don't find it.

"Is this all you brought?" the girl asks, poking my carry-on.

"Sì," Noting the puzzled looks I add, "I thought I'd take advantage of being in Milan and pick up some new wardrobe staples."

And I was only given one hour to pack a bag.

"Wonderful idea!" Marco says, clapping his hands. "There's a market the nannies go to near Sant'Ambrogio. I can give you directions."

I keep my face neutral, but the thought of picking through clothes in an outdoor market like a poor housewife makes my lunch twist menacingly in my stomach.

"Or better yet," he continues, "when Carmen calls, she can take you herself." His smile is huge, and there's something in his teeth. A bit of pepper, I think. I tear my eyes away and focus on what he's saying.

"I'm sorry, who is Carmen?"

"One of your new friends. She reaches out to all the nannies when they get here. Shows them around, introduces them to other young people in the area."

I pretend he didn't just lump me in with all the other nannies. Despite how this looks, I am not the help.

"In fact, here's the phone she'll call. It's the one all the nannies use. You can pay to add minutes to the sim card." He pulls a black phone out of his jacket and offers it to me.

I stare at him, confused.

Am I meant to take this dingy old phone? And use it??

It looks like the cheap phone our maid uses when she thinks no one's looking.

"I actually have my own," I reply.

"Of course," Marco says. "But you can hang on to this one so your new friends can reach you." He's still holding it out to me, and I have no choice but to take it.

"Thank you." I give him a smile that would make my father proud and accept the phone like it's a bouquet of flowers.

The four of us stand in the living room for a beat, then I flash my most gracious smile. "I better start unpacking."

"*Tesoro,* why don't you show Lydia her room?" the mom says.

The girl takes my hand and leads me down the hall while I try to guess why her fingers are so sticky.

Frosting from a recent snack? Blood from an animal sacrifice?

With kids, you never knew.

We pass two bedrooms and a bathroom, then stop at a room at the end of the hall. My prison cell for the next year.

A dark wardrobe fills one corner, and a small bed is wedged into the corner opposite next to a wooden nightstand. That's it. That's the entire contents of the room.

I set my bag on the worn comforter. I'm twenty-two years old and sleeping in a twin-sized bed like a toddler.

"Want some help unpacking?"

I jump. The child is still standing there like something from a horror movie.

"That's okay. I can manage."

"I'm seven now," the child says, and despite my exhaustion I make sounds like she invented a smear-proof mascara. "I'm a good helper."

"I'm sure you are," I say, but my smile says, *"Get out of my room, small human."* She ignores it.

She unzips my bag and paws through my clothes.

"What are you doing?" I yelp as she yanks out my Dior blouse like it's a T-shirt from Target.

"Helping." Several items fall out of the suitcase and onto the murky beige carpet. "Wow, you have nice clothes."

She pulls out a black evening gown with a sweetheart neckline and an open back.

"Thank you," I say, taking the dress from her and putting it on a metal hanger in the wardrobe. When I turn around, she's pulled out my favorite cashmere sweater and is rubbing it against her face. I take it from her before it gets ruined by jam or chocolate or whatever other food children keep on their faces.

"That's cashmere," she says, eyes sparkling.

"Yes."

"None of the other nannies had cashmere."

What can I say? I like to bring a little style to my indentured servitude.

She finds my Kate Spade high waist dress pants and lays them out on the bed.

"I know a lot about fashion," she tells me.

"I'm sure you do."

"Your Italian is better than the other nannies."

Of course it is. I've had an Italian tutor since I was ten, and my family spends a month in Tuscany every spring.

"Do you know any secret handshakes?" she asks.

I glance at my watch. It's been a long day, and my manners are hanging by a thread.

"What time is your bedtime, sweetheart? Wouldn't want you to be tired for school tomorrow."

Miraculously, she seems to pick up on the fact that she's not wanted and stomps out of the room.

Finally.

I slip my boots off and line them up inside the wardrobe, then sink onto the bed. The springs creak under me as I bring my knees to my chest and wrap my arms around my legs. The thin walls let in the muffled sounds of the family speaking in rapid Italian.

I am no longer a sophomore at Engleman University. I am some family's live-in help.

A powerless fury rises up from my toes, gaining strength as it reaches my mouth. I want to scream until someone hears me.

Instead, I close my eyes, clench my fists, and shove the feeling down.

There's a knock on the door, and my eyes fly open.

"Come in," I call, voice straining to stay calm.

It's the wife. *What is her name?*

"I wanted to make sure you have everything you need."

What I need is a father who lets me run my own life. What I need is my boyfriend, Chad. What I don't need is a year as a babysitter in a country full of people who haven't discovered deodorant.

I give the woman my brightest smile. "I'm all set."

"Good. Tomorrow I'll go with you to Isabella's school and show you which bus to take."

Isabella = small child. Got it.

"Sounds great," I reply, happy mask intact.

"We're so glad you're here, Lydia."

"I'm glad too," I say, the lie rolling off my tongue with practiced ease.

I rack my brain for some memory of her name but find nothing.

"*Buonanotte.* We'll see you in the morning."

"*Buonanotte,*" I echo.

She stands in my doorway a second longer then says, "Isabella can take some time to appreciate. She's an only child, and I'm afraid she's become a bit spoiled. We're working on it. But I think with time, you will grow to love her."

The raw vulnerability on her face is hard to look at.

"Isabella seems wonderful," I tell her. "I'm sure we'll get along just fine." The easiest lies to tell are the ones people want to believe.

I wait until she's closed my door and I hear the latch on her own door click shut, then I pick up my phone and dial Amex travel services.

"This is Lydia St. Clair. I need a flight from Milan to New Haven, Connecticut. For tomorrow morning."

Chapter Two

Dust swirls in a beam of light streaming through the gauzy kitchen curtains. I'm seated at the breakfast table, showered and dressed with my hair and makeup done, finishing the last sip of my espresso.

At least the coffee here is decent.

The city sounds of traffic and construction filter in through the window.

"Good morning, Lydia," the mom says, coming into the kitchen. Isabella scowls at her side, hair wildly disheveled, like she's been wrestling a small, determined octopus.

The woman prepares breakfast for Isabella, and the kitchen feels even smaller with three people in it. It's like a reality show where contestants are forced to survive a week in a tiny Milan apartment.

I move to the living room and check my phone. My flight home leaves Mal Pensa airport at noon, which gives me plenty of time to drop Isabella off at school, return, repack my suitcase, and Uber to the airport.

With a firm exit plan in place, I look at the apartment with a more generous gaze. It's small, but beautifully decorated with vibrant colors and mismatched textures. There's a midnight blue throw blanket on the armchair, soft as rabbit fur, and the couch is a deep red that's bold without overwhelming.

Once Isabella has eaten and dressed, she prattles on obnoxiously while I plaster an interested look on my face.

"I get to pick whatever clothes I want for school," she tells me, standing tall with pride. "And I have a new backpack this year. It has sequins."

Sequins are an abomination. But based on the outfit she chose, pink pants with a matching pink unicorn shirt, I'm not surprised.

"Lovely," I tell her, checking the time to see when I can drop this child off at school.

"I'm going to the same school this year, but a different classroom. And my teacher is different. And there will probably be different kids in my class."

Her voice has the bossy, authoritative cadence that comes naturally to only children, but she's clenching and unclenching her fists at her sides.

It reminds me of every time I went to school on the first day. The carefully chosen outfit, the nervous chatter.

And even though I don't care about this kid, the tiniest bit of empathy flickers through me.

School is basically an anxiety theme park.

"Do you know the secret to nailing first grade?" I ask.

The expression on her face is both hopeful and skeptical. "What?"

"Act like you're in second grade."

Her brow furrows. "That doesn't make sense."

"Sure it does. Are second graders nervous around a bunch of first graders? No. Do second graders worry if first graders want to play with them at recess? No."

The child looks at me like she can't tell if I'm brilliant or bonkers. I don't care either way.

"Buongiorno, tutti," Marco says walking into the living room. Hello everyone. "Lydia, how did you sleep?"

"Well," I reply.

After I successfully plotted my escape from your house.

"Perfect. Sofia will assist you this morning bringing Isa to school, and then you'll have the morning and afternoon off until you pick Isa up at 4pm."

Sofia is the wife's name. Good to know.

I'll send Marco a text from the Uber letting him know my change of plans, and they'll have plenty of time to find someone to pick Isabella up at 4pm.

"Sounds great," I say.

Sofia, Isabella, and I make it out the door and onto a city bus.

It's crowded, the air thick with cigarette smoke and body odor. I move toward Sofia who, unlike the man on the other side of me, isn't checking out my butt.

I grip the metal pole as the bus lurches forward, tires scraping against the cobblestones. A man with a briefcase bumps into me and smiles apologetically. His suit is cut beautifully, his tie real silk.

Within fifteen minutes, we arrive at Isabella's school, a giant block of a building plunked down on the corner of a busy intersection. The shrieks of running children ricochet off the concrete walls as parents sniffle and cry.

I can only assume they're tears of relief that school is starting again.

Sofia wipes her eyes and gives Isabella a hug and a kiss on the cheek. Isabella nods, face pale, eyes unblinking.

We're not big on physical affection in my family, but I muster up an arm pat for her. And then she's off, mixing in with the other small creatures as they run screeching into the building.

"Well, I'd better get to work," Sofia says, blowing her nose, cheeks pink with embarrassment. I pretend I don't notice. "Can you find your way back here at 4pm?"

I made it from Monte Carlo back home to Connecticut when my dad got called away on work during our last family vacation. Yes, I can make it from the apartment to the school.

"Don't worry about a thing," I tell Sofia. "Everything is going to be fine."

By that, I mean my life is going to be fine. No idea what she's going to do about hiring a new nanny.

But she seems the resourceful type. I'm sure she'll figure it out.

I head back to the apartment and pack. Just as I'm rolling my suitcase toward the door, my phone rings. It's Karen, my father's personal assistant and my personal tormentor. If there was a vote for who should be dropped into a pit of wild hyenas, I'd nominate Karen and write a very persuasive letter of recommendation.

"Hi Karen!" I say in an over-the-top perky voice. "How kind of my father to take you off butt-kissing duty so you could make a personal phone call!"

"How kind of you to take time off from your life of reckless indulgence to answer your phone."

Oh, how I loathe this woman.

I give my suitcase an extra jerk to get it over the living room rug.

"As much as I enjoy these chats Karen, I'm in the middle of something." I maneuver my suitcase out the front door and toward the elevator, then remember the keys.

Can I slide them under the door after I lock it? Will they fit?

"On the way to the airport I'm guessing." Her voice is smug and I stop, a bad feeling creeping into my stomach.

Karen takes my silence as confirmation.

"Let me save you a trip. I canceled your ticket."

Panic floods my veins. "How did you—?"

"Your father monitors your credit card. All international flights have been flagged for notification."

My throat tightens, and my palms are slick against the handle of my suitcase. I know my father checks the credit card occasionally, but he's never canceled a transaction before. Not even when I bought a small boat on a girls' trip to Martha's Vineyard.

As though reading my mind, Karen says, "He's taking a hard line this time and will not tolerate any of your shenanigans."

"Returning to my own home is shenanigans?"

Karen ignores my question and says, "If you try to book another ticket, I'll simply cancel it. Your father cares about you and thinks this year abroad will be a transformative experience for you."

My parents are always looking for "transformative experiences" for me, which begs the question: What is so wrong with me that I need to be transformed?

And if my father cares about me, why am I talking to you, Karen?

"I see," I tell her.

"I truly hope you do, because it's time you grew up and started—"

I hang up before Karen can get to the part about "getting my pretty little head out of the clouds."

Despite what Karen and my parents think, the chances of me staying here are smaller than a Brazilian bikini. I will find another way to get home.

"Hey, Chad, it's me." I plonk onto the Rossi's stupid red couch. "I need your help."

"Babe! I'm so glad you called! Heidi said you flew to Europe yesterday. And I was like, 'No way. My girlfriend wouldn't just fly to Europe without telling me.' And she was like, 'Well she did, because she's in Italy right now." And I was like, 'Which one is it, Heidi, Italy or Europe?' And Heidi was all, 'Italy is *in* Europe.' And I was like, 'Are you sure?' And she was like, 'Yes, look at a globe.' But you know how those things are, all tiny and confusing. Like, why is Australia just floating out there?"

A headache starts at the base of my skull, and I rub at it, annoyed.

"Chad, I need your help to get home."

"Sure, Babe. I'll pick you up from the airport, just tell me when. Everyone's doing a bonfire at the point tonight, and Marcus says Brett grew a horrible mustache over the summer. I'm dying to see it."

"I don't *have* a flight home," I say, trying to mask my annoyance. "My dad canceled it. I need you to get me a flight."

"Ooh. That's a bummer. I'd totally book you a flight, but my parents took my credit card after that thing in Atlantic City."

By "thing," Chad means losing nearly $30,000 at the casinos in one weekend.

"I read this comic book about a guy who hitchhiked from Europe to Texas." He pauses. "But also, he had special gills and could swim across the Atlantic. So maybe that's not very helpful for you."

"Not helpful," I agree, flopping back into the plush cushions of the couch.

"Don't worry Babe, I'll think of something. Whatever it takes, I'll get you home."

He's switched to the dramatic voice he uses when he's been watching a lot of action movies, and I dig through my purse for some Excedrin.

I swallow the pill dry and tell him, "Good, I'll call you later to get the details."

Then I stomp down the hall to my room, crawl into bed and sleep for the next four hours.

The doors to Isabella's school are still closed when I arrive just before 4pm. I wait with a crowd of parents, grandparents, and caretakers, none of whom look thrilled to be there, until the doors open, and a flood of children rushes out. I spot Isabella and give a whistle like I'm hailing a cab in Manhattan. She runs over, cheeks flushed with excitement.

"You'll never believe what happened at second recess," she says, dropping her backpack at my feet. "I was on the swing and Sylvia, who's still only six, told me to get off." She looks up at my face to make sure I appreciate the absurdity. "I had only been on for like, five minutes."

I nod like I'm captivated by her recess drama but focus on coming up with a Plan B in case Chad doesn't come through for me.

Marrying a wealthy Italian man? Faking my death and starting a new life in Switzerland?

"I told her no," Isabella continues. "But then she hollered for the teacher, and *Signora* Macaluso made me get off and give her a turn. Which wasn't even fair!"

A man twenty years my senior is gazing lecherously at me and my hair, and I lead Isabella out of the crowd to the sidewalk. When Isabella's done whining about the unfairness of it all, she concludes with: "So I told Giuseppe and Maria that she still wets the bed."

Guilt flashes in her eyes as they meet mine.

"Well done," I say.

Look at me being supportive and encouraging.

Isabella smiles in surprise and directs me to a pizzeria on the corner. We squeeze into the crowded shop and are enveloped by the smell of fresh bread and garlic. After pushing through a long line of kids and caretakers, I order two squares of pizza and take them to a table by the window.

"Did you know," Isabella says after taking a bite of pizza, "my last nanny split her pants right open in the middle of this pizzeria?"

"Is that so?"

Isabella nods happily. "She bent over to get something from my backpack and split a giant hole in her Levi's."

I wrinkle my nose. "Why was she wearing Levi's in the first place?"

Isabella nods in agreement. "I know, right? She wore jeans and T-shirts All. The. Time."

I shake my head. "Sounds like a monster."

Isabella stops nodding. "She wasn't a monster."

I shrug. I don't care either way.

"She wasn't," Isabella insists. "She was cool. She even had a boyfriend while she was here."

As though a boyfriend makes you a good person. I shake my head. The miseducation of women starts young.

I take a bite of my pizza. The sauce is hot enough to burn my tongue, and the crust is the perfect combination of crisp and chewy. It tastes like the pizza our chef used to make on Fridays when I was younger. Before Mom switched everyone to a paleo diet.

Isabella keeps up a steady stream of conversation while she eats her pizza and all the way home. I nod occasionally, but I'm running through exit plans in my head.

"Do you want to play Uno?" Isabella asks as soon as we walk in the door. "I'm really good at it."

Her eyes sparkle like she's suggested we browse a Chanel catalogue.

My life is in shambles. No, I do not want to play the world's boringest card game.

"Maybe another time."

"How about Barbie dolls? I have twenty-seven."

I groan. *Doesn't this child know about television?*

"I'm going to have a little rest in my bedroom. Why don't you find something great to watch on TV?"

She looks at me for a moment, like she can see right into my head, then walks over to the couch and picks up the remote. I escape to my bedroom.

Kids are so clingy.

Chad promised he'd get me home, but I have my doubts. For one thing, Chad isn't smart. It's one of the reasons I like spending time with him. He isn't one of those annoying men who interrogate you on books you're reading or bore you with the details of some documentary they watched.

However, his lack of brains makes these sort of rescue endeavors harder to pull off. I settle onto my tiny bed and give him a call.

"Hey, Chadman," I say, using the nickname he loves.

"Hey Babe." His voice sounds like he was sleeping. "What's up?"

Is he serious right now? Did he forget that I'm stuck here in Italy, and he's supposed to be getting me home?

"I'm calling to see if you found a way home for me." My irritation leaks into my words so I add, "I can't wait to see you."

"Right! The rescue mission! I've totally got you."

"Yeah?"

"Yeah! Brett's dad is in Prague for work, but he's coming home this weekend, and he's stopping by Milan to see an opera at The Scale."

It's La Scala, but I don't correct him. I'm smiling too much to care. This is exactly what I need.

"All you have to do is meet him at the airport Friday morning at ten, and he'll give you a ride home in his jet."

The shrill sounds of Isabella's TV show filter in from the living room.

Today's Monday. Four more days of this and then I'll be home.

"Chad, you're amazing!"

"What are you going to tell the family you're bailing on?" Chad asks. Annoyingly.

"Whatever I want. Family emergency. Accidental pregnancy. I'll come up with something."

"What are you going to tell your dad?"

I blow out a frustrated breath.

"Nothing, Chad. I don't want my father to know. That's why I'm bumming a ride off a stranger instead of using my credit card to buy a ticket. For all he'll know, I'll still be in Milan working as a babysitter."

"Babe! I've got a brilliant idea! Why don't you come live with me in the pool house? It will be epic!"

Chad's enthusiasm is not contagious. I haven't exactly worked out where I'll stay for the next nine months, but Chad's parents' pool house is low on the list.

Congress is in session and my father is at his apartment in DC. My mom is with him, ostensibly to show support, but actually to keep him away from the other DC wives. His affairs are an open secret, but my mom pretends she doesn't know about any of them so she can stay married to a senator.

All that to say, my home in Connecticut is empty. But the housekeeping staff are so loyal to my father they'd rat me out the first chance they got. And probably get a raise for it.

Still, staying in Chad's pool house, which closely resembles a frat house, is not a good option. I prefer Chad in much smaller doses.

"It's going to be so fun," he says as I gaze out the window at the little neighborhood park. "I'll teach you foosball, and we can watch all the Marvel movies from the beginning of the franchise."

Somewhere below, a Vespa roars down the street.

"Aren't there like twenty of those movies?" I ask.

"Twenty-five," Chad says.

"Can't wait. And thank you for setting this up."

"You're welcome, Babe. You know I'd do anything to get you back here."

To be clear, he called one person. But still, it's a nice sentiment.

"Want me to bring you back something special from Milan?"

"Yes! Do they have those Toblerone chocolate bars there?"

"Those are Swiss, and you can get them in America—"

"I love those!" he interrupts, and I promise him I'll bring some home, then end the call.

I've got a ride back home. Relief mixes with anxiety as I contemplate where I can live for nine months without my father knowing about it.

I rummage through my Louis Vuitton bag and pull out my sketchbook and pens. Most of the pages are filled, but I find a blank page near the back. I let my mind relax, relishing the calm that comes as pencil meets paper.

There was a gorgeous camel-colored coat hanging in a shop window on the way home from Isabella's school. I sketch it from memory but give it a fuller skirt and double-breasted buttons. Then I add knee boots and a jade scarf like the one my Grandma Lottie used to wear.

She said life was a battlefield and clothes were a woman's armor. She's the one who taught me to sew. Lottie was the one person in the St. Clair family who never cared what my father thought.

Next to the trench coat, I draw an evening gown with yards of gleaming velvet, like something you'd wear to the opera. Velvet can be slippery, but it's one of my favorite materials to work with.

Of course, it's been ages since I've actually sewn a full dress. The last time was for a history project my sophomore year of high school. Grandma Lottie helped me sew six different outfits showing how women's fashion changed in the years during World War II. I'd gotten my friends to model them, and I'd felt so proud when I gave the presentation.

My dad had been proud of me too. He'd seen the A on my poster and given me a hug. And John St. Clair III did not give away hugs for nothing.

It had given me a false sense of hope. A hope that was crushed when I asked to take home economics the next year.

"They still teach that class?" my father had said. "What a waste of time. That class is for housewives who do their own cooking and sewing. Is that going to be you, Lydia? Are you going to cook meals and sew clothes and take care of five kids?"

I tried to explain I was interested in the design part of sewing clothes, but my dad was laughing too hard to hear.

My lines have grown thicker and darker, and I take a second to erase them and start again. The velvet dress needs a pair of stilettos that lace up to mid-calf. And a purse. A smooth patent leather that will complement the softness of the velvet.

Marco and Sofia come home, yanking me out of my sketching Zen. I suppose I should at least *pretend* to nanny their child. I go back to the living room and there are greetings and questions. I put my brain on autopilot and give them charming and reassuring answers.

We spend a mind-numbingly boring dinner together as Isabella chatters nonstop about school. I'm *this close* to fake choking on my chicken just to get away when Isabella declares she's done. I gratefully escape back to the closet they call a bedroom.

I pick up my phone to call Heidi or Jaclyn or a dozen other girlfriends who'd love to hear the juicy drama of my current life. But at the last second, I punch in my brother Robert's number.

We're not close. I mean we used to be, but now he's busy with his third year of med school at John Hopkins, and we don't talk much. Still, he's a good guy.

"Hey Eggplant, how are you?"

Eggplant is his nickname for me. Charming, isn't it? When I was ten, I got a black eye during an archery lesson and my whole face swelled up and turned blackish purple. He likes to remind me of the two weeks in my life when I wasn't beautiful.

"Fine. How's school?" I flop onto the bed feeling every spring in the thin mattress.

"They don't let me sleep and they yell at me a lot. How's school for you?"

"I'm not at school actually."

"I thought you were returning to Engleman this year."

I pick up my sketch pad again and start doodling. "Change of plans."

I assumed my father would have told Robby, but apparently, John St. Clair III doesn't divulge embarrassing family information, even to his own children.

Engleman was even worse than Cornell, and that's saying something.

"Where are you now, Eggplant?"

I sigh and try not to sound like a petulant child when I say, "Milan."

"Milan, Italy?"

"No, Milan, Texas. Yes, Milan, Italy."

"But why?"

Silence.

"What happened at Engleman, Lydia?" His voice has gone soft, and he's using my real name, which means I have about fifteen seconds until this turns into a *serious talk*.

"It didn't work out," I say briskly. "I'm looking for a place to stay for the next few months. I thought maybe you'd like a roommate. You work so much, you'd barely have to put up with me. Plus, I could cook you delicious meals when you come home."

Robert barks out a laugh, and I smile. I am a notoriously bad cook. Although I do make delicious, buttered toast.

"It could be fun," I continue. "Like old times, before..." I don't have to say the words "before Dad got elected." It's implied.

"That does sound fun, Eggplant, but I can't swing it. Katie moved in last month."

"Oh." Kate Bradshaw has been Robby's girlfriend since undergrad.

"The apartment's pretty cramped with all her stuff, and you know how she is with people."

I do.

"Besides, I thought you said you were in Italy."

"Yes, but I don't *want* to be."

"Oh." There's a long pause. "Why don't you try this place out? You don't have to leave *every* time things get hard."

"It's been nice catching up," I say. "Tell Kate I said hello."

"Wait, Egg, I didn't mean it like that. I just think sometimes—"

"Love you. Bye."

I hang up and flop back onto the bed. A crack in the ceiling meanders to the window and I follow it with my eyes. There's a gnawing heaviness in my gut when I think of what I'll do once I'm home. But I'll figure that out later. The most important thing is getting out of here.

Chapter Three

A shrill ring cuts through my sleep, interrupting a delicious dream about sailing through a sea of caviar with Pedro Pascal. Isabella and I came back from school an hour ago, and I crawled into bed fifty-nine minutes ago. That child is exhausting.

I'm willing to admit it's not all her. I have as much business taking care of a child as I do performing open-heart surgery. Blindfolded. On roller skates.

Now I reach for my phone, eyes still closed, and push several buttons. The ringing continues, and finally I crack an eye open, wincing against the late afternoon sun streaming in through the window. The black nanny phone vibrates on the floor where I left it. I pull a pillow over my head to muffle the annoying ringtone. The pillowcase is scratchy against my face. There's no way the thread count on these sheets is higher than 200. I'm pretty sure they get nicer linens in prison.

Finally, the ringing stops, then a few seconds later there's a short beep.

Did someone leave a voicemail? People still leave voicemails?

I'm rearranging the pillows and trying to get comfortable in this ridiculous bed when Isabella bursts through my bedroom door like a horde of Phi Beta Kappas at a pledge party.

Honestly, does this child have any boundaries?

"Look what she sent me!" she hollers, waving a thick book in the air and leaping around like a monkey after its second espresso.

"It's the second *Glitter the Mermaid* book!" Not bothering to ask, she climbs onto my bed next to me, jabbing me in the arm with her pointy elbows. "Juliet sent it to me! Because we finished the first one together."

"Juliet the fat nanny?"

"She wasn't fat," Isabella replies sharply. "She just liked food a lot."

I like food too. That doesn't mean I eat until my pants split open in the middle of a pizzeria. It's called self-discipline.

"So can we read it?" She bounces with excitement as she waves the giant book, sending it crashing into the wall.

"No," I say.

"What? Why not?" Her voice turns from excited to whiny.

"Because. I don't want to."

"You don't want to read *Glitter the Mermaid*?" Her eyes are wide like she can't comprehend such a thing.

"Books are a waste of time."

She stares at me, hurt and disappointment etched into her downturned lips.

"You're not a good nanny," she says, making direct eye contact with me.

I don't break eye contact, and I don't flinch at her words. "I'm not," I agree.

I don't sing songs, or dance with penguins, or wear a stupid hat.

Isabella slides off my bed and shuffles out of the room.

I can't sit through another family dinner, so I tell the Rossi's I have errands to run and catch an Uber to a steakhouse downtown. After the last two days, I deserve a Michelin-starred meal.

The rich scent of sautéed garlic mingles with the aroma of charred meat. I'm escorted to a small candle-lit table near the back, and shortly after I'm seated, an Italian man stops by my table to offer his company for the evening. I decline.

Does he honestly think a woman like me would be eating alone if she didn't want to? These people are absurd.

My steak, perfectly cooked and paired beautifully with grilled asparagus, does not actually make me feel better about my life. So, I find a salon a block away and treat myself to a pedicure. It only helps a little.

The apartment is quiet when I return, and I tiptoe to my room so I don't have to interact with anyone. A shrill ringing breaks the stillness and I jump. The nanny phone, still lying on the floor near my bed, rings again before I snatch it up and send it to voicemail. A few seconds later, there's another beep.

What in the world is so important someone would leave two voicemails?

I jab at the buttons and pull up the messages.

A perky voice, heavily accented with Spanish, fills the room.

"*Ciao!* This is Carmen! You don't know me yet, but I hope we'll be great friends!" She sounds like the annoying RA at Engelman. "I know you're new to town and don't have any friends, and I wanted to let you know that we've got people here that are excited to meet you. Give me a call back, and we'll make plans to get together."

Sorry perky Carmen. That's not going to happen.

I resent the assumption that I don't have any friends. They just happen to be on the other side of the world.

I delete the message and listen to the second one.

"Hi! This is Carmen again!" I turn the volume down because her voice is seriously too much. "I wanted to invite you to hang out with all of us this weekend. We're getting together for dinner on Saturday night. It's a new place that just opened, but don't worry, it's not too expensive."

Are the nannies always poor?

"Anyway, we're meeting at *Il Duomo* at 7pm. If you don't know how to get there, give me a call and I'll help you find your way. We're all looking forward to meeting you! *Ciao!*"

Thanks for the invite, I say to Carmen in my head, *but fortunately, by Saturday night I'll be long gone.*

Chad wasn't kidding, Brett's new mustache is revolting. He looks like he's trying to sell a used car and date your underage daughter.

It's Wednesday morning after school drop off, and I'm in bed scrolling through Instagram. It's the usual feed from the usual people. Frat parties, selfies from around campus. It's not that I miss being at college—I don't. But I miss...something.

Grandma Lottie's cottage pops into my head. When she passed, my father donated all her stuff to charity, but I managed to retrieve her sewing machine and kept it in my closet. When school sucked or my father yelled, I would sit in the closet and sew until I felt better. I even brought the sewing machine to Cornell and Engelman.

As silly as it sounds, I wish I had brought it with me here.

My phone rings, but I don't recognize the number. Probably Heidi calling from some new boyfriend's phone. It's about time she called to see how I'm doing. I've been gone for four days.

"This is Lydia St. Clair," I say, the way I was taught when I was twelve.

"Lydia? It's Marco." The words come out fast, edged in panic.

"Marco, is everything okay?"

I dropped Isabella off thirty minutes ago and she was fine. If she threw up at school, and I have to go pick her up, I will quit right now and stay in a hotel until Friday. I do *not* deal with other people's vomit.

"I have a favor to ask. I left work papers at home, and I need them ASAP. Could you bring them to my office?"

Before I can answer he continues. "I know this isn't part of your normal nanny duties, and I wouldn't ask if it wasn't an emergency."

I smother a groan.

You're an adult for crying out loud. Keep track of your stuff.

But I don't technically have anything to do this morning. And maybe it will bring me some good karma since I'm planning on bailing on them in three days.

"Sure, Marco."

His sigh of relief is audible. "*Grazie mille.* There's a black folder on the kitchen table. I'm sending an Uber to pick you up. They should be there in seven minutes. Thank you, Lydia. You're saving me."

"Happy to help," I lie.

I hang up with Marco and grab the folder from the kitchen table. By the time I reapply my Red Royalty lipstick and grab my purse and sunglasses, the Uber is waiting outside.

In the short trip to Marco's office, the Uber driver runs two red lights, swears at a young man on a Vespa, barely avoids hitting an old woman crossing the street, and asks me out to dinner. I climb out of the car as quickly as possible onto a busy sidewalk.

A discreet sign on the gray stone building in front of me says Rossi and when I push through the heavy iron door, Marco is waiting in a light-filled lobby. His shoulders melt in relief when he sees the black folder in my hand.

I should be curious about why this folder's so important, but computer programming software logistics or whatever it is Marco does for a living, is of very little interest to me.

"*Grazie* Lydia," he says, taking the folder from me. "I really appreciate this."

"It's no problem," I say.

"Can we get you a coffee? Call you another Uber?"

"That'd be great," I say, taking in the rest of the space. The lobby is all glass and steel, cool and modern, with giant abstract art on the walls. The faint scent of espresso hangs in the air, mingling with something sharper—leather, maybe.

A young woman with red hair and a round face sits at a giant white desk. She has nice features, but the oversized glasses perched on her delicate nose give the appearance of a surprised turtle.

"Chelsie," Marco says to her. "Would you mind making a coffee for Lydia? She saved the day for us."

"Sure thing, boss," she says, and asks how I like my coffee.

"Cream and sugar is fine, thank you."

"I've got to dash to my meeting now," Marco says, "but thank you again. And Chelsie will call an Uber for you when you're ready."

He slips through a frosted glass door before I can reply.

Moments later, a tall plumpish woman with a severely cut bob comes through that same door. She stops when she sees me.

"Are you new?" she asks, eyes open in surprise.

"Yes."

She nods, looking me over, sharp gaze lingering on my bust and hips. "I would guess 34-24-34, but we'll measure once we get you undressed."

My eyebrows shoot up. “Excuse me?” I take a small step backward toward the door.

“Bianca, this is Lydia,” Chelsie says, returning to the lobby and handing me a steaming mug. “She brought us the Vangarten measurements.”

“Oh!” Bianca’s hands go to her cheeks. “You’re the nanny!”

“I am,” I confirm.

“My apologies. I thought you were one of the models.” She looks me up and down again. “Have you considered modeling? Your build and skin tone are exceptional.”

“And that hair,” Chelsie adds, eyes wide. The reverence in her voice makes her sound like a member of a cult.

I add “start a cult” to my mental list of possibilities for my future.

I’d be a great cult leader. I wouldn’t make the women wear those hideous pioneer dresses you see on the news.

Chelsie settles in behind the giant reception desk, and I look back to Bianca.

“I’m sorry, what is this place?”

My question goes unanswered because the door to the street opens and an absurdly attractive man walks into the lobby. He’s tall, at least six and a half feet, with the chiseled facial features of a Viking God. Light gleams off his blond hair, and when he glances my way, cool blue eyes sweep over me and full lips curl into a smile. He’s flanked on either side by two smaller blond men with serious expressions, like they would throw themselves in front of a bullet to protect that face.

“Mr. Vangarten!” Bianca says rushing toward him. “Good morning. Marco is all ready for you. I’ll escort you to his office.”

Before I can close my mouth, Bianca has whisked this beautiful specimen away.

What in the world?

“That was Noah Vangarten,” Chelsie says, answering the question written all over my face. “The most beautiful man in Norway. Possibly the continent.”

“What’s he doing here?”

“They’re doing a first fitting.” She tucks a lock of red hair behind her ear.

“I’m sorry, *what* is this place?”

Chelsie's eyebrows furrow. "This is Rossi Designs."

"Marco is a...fashion designer?"

Chelsie straightens, as though personally offended I didn't know.

"He is a rising star in the Milan fashion scene." She sounds like she's quoting someone. "And after this year's spring collection, Rossi will be a household name."

No.

I cannot reconcile the short, chubby, messy-haired man with "rising star." Computer nerd, sure. Jolly chef, absolutely. But never in a million years would I guess that Marco, who wears a nightgown to bed, is a fashion designer.

Bianca comes bustling back before I can ask any further questions.

"Thank you for bringing those measurements in," she says to me. "I keep telling Marco not to bring his work home, but does he listen to me? No, he does not." She shakes her head, and a crease forms in the middle of her forehead. "Chelsie can call you an Uber."

But suddenly I don't want to go home and sit in that tiny apartment. Or walk around the city alone. Or even go shopping. I want to see what's on the other side of that frosted glass door.

I turn to Bianca with a charming smile, ready to sweet-talk my way in, but she's looking at a clipboard like it holds the key to the universe. The efficient energy radiating off her does not give "impromptu tour" vibes.

"Don't worry about an Uber," I say. "I'll walk."

I stroll the leaf-strewn sidewalks, wracking my brain for how I can get back into that studio.

Could I steal something from Marco's briefcase and then show up tomorrow to "return" it? Does he even carry a briefcase?

I haven't been paying enough attention to notice.

Could I tell Bianca I changed my mind, and I do want to be a model? Only then I'd be stuck modeling.

I keep plotting, undeterred. This is something, I can feel it.

What are the odds that of all the families I could work for, I landed in one with a fashion designer?

Okay, it's Milan, so the odds are better than most places, but still. I'm taking it as a sign.

As soon as I get back to the apartment, I grab my sketchpad and settle onto my bed. I run a finger over the crisp paper and pull up Noah Vangarten in my mind—his sharp cheekbones and cool blue eyes.

The pencil glides across the paper, soft and certain, leaving behind bold lines that flow into sharp angles. A crisp white button down with an embellished collar. A snug fitting vest in midnight blue.

I pause to imagine the texture of leather under my fingers, the weight of a fur-lined collar.

Then I move onto pants—a simple pair of dark wash jeans, tight through the hips and thighs, slightly flared. Shoes are my favorite, and I take my time sketching out a chunky black boot that laces to mid ankle.

The room is quiet except for the rhythmic scratch of graphite on paper, and for the first time in days, the muscles in my shoulders loosen.

The alarm on my phone rings and I startle, drawing a jagged line through what was otherwise a nice hat.

Is it 3:30 already?

Somehow I skipped lunch and spent the whole day drawing.

Grabbing my phone and purse, I zip out the door and head to Isabella's school.

"Why are you in a good mood?" she asks as soon as she sees me. Her face is scrunched up like a skeptical raccoon.

"What makes you think I'm in a good mood?" I ask.

"You're smiling."

"I smile all the time," I say, hustling her out of the crowd and onto the sidewalk.

"Yeah, but not like you mean it."

I stop and look at her. She shrugs.

"Well," I say. "Your dad asked me to drop something off at his office, and helping people makes me happy."

"You got to see Dad's studio?" she asks, voice accusing.

"I was doing him a favor," I say defensively. "I didn't even see the studio." I pause. "Why, have you seen it?"

The answer is obvious from Isabella's scowl.

"Well, lots of kids don't go to their dad's office," I say. "I've never been to my dad's office."

"Your dad probably has a boring office."

She's right. My dad was a lawyer before he got into politics, and though

I've never been to his D.C. office, his study at home is a mahogany snooze fest.

"But my dad has an amazing office," she continues.

The longing on her face is intense, and a plan takes shape in my head. This annoying kid may be the key to getting exactly what I want...

Chapter Four

By the time Sofia comes home from work, I'm like a cat ready to pounce.

"*Ciao, tesoro*," she says, setting her bag next to Isabella with a soft thump. The faint smell of her floral perfume—something light and expensive—drifts in with her. "How was school today?"

"Fine," Isabella says, not taking her eyes off the television.

Marco usually comes home within a few minutes of Sofia, and it takes everything in me not to hover by the door.

"Do you have any homework?" Sofia asks.

Isabella doesn't answer, which is answer enough.

"Why don't we work on it together?" Sofia says in a coaxing voice.

"It's reading and it's terrible," Isabella says, still laser focused on the animated figures leaping around the screen like demented bumble bees.

"Maybe, um," Sofia glances at me. "Maybe Lydia will help you."

I'd rather get a bikini wax from Karen than help that child with her reading homework.

"I don't want her help," Isabella says, which is highly convenient, because I was going to look like a *cretina* when I refused.

"Listen, *amore*, Dad called. He's staying late at the office."

My heart deflates.

"So, we're on our own for dinner." Sofia turns to look at me. "Lydia, are you joining us for dinner tonight?"

"I'd love to," I say, just the way my mother does when she's turning down social invitations from people beneath her. "But I have some things I need to pick up downtown. Perhaps tomorrow night."

I leave quickly, the door clicking shut behind me, and catch an Uber downtown. The city hums around me—cars zipping past, laughter from an open café—and a cool breeze plays with my hair. My heels tap against the cobblestones as I head toward a little bistro I spotted on Jaclyn's Instagram from last year. I almost call her on the way but decide against it.

Dinner is exquisite, the creamy crème brûlée nearly as good as the one I had in Paris, and by the time I get back to the apartment around 9pm, Marco is there. He's sitting on the couch with his coat still on, like he just got home.

"*Ciao*, Lydia," he says.

His face is puffy, and his eyes look tired.

Has this man never heard of La Mer eye cream?

Still, after today's revelation, I can't help looking at him in a new light.

"Thanks again for dropping that folder off," he says.

"Of course," I say, taking a seat in the armchair diagonal to him. "I was hoping I could talk to you about something. Maybe it's not my place..." I trail off and wait for him to urge me on. When he does, I say, "I know your work schedule is hectic right now, and there will probably be a lot of nights like tonight, where you come home after Isabella has gone to bed."

Guilt flashes across his face. *Bingo.*

"I know you can't change your workload, but Isabella mentioned she's never been to your studio, and she'd love to see it."

Marco looks at the hardwood floor, rubbing the back of his neck.

"I thought," I continue, going for wholesome nanny whose only concern is Isabella's relationship with her dad. "Instead of going straight home after school tomorrow, I could bring Isabella to the studio. Let her see where you work and what you do."

He's nodding slowly now, almost there. I make my closing argument.

"That way, Isabella would have a picture in her head of where you are all those nights you don't come home until late."

Marco's guilt and love for his daughter are written in the flat line of his lips and the furrow of his brow.

Manipulating parents is almost too easy.

"She has asked to see the studio," Marco admits. He looks over at me. "Why don't you drop by around 4:30pm? My meetings should be finished for the day."

"Absolutely," I say.

He stands and runs a hand down his sagging cheeks. "Thanks for thinking of this," he says. "And looking out for Isa."

I smile. "That's what I'm here for."

Isabella starts ranting as soon as I pick her up from school—something about her teacher and show and tell—and I have to wait a good four minutes before I can share my news.

"Guess where we're going this afternoon?"

"Where?" she asks in a bored tone.

"To your dad's work!" I expect a smile or a high five or something, but Isabella is annoyingly annoyed.

"What? Why?"

"What do you mean why? You were telling me yesterday how much you wanted to go, so I talked to your dad."

Honestly, children are ridiculous.

She still looks grumpy.

"Why are you all scowly? You'll have wrinkles by the time you're thirty."

"I'm not scowly," she says, scowling even harder. "I just don't get why he said no all the times I asked and said yes when you asked. You've been here like a day."

"I don't know what to tell you, kid. But you get to go. You're welcome."

"*Grazie*," she mumbles.

Bianca is waiting to greet us in the lobby, all smiles and sweetness for the boss's daughter.

"*Tesoro*!" Marco says, coming through the glass doors and scooping her up. Honestly, it's a little over the top. "Are you ready to see my work?"

"*Sì!*" she yells, and he leads us into the main studio.

Natural light pours through floor-to-ceiling windows and skylights in the vaulted ceiling, bathing everything in a golden afternoon glow. The air smells faintly of linen. Four large tables command the open space, filled with sewing machines, fabric swatches and scissors that gleam like surgical tools. Mannequins stand at attention along the periphery, clothed in layers of satin and lace that ripple like water. It's peaceful and exhilarating all at once.

Forget Milan's cathedrals. This is my church.

"So, this is where we keep all of our fabric samples," Marco says, leading Isabella over to a big storeroom. I follow, trying to make my steps look dutiful, not excited. Marco shows us bolts of satin, chiffon, linen, leather, and lace.

"Where did you get all of this?" Isabella asks, looking as starstruck as I feel.

"We have a wholesaler we work with to get most of this stuff. I get some of the more unusual fabric myself." He pulls out a heavy bolt of ruby red silk, the fabric whispering as it slides off the shelf. The sheen catches the light, glowing like molten glass. "Remember that trip I took to Turkey last month? When I brought you back that teddy bear? That's where I got this."

The ridiculous grin on my face is wrecking my plans to play it cool, so I imagine Chad talking about video games until my expression slips into boredom.

"What are you going to use it for?" Isabella breathes, taking the words right out of my mouth.

"I don't know yet," Marco replies. He puts it back, a discouraging tilt to his eyebrows. "I was looking for a special tweed fabric they make with Turkish cotton. Then I saw this piece and knew I had to have it."

"I think it should be an evening gown," Isabella said.

"That sounds sensational, *amore*," Marco says.

When he looks away, I reach out a hand to touch the fabric. It's cool and smooth under my fingertips.

"Would you like to see some of my designs?"

"*Sì!*" I say, then blush crimson when I realize he was talking to Isabella.

He leads us to a glass-walled conference room with a corkboard covered in sketches and scraps of fabric.

I listen, ensorcelled, as Marco talks about his creative process, his voice low and thoughtful. The air conditioning kicks on, sending goosebumps down my skin, and causing the sketches on the corkboard to flutter. I lean in, not wanting to miss a word out of Marco's mouth. He describes the weight and feel of quality fabric, while Isabella rolls around in an office chair, wheels squeaking on the polished floor.

"Should we go look at the mannequins?" Marco asks when Isabella rams into the wall for the third time. Isabella nods and darts out of the conference room and into the studio.

"She seems to have a real love for fashion," I say to Marco.

He nods. "She's always been interested in my work. Thank you for bringing her here. It's wonderful to see her excitement."

By the time we make it over to the mannequins, Isabella is flopping their arms around like they're having seizures. Marco tells her how they use the mannequins to make the clothes fit. I step away, ostensibly to let them enjoy this father-daughter time, but really so I can scope out the rest of the space.

A wall by Marco's office boasts framed magazine articles and photos from runway shows. The models seem to float above the catwalk in glimmering gowns and tailored suits. My pulse quickens as I take in each piece, my fingers itching to trace the elegant lines and folds captured in the photos.

"That could be you," Bianca says from behind me, and I jump. "There are a dozen agencies in this city that would sign you in a second." She frowns. "Of course, we'd expect to be your studio of choice."

I've gotten similar offers since I was twelve, but I'm not interested in smiling and posing. I do enough of that as a senator's daughter.

"I appreciate the offer," I say, "but modeling is not for me."

She opens her mouth like she wants to convince me, then changes her mind and smiles stiffly. "I understand." She walks away, black bob bobbing as she goes.

The whir of sewing machines and the smell of fresh linen wrap me in a feeling of comfort and safety. I'm back in Lottie's cottage. And it doesn't matter if I've failed another exam or got yelled at for my report card. Because I can bring fashion to life in a way that makes me feel brilliant.

My heart squeezes with longing. It's not just that I miss my grandma—the only one in the St. Clair family who saw me for who I was and deemed it enough. I miss the part of me that died when she did. The part of me that believed I could break out of the St. Clair mold and live my dream.

The sudden scrape of a chair draws my attention to a nook by the window. A man and woman work at sewing machines, fingers carefully feeding the fabric through.

I wander over to where Bianca is sorting patterns on a table. "How many people work here?" I ask her.

"We're a small team," Bianca says. "I'm Marco's personal assistant and operations manager, Chelsie handles reception, and we have three junior designers, Danilo, Clara, and Luigi." A wrinkle furrows her brow.

I eye the junior designers.

Who did they bribe to get to work in this magical place? And does that person still need cash?

Across the room, Marco is wrapping a velvet cape around Isabella while she giggles. Bianca glances at her watch, and I suspect I can garner some goodwill by cutting this tour short.

"I better collect Isabella, so you guys can get back to work," I say. "Thank you so much for clearing Marco's schedule for this. I know it meant a lot to her."

"Anytime," Bianca says in a way that means 'please don't ask again'.

Isabella kisses her dad goodbye, and he waves us off. All the way home, she talks about how cool her dad's studio is and all the amazing stuff she saw. I nod, trying to bring order to my swirling thoughts. My blood is fizzing like my veins are filled with champagne.

The St. Clair's are a mix of doctors, lawyers, and politicians, with a few engineers thrown in. They are not actors or athletes. They don't become writers or florists. They get an education at a respectable institution, choose a career in a respectable field, and marry someone of equitable status.

But maybe I could do things differently.

The ride Chad lined up for me leaves tomorrow morning. In less than twenty-four hours, I'll be out of this nanny mess. Back in Connecticut. Living in Chad's pool house. Killing time until...what? My dad bribes another university to take me next fall?

Or I could stay here. Work for Marco. Learn about fashion. See if I have what it takes to be a designer. If I do well, Marco might write me a recommendation, and it could be enough to get a real job back home.

"Can you walk faster?" Isabella whines. "I have to pee."

Of course, staying means watching this ridiculous child. For a whole year.

Could I pay someone else to watch Isabella? No—she'd tattle. Maybe pay Isabella to keep quiet? Probably not, I don't trust her.

We make it to the apartment, and I push through the heavy glass doors.

Honestly, I could endure the indentured servitude in the morning and afternoons, if it meant I got to work in that studio all day.

I try to shake the idea as I put on the TV for Isabella and hop in the shower. But the idea won't let go of me.

What if I stayed?

I turn the water on, and the pipes rattle like an angry ghost. Water comes out freezing cold, then piping hot.

What if instead of living with a guy who thinks Crocs are acceptable footwear, I lived with a real-life fashion designer?

If Marco took me on as an intern, I'd learn more in a month than in a year at school.

I work a healthy amount of Pureology shampoo into my hair.

Would Marco want an intern who's also his nanny? Asking might give off stalker vibes.

But I have to at least try, right? I won't have another chance like this.

I rinse the shampoo from my hair and wrestle my excitement into submission so I can hear my rational brain.

If I blow off my ride tomorrow and Marco says no, I'll be stuck here doing nothing but nannying. And I will stab my beautiful eyes out.

By the time I climb out of the shower, I've made my decision.

It's too risky. That private jet is my ride home, and I'm taking it.

Chapter Five

Isabella is asleep, and the whole house is quiet except for the low murmur of Marco and Sofia talking in the living room. My bag is packed and tucked under my bed, and I rehearse the plan for tomorrow in my head.

I'll drop Isabella off at school, come back, and grab my things and Uber to the private aircraft section of Linate airport. Once I'm on the plane, I'll call Sofia and let her know there's been a family emergency. She'll have plenty of time to pick up Isabella from school.

I'm not sure what they'll do for the rest of the year without a nanny, but that's not my problem.

Didn't Isabella mention grandparents that live...somewhere? I'm sure they'd love to take care of their sweet tesoro.

I scan the room for anything I might've left and spot one Gucci sneaker by the wardrobe. Isabella was flying the other one around like an airplane.

Did it end up in the living room?

All the more reason to leave this house. For someone obsessed with designer clothes, that child does not treat them well.

I tiptoe down the hall toward the living room.

Should I mention something to Sofia and Marco about family drama developing at home, to back up my lie tomorrow?

My thoughts are interrupted by Marco's raised voice.

"We're a month out, Sofia!"

Sofia's response is too soft to hear, and I tiptoe closer.

"Danilo and Clara are hard workers," Marco says, "but there's so much left to do, and I was counting on Luigi." His voice sounds desperate, and a tingling feeling creeps up my spine.

"He didn't tell you he was leaving?" Sofia asks.

"He didn't tell anyone. He just eloped."

"Doesn't one of your models do extra work around the studio during busy season?" Sofia asks.

"Nico," Marco says. "But that's only two days a week. I'm not sure it will be enough."

There's silence, and I lean forward, heart pounding so loud I'm sure they hear it.

"I know how important this collection is to you," Sofia says. "I'm sure you'll find someone."

There's a shuffling sound like they're getting off the couch, and I race back to my room.

My thoughts trip over themselves, and I can't keep the grin off my face. Luigi left. Marco is desperate for help. This is my chance.

I pull my carryon out from under my bed and start unpacking.

The sunrise paints the trees outside my window in fiery silhouettes, and I run through my diabolical plan to get hired at Marco's studio. Something I learned from my father—if you want a yes out of someone, make them think it was their idea.

I dress in my beautiful Kate Spade pants and cashmere sweater then walk into the kitchen. Marco sits at the table finishing his coffee while Sofia scrambles eggs on the stove. Isabella won't be up for another fifteen minutes. I make myself a cup of coffee and join Marco at the table.

"I think Isabella enjoyed her visit yesterday," I start.

"Yes, she's already begging to come back."

"Chelsie was raving about the upcoming collection," I add. "She said it's your boldest vision yet. And if you pull it off, Rossi will be a household name."

Marco laughs nervously. "Yes, well. If we pull it off."

"I'm sure you will."

I leave Marco at the table shredding his napkin and rinse my coffee cup at the sink.

"Could I talk to you about something?" I ask Sofia.

"Of course," she says, turning the stove off and looking at me.

"With Isabella's school schedule, I have a lot of free time during the day. I wondered if you might know of any job opportunities. Teaching English or walking dogs. Just something to fill the time before I pick up Isabella in the afternoon."

Even though the kitchen is tiny and Marco is only a few feet away, he seems lost in his own thoughts. I raise my voice.

"It wouldn't even have to be paid. It could be volunteer work or something like an internship."

"I see," Sofia says.

"It's not urgent, of course. I simply want to make the most of my time in Milan. And it seems a shame to wander around shopping, when I could be helping an *organization that really needs it.*" I raise my voice another notch.

Sofia nods. "That makes sense. I'll ask around at work, see if anyone knows of something part-time."

"*Grazie,*" I say.

After school drop off, I call Chad from a café near Isabella's school.

"Hey Babe! So excited to see you today," he says. "I told all our friends you were coming back, and they're stoked! There's a kegger at Point's Place to celebrate."

I tug on my hair. I made it perfectly clear that when I came back, I'd have to lay low. Plus, I hate keggers.

"There's been a change of plans," I say. "I'm not coming home today."

"What? Why not?"

"It's too risky. I can't bail on the family."

"But. Like. I got you a flight home and everything."

"I know. And I appreciate it. But my plans changed."

"How? Why? I don't even understand."

And he wouldn't, even if I tried to explain. So, I don't mention fashion or Marco's studio, or the euphoric feeling of possibility bubbling inside me.

"If I bail on this family, my father will hear about it," I say like I'm explaining it to a toddler. "Then I'll be in even more trouble than I was a month ago."

Now that I'm saying it out loud, I hear how true it is. My plan of going back home would never have worked. My dad would have found out immediately and shipped me off somewhere else. Or worse, made me go to work for him.

"I just," Chad's voice grates on my ears and I move the phone away. "I thought we were going to live together this year. I was really excited. I even cleaned the pool house and everything."

"That was sweet of you," I say, and almost mean it. "I'll keep you posted if anything else changes."

I hang up before he can ask any more annoying questions.

I order a cappuccino, extra foam, and drink it slowly while I watch the minute hand on the café clock tick by. My anxiety slowly rises and then peaks at 10:30am, when I've officially missed my ride home. Whatever happens now, I'm stuck here.

The day drags on like a politician's speech and by the time bedtime rolls around, my nerves are ragged. This whole thing was a gamble, and as I crawl into bed, it looks like I bet on the wrong horse.

Was I too subtle? Or maybe Marco doesn't want his nanny working in his studio—desperate or not.

A soft knock interrupts my thoughts and sends hope zipping through me.

"Come on in," I say, leaping out of bed and smoothing my pajama pants. I try to look fashionable, humble, and hardworking. Only one of those comes naturally.

Marco opens the door and comes in, Sofia right behind him.

"Sofia and I were talking about your interest in doing something else while Isa is in school," Marco says, "and I had an idea."

I keep my face neutral, but my heart takes off at a sprint.

"You can say no, and I assure you there will be no hard feelings," Marco says.

I nod encouragingly.

"It may sound a little unorthodox, and we've never done this with the other nannies. Of course, that's because, with the exception of Juliet, all of them were home with Isabella full-time. But now that Isa's in school..."

For the love of Versace come out with it, Marco!

Sofia gives him a nudge and he says, "Might you be interested in helping out at my studio? As a sort of internship?"

I take a moment to answer and before I do, Marco rushes to add, "It would just be for the next month leading up to the show. And I wouldn't be able to pay you. Unfortunately, when Luigi left, I bought some ridiculously expensive velvet in a fit of anger." The look on his face is so sheepish I nearly giggle.

"If you don't feel comfortable working in Marco's studio," Sofia adds, "since you're already living in his house, you can decline. It's okay."

I pretend to think it over, like this is a new idea, and I haven't orchestrated this entire conversation. After a beat, I say, "I would be delighted to work in your studio."

Marco breaks into a relieved grin.

"And don't worry about the unpaid internship part," I continue. "My nanny salary is plenty for me to live on." The nanny salary is a joke, but since I have my own funds, it's irrelevant.

"Well, that's settled then." Marco grins so big his eyes become slits. "Welcome to Rossi Designs. You can come to the studio straight after you drop off Isa on Monday, and Chelsie will get you the paperwork to make it official."

"Wonderful," I say, and Sofia nods, apparently relieved that Marco's offer hasn't driven me away and left them nanny-less.

"And thank you," Marco says as he leaves my bedroom. "I think you'll be a big help to our team."

"I'll do my best," I say, trying to look grateful and supportive, and not like the puppet master that I am.

My heart pounds out a victory anthem as I lay in bed staring at the ceiling. Yes, I'm still sleeping in a tiny bed. In a tiny apartment. Babysitting a tiny human. But life suddenly feels big, brilliant, and bursting with possibility.

Chapter Six

Every item of clothing I brought to Milan is strewn across my bed, but none of them feel right for my first day at the studio.

Why didn't I bring more clothes? Or buy new ones?

I rifle through the wardrobe again.

Because you planned to flee Milan at the first available opportunity, my brain reminds me.

Whatever. That was yesterday. And rude of you to bring it up.

I select a pair of black ankle-length pants but instead of pairing them with my usual fitted blazer, I grab a loose-fitting sweatshirt. It's one I bought on vacation in Paris and has a watercolor picture of the Seine. I usually only wear it when I'm lounging around the house, but today I pair it with my black ankle boots and gold bangles. The bracelets slide over my wrist with a delicate clink, cool against my skin. I add some hoop earrings and evaluate the outfit.

Professional, but fun.

Coco Chanel's advice to take off the last accessory pops into my head, and I ditch the earrings.

Better.

My fingers tremble as I run them through the thick waves of my hair, snagging on a stubborn tangle near the nape of my neck.

The last time I was this excited was senior prom. I'd found a vintage Oscar de le Renta dress, and it fit me perfectly. But then I'd been crowned prom queen and the runner-up "accidentally" spilled red punch all over it.

I'm hoping today goes better.

My father thinks I'm a failure, and technically, I have failed at the internship he lined up with his crusty law school friends and both the Ivy League schools he got me into.

But I've always told myself it's because those things weren't right for me. If I had the opportunity to work in fashion, I wouldn't fail. I'd succeed spectacularly.

Today we'll see if that's true.

Dropping Isabella off takes longer than usual because her teacher insists on talking to me. I explain that I'm just the nanny, but she ignores my protests and informs me that Isabella has yet to turn in a single piece of homework and is proving to be disruptive in class, especially during reading time.

"I'm not her mother," I repeat. "It would be better to have this conversation with Sofia or Marco."

She eyes me for a moment and then nods. "Perhaps you're right."

Of course I'm right.

Fifteen minutes later, I'm standing in front of Rossi Designs. I checked my lipstick in the cab, and I am Red Royalty ready. I take a deep breath to compose myself, then walk through the ornate iron door into the office with all the confidence of a St. Clair.

"*Buongiorno*, Chelsie," I say, smiling brightly. Then I rein in my smile. No need to get too chummy. I'm one of the fashion interns, and she just answers the phone.

"*Buongiorno*, Lydia," Chelsie says with a smile. "And welcome."

"*Grazie*."

"Marco has prepared a simple contract for you. If you don't mind signing here, we'll be all set."

My palms are damp, so I swipe them against my pants, pretending to smooth the fabric. I scan the one-page document briefly, then sign at the bottom.

"I know you must get asked this a lot," Chelsie says, "but what kind of product do you use to get your hair to look like that?"

She's right. I do get this question a lot. From friends, from strangers, from a cop who pulled me over for speeding.

There's not a product on this big blue Earth that could make Chelsie's shaggy red hair look like mine. My glossy chestnut tresses are a miracle that can't be replicated. But women don't want to hear that, so I go with the usual lie.

"Pureology shampoo and conditioner and a deep conditioning treatment once a month."

Chelsie nods as though that explains it, and I smile and hand her the signed contract.

"You can head to the conference room."

"*Grazie*," I say again and take another deep breath before pushing through the frosted glass doors.

The scent of leather and fabric glue lingers in the air, blending with the faintest trace of expensive cologne.

You're Lydia St. Clair, I remind myself. *You have the hair of a goddess and the fashion sense of Versace himself.*

With confident strides I cross the studio to the conference room where Marco, Bianca, Danilo, and Clara are already gathered. Marco stands in front of the board filled with sketches and samples and Bianca hovers next to him, clipboard in hand. Clara and Danilo lean toward each other, whispering.

Both of them are younger than I thought, probably only a few years older than me. Danilo's dark hair is gelled stiff, his goatee pure cartoon villain. Clara's eyes are too small for her face. Or maybe her nose is too large. There's something not quite right there, but I don't care enough to figure out what.

"Perfect timing," Marco says when I enter. "Danilo, Clara—Lydia is joining us for the next month and helping us prepare the collection for the show and catalog shoot."

A soft chorus of *grazies* and *benvenutas* follows.

"She doesn't have a background in fashion," Marco says, and I frown.

I've spent more time in designer boutiques than most fashion students spend in class. Does that count for nothing?

"...but she'll be a big help in the detail work, especially for menswear."

I have no idea what he means by detail work, but I keep my expression neutral and give away nothing.

Maybe this is what he meant by 'no background in fashion'.

"We have exactly one month until the show." He turns to look at me, and I assume everyone else in the room already knows this information. "This is our spring collection. In the fashion world, the spring collection comes out in fall, and the winter collection comes out in early spring."

I know this from having attended fashion shows in New York, London, and Paris, but I nod as though hearing it for the first time.

"Our theme for the collection is Midnight Garden, and it is inspired by our lead model, Noah Vangarten's Nordic heritage. Our collection showcases twenty-one ensembles. Of these, seven are completed, nine are in the last stages of completion, and five still need a fair amount of work."

A bead of sweat slides down the side of Marco's face, and he brushes it away.

"The week following the runway show we'll have our official photo shoot, and then the catalog will go into circulation." Another bead of sweat drips, and he doesn't bother to wipe it away. It rolls all the way down to his soft jaw and drops to the floor.

"We have a lot to do to make these deadlines, but if we stay focused, we'll get it done. Now enough of the big picture, let's jump into details. Clara—I'd like you to double check the measurements for our female models. For some reason, the inseam for Federica wasn't hitting quite right at her last measurement. Their measurements are in the database, you can check them against the numbers we've been working with."

Marco takes a breath and looks at Danilo. "Can you go through the nine nearly finished ensembles and get me a punch list of what needs finished on each, as well as an estimate on when you think our team can complete those? Keep in mind, we have Lydia now, and she can take some of the more menial work off your hands."

I'm beginning to feel the teensiest bit in over my head, so I perk up at the mention of menial work.

Please give me something easy.

"Bianca, you and I talked this morning about next steps going forward with Vangarten, please keep me posted on your progress."

"Got it boss." She looks like she wants to salute.

"Any questions?" Marco asks, and even though there are a dozen racing through my head, I don't dare ask one.

"I have a question about the leather on the vests," Danilo says. "What came in is two shades darker than we wanted, and I'm wondering if it throws off the aesthetic. Can you take a look?"

Danilo brings one of the mannequins over and drapes a sample of dark brown leather over the white dress shirt and brown pants. It doesn't look bad...but it's not quite right either. It's fine that the browns don't match, but they don't complement each other. In fact, the leather makes the brown pants look muted and dull.

"I see what you mean," Marco says, circling the mannequin. "And we talked to the supplier?" he asks Bianca. "They can't send us a replacement?"

Bianca shakes her head. "I called this morning. They said this is all they have."

"This wouldn't be all they had if we were Armani," Danilo mumbles, and Marco's lips curl the slightest bit.

"The problem with being a smaller label is you do not get the same accommodation as a well-known designer," Marco agrees. "The advantage is we are nimble and innovative."

He fingers the dark leather, then takes the whole sample off and examines it, turning it over. The underside is rough and two shades lighter. Marco drapes it back over the mannequin, raw side up and takes a few steps back. No one says a word until Marco asks, "What do we think about this?"

"The coloring works better," Clara says.

"The rougher leather alters the look," Danilo says, "but if we scuff the boots a bit, it could give the whole outfit a grittier feel."

"I like that," Marco says. "Can you make me a prototype today, of both the vest and the scuffed boots and we can see how it looks?"

"On it," Danilo says, and jots down a couple of lines in his notebook, then grabs the leather sample and heads to a workstation.

Clara picks up her notebook and brings it to a computer where she inputs something. Bianca hustles off to do whatever it is she does. And I stay sitting in my chair because I'm paralyzed with nerves. My heart is pounding, and sweat is collecting along the back of my neck. I try to reframe my anxiety as excitement. I am paralyzed with excitement.

"Okay, Lydia," Marco says, coming over. "If you'll follow me to a workstation, I'll show you the detail work I mentioned."

"Of course," I say. It's the first thing I've said since the meeting started.

Marco brings me to a large table in the corner on which sit four boxes. "We have several ensembles featuring pearl beads."

Marco opens the first box and pulls out a four-foot strand of pearls. "Unfortunately, we were not able to get any pre-cut, so all of our beads will need to be cut." I peer into the box. There are more than a hundred strands in there.

"Do all these boxes have pearls in them?" I ask, eyeing the stack.

"Yes."

"I see."

Marco mistakes my expression for disappointment and gives me an encouraging smile.

"I know it's not glamorous. And it may take you all week to get through them. But it makes a big difference, freeing up Danilo to finish the pieces we need completed."

It's not disappointment I'm feeling, it's elation. The chances of screwing this up and getting thrown out of the studio on day one are extremely low.

Once Marco has found me a pair of scissors, he leaves me to my task. The steady hum of sewing machines blends with the occasional snip of scissors and rustle of fabric.

Carefully, I begin snipping pearls off the string, enjoying the soft snick of the thread and the satisfying plink as the pearls fall into the bin. It reminds me of Grandma Lottie teaching me to use her sharp sewing scissors when I was seven.

This task requires exactly 10% of my brain, and I use the rest to imagine the outfits these pearls will complement. With the Midnight Garden theme, I dream up silky gowns in deep blues and flowing skirts in dark purples. To capture the Nordic inspiration, I add fur-trimmed capes and the dark greens of a pine forest. Ooh, with some pops of red. But I don't want it to look too Christmassy, so I adjust the red to burgundy.

It takes me an hour to finish one box, and when I do, a thrill of genuine satisfaction ripples through me. Yes it was a simple task, but I nailed it.

I zip to the bakery across the street and pick up half a dozen croissants. When I come back to the studio, Clara and Danilo are huddled together at a desk by the window. They stop talking when I come over. Danilo's eyes snag on my hair and Clara's lips pinch.

"I brought some pastries," I say, offering them the box. Silence. Chelsie's keyboard clacks softly from the lobby, and Bianca's and Marco's muted voices murmur from inside his office.

"We can't eat while we work," Clara says, each word sharp enough to cut fabric. "We'd get crumbs on everything."

Danilo doesn't respond.

"Well, maybe for your lunch break then." I leave the box on the stool near their desk and walk back to my table. A quiet snicker slithers between them, like a secret I'm not invited to hear. But I refuse to feel embarrassed. I made a thoughtful gesture, and they responded ungraciously. My mother would have words with them.

While I cut the next box of pearls, I watch Marco at work. He drapes fabric pieces on a mannequin, then sketches something on a pad. Creativity radiates off him in waves.

I want to crawl into his head and roll around in his thoughts. There is no way a month will be long enough for me to learn everything I can from him. I've got to convince him to keep me on as an intern after the show, even when he's no longer desperate.

And it might help to have some allies.

Swallowing my irritation at their response to my pastry sharing, I pick up a box of uncut pearls and make my way to the table in the middle of the studio where Clara and Danilo are working at sewing machines.

"Mind if I join you?" I ask.

Danilo opens his mouth to say something, but Clara beats him to it.

"This station is for junior designers," Clara says, eyes narrowing.

"I didn't realize seats were assigned," I say, holding her gaze.

"They are." Danilo points at my table with his scissors. "Nannies and interns sit there." Clara covers her mouth with her hands and snickers.

Well, now.

I prefer allies to enemies, but if I can't have one, I'm not afraid of making the other.

I look at the table, then back at Danilo, moving my gaze slowly from his heavily gelled hair to his last-season shoes. "It must be embarrassing," I say.

His head tilts, but his hair doesn't move. "What's embarrassing?"

"To be so bad at your job your boss has to hire his nanny to get things done."

Clara's mouth drops open, and Danilo's eyes go wide. I leave them at their junior designer workstation and return to my table to continue snipping pearls.

Chapter Seven

The studio hums with activity when I arrive the next morning. Sewing machines chatter and Marco's footsteps tap a steady rhythm as he paces in his office. Bianca barks orders at a terrified delivery man, and Chelsie fields multiple calls from her sleek white desk. The energy of this place is better than a triple shot espresso. It feels like all my senses are waking up for the first time in years.

I hang my coat on the hook by the door, then head to my table. Only my table isn't there. The boxes of beads are there, sitting on the floor, but the table and chair are mysteriously missing.

A muffled giggle draws my attention to Clara and Danilo. She's holding onto his arm and covering her mouth, and he's looking at me with undisguised glee.

I've seen this sort of thing in movies and shows but never experienced it myself. No one back home would dare treat a St. Clair this way. The repercussions would be swift and devastating.

With sudden clarity, I realize that being a St. Clair means nothing here. No one knows that my father can ruin a man with a phone call or that our family has more money than a small island nation.

An unfamiliar sense of freedom spreads through me. For the first time ever, I'm not representing the St. Clair family. I'm just me. And sure, I don't have the safety net of people propping me up or paving my way, but I managed to mastermind my way into this internship on my own, surely I can make it a success.

And if it is a catastrophic failure, at least my father won't know about it.

When I turn to Danilo and Clara, the smile on my face is genuine. There is something comforting about their direct antagonism. It's transparent, and I know it's coming. Not like the time I told Jaclyn I was nervous about my driver's test, and it ended up splashed all over the tabloids.

Instead of searching for my table and chair like a fool, I grab a nearby stool and sit down, exuding the dignity of a queen whose throne has mysteriously vanished.

At least they didn't hide my scissors. I grip the cool metal and begin my work.

A snip-plink melody plays while I imagine what I would do to Danilo and Clara if we were back home.

Blacklisted from every social event, to start. Then a rumor that they're dating each other even though they're secretly brother and sister.

I've done worse for less.

But we're not home. And I have to accept both the advantages and disadvantages of that.

Besides, at the end of the day, those two mean nothing to me. I'm working in a fashion studio with a brilliant designer. Nothing else matters.

A shaft of golden light cuts across the polished floorboards, and I move my stool into the warmth. I'm getting into a groove, almost finished with the third box, when the door to the studio opens and beautiful men file into the room. Vangarten is there, along with five others.

Bianca's heels tap a quick staccato against the hardwood as she hustles around the studio, pulling out stools and full-length mirrors.

Marco strides out of his office into the main studio and kisses cheeks while Chelsie distributes coffees. When each model has been set up with a chair, stool, mirror, and coffee, Marco issues instructions to Danilo and Clara, and they each head over to a model. The other models settle into their armchairs, pull out their phones, and wait. Since no one has given me any new instructions, I continue to snip pearls.

On the far side of the studio, Marco's deep voice rises and falls in rhythmic Italian, punctuated by wild hand motions. He's got a measuring tape under Vangarten's armpit, but the two of them are laughing like they're having a drink at the pub. Despite being a fashion genius, Marco's refreshingly unpretentious.

"'*Scusi*, do you know where I can get a stool like that?"

I look up into a pair of chocolate brown eyes and my breath catches. Wavy dark hair covers part of an olive-toned forehead, and I want to brush it away to get a better look. A chiseled jawline leads to a pair of full pink lips.

If I hadn't had years of rigorous training, I would gawk like an ostrich at this beautiful face.

Fortunately, my social reflexes kick in, and I smile and say, "I don't believe we've met. I'm Lydia."

"Nico." The young man bends down to kiss both my cheeks, sending a tingle all the way to my toes. I get a whiff of something warm and citrusy, like grapefruit picked right off the tree. It lingers in the air as he leans back. "It's a pleasure to meet you."

"Likewise," I say, maintaining eye contact.

Nico smiles at me for a moment, then seems to remember himself. "Marco is going to come over in a few minutes to re-measure the hems. We've measured the hems three times, but he's Marco, and he's going to measure again. So, I need to get my hands on a stool like yours."

"I see. Well, it looks like this little wooden stool has become quite valuable." I let my smile stretch a little wider. "What can you offer me?"

Nico grins, and dimples pop out in each cheek. My stomach flutters. Dimples are a personal weakness of mine.

"I can offer you a variety of things." He straightens his shoulders and clasps his hands behind his back in a negotiating pose. "I can get you a fresh hot coffee. I can get you my very comfortable armchair to sit in. And if you can distract a couple people, I could probably grab that purplish dress hanging over there."

I grin back at him. "I'll take the armchair."

"Wonderful."

I stand, and he takes my stool and moves it to the mirror ten feet away. Then he picks up the armchair as though it weighs nothing and carries it over to me.

His T-shirt stretches across his broad shoulders as he lifts and rides up a little on the left side revealing a sliver of tan torso. I briefly forget the concept of language. My only thoughts are in emojis: 🔥🔥🔥.

"As promised," he says, setting the chair next to me.

"Thank you." My response is neither clever nor creative, but I'm still recovering from watching him carry that chair. It was way hotter than it should have been.

"You're new here, aren't you?" His eyes have fallen to my hair, and I brush it away from my neck and send it cascading down my shoulders.

"This is my second day." I sink into the armchair, its dark green velvet warm and soft against my skin. He towers over me like an extremely attractive pine tree.

"Did Marco hire you for your advanced snipping skills?"

I tilt my head to the side, and he points to the box at my feet. "I was watching you work. You have a real gift." His face is deadpan, but his eyes twinkle.

"Yes, well. A gift like mine doesn't come cheap. You wouldn't believe what Marco's paying me."

"Whatever it is, I'll tell him to double it."

Nico smiles again, and I resist the urge to put my pinky finger in the dimple of his left cheek.

"Sounds like you have a lot of sway with the boss." I scoot to the edge of my seat, wanting to be closer to him.

"What I have are incriminating photos of the summer he tried to straighten his hair," Nico chuckles. "He looks like one of the Beatles."

I smile at the mental image.

"Of course, he has pictures of me wearing underwear like a hat, so if I launch the first attack, it'll be mutual destruction."

I hold up a hand. "Why does Marco have pictures of you with underwear on your head?"

"Sometimes five-year-olds wear underwear on their heads," Nico says defensively. "It's a perfectly normal developmental phase. As for how Marco has photographic evidence—he was best friends with my dad. He's known me since I was a baby."

"I see."

"Which is also the reason I've got this gig."

"Sure. Only a family friend would look past your hideous face and hire you as a model."

His eyes open in surprise and for a second I think I've gone too far. Then he laughs and his eyes crinkle, and my heart continues beating.

"Exactly. Pity from family friends is all you need to get ahead in the world."

He tips his head to the side and looks at me. "How did you get here?"

"A friend of a friend arranged the nanny job with the Rossi family, and then Marco needed some extra help before the show."

"So, you're Isa's new nanny?" His lips quirk like he's familiar with Isa.

"Yes," I confirm, making sure my expression doesn't give away my feelings for the child.

"Welcome to Italy," he smiles again and my breath catches. He is Just. So. Beautiful. "And to Rossi Designs."

"Thank you. I'll let you get back to the pants hemming," I gesture back toward his mirror and wooden stool.

Nico keeps looking at me. "Marco always does my stuff last. Why don't I help you cut some of those beady strings?"

"Oh, you don't have to—" but he's already waving Clara over. Her face lights up, and she drops what she was working on to walk over. Her legs are weirdly bendy, and her hips keep jutting out in unnatural ways.

Is she trying to walk like she's a runway model? Oh, this is hard to watch. Without popcorn.

My lips curl into a wicked smile as she continues her sad sashay toward us.

"*Ciao*, Nico," she purrs. She doesn't look at me.

"Would you mind fetching me another pair of scissors?" he asks.

Clara stares at him blankly.

"I'd like to help Lydia while I wait."

Clara gives him a single nod and comes back a minute later with scissors. She gives Nico a look that says she'll also have his babies, if he's interested.

If Nico notices, he doesn't let on, simply thanking her and picking up a string of pearls.

"So how long have you been modeling?" I ask, grabbing a string for myself.

"About five years. Marco started his own studio the year I turned eighteen and needed models. I needed the money for college, so it worked out well."

"And what are you studying at college?" I ask.

"Engineering." The pride on his face is adorable. "I graduate in the spring, and then I'll be done with modeling."

What? No! Why?

"How about you?" he asks. "Are you going to college?"

"Right now, I'm a nanny and professional pearl snipper," I remind him. "Why don't you want to keep modeling after you graduate?" I ask, trying to get us back on the subject of things that matter.

He shrugs. "I don't love it the way I love engineering."

"*Come va ragazzi*?" Marco asks, coming over.

"We're doing great," Nico says, smiling at me in a way that makes my heart flutter.

"Sorry to keep you waiting," Marco says.

"That's what you say every time," Nico grumbles, but he's still smiling.

Marco leads Nico back to the short stool and mirror and starts taking Nico's measurements. Nico catches me looking and winks.

There's something decadent about his smile—like the first bite of tiramisu, light and rich all at once.

I tear my gaze away, but I can't keep the smile off my face. This studio keeps getting better.

Chapter Eight

The nanny phone rings loudly from under my bed, it's sharp, tinny chime slicing through the quiet and startling me out of my sketching trance. Nico's smile has been living rent free in my brain for the last four hours, and it's got me in a good mood. Fishing the phone out from under the bed I jab at the green button.

"*Pronto*?" I say.

"*Ciao*! This is Carmen. We haven't met, but I know you're the new nanny for the Rossi family, and I thought you could use some friends." Her Italian has a strong Spanish accent, and it takes me a moment to parse her words.

Thanks, Carmen. But I'm not a sad lonely girl who needs friends. I have a whole entourage back home.

Before I can respond, she continues.

"We're going out dancing tomorrow at a club downtown. It's free for foreigners on Wednesdays."

Venues that let people in for free are not usually the places I frequent. I get the distinct feeling Carmen and her friends are not my people.

"Thanks, Carmen, but—"

A muffled shriek interrupts my reply, followed by a thunk, like a backpack thrown against a wall.

“I’m *not* doing homework,” Isabella’s shrill voice declares.

Sofia’s soft voice responds, “I’ll help you, *amore*. It’s just one page.”

On the other hand, it might be nice to get out of the house.

“Why don’t you text me the address, and I’ll see if I can make it,” I tell Carmen.

“Okay. We usually get there around 8:30pm.”

“Who’s we?” I ask.

“Oh. It’s me, my best friend Valentina, and her boyfriend Paolo. We had a bigger group last year, but—it’s just the three of us now.”

“I’m Lydia, by the way.”

“Welcome to Italy, Lydia. I can’t wait to meet you.”

I didn’t say I would come, I tell her mentally. *I only said you could give me the address.*

Chances are slimmer than a spaghetti strap that I’ll actually show up tomorrow.

I showed up.

It’s nearly 9pm and the throb of bass spills out onto the street where a garish fluorescent sign casts neon streaks on the pavement. It looks like the kind of place that attracts people who wear body glitter.

“I’m here,” I text Carmen, trudging toward the entrance.

But why am I here?

Immediately after we got home from school, Isabella staged a rebellion, refusing to watch TV and insisting I play with her. I ignored her for as long as I could, but when she unearthed a recorder and started the world’s worst serenade, I caved and we played Barbie dolls for an hour.

You’d think she would have been happy, having won our little standoff, but instead she complained the whole time that my Barbie was too mean.

Do you think Barbie got that *man and* that *dreamhouse and* that *car by being nice?*

I left as soon as Sofia got home, and after a nice dinner and a walk through the park, I’ve stopped fantasizing about burning all of Isabella’s toys in front of her.

But I can’t go back to that apartment.

Which I guess means I'm spending the night in a club that looks like a scene from a teen movie from the 2000s.

I consider blowing it off to get another manicure, but my nails already look fantastic.

So we're doing this.

There's a long line to get in, but I smile at the guy at the door and walk confidently past. Inside, the music pounds against my ribcage and the smell of cheap beer and hot bodies makes my eye sting. Large, multi-colored chandeliers fling light over a sea of dancers.

Steering clear of the flailing limbs, I walk along the periphery of the room, sticky floor grabbing at the red soles of my shoes. People wait three deep at the bar, but I catch a bartender's eye and mouth the word Coke. He reaches over a couple of heads to hand it to me, and I fight against the press of bodies, their skin damp and warm against my own, to pass him some Euros.

Then I retreat to a pillar and take a cold drink. Men and women fill the dance floor, and booths line the far wall. The booth nearest me is crammed with what are certainly American frat bros. Their polo shirts glow faintly under the blacklight, collars popped, as they aggressively high-five each other between shots of tequila.

The next booth has three blondes, each making out with a dark-haired guy. The third booth contains two people, on what appears to be the world's most awkward first date. An untouched plate of nachos sits between them on the table as they avoid eye contact. The last booth has a couple on one side and a dark-haired girl on the other. The three of them are building a pyramid out of plastic cups.

Where are we, the junior high cafeteria?

I check my phone and see a text from Carmen.

> Yay! We're in a booth in the back, the last one, closest to the stairs.

I sigh. *Of course they are.*

A big part of me wants to turn around and walk out. But I can't go back to that apartment. Even if Isabella's asleep, she still feels annoying.

Decision made, I walk across the crowded dance floor and slide into the booth next to Carmen.

"*Ciao ragazzi*. I'm Lydia."

The three of them startle. No one speaks.

"Carmen?" I ask the woman sitting next to me. She nods, black hair falling into her heart-shaped face.

"Paolo and Valentina?" I say looking at the couple across from me. They're well suited for each other. He's absurdly handsome, with wavy hair, a strong nose, and full lips. She has beautifully delicate features and glowing skin.

"*Sì. Ciao.* Sorry," Valentina says. "You're just not who we expected."

I frown.

Paolo smiles. "The American nannies are always easy to spot because they look like lost puppies, waiting for someone to scoop them up."

"You're like a jungle cat," Carmen whispers, then blushes, like she didn't mean to say that out loud.

"I'm glad you made it," Valentina says. "And I love your hair."

"Thank you. And thank you for inviting me." I smile, but I'm looking for the nearest exit.

These are not my people. Carmen's cheap lipstick clashes with her skin tone, and her frizzy hair is in desperate need of a deep conditioning treatment. Valentina's lavender cardigan screams 'stolen from a librarian'.

Paolo's presence is reassuring—he's wearing a vintage Cartier watch and smells like Armani cologne. But it makes me wonder, what's his big flaw if he's hanging out with these two?

"How are you settling in?" Carmen asks. "Do you need anything?"

"I'm settling in fine, thank you," I reply.

Settling is right. Last year, I was lounging with friends on a sailboat, and now I'm hanging out with these weirdos in a dilapidated night club.

"How is Isabella treating you?" Paolo asks. His sly grin tells me he knows about Isabella.

"She's fine." I don't want to waste time talking about her. But I am curious about the previous nannies.

Who are these people that voluntarily come here to work as live-in babysitters? Are they also being forced by their fathers to spend a year in Europe so as not to further embarrass their family?

"So, you guys were friends with all the nannies?" I ask.

"*Sì*," Valentina says.

"It must be hard when they go back home every year."

"Some are easier to miss than others," Paolo says with a smirk.

"Tell me about the last one," I say.

"Oh! Juliet was the best," Valentina gushes.

"Isabella told me she gained a lot of weight and split her jeans in the middle of a pizzeria," I mention.

Paolo bursts out laughing. "That's true! Oh, we made fun of her for weeks."

"I heard she's visiting Jake this weekend," Valentina says. Then she turns to me. "That's her boyfriend. They met here last year."

I truly don't care.

"How about the nanny before her? What was she like?"

Valentina shakes her head. "Christie. We didn't get to know her as well. She was only here a few months."

"What happened?"

Carmen opens her mouth, but Paolo gives her a sharp look, and she closes it.

What?

"Marco killed her and dumped the body?" I guess.

"No!" Valentina says. "Nothing like that. She just...went home."

Paolo gives an impatient sigh. "That tiny monster tormented her until she quit. Or did she get fired? In any case, Isabella is not to be underestimated."

A ribbon of worry weaves its way through me. *Sure, Isabella and I haven't really connected. But she wouldn't get me fired, would she?*

"Maybe she's changed," Valentina offers. "After Juliet, she was doing much better."

Marco would never fire me. He needs my help in the studio. I take a sip of my Coke.

But he won't need me after the show. And Marco and Sofia give Isabella whatever she wants. If she decides she doesn't want me...

"So how did you end up with the Rossi family?" Carmen asks.

"Oh, it was just one of those opportunities that fell into my lap."

Completely against my will. "What do you guys do?" I ask, then tune out their answers.

Surely, I can win over a small child. I'll give her candy and let her brush my hair. Done.

Paolo's talking about his work at a bank. He's definitely new money, which isn't my preference, but new money is better than no money.

"I'm in my second year of nursing school," Valentina says.

"She's going to be a wonderful nurse," Paolo says. The love glowing in his eyes is obvious. And a little pathetic.

Valentina talks about her classes and professors, and I feel an overwhelming relief that I'm not going to school. As much as I loathe nannying, it's a million times better than the nine months I spent at Cornell and seven months I did at Engleman.

"How about you?" I ask Carmen. "Are you working? Going to school?"

"I'm working," Carmen says. "This is my third year teaching elementary school, but it might be my last."

"You say that every year," Valentina says.

"And I mean it every year," Carmen responds. "But it pays the bills, with enough left over for Sant'Ambrogio."

"What's Sant'Ambrogio?" I ask.

"It's this amazing market they do every Saturday near Sant'Ambrogio church," Valentina says.

"We should go this Saturday!" Carmen's eyes light up like we're planning a trip to St. Tropez.

I'm physically repulsed at the thought of buying clothes out of bargain bins at an outdoor market.

As though he can read my mind, a wicked gleam pops into Paolo's eyes. "You should come, Lydia. You would love it."

I don't know how he knows, but the grin on his face and those raised eyebrows tell me he has sensed my aversion to market shopping.

"I'll see what my Saturday looks like," I say politely.

We chat for a while and when enough time has passed, and the lipstick on Carmen's teeth proves too irritating for me to bear, I thank them for a lovely evening and make my exit.

Honestly, the best part of the night was the Coke from the bar.

Chapter Nine

Thursday dawns gray and cold, and I'm grateful for the warmth and coziness of the studio. The hum of sewing machines mixes with the clank of scissors, and my muscles relax in contentment. I even picked up a package of mint candies to suck on while I work. They don't taste exactly like the ones from Grandma Lottie's porcelain dish, but they're close.

I noticed the weekly calendar in the conference room listed fittings for today and anticipation shoots through me at the thought of seeing Nico.

A little after 9:00am, the door to the lobby opens and six models enter in a parade of long legs, full lips, and glossy hair. Unfortunately, they're all female. My shoulders slump, disappointment replacing my anticipation.

"Expecting someone else?" Clara says beside me, and I adjust my posture, annoyed that she's read me so easily.

"No." The lie is not convincing.

"Marco schedules the male and female models on different days. Obviously."

"Obviously."

Her mission to make me feel dumb accomplished, Clara saunters back to her table.

It's fine. Maybe I'll see Nico next week. Or not. Either way it's no big deal.

After I finish all four boxes (with only a few hand cramps), Marco promotes me to braiding strands of leather to make tassels. We need approximately 4,382. It's trickier than cutting, but I follow his example and pick it up fast. It reminds me of making friendship bracelets at girls' camp as a kid.

Of course, the girl I gave my bracelet to cut it to pieces when I stole her boyfriend later that summer.

"You finished the beads without me?" Nico's voice, low and playful, startles me and sends my heart racing. He leans an arm along the top of my chair, eyes twinkling.

"Nico!" He leans down to kiss my cheeks, and I resist the urge to wrap my arms around his neck and pull him into me. Today his citrus smell carries a hint of strong coffee.

"Lydia!" Just hearing him say my name makes my toes tingle.

"I thought the male models come in on Tuesdays."

"True. But I'm not just a model. I'm Marco's favorite." He grins. I suspect he's a lot of people's favorite. "He pays me extra to come in on Thursdays and help out with whatever needs done. Sometimes I'm a human mannequin, sometimes the photographer uses me to check the lighting."

He grabs a chair from nearby and sets it next to me.

"What about school?" I ask.

"I don't have classes on Tuesday or Thursday mornings."

"That's excellent news." *Tone it down, Lydia.* "So I don't have to do all these tassels myself," I add.

Nico picks up some skinny strips of leather, watches me for a moment, then starts braiding them together like he's done it a million times.

We work in companionable silence for a moment and then Nico asks, "Any idea what Marco is using these for?"

"None at all."

"I'm hoping he puts them on the long sleeve shirts. You don't see enough elbow tassels on men."

"Elbow tassels? Is that a thing?"

"No. But it should be." He uses a safety pin and clips a braided tassel to his long sleeve sweater. "Look how fancy I look." He swings his arm a little and the tassel swings. He looks ridiculous, but also somehow hot? I'm not sure how he's pulling that off.

"Very fancy," I say.

He gets another tassel and a safety pin. "These are really a men's accessory, but let's see how they look on you." My body stills as he steps toward me. And even though his skin doesn't touch mine, I can feel the heat of his fingertips through my cashmere sweater as he fastens the tassel to my sleeve.

"There." Nico straightens and stands back to look at me. "You look amazing."

I've heard those words plenty, but from him, they land differently.

He slips his phone out of his pocket. "We need to record this so no one steals our idea."

"Absolutely," I confirm.

He takes a selfie of the two of us, elbows on proud display, then shows it to me.

"It totally works, right?"

My arm tingles from his touch, and I breathe in his scent. *Yes, this totally works.*

"It's a fashion game changer," I tell him.

"Give me your number, and I'll send it to you," Nico says, handing me his phone. "You can have a piece of fashion history." I punch my number in, enjoying his nearness as he leans over my shoulder to watch.

"So, did you grow up in Milan?" I ask.

"No way," he says, shaking his head. "You asked all the questions last time, now it's my turn."

I've found that most men will talk about themselves indefinitely if you let them. It's always boring, but it's easier than answering questions about my life.

"Fine. A question for a question," I offer.

"That's fair, but I get to go first."

I switch into "politician's daughter" mode and review my collection of carefully curated answers to personal questions.

"Would you rather fight one horse-sized duck or a hundred duck-sized horses?"

I burst out laughing. "What?"

"It's a valid question. I'd like to know what I'm working with if we ever end up in that situation together."

An image of Nico and me surrounded by tiny horses pops into my head and I smile. "I'd take on the horses. And after I conquered them, I'd train them to be my spies."

Nico raises his eyebrows. "See? You learn a lot about a person from that question."

"Okay, my turn. Have you lived in Milan all your life?"

"Yes. What is your favorite cheese?"

I scowl at him for his short answer, then answer his question. "Pecorino Romano. That's the one they use for *cacio e pepe*, right?" It's one of my favorite Italian dishes.

"Yes, it is. My mom makes an amazing *cacio e pepe*."

"Tell me about your mom," I say.

"She's the best. She works as a cook at Tavola Grande and still cooks delicious food for us when she gets home. And that counts as a question, so now it's my turn again."

For a second, I panic thinking he'll ask about my parents, but instead he says, "What's your most embarrassing childhood nickname and can I start calling you that?"

A mortified blush creeps into my cheeks at the thought of Nico calling me eggplant. "Absolutely not."

Nico's eyes light up "So, you do have an embarrassing nickname!"

"Nico," Marco calls, "I need you."

Nico puts his braided leather on the table and stands. "Don't go anywhere. When I get back, I have three more soul-revealing questions for you."

I shake my head smiling as he walks to Marco. His sweater isn't snug, but I can still see the defined muscles of his arms and shoulders. I wonder if Marco might be talked into putting Nico in a tank top for the show...

The next morning, I braid leather strips and replay yesterday's conversation with Nico for the millionth time. He didn't ask me about my family background or education plans. Unlike getting-to-know-you conversations I've had back home, it didn't feel like he was interviewing me to see which boxes I checked.

The sky is overcast and the muffled patter of rain against the skylight blends soothingly with the rustle of fabric and slice of scissors.

Nico kissed my cheek before I left yesterday, and I felt it all the way to my toes. It's been a long time since I've felt something like that.

"Still braiding?" Clara says walking over. She makes braiding sound like rummaging through the gutter. Danilo comes up behind her, his goatee looking especially cartoonish this morning.

"Yes." I answer, wary that they're talking to me.

"Too bad you have to do it all by yourself today," Danilo says.

"You and Nico looked so cute together yesterday," Clara says. Her face is innocent, but I've seen that expression on too many girls like her to fall for it. I shrug noncommittally.

"Too bad he's got a girlfriend," Danilo says.

"She's a model too," Clara adds. "Swedish. He likes blondes."

"Good for him." The expression on my face is bored, but I squeeze the leather strips tighter in my hands.

"Sorry if you were hoping he would ask you out," Clara says, narrowing her already tiny eyes. She's waiting for my reaction, but I don't give her one.

"I don't think my boyfriend would appreciate that," I reply, as nonchalant as a breeze.

Honestly, I haven't thought about Chad since I told him I was staying. But I suppose, technically, he's still my boyfriend.

Danilo and Clara wear matching expressions of surprise and disappointment.

I smirk. "You really thought I was single?" I shake my head at their ignorance, letting my gorgeous hair catch the light, and go back to braiding leather. They stand there a moment longer, but I refuse to acknowledge them.

After they wander off, I turn my chair the tiniest bit so they don't have a view of my face.

Why in the world did I think an Italian male model would be single? That's like assuming a politician would be faithful to his wife.

I put Nico out of my mind and focus on the fact that I'm working in a real fashion studio. Marco comes out of his office and starts adjusting the clothes on one of the mannequins. He layers a linen shirt, then vest, then scarves. The effect is Nordic street poet, and I absolutely love it.

A female version of the outfit takes shape in my mind. Full flowing skirts in dark winter colors, a fitted blouse with a drawstring V-neck neckline, and tassels.

Yes! This is where some of my tassels should go!

I'm itching to get it down on paper, but I don't want to stop braiding and look like a slacker.

A few hours later, while I wait for Isabella to be released from school, I pull my sketchpad out of my bag and draw the design I imagined back at the studio. All I have is a black pen, and this calls for deep, vibrant colors, but I can fill that in when I get home.

"What's that?"

Isabella is standing next to me, like a tiny, creepy ninja. I snap my pad closed.

"Nothing."

"It looks like the kind of drawings my dad does."

I shrug. "How was school?"

"Boring. Why are you making fashion drawings?" Her eyes narrow and her small fists clench at her sides. "Are you stealing my dad's ideas?"

I give an exasperated sigh. "No."

"Then what are you doing?"

"I'm just drawing!" I turn and walk out of the building, counting on Isabella to follow me.

The rain has stopped, but raindrops linger on the trees and puddles litter the sidewalk and street. A taxi zips past, and I barely avoid the splash it leaves in its wake.

"I don't want to go home," she says, catching up to me. "It's boring there."

"Too bad. That's where we're going."

"I want to go to the park. All my friends go to the park after school."

"Well, I don't want to hang out with a bunch of moms or other nannies. We're going home. You can watch TV."

"I don't want to watch TV."

"I don't care."

I sound heartless, but it's not like watching TV is a hardship. I would have killed for that kind of childhood. My parents were strict about screen time. "Your brain is precious. You must protect it," my dad used to tell me. Back when he thought I had a brain worth protecting.

I pick up my pace and walk in the direction of home. Isabella jogs along next to me, her eyes squinting in concentration.

She stops and turns to me. "You love fashion."

"Yeah." I keep walking but she doesn't move.

"You wear beautiful clothes and draw pictures like my dad."

"Yes. Is there a point to this?"

"You probably love working in my dad's studio." She flings it out like an accusation. Like I probably love embezzling money from senior citizens.

"Yes, I love working in your dad's studio. Now let's move."

"We're not going home," Isabella announces. "We're going to the park."

This child is high on glue sticks if she thinks she can boss me around. I shake my head and continue walking to the apartment.

"We're going to the park or *you're* going home," Isabella calls after me. "Home to America."

I walk back to her, keeping my face neutral. "Explain yourself."

Her eyes shine with power as she lays it out for me. "You want to be here. Not as my nanny, but as a fashion person. And all I have to do to get you sent home is tell my daddy what a terrible nanny you are." Her hands go to her hips, and she steps closer to me. "So, if you want to stay here, and keep working in my dad's awesome studio, you will do everything I say."

My blood runs cold, but I cross my arms and call her bluff. "Your dad won't fire me. He's desperate for help at the studio."

"Only until the show's over."

Panic tightens my chest, but my face gives away nothing. "There's no way he can find another nanny on such short notice. Who will drop you off and pick you up from school?"

The smug look on her face makes my stomach clench.

"I guess you weren't paying attention." She takes a step closer. "I'm the only child of two only children. I have four grandparents and any one of them could look after me this year."

This is not good. NOT good. My only hope is bluffing my way out of this.

"I seriously doubt that," I say, filling my voice with skepticism.

"That's what happened when Christie went home," she replies. "Oh, and why did she go home? That's right, because I DIDN'T WANT HER HERE." Her face is red, nostrils flared, like a furious little dragon.

Sweat pricks at the back of my neck as I realize how badly I misjudged this situation. Isabella has all the power. And from the fiery look in her eyes, she knows it.

A strong wind shakes the tree branches sprinkling us with rainwater.

"Fine, if you want to go to the park so badly, we'll go. Who cares?" I play it off like it's not a big deal, but we both know the truth. She owns me.

"I told you she was a devil creature," Paolo says on Saturday morning. We're walking toward the market, and I've just finished explaining my predicament with Isabella.

I didn't plan on seeing these people again, but I have no idea what to do with Isabella, and I'm hoping they might have information on how to tame this monster. Surely Juliet the Great shared some of Isabella's weaknesses that I can use against her?

My arms ache from the hours I spent pushing Isabella on the swings at the park. Then she demanded I make her favorite snack, bruschetta. The whole kitchen filled with acrid smoke and the tomato olive mixture looked like something our gardener would scrape off the bottom of his shoe. I don't think Isabella was even hungry, she just liked watching me fail.

Even after Sofia got home, Isabella wouldn't let me escape to my room. We played with dolls, and she brushed my hair, raking the comb across my scalp with a vengeance. Sofia was thrilled to see us playing together. I wanted to strangle everyone within a five-mile radius.

The only bright point in the day was getting a text from Nico. He sent the tassel picture of us with the words "Nico and Lydia—fashion pioneers." I stared at the picture, enjoying the way our names looked together, until I could almost forget about the Swedish girlfriend.

"It's like she was trained by my own family," Paolo says. His expression is one of pride mixed with pity. At first, I think he's talking about the Swedish supermodel, but then I remember we're discussing Isabella.

"It will all work out," Valentina says. "I know she can be difficult, but there's also a lot of good in that child."

Her comment is too stupid to acknowledge.

"Marco won't really fire you, will he?" Carmen asks unhelpfully. I shrug.

"Maybe you could do something nice for her," Valentina suggests. "Win her over so she doesn't make your life miserable."

These people are idiots, and their advice is the worst.

"You have to meet force with force," Paolo says, and my ears perk up. "Let me tell you about my *Zio* Franco and the barber."

Paolo launches into a detailed retelling of the battle between his uncle and the barber in their small Sicilian village. Wild hand motions punctuate his storytelling, and his face beams with pride.

"And now he always gets his hair cut exactly the way he likes it," Paolo concludes.

"How does that help Lydia?" Carmen asks. "Isabella doesn't have a cat she can kidnap!"

"I'm just saying," Paolo says with a shrug.

"You're talking a lot and saying nothing," Carmen grumbles.

We turn a corner, and the market comes into view. Tacky white tents hover over rickety tables where clothes are heaped like piles of garbage. Haggling voices mix with the rustle of plastic bags.

I recoil and step on Carmen's feet behind me.

"I'm actually going to grab a cappuccino," I say, stepping off the sidewalk so the group can move past me. "I'll catch up with you...later."

"What? Why?" Carmen asks.

"Because she'd rather shop in a designer store than dig through clothes at the market," Paolo says.

"Some of them are hung up," Carmen says defensively. And even though I didn't say anything, she gives me a hostile look.

If she *wants to dig through cheap, musty clothes that's fine, but* I *don't want to.*

Valentina takes my hand. "It's an experience. You should give it a try."

Running naked through the streets is an experience. I don't plan on trying it.

"Or you could go home and hang out with the vindictive child-God who wants to make your life miserable," Paolo says with a smirk.

He's not wrong about my options, but I still don't like it.

"I'm looking for a new pair of boots," Valentina says. "With all your fashion knowledge, you can help me find the perfect ones."

So that's how I end up surrounded by cheap knockoffs in an outdoor market that smells like city dumpsters.

"Aren't these gorgeous?" Valentina gushes. She's holding an ugly brown boot that bares only a vague resemblance to Prada's brown leather riding boots. That has not stopped someone from stitching Prada down the side. On closer inspection, it's actually Prado.

"And only twenty Euro! Can you believe it?"

"I cannot," I manage.

We're twenty minutes into this shopping trip, and I have exhausted all my polite excitement for the pieces Carmen and Valentina pick out. Paolo, who might have helped me with these two, has wandered off to look at belts.

"What do you think of this?" Carmen asks, holding up a black dress with sequins all over it. It screams reality-show divorcee, moments before she hurls a drink in someone's face. Valentina squeals with delight.

"It will definitely get Lorenzo's attention," she says.

Carmen blushes and holds the dress against her. The color is wrong. Very few people look good in black. And the cut of the dress is not doing her any favors. She has a curvy body, and she'll look like a stuffed sausage in that thing. What she needs is a classic A-line to accentuate her tiny waist and give her hips and butt the room they need. But I don't know how to tell her that, so I say, "Tell me about Lorenzo."

"It's nothing," Carmen says, grinning like it's definitely something.

"He works the bar at Calypso," Valentina says, picking up another boot, somehow more hideous than the last. "He's been super flirty with Carmen lately."

"He's a bartender," Carmen protests. "That's like, fifty percent of his job."

Still, her eyes have that hopeful look I've seen in girls who don't know how to read boys.

"What about you?" Carmen asks me.

"What about me, what?"

"Do you have someone you're dating or crushing on?" Valentina asks.

I texted Chad on Thursday night to let him know we were breaking up. His response was an emoji thumbs up which made me question why I dated him in the first place.

"No," I say. But Nico's smile with those adorable dimples pops into my head, and it feels like a lie.

Crushing on that guy will lead to nothing good, I tell myself.

Myself, who is sometimes an idiot, refuses to listen.

Paolo's story about his uncle comes to mind as I walk past Isabella's room later that day. She's out on a walk with her parents, and there's a giant blue unicorn sitting on her bed. I don't know if this is her favorite stuffed animal because I don't care enough to notice these things. But it has the place of honor on her bed, so I take it.

Once I'm back in my room, reason returns.

What am I doing? I can't take this.

Then I remember how bad my arms hurt from pushing her on those swings and the way she brushed my hair for an hour.

She deserves it.

A key turns in the lock, and I freeze.

I'm seconds away from being discovered stealing a child's toy. There's nowhere to hide the dumb thing, so, panicked, I shove it into my carry-on bag and slide the whole thing under my bed.

Everything's fine until bedtime when Isabella's screams ricochet down the hallway, sharp as sirens.

"Where's my unicorn?!"

"I don't know, *amore,*" comes Sofia's soft response.

Furious footsteps pound down the hall, and my door bursts open.

"Where's my unicorn?" Isabella demands.

Sofia rushes behind her, mortified. "I'm sure Lydia doesn't have your stuffed animal, Isa."

"Yes, she does!" Isabella insists.

"Did you lose something?" I ask, my voice the epitome of concern.

"I didn't lose it. You took it."

My face morphs into a mask of patience and kindness. "I'm so sorry. I hate when I lose things. Do you want me to help you look for it?"

Ignoring me, Isabella flings open my wardrobe and starts digging through my clothes like a customs officer convinced I'm smuggling exotic lizards.

"Isa!" Sofia scolds. "That's not okay. Those are Lydia's things."

"It's fine," I tell Sofia reassuringly. "I know she's upset." I stand in compassionate grace as Isabella looks through all my clothes, pulls out the drawers in my nightstand, and checks under the bed.

"Why don't I help you look in your bedroom?" I offer quickly, before she can drag my suitcase out and open it.

Isabella grunts and storms out of my room. I spend the next thirty minutes sorting through toys, books, clothes, and games in her bedroom. Unsurprisingly, we do not find the blue unicorn.

"I think we'll have to sleep without him tonight," Sofia says.

Isabella's chin quivers, and her eyes fill with tears.

I slink back to my room. I've stolen boyfriends, cheated on exams, and lied about crashing my dad's car. But I have never felt as ashamed as I do in this moment.

As soon as I drop Isabella off at school tomorrow, I'll put the stuffed animal back on her bed. And I'll be extra nice to her all day.

My promise is short-lived. When I go into the bathroom the next morning, my *Cle de Peau* face cream is floating in the toilet.

This stuff costs more per ounce than cocaine!

I plunge my fingers into the cold water and retrieve the tiny jar, then stomp into the kitchen where Isabella and Marco are eating breakfast. My hands tremble with rage, and I take a breath to calm down. It doesn't work.

"Isabella, do you know what happened to my face cream?" I think she'll deny it, but instead she hangs her head and slumps her shoulders.

"I'm so sorry," comes her soft reply. "I accidentally bumped it off the shelf. I didn't mean to."

Marco looks up from his newspaper and tunes into what's happening. Isabella looks at me, giant eyes even wider, mouth turned in a frown. "You're not mad at me, are you?"

Oh, this one is good.

My hands squeeze into fists at my sides, and I clench my teeth with a ferocity that may lead to permanent damage. "Of course not. It's fine."

Marco goes back to his newspaper, and Isabella flashes me a smile so smug I want to pour her cereal over her head. Instead, I retreat to my room.

Well played, small child.

I've never been happier to drop her off at school.

At the studio, Danilo and Clara are filing into the conference room. I follow them, but Clara stops me with a hand.

"This meeting is for designers only."

I don't say anything, but I stare at her giant nose until she touches it self-consciously. Victory in hand, I head to my table and braid furiously while my brain plots.

If I'm going to keep Isabella from firing me, I need to impress Marco. And that's not going to happen if I'm braiding strips of leather while everyone else is in important meetings. As soon as the meeting ends, I march to Marco's office and knock.

"Come in," he hollers without looking up.

"I finished the leather braids. What else can I take off your plate?" I stand tall, shoulders back, like the kind of young woman who can be trusted with important tasks.

"You finished the braids already? That was fast."

I smile. "I'm a fast worker."

"Perfect, because I could use your help with this." A pile of velvet sits on his desk, and as he holds it up, it takes the shape of a dress.

"Clara used an overlock stitch, and I need this hand-stitched so the seams lay flatter. I take all the blame for the miscommunication, but it means we'll need to undo it." He looks at me. "Have you done any seam ripping?"

I stifle a smile. Grandma Lottie made me rip the seams of every stitch I got wrong, and at the beginning that was a lot. I'm basically an expert.

"*Sí*," I reply.

He hands me a seam ripper but holds on a moment before releasing it to me.

"I know this is tedious work, but I need it done carefully. Unfortunately, we don't have any other velvet. If this ends up full of holes, we'll have to scrap the whole piece."

"Understood." I take the garment back to my workstation and smile viciously at Clara before carefully ripping out each of the stitches she sewed.

I finish just before it's time to pick up Isabella. But instead of returning the velvet to Marco, I wait until no one is looking and slip it into my bag along with a needle and thread. I need a way to impress Marco, and this is it.

I'm feeling smug as I pick up Isabella. Then I see her expression and my heart plummets. Her eyes are narrowed, and her mouth is set. It's clear she's had a bad day, and she's about to take it out on someone. I consider faking amnesia and walking right past, but it's too late. She's seen me and is stomping my way.

Chapter Eleven

Isabella drops her backpack at my feet without a word. Normally, I would refuse to pick it up or make her at least use manners to ask me, but the glint in her eye has me picking it up without comment.

"So...are we heading to the park?" I jog to catch up, my Chanel ballet flats slapping against the cold sidewalk.

She doesn't answer. Up ahead a motorbike revs before zipping around a corner.

"Park?" I ask again, because at this point, I'm hoping some fresh air and swing time will wipe the homicidal look off her face.

"No, I have a new plan."

I follow as she marches toward home, dread growing with each step. There is zero chance this new plan is a good plan. A cool breeze carries the scent of dying leaves, and I button my coat to the top. As soon as we walk in the door, she takes her backpack from me, and dumps it out, spilling crayons, markers, and piles of papers onto the floor.

"*Signora* Macaluso made me miss recess. She said I haven't turned in any homework."

"Have you?"

"No."

"Well, there you go."

"She said I'll miss recess every day unless I turn my homework in."

"So do your homework."

"No."

"Fine. Miss recess, I don't care."

Honestly, why are we having this conversation?

"I'm not going to do my homework." Isabella pierces me with an icy glare. "You are."

I laugh. "I'm not doing your homework."

"Yes, you are. If you want to stay here and work in my dad's fancy studio, you have to do my homework."

"I think it'll be a little obvious to your teacher that a twenty-something is doing your homework."

"I don't." She grabs a piece of paper off the pile at random. It has triangles and squares. "My teacher can't tell who colored a dumb triangle."

She picks up another one with letters on it. The example shows a circle around some of them. "Can you draw a circle like a first grader?" She drops it back on the pile with disdain and picks up a page with numbers. They're out of order and need to be cut and glued in the right order. "Can you cut and glue like a first grader?" She crosses her arms. "It all needs to be done by the end of the week."

"The end of the week?" I yelp. There are at least fifteen different homework assignments.

"Yes. And make it look good. I don't want a bad grade."

This is ludicrous. I can't actually do this. Besides the fact that I very much don't want to, it wouldn't be...right.

"Isabella." I make my voice the voice of reason. "I can't do your homework for you. It wouldn't be ethical."

"I think ethical went out the window when you stole a child's stuffed animal," she replies, then picks up the remote and turns on the TV. "I want my unicorn back by the way."

The fantasy of tossing Isabella and all her homework out the window is so enticing I leave the room. I march to my bedroom, yank my suitcase out from under the bed, and toy with the idea of ripping the unicorn's head off and leaving it in Isabella's bed, Godfather style. It's only the conundrum of explaining it to Marco that keeps that animal's head attached.

I return to the living room and toss it on the couch next to her. "Here's your unicorn."

"Here's your homework." She hands me a stack of crumpled papers.

I glare at her with every ounce of rage I have. And then I take the papers from her.

In less than an hour I'm finished. I snapped a couple of crayons out of anger, and it made the work look more child-like.

Part of me wants Isabella to get caught. The smarter part realizes it will be so much worse for me if she does. Of all the black spots on my record, faking a first grader's homework would be the most embarrassing.

My plan to spend the afternoon hand-sewing the velvet dress was sabotaged, so I have to work on it late into the night. As tired as I am, my body vibrates with happiness. This comes easy to me in a way that reading and math don't.

When I walk into the studio the next morning, I'm yawning, but bursting with pride.

"*Buongiorno,*" I say, stepping into Marco's office.

"*Buongiorno.*" His eyes are purple and puffy, like he spent the night at a basement fight club instead of sleeping.

"Just dropping the velvet dress off." I hold it up so it's obvious it's been sewed back together.

He frowns. "I thought I asked you to rip the seams..."

"Yes, to be hand stitched." I hand him the dress and shove my hands in my pockets to keep them from shaking.

"This is beautifully done," he says after an eternity. He looks at me like he's seeing me for the first time. "How much sewing have you done before?"

"A lot," I say. "My grandmother taught me."

"I had no idea," he murmurs. "Well. This is excellent news. Between you and me, we're falling behind schedule, and I could use a talented seamstress to lighten the load." He seems to remember at this moment that he's not paying me, because he adds, "If you're up for it. I don't want to overwork you."

"It's not a burden at all," I assure him.

When I leave his office, my arms are full of silk skirts to be hemmed, and I feel like leaping for joy like the women in those unrealistic tampon commercials.

Nico is at my worktable when I get there. He's wearing a dark green shirt that makes his eyes look hazel. And makes his muscles look like I should be running my hands all over them. I force myself to look away.

"*Buongiorno*!" he greets me, leaning in and kissing each cheek. Is it just me or does he linger a moment? I drink in his smell and let it soak into my bloodstream. I'm struck all over again by how handsome he is. I tried to forget over the weekend, but it's impossible to ignore when he's standing right in front of me.

"*Buongiorno*," I say as I settle into my chair.

"You look lovely today."

He may as well have confessed his love for the way my body responds—palms sweating, heat flooding my cheeks.

"*Grazie*." I swallow against the dryness in my throat. "I like your shirt."

"*Grazie*. It's my favorite."

Did he wear his favorite shirt for me? Or am I reading too much into this?

I lay out a satin skirt on the table, smoothing the wrinkles from it, and Nico lays out the others, copying my smoothing motions.

"What are you doing with these skirts? Adding leather tassels to them?" The excitement in his eyes is adorable.

"I'm hemming them."

I try to keep my voice casual, but my smile must ruin it because Nico says, "You really like this stuff, don't you?"

Happiness is pulsing through me like electric current, but I shrug. "It's not bad."

The last time I admitted liking something, I ended up blackmailed by a first grader. Better to keep my true feelings to myself.

"What do you like?" I ask Nico.

"Bridges," he answers immediately, and dimples pop in each cheek as he smiles.

The other male models file into the studio, and Marco goes to work with Vangarten first.

"Bridges? What do you like about bridges?" I check the settings on the sewing machine Bianca brought over and do a test run on a scrap of fabric.

"What do you mean, what do I like about bridges? Everything! They are the most important structure there is!" His hands wave emphatically, and I smile.

Could this guy be any cuter?

I pause my sewing to watch him.

"Giant river blocking your way? Bridge. Boom. Problem solved. Massive canyon standing between you and the place you want to go? Bridge. Boom. You're welcome." His cheeks are flushed, and his eyes sparkle. "Need a dramatic place to stare into the distance while contemplating your life choices? Bridge. Boom. I got you."

"Clearly, I have not been giving bridges the appreciation they deserve."

"You have not. And that is a shame, because you have amazing bridges in your country. The Brooklyn Bridge is my favorite. The sheer number of cars crossing that bridge each day is incredible." He shakes his head in wonderment, and I bite the inside of my cheek to keep from smiling.

"Now, our bridges don't do the same heavy lifting as the ones in metropolitan America," he continues, "but for beauty, we may have you beat." He starts ticking his fingers. "Rialto Bridge in Venice. Ponte Vecchio in Florence. Vittorio Emanuele in Torino. And those are just the ones in the north."

"Nico," Marco calls. "Can you help us with a lighting test?"

"Coming, boss," Nico says, getting up. "This is so sad for you Lydia, because I was just about to tell you about all the bridges of the south." His smile is contagious, and I smile back at him.

I try to finish the last skirt, but my eyes keep staring longingly at Nico. There's an unfamiliar sweetness to him. He's clearly never "forgotten" to invite a friend to a Hamptons weekend, then posted just the right amount of Instagram stories so they'd see. Or stolen his best friend's girlfriend and then brought her as his date to said best friend's birthday party.

Thinking of Nico in the Connecticut social mix makes my heart hammer. They'd eat him alive.

I'm staring so much I accidentally prick myself.

Focus, Lydia. This is a terrible time to get distracted by a gorgeous Italian guy.

Is there ever a bad time to get distracted by a gorgeous Italian guy? I counter.

Yes! the voice in my head responds. *And this is it. Focus.*

I focus on sewing perfect French hems, the satin smooth beneath my fingertips, delicate as butterfly wings. And then I hear Nico's laugh, deep and joyful.

He's joking around with Marco and while I can't hear what they're saying, Nico's happy rumble sends tingles down my spine. He looks over at me and winks, and my lips curve to match his smile.

Then I remember his girlfriend, and my smile vanishes.

Focus on your sewing.

Chelsie hustles into the studio to pass a note to Marco and then hustles past me toward the reception area. Unlike Danilo and Clara, Chelsie's been nothing but decent to me.

"Chelsie," I say, quick and quiet as she dashes past. She stops and adjusts her glasses.

"Yes?"

I lower my voice, suddenly embarrassed.

What am I doing?

Sensing my rational mind is about to talk me out of this bad idea, I blurt out in a rush, "Does Nico have a girlfriend?"

Chelsie smiles knowingly and heat rises to my cheeks, but I wait for her response.

"Yes. Some Swedish model. Sorry." She sounds like she means it, and I nod my head.

"Okay. Thanks."

I go back to my sewing, face burning, grateful that Danilo and Clara didn't hear. I keep my eyes on my work the whole time Marco measures Nico and only look up when Nico returns.

"*Ciao, bella.*"

Nico smiles at me and launches into the old Italian song "Bella Ciao." It sounds like a drowning cat.

"That's some interesting singing," I tell him. "You have a lot of..."

"Talent?"

"Guts."

His eyes crinkle. "I know I'm a terrible singer. My sisters tease me mercilessly about it. But I like singing, and I won't stop."

I am absolutely puzzled by this person next to me. Men who look like Nico don't act like this. Goofy and sweet. Honest and self-deprecating.

How did Nico turn out this way? Was he fat as a child?

"Tell me about your sisters," I say.

"They are the best." He grins. "And the worst."

I adjust one of the pins and then line up the skirt again. "How so?"

"Well, there are three of them and they all hog the bathroom, which is tough because we only have one. They leave make-up and hair things all over the house."

I step on the pedal of the sewing machine and feed the skirt through as Nico keeps talking. I can hear the smile in his voice.

"They all share a room so I can have my own room, but they fight over who borrowed whose dress and why their sweater is missing. My mom works full-time, so I do a lot of the refereeing."

It clicks.

He's poor. That's why he's gorgeous but still sweet and funny. He's poor and raised by women.

"What about your dad?" I ask, carefully feeding more fabric through the machine.

"He's not in the picture anymore."

I stop sewing and look at him. "I thought he and Marco were friends."

"College roommates, actually. But five years ago, my dad took off. Left a note for my mom saying family life wasn't for him." He coughs. "No one's heard from him since, not even Marco. It's another reason Marco hired me. He knows we could use the money."

My chest squeezes. I don't know what to say, so I keep my mouth shut.

Nico runs a hand along the back of his neck. "It's been hard. Julia, that's my youngest sister, was only two when he left, so she doesn't remember him. But Camilla was eight and Benedetta was twelve. There's still a lot of anger there."

Back home, no one would willingly share unflattering information about their family. Pretense is everything and secrets are traded like currency.

"Nico, I'm so sorry," I say. It's inadequate, but I say it anyway.

Nico shrugs but doesn't say it's okay. I can tell it isn't.

"The funny thing is," he says after I continue sewing, "I have a lot of great memories with my dad. I guess that's why it hurt so much. I thought our family was great, and I assumed he did too."

I imagine seventeen-year-old Nico bewildered by his dad leaving, and my heart breaks wide open.

"You okay?"

I look down and notice I've been stabbing a needle into the pin cushion like it's a voodoo doll of a deadbeat dad.

"Just testing out the needle strength," I say embarrassed. Nico smiles.

"Tell me about your family," Nico says, obviously ready to move on. Which I get. Only I don't want to talk about my family. At all.

"Did your mom teach you how to sew?" he asks.

"That was my grandmother actually. She lived in a little cottage on our property, and I spent as much time as I could there growing up." My shoulders relax as I talk about Grandma Lottie, and Nico is such a good listener I end up telling him about the ridiculous hats she wore and the special mints she kept in a dish and how she always smelled like chamomile.

"She sounds awesome," Nico says.

"She was. She passed away five years ago."

I swallow, clear my throat, then slide the skirt out from the sewing machine and snip the threads.

"One down, three more to go," I say.

Satin is tricky to work with because it shows every mistake, but this skirt is just about flawless. I smile in admiration.

"You look pretty proud of yourself," Nico says.

"I am."

When was the last time that happened?

Chapter Twelve

A crowd of parents clusters near the entrance to Isabella's school. I hang near the back, shifting on the uneven pavement, hands clammy. Sweat trickles down my spine, despite the crisp autumn breeze.

Isabella and I battled over how much homework to turn in this morning. She wanted to dump the entire stack on her teacher's desk and secure her recess privileges, while I pointed out that going from zero completed assignments to fifteen overnight might raise suspicions. We settled on five pages—enough to show her teacher she's taking this seriously, but not enough to blow our cover.

Isabella is smiling when she comes out, but I don't relax until she tells me the news.

"Mrs. Macaluso gave me stars on my homework," she announces. "And as long as I turn in an assignment every day, I can go to recess."

I exhale in relief. "Excellent news." She holds her hand out for a high five, and I can't help but comply.

Whether good or not (okay, I know this falls squarely in the "not" category) doing Isabella's homework has changed the dynamic between us. I'm still her servant, but she's stopped trying to make my life miserable, which I appreciate. When we get back to the apartment, she settles onto the couch to watch television, and I head back to my room.

I'm thrilled Isabella's teacher didn't notice our cheating, and I'm buzzing from getting promoted to seamstress at the studio.

Settling onto my bed, I scroll through my phone, looking for someone to share my good news with. Heidi and Jaclyn still haven't called, and I stubbornly refuse to call them first. Instead, I call my brother.

I don't bother calculating the time difference. Because of his schedule as a med student, day or night means nothing.

"Hello?" he answers groggily.

"Hey, Robby. How's it going?" A fierce wind whips the tree branches outside my window and orange and red leaves fall like a fiery rainstorm.

"Eggplant? Hey!" His voice perks up. "How is Italy surviving your reign of chaos?"

"Italy is honored to have me," I inform him. "Don't be surprised if they erect a statue of my likeness before the year is out."

"When it comes to my favorite Egg, nothing would surprise me. How are you doing?" His voice says he's sorry he couldn't help me get home.

"Nannying is the worst, but I'm making an opportunity out of it."

"Dad would be proud," he says with a snort.

I pause. "Maybe..."

"Egg?" The concern in his voice is immediate, like maybe I've joined the mafia.

"I talked my way into an internship with a fashion house."

"Fashion? That sounds right up your alley."

"I've only been working there a week, but the place is incredible." I hop off my bed and walk around my room. "Marco, the head designer and dad of the kid I nanny, is brilliant. He's doing this collection with all this fur and velvet and pearls. It's incredible. And today he let me hem some of the skirts for the collection."

"Wow. You sound really excited."

"I am."

There's a "but" hanging in the air between us, and I close my eyes as soon as he says it.

"But you know Dad's not going to let you study fashion."

"Rob, I'm twenty-three years old. Dad doesn't let me do anything."

"I know. You're your own person, I just...if you were thinking of coming back here in the summer and studying fashion...I'm not sure it's a good idea."

"I didn't say I was going to go home and study fashion. It's just something I'm doing here. To kill time. It's not a big deal."

The lie feels heavy, and I slump onto the bed.

"Okay, well I'm glad you understand."

"Yeah. I'll let you get back to sleep, Robby. Talk to you later."

"Love you, Eggplant."

"Love you too."

I stare out the window, my good mood trickling out of me like water down a shower drain.

The air at Calypso is humid and thick with cheap cologne and cigarette smoke. I wasn't planning on coming back here, but, well, after my conversation with Robert, I thought some dancing might cheer me up.

I spot the gang immediately. Partly because they're in the same booth by the stairs and partly because the sequins on Carmen's dress are so bright they can be seen from space.

I greet the three of them with *ciaos* and cheek kisses.

"You're wearing the new dress," I say, squeezing in next to Carmen. I lift my voice, so it sounds like a compliment.

"Thanks, I am." She fidgets under my gaze, tugging at the hem of the too-stretchy fabric.

"Is Luca working tonight?" I ask.

"Lorenzo, and yes." Her tone is that of a woman who not only knows Lorenzo's work schedule but also his home address and closest relatives. "He's at the far left of the bar wearing a blue shirt."

I casually turn my head and scan the bartenders. They all look the same, like whoever runs this place ordered a set of generic Italian bartenders from a factory. I spot the guy in blue. A little shorter than I like, and I'm not a fan of facial hair, but I can see why Carmen would like him.

"He's cute," I say.

Carmen nods.

"So how does this normally go?" I ask.

"Like this," Paolo says, waving his hand toward Carmen. "She watches him the whole night and does nothing about it."

"Says the guy who was in love with Valentina for a year before he asked her out," Carmen shoots back. Paolo goes quiet.

"Why don't you go order us some drinks?" I say. "You can talk to him."

"Oh. The drinks here are really expensive."

I forgot. All these people are poor.

I slip my credit card out of my wallet and hand it to her. "Drinks are on me."

She takes the card but doesn't move, instead glancing at Paolo and Valentina.

"We, uh, don't really drink."

I tip my head back, exasperated. "Then order some sparkling water. I don't care what you get, just go to the bar and make sure this guy notices you."

Carmen nods, a look of determination on her face. "Okay."

"How are things going with Isabella?" Valentina asks.

"Not well." I glare at Paolo. "All because I took your advice."

"Excuse me?" His eyebrows raise.

I tell them about Isabella's unicorn and my drowned moisturizer. Valentina looks horrified that I would steal a child's stuffed animal, but she's clearly never known a child like Isabella Rossi. When I get to the part about the homework, Valentina's eyes grow as wide as bangle bracelets, and Paolo laughs so hard he bangs his elbow on the table.

"That is a conundrum," Paolo says, still grinning. He squints his eyes. "I have a cousin in Palermo—"

"I can't listen to your stories, Paolo. It'll only make things worse."

He opens his mouth to protest but stops when Carmen arrives at our booth. She's carrying a tray with two bottles of sparkling water and three large pickles. We stare at it for a moment without speaking.

"I know," Carmen says, face beet red. "I panicked. I ordered the water and then he asked if I wanted anything else, and I didn't want our conversation to be over, but I didn't know what else to order."

Paolo picks up a pickle and looks at it. "I didn't even know they served pickles here."

"I'm not sure they do," Carmen says, shaking her hands out nervously. "I spotted them behind the bar. I think someone brought them from home? He didn't even charge me for them, just handed them over."

"Oh, Carmen," Valentina says, and Carmen drops her head to her hands. "I think it was very sweet he gave you free pickles."

Paolo opens his mouth to say something, but Valentina elbows him and he shuts it.

I burst out laughing, but Carmen looks so embarrassed I clap my hand over my mouth. "I'm so sorry. It happens to the best of us."

Her embarrassment turns to a scowl. "Not you," she mutters.

"You're right, Carmen. I've never panicked and ordered pickles from a cute bartender. But I've done other dumb things."

Carmen shakes her head, unconvinced. "Like what?"

I wave her question off with a shrug, but she leans toward me until our faces are only inches apart.

"I need you to name one dumb thing you've done, and I need you to do it now." Her voice is low and shaky. Tears glisten in her eyes.

Her raw vulnerability is too much for me, and I blurt, "I let a dozen chickens loose in the dean's office at Engelman University."

Carmen's eyes go big. Valentina gasps. Even Paolo looks impressed.

"Why?" Valentina says eventually.

I shrug. "I had my reasons."

"Oo-kay. Well, I am feeling a little bit better about my life," Carmen says. "So, thank you for that."

I can tell Valentina wants to ask a question, like why would a perfectly normal girl do something like that? But I don't want to answer. Fortunately, Paolo senses it and asks Valentina what exciting things happened in the nursing world today.

I should not have shared that.

It's the kind of information that would spread like wildfire back home.

I wait for regret to wash over me. But Carmen squeezes my hand in gratitude, and Valentina talks about a sweet pregnant woman at work, and the regret doesn't come.

Instead, I feel a little bit lighter.

I have no clue what to do with Isabella, but in the studio, everything feels easy. My fingers guide the cool satin under the needle of the sewing machine with steady precision, and my toes work the pedal with confidence.

I've seen enough of Marco's finished ensembles to trust that whatever he's got planned for this simple skirt is perfect. But for fun, I add some embellishments in my head.

"*Ciao, Bella,*" Nico says, and I jump.

Is my heart going to do this obnoxious racing thing every *time he's near? It feels over the top.*

"*Ciao,* Nico."

"Daydreaming at work?" he teases. "Very unprofessional."

"Unless your job is dreaming up amazing outfits, then I'm killing it."

"Tell me all the things you're dreaming about," Nico says, eyes sparkling, voice rich and warm like melted caramel.

I cough. "Well, I would lengthen the skirt a bit."

"Lengthen? Are you sure that's the direction you'd go?" His dimples make another appearance.

"Yes," I say, giving him a light swat. "Maybe six inches longer, so it swirls around her calf. And I'd add a big girly bow at the back and a little bit of tulle peeking out at the bottom. Really feminine, you know?"

Nico nods. "I hear Marco's pairing this one with combat boots."

My jaw drops.

"Kidding!" he says, and my cheeks flush, embarrassed. "You should talk to Marco about your ideas."

I want to tell him my diabolical plan to get into the Friday design meeting, but I don't. As I discovered on Tuesday with my embarrassing gushing over my grandmother, Nico's easy smile and gorgeous eyes trick you into telling him all kinds of things. It's a mistake I won't repeat.

"So, tell me more about bridges," I say. "How do you build them? What did they do wrong with the London Bridge?"

"I can see you're using my love of bridges to avoid this conversation.

And it's a wise move, because now that you bring it up, I'm dying to tell you what they got wrong in London."

I smile and sew while Nico talks, until Marco calls him away for a fitting. I can't take my eyes off the hem I'm working on, but my ears cling to Nico's low laugh, and I break out in giggles when he starts singing the Italian version of "Bridge Over Troubled Waters."

He really is a terrible singer.

He catches me at the door just as I'm about to leave to pick up Isabella.

"I was thinking," he says, helping me into my Burberry trench. "What are you up to this weekend? A friend gave me tickets to see this horrible play. Do you want to join me?"

Excitement sparks through me, but a dull ache settles in my chest.

Chelsie confirmed two days ago that he has a Swedish model girlfriend.

"Are you asking me out on a date?" I say, just to be sure.

"Yes." He doesn't break eye contact, and the hope in his brown eyes is obvious.

He doesn't strike me as the cheating type. Which sounds naïve now that I think of it.

He's a gorgeous Italian model. How surprised should I be?

A lump lodges in my throat as I force out the words. "I don't think that's a good idea."

"Oh." Nico's eyes dim, like someone flicked off a light. I want nothing more than to spend every second I can with him. But the image of my mother's tear-streaked face slams into my mind, and I square my shoulders. I won't get sucked into a situation like that.

The hum of the city outside—buzzing mopeds and distant laughter—feels sharper against the silence stretching between us.

"Is it because of the horrible play?" Nico asks. "Because we could do dinner instead."

It's a tempting offer, but I resist. I learned my lesson at girls camp—stay away from other people's boyfriends. And Lydia St. Clair may be a screwup, but she's nobody's side piece.

I shake my head. "I don't think it would be...appropriate. I don't want anyone getting hurt."

"I see. Of course."

He gives me a half-smile and a wave, and I walk out the door onto the street.

My heart is unreasonably sad, like the time I showed up late to a sample sale and they'd already sold out of the best boots.

It's not a big deal, I tell myself as I walk to Isabella's school. *He's a fun guy, who, like most guys I know, is also a little bit scum. You'll get over this.*

By the time I pick up Isabella, I almost believe it.

Chapter Thirteen

"I want focaccia," Isabella announces when I pick her up from school. She drops her bag at my feet and heads off.

She is the most entitled child I have ever known. And I lived down the street from the Kennedys.

I scoop up her backpack, and we make our way down the crowded sidewalk toward the pizzeria on the corner. I elbow my way through the mob of after-school snackers and buy us two slices of focaccia.

Isabella is waiting for me at a table by the window where we have a mesmerizing view of scaffolding and construction.

I pass her a slice of oily bread and some napkins. "What did you first graders get up to today?"

"Nothing." She sounds offended that I would pry into her business, never mind the fact that I'm doing her homework.

I tear off a piece of warm focaccia, the crisp edges crackling beneath my fingers. The scent of rosemary and olive oil fills the air, and I take my first bite. It's warm and salty, and if they made couture clothing bigger than a size four, I would order three more slices.

Emotional eating due to idiot men is lame and cliche, but after my conversation with Nico, I'm letting myself indulge.

What did he mean by asking me out? Does he know that I know he has a girlfriend? Does he think I would be okay with—

"I want to go to the park," Isabella says, ignoring the napkin in front of her and swiping a hand across her oily mouth.

"Of course, *principessa.*" If she detects the sarcasm in calling her princess, she ignores it.

The park is packed with screaming kids and gossiping moms. Probably because it's the first warm day we've had in weeks. The sun is shining, casting shadows on the leaf-strewn ground, and the air is filled with yelling, the rhythmic creak of swings, and the occasional car horn.

Isabella heads to the swings, and I sit on a bench in the sun and pull up Instagram. There are all my friends. Having a great time without me. Not seeming to notice or care that I now live on a different continent.

And yeah, it's working out okay because of the fashion thing, but they don't know that. I scroll through Chad's feed of endless boat selfies and Marvel memes and wait for something to stir inside of me—longing, affection, nostalgia. Nothing stirs.

The wooden slats of the bench are hard, and when I shift my weight, my hand lands in something sticky, like gelato that's melted and dried.

Gross.

I head over to the playground to see if Isabella's ready to go home. She's by the slide playing with a blond boy and a brunet boy. Well, not playing, more like yelling.

Does she treat her school friends as poorly as she treats the rest of us?

The boys are yelling back, which I appreciate.

Someone needs to put that tyrant in check, and who better than her peers?

Their shrill voices blend with the frenetic playing of the other kids, angry but incoherent from this far away. The blond takes a step closer, his face screwed up in fury. The groan of the swing drowns out his words, but their impact is clear as Isabella's face turns red and her chin quivers. Her fists clench at her sides.

Maybe I should go over there...

Before I can take a step, Isabella lands a right hook to the blond kid's face. The dull thwack is loud enough to be heard over the din of the playground.

My mouth drops open. *What did my eyes just see?*

Isa's eyes go wide like she's as surprised as everyone else. Silence hangs for a moment, like a crystal vase suspended in midair, then it shatters. The blond boy shrieks and grabs his face. His friend sprints to tell the grown-ups. Two dark-haired women charge toward Isabella like mama rhinos.

I sprint toward Isabella and make it to her side at the same time as the angry moms. The larger of the women waves her hands wildly in Isabella's face. Isabella stands there frozen. The second mom checks her son's face, then joins the first mom in yelling at and berating Isabella. Their Italian is too rapid and angry to understand, but their accusatory tones are clear.

The large woman jabs a finger toward Isa's face, and my protective instincts flare.

"*Scusi*," I say loudly. "What seems to be the problem here?"

"Mind your own business," the large woman says. They both glare at me, and if I hadn't been raised by New England's scariest litigator, I would be intimidated. But I was. And I'm not.

"I'm Isabella's nanny. This is my business."

"If you're the nanny, you're doing a terrible job."

I ignore her comment and repeat my question. "What is the problem here?"

"The problem is this child just punched my son in the face."

Based on the mama bear vibes coming off this woman, she would have been over here in seconds if she'd actually seen Isabella punch her son. But the skinny boy ran off to fetch her, which tells me this mom didn't see anything.

"Did you actually see Isabella punch your son?" I ask. There's so much skepticism in my voice I sound like my father.

The woman opens her mouth, closes it, then opens it again. "Luca said she did. And my son has a huge red mark on his face."

I tilt my head. "So, you *didn't* see anything."

It's a punk way to treat a mom whose kid just got punched, but I don't care about this woman. I barely care about Isabella and should probably let her face the consequences of her actions. But this feels out of character for her. She's clever and devious. More likely to sabotage you quietly than throw a punch.

The other woman starts to speak, but I cut her off. "What I see is two grown women bullying a small child. And I've seen enough. Come on, Isa, we're going home."

Isabella nods and goes to pick up her backpack. "I hope your face feels better," I say to the blond boy. "Whatever happened to it."

Isabella is smart enough to walk away quickly, and I have to jog to catch up with her. Once I do, she slows down. We walk in silence for a minute and then Isabella says, "I did punch him."

"I know. I saw the whole thing."

Isa's head snaps up to look at me.

"So why...?" She lets the question hang, and I don't quite know how to answer it, so I dodge.

"Want to tell me what happened before you threw that punch?"

"Not really."

"Well, tell me anyway, because I just defended you against two terrifying Italian mamas."

Isabella's shoulders slump, and her head drops. Her answer is so quiet I have to lean down to hear it.

"He called me stupid."

And just like that I'm back in the second grade, the first time someone called me stupid. I didn't punch them, but looking back, I wish I had. Instead, I went home and cried. Instead, I believed them.

"That's ridiculous," I say matter-of-factly. "You're the smartest seven-year-old I know."

"How many seven-year-olds do you know?" she asks.

"See there? That's a great question. The kind only a smart seven-year-old would ask. I know many seven-year-olds. I have twin cousins who are seven. Sweet as can be. Not very bright. My dad's executive secretary has a seven-year-old. I met him once. Dreadful. He burped the ABCs. And then there is the neighbor across the street who just turned seven this year. She's not an idiot, but she's not as smart as you."

"How do you know?" Isa asks. "How do you know I'm smart?"

I give her a raised eyebrow. "Because I'm smart. I recognize it in others."

We continue home in silence and just as we reach the apartment, she asks. "Are you going to tell my parents?"

It's a testament to her mental state that she's asking instead of forcing me to do whatever she wants. I think about it for a moment, but not long enough for her to remember she has the power in this relationship.

"How about this: You promise not to punch anyone else, and I'll promise not to tell your parents?"

"I promise," she says quickly. "It really hurt." She rubs her tiny knuckles, the olive skin tinged red and angry.

"I bet." I open the door with my key, and she follows me into the lobby and into the elevator. "You never want to throw a punch. It's hard to do well, and it almost always hurts. Better to outsmart your opponent, because as I mentioned earlier, you're a very smart girl."

The elevator opens on our floor, and we step out into the hall.

"However, if you must hurt someone, and sometimes it's necessary, I've found a good kick to the crotch is the best option."

Her eyes widen.

"The crotch kick is effective, inflicting maximum pain while minimizing your risk of getting hurt. And kick them twice just to be sure."

Our neighbor has stepped out of her apartment and is listening to my conversation with Isabella. She gives a nod, apparently a "kick them twice" woman herself, then waters the potted plant by her door and goes inside.

As soon as we walk in the door, Isa plunks onto the couch and stares at the blank TV. I wait for her to pick up the remote, but she doesn't.

Picking up her backpack, I go through her homework folder and pluck out her homework assignment. She's already caught up, so I only have to do the daily homework she brings home.

"Thank you," Isabella mumbles from the couch, and I look up, startled. I've completed seventeen assignments for her, and she's never said thank you.

"For defending me in the park," she says. "Even though I didn't really deserve it."

"Thank *you*," I say. "For punching that boy and defending yourself. You never deserve to be called stupid."

I head to the kitchen to make Isa some of my famous buttered toast, and Sofia comes home a short time later.

"How was school?" she asks Isa as I put the toast on a plate. "Anything exciting happen?"

I hold my breath for Isa's answer.

"Fine. No."

I bring Isa her toast and sit next to her on the couch.

"How was work?" I ask Sofia, urging my facial muscles not to give away the fact that her daughter punched a kid at the park today.

"It was fine," Sofia said. "Pretty slow this time of year. Which is nice, my slow period coincides with Marco's busy season."

She leans over and gives Isa a kiss on the head. "Only three more weeks."

"Plus the catalogue shoot," Isa says.

"Okay, four more weeks. And then we get Papa back."

My chest tightens painfully, like a fist closing around my ribs.

Four weeks. That's all I have left, and then Marco won't need me anymore.

The thought sends panic shooting through me. There's still so much to learn. And I'll never have a chance like this again. I have to find a way to stay. I have to show Marco that I can be a real asset to his team. And it starts with getting into that design meeting.

Chapter Fourteen

The mood at the studio on Friday is weird. Chelsie's fielding half a dozen calls at reception, and Danilo and Clara are huddled at a table whispering. Marco and Bianca pace his office, their silhouettes just visible behind the closed blinds.

What's going on?

It doesn't matter. I'm laser-focused on my goal. After a double espresso and a pep talk given to me by me, I'm ready to talk my way into the designer meeting today.

When I finally lay eyes on Marco, he looks like a raccoon that got in a fight with a honey badger. The bags under his eyes are puffy and purple, and his curls stick up in every direction.

It's not a good time. Ask him next week.

No, the stubborn part of me speaks up. *It has to be today. You're running out of time.*

"*Ciao*, Marco," I say, falling into step with him as he heads in the direction of the conference room.

"*Ciao*, Lydia." His tone is polite, but signals he does not have time for superficial conversation. I go direct.

"I'd like to attend the meeting this morning."

He looks at me, eyebrows furrowed. "That's for designers."

"I understand." I shut my mouth and wait. My father taught me to never say too much in a negotiation.

"You want to come?" Marco finally asks.

"Yes."

A pause. "Okay."

I nod professionally, resisting a triumphant grin, and head toward the conference room. Warmth spreads from my chest to the tips of my fingers.

I'm in!

The urge to pump my fist in the air like a jock in a sports movie is surprisingly strong, and I barely manage to restrain myself. Summoning all my chill, I enter the conference room and take a seat in a tall leather chair. A few minutes later, Clara and Danilo file in, stone-faced and silent.

Yeah. I'm at your precious designer meeting. Get over it, you human equivalents of cargo pants.

Then Marco walks in, followed closely by Bianca, and I know something bigger than office rivalry is going on here.

"Some of you may have already seen it," Marco says, sinking into the chair at the head of the table, "but I'll summarize our situation." He runs a hand through his hair, making the curls stand up even wilder. "One of our models, Giovanni, posted a short video on social media yesterday. It's gone viral. He was here at the studio when he took it, and he's wearing his third ensemble for the runway show."

"How bad is it?" Danilo asks.

"The video shows everything; shirt, vest, pants, scarf, and accessories."

"Do we suspect foul play was involved?" Bianca asks like an inspector on a TV show.

Marco massages the bridge of his nose. "We suspect a twenty-something male with underdeveloped cognitive function was involved."

Chelsie covers a snort.

"So, what do we do?" Danilo asks.

"By the time the show hits in three weeks, there will be copycat outfits online. We need something entirely new. The shoes can stay, but the rest of the ensemble has to be reworked."

Marco runs another hand through his hair, now resembling a dark-haired Einstein. "Unfortunately, we are limited by both time and budget.

We'll need to work with the material we have, and we'll need to start creating and fitting the new outfit on Monday."

He stands, paces two feet in each direction, then leans on the table, bracing his weight on the tips of his fingers. He looks at Danilo and Clara. "I'd like to see ideas from both of you by Monday morning. Keep in mind, we need something entirely new, but it still has to work with the rest of the collection."

Clara nods and Danilo squeezes his eyes shut as though he's trying to come up with the perfect ensemble that second.

"Lydia," Marco says, and my head snaps up. "I'd like you to work on deconstructing the pieces we have so the material will be ready to go Monday. It'll be slow going, but that's fine, we just need clean seam rips and as many large pieces as possible."

"Got it."

I spend the rest of the morning carefully deconstructing the outfit Marco worked weeks to design and create. The original ensemble consisted of tan linen pants, a dark brown leather vest, a short-sleeve white cotton T-shirt, and a midnight blue cashmere scarf. I'd seen it on the model last week, and it looked amazing. Now most of it sits in a heap on my table while I carefully rip the seams from the leather vest. Danilo and Clara sit at their tables sketching frantically.

The leather in my hands is thick but soft, and the kind of battered that looks like someone wore it through the desert. It's a tragedy to take it apart, but I do, getting every piece back to the original material. Before I leave the studio, I bring the pile of fabric to Marco's office, carrying it like it's a fallen comrade pulled from the battlefield.

Nico texts me when I'm on the way to Isa's school.

Just heard about the design leak. Is everyone freaking out?

Yes!

My thumbs fly across the keys as I tell him everything I know about the redesign and find the video on social media to send him.

His response comes back immediately.

That's crazy! What's Marco going to do?

I'm still texting Nico when Isa comes out, looking like it's been a long day. I slip my phone into my pocket.

"Should we go to the park?" I ask innocently. She gives me a panicked look that turns into a scowl when she realizes I'm teasing.

"Seriously, how did things go at school today?"

"It wasn't great."

"Do you want to talk about it?"

"No."

I give her some space. For now.

Once we get to the apartment, I get my pen and notepad and start sketching. How do you change the outfit enough to look substantially different from the original, but still make it fit with the rest of the collection? And how do you do that with a very limited supply of materials?

I pull up the model's video, and he springs to life, staring soulfully into the camera. "*Maria, ti amo,*" he breathes, like he's narrating a perfume commercial. Then he recites an original poem where he compares her body to a majestic mountain. If I'm Maria, I'm not loving that. At the end, he tears up, begging for her forgiveness and promising to do better. All while wearing Marco's ensemble.

This guy's a tool. I hope Maria steals his favorite sweatshirt, then dates his brother.

I admire the fit of the pants, snug, but not tight, and the contrast of the dark leather vest. The outfit looks perfect. And trying to redesign it feels like trying to remake a Beatles song. *Where would you even begin?*

I watch the video three more times, muting it to avoid Giovanni's annoying declaration of love, and nudge my brain to think of alterations.

The most dramatic way to change it is to change the pants. But we don't have enough material to do the pants out of anything but linen. Unless we did shorts...but the collection has a very cold vibe.

Marco said we're keeping the shoes from the original outfit, fur-lined hiking boots in a light tan, with darker accents. They look like the kind of shoes you'd wear hiking through a jungle. I sketch a T-shirt with layers of leather braided necklaces over it, but it looks too Johnny Depp circa 2002, and I turn to a new page.

Maybe we could use the leather for a satchel of some sort?

Isabella sits next to me on the couch watching TV, and I close my eyes and imagine linen, leather, cotton, and cashmere as a shrill cartoon voice chatters about cheese.

The leather is the most captivating of the materials. If I can figure out the right way to use it, the rest of the outfit might fall into place.

Maybe a—

"I'm bored."

I open my eyes to see Isa staring at me.

A brilliant idea is hovering on the tip of my brain, I can feel it, but Isa's big eyes lock on me and I put down my pen.

"What do you want to do?"

"I want to play a UNO," she says.

UNO is a ridiculously dull game, but she's had a rough week, so I rummage through the cupboard and find it.

She deals the cards onto the coffee table, and I beat her in two minutes. I shuffle the cards and then deal. This time I beat her in one minute.

"I thought you might let me win," she says.

"No."

"The other nannies let me win."

"Then they did you a disservice." I shuffle the cards again but don't deal them. "If you want to win, play a game that doesn't depend on luck."

Isa's eyebrows smoosh together, confused.

"Let me teach you poker."

We spend the next hour using dried beans as chips as I teach Isa Texas Hold 'Em. She's a fast learner with a natural gift for bluffing. The beans clink softly as we push them into the center of the table, and when she places her bet, the tap of her fingers against the table carries the confidence of a Vegas regular.

"This is fun," she says, scooping the beans from the middle after I fold yet again.

"You have a knack for it."

I watch her shuffle the cards for a minute, then say, "Can I ask you a question?"

Her shoulders hunch protectively, and her lips go flat. "What?"

"Why did you get so angry when that boy called you stupid?"

It seems almost cruel to ask. But there's a part of me that wishes someone would have asked me the same question when I was her age. That someone would have helped me make sense of what I was feeling and why.

Isa shakes her head, the fire burning in her eyes doing its best to keep the tears at bay.

"You might feel better if you talk about it."

Isa opens her mouth, and before she can even get the words out, the tears are falling.

"Because he's right. The other kids can read, but I can't. Not even little words. I try, but it doesn't work."

Her shoulders curl inward as she sucks in sharp, uneven breaths. Tears spill slowly at first, then faster. A lump rises in my throat, thick and heavy, and I want to tell Isa she's not stupid or broken.

Instead of saying anything, I scoop her onto my lap and wrap my arms around her. She's probably too old for laps, but she doesn't resist as I hold her tight and let her cry herself out. I rub small circles on her back, trying to soothe something that words can't fix.

My blouse is getting soaked in snot and tears, but I try not to think about it. I make soft shushing sounds like my mom used to do with me, until I outgrew it at the age of four. Finally, the crying slows and her body relaxes.

"I hate crying," Isa says. "I feel like a baby."

"You're not a baby," I say. "And you're not stupid either."

"I think I might be."

A piece of dark hair is stuck to her tear-stained face, and I pull it away.

"Albert Einstein, a crazy smart scientist, said, 'If you judge a fish by its ability to climb a tree, it will spend its whole life believing it is stupid.'"

Isa giggles. "A fish climbing a tree would be so funny!"

"It would! And even though the fish is a great swimmer, it might feel stupid because it can't climb a tree."

Isa nods slowly.

"Your dad is an amazing designer. But maybe he'd be a terrible doctor."

"He hates blood," Isa says. "Mom has to put on my Band-Aids."

"See?"

"You're good at designing too," she says, glancing at my sketchpad on the couch.

"Thanks. Can I tell you something I'm bad at?"

Excitement creeps into her eyes. "*Sí.*"

I swallow. Open my mouth. Close it again. This is harder than I anticipated. Squeezing my eyes shut, I say, "Reading."

Her nose scrunches. "But you're a grown-up."

Heat rushes to my face, and embarrassment prickles on my skin.

"I know. And do you want to hear something else? Something I've never told anyone?"

She's still sitting in my lap, and when she looks up at me, I can see the gold flecks in her eyes. "*Sí*," she whispers.

"I'm dyslexic." It's the first time I've said it out loud, and my heart hammers at the words.

Isa's eyes go huge. "You can read minds?"

I burst out laughing, shaking Isa's body so hard her head bonks my chin.

"No," I say, still laughing. "I wish. Dyslexic means I have trouble keeping the letters in the right order when I'm reading. They switch places in my brain. It makes reading hard."

"Oh. That's worse."

"It is worse."

"What did you do in school?" she asks, wiping her nose on her sleeve. *Better hers than mine.*

"Faked it. Pretended I knew what the words meant, even when I didn't. School was pretty awful for me. I got terrible grades."

"That's not fair! It wasn't your fault."

"No. But I didn't know that. I was only diagnosed a few months ago. I spent a long time thinking I was stupid."

"But really you're a fish in a tree."

"Yes." I look at her face. "Do the letters ever do that switching thing on you?"

She shakes her head. "No. They stay in the same spot. I just don't know what they *mean*. I learned the alphabet and the sounds, but when I try to put them together, I forget. I can't keep it in my head."

I nod. "I can see how that might happen."

"Do you want to play another round of poker?" she asks. And so we do. By the time Sofia gets home, Isa's got most of the beans in front of her, and her tears have dried.

"Ciao, tesoro," Sofia says when she comes in. "How was your day?"

Isa glances at me, and I can tell she hasn't told her parents she's struggling in school.

"Good," she tells Sofia. "Lydia taught me Texas Hold 'Em."

Sofia looks between the two of us. "Didn't Juliet and Jake teach you that last year?"

Isabella's innocent smile turns into a wicked grin.

"You hustled me!" I say, looking at her giant pile of beans and remembering how quickly she picked up the game.

"Maybe a little."

I shake my head, laughing. *What am I going to do with this child?*

Are you free tonight? If I watch Valentina and Paolo make kissy faces at each other a second longer, I'm going to lose it.

Carmen's text comes just after dinner. I hadn't planned to join the Rossis for dinner, but Isa insisted, and I'm starting to understand why it's hard to say no to this child. Anyway, it wasn't so bad. Sofia made grilled chicken and a green salad, and they were both delicious.

Sofia and Isa are reading a book on the couch, and Marco's still at the studio. Carmen's not my favorite, but I don't have anything going on tonight, so I text her back.

Sure.

Forty-five minutes later, the two of us are tucked into a cozy café, sipping Italian hot chocolate. Espresso machines hiss, ceramic cups clink, and the air is thick with the scent of roasted coffee beans and chocolate. A fierce wind whistles outside, and my cold hands curl around my hot mug.

"I'm tired of being single," Carmen says. "There are a million single men in this city, but none of them are interested in me."

I take a sip of my chocolate. It's dark and rich, with a hint of vanilla.

"My job is terrible," Carmen continues. "Because teaching small children anything is impossible."

Agreed. I wouldn't even try.

"But I also have no idea what else I would do." The napkin in front of her is slowly shredded as she speaks. "Plus, I think I've gained five kilos."

From the hot chocolate, I'm guessing.

"Which is probably why I'm still single."

Her problems are trivial, and I make a mental list of how she can fix each one, waiting until she stops talking so I can tell her.

Finally, she lets out a sigh. "Sorry for venting. Sometimes it just gets to be too much, you know?" She finishes the last of her hot chocolate. "Thanks for listening. And for not offering any "helpful" advice. I hate when people do that."

"The worst," I agree.

If she doesn't want advice, why is she telling me all this stuff??

"So how are you doing?" she asks. Her face is expectant, as if she thinks I'm also going to share all the ways my life sucks.

That's not happening.

My phone buzzes, and a text from Nico pops up.

Just heard from one of the other models that Giovanni got fired.

"Want to hear some juicy drama from the studio?" I ask Carmen.

She nods her head vigorously.

I pull up Giovanni's video and fill her in on what it means for Marco.

"And he's getting fired now?" she asks.

"That's what Nico said."

"Who's Nico?"

"Oh. He's a friend from work."

"A friend, huh?" She's looking at me closely, and I will myself not to blush.

"*Si.*"

"Then why are you twirling your hair around your finger like you're thirteen years old with your first crush?"

I yank my hand out of my hair so fast it hurts.

"Let's see a picture of him," Carmen says, holding her hand out for my phone.

"I don't have a—Oh."

Carmen's eyes go big, and so does her smile. "You *do* have a photo of him!"

"It's just a dorky one he took with elbow tassels."

Carmen reaches out her hand for my phone. I consider refusing, but the glint in her eye says she will wrestle it from me if necessary. I pull up Nico's photo and hand it to her.

"This is the most beautiful human I've ever seen," she says, expression dead serious.

"*Sí*," I agree. The espresso machine behind the counter hisses, releasing a cloud of coffee-scented steam.

"So...why don't you work your gorgeous hair magic on this man and snatch him up?"

"He's dating a Swedish supermodel."

"Oh." Carmen's whole face falls. "That is bad luck."

"He did ask me out, though," I can't help adding.

"Really?!" Carmen leans back in like she's watching a movie. "What did you say?"

"No."

Her eyes go big. "Are you crazy?"

"I'm not going out with a scumbag who cheats on his girlfriend." Although even as I say the words, they don't feel like Nico.

"And you're sure he's got a girlfriend?" She sets her mug onto her saucer with a clang.

"Confirmed by three sources."

Carmen's brow crinkles. "Maybe his girlfriend will fall off a mountain. And then get trampled by goats. Don't they have a lot of mountains and goats in Sweden?"

"Pretty sure you're thinking of Switzerland."

"Hmm. Well then, hit by a bus or something. I'm sure they have buses in Sweden."

She looks at the photo again. "What are those things dangling off your elbows?"

"Elbow tassels." I tell her about his design idea.

"He sounds funny," she says.

"He is."

"And sweet."

His face when he talked about his sisters pops into my head. "He is."

Carmen raises an eyebrow, clearly wanting more, but that's all I'm ready to admit. Catching feelings for Nico would be like walking on cobblestones in stilettos—inevitably ending in disaster.

"I love your sweater," I tell Carmen. It's black and fuzzy and says Dolce & Gabbana across the chest in white letters.

"Thanks. It's not really Dolce & Gabbana."

I hold back a smile. There was never any doubt.

"It must be nice to buy real designer clothes," she says.

I nod. It is.

"It's not always about the designer, though," I say. "It's about dressing for your body. Finding the cuts and styles that are the most flattering on you." I want to bring up the black sequin dress that makes her look like a sausage, but she's already depressed.

"I love clothes, but I don't always know what looks good on me."

"You should come over sometime. We can look through my wardrobe and get an idea of what works best on you." Carmen has about ten pounds on me, but if we leave things unzipped, we could still get a sense of what works. She has so many feminine curves, it would be fun to dress her. Runway models are so thin, it can be limiting. My fingers itch to sketch out some ideas that would look great on Carmen.

Carmen's eyes fill with excitement. "Really?"

"Yeah, it'll be fun."

"Okay!"

While I pay for our drinks, I go over our conversation tonight. Carmen sharing all her problems, talking about Nico, inviting her over to try on clothes.

Dang. Did I become friends with this girl?

"Thanks for meeting up tonight," Carmen says outside on the sidewalk. "It was fun."

"It was," I agree, surprised that I mean it.

She gives me two quick cheek kisses, then dashes off to catch her bus.

On the way home, I think about what I have in my wardrobe that could work for Carmen. Definitely the Armani blazer. She'll have to wear it open, but that's okay. I'll pair it with my Balenciaga T-shirt. Isa was just admiring it the other day.

Her tear-streaked face pops into my head, and I feel a pang, wishing there was something I could do to help her.

Then out of nowhere, a brilliant idea jumps into my head.

"*Scusi*," I say to the Uber driver. "I need to make a stop please."

When I sneak into the Rossi's apartment thirty minutes later, my arms are full of fashion magazines and white posterboard. Everyone's asleep, and I tiptoe down the hall and start working on my project.

Creative energy buzzes through me as I cut out pictures from the magazines and glue them to the whiteboard.

This is the best idea I've ever had. Isa's going to love it.

The next morning is Saturday, and Isa wakes up late. I fidget on the couch while she eats breakfast, listening to the clank of her spoon and the slurp of milk, while I try to shake the "school presentation" feeling in my belly.

This is the worst idea I've ever had. Isa's going to hate it.

Finally, she stumbles into the living room, dropping onto the couch beside me smelling like sleep and Chocopuffs.

"What are you working on?" she asks, eyeing the poster board lying face down on the coffee table.

"I made something for you." Suddenly I don't want to show her.

Not like I care about her opinion. She's just a kid. And it's a silly project.

"What is it?" She flips the poster, the paper rustling as the glossy images catch the light. My carefully cut-out ads gleam against the white board, their edges curling slightly.

"It's an...alphabet," I tell her. Her eyes dim with boredom.

She hates it.

"I thought it might help," I explain.

She squints at the poster, hovering over the ad at the top left. "What does a model in a suit have to do with the alphabet?"

"Can you tell what kind of suit he's wearing?" I ask.

Isa leans in closer. "I think Armani."

"Correct!" I point to Armani written in large careful letters underneath. The A is especially big.

"This one's trickier," I say, pointing to an ad for sneakers. "Do you know Balenciaga?"

Isa nods. "I've heard of them."

Before I reach the third photo Isa shouts it out. "That's a Chloe purse!"

"It is."

"And that's the perfume my mom wears." Isa points to a picture of a teardrop perfume bottle. "It's Dior."

"Right again. A is for Armani, B is for Balenciaga, C is for Chloe, D is for Dior."

"It's the alphabet!" Isa says, her eyes bright with delight. "But with designers!"

"It is." I smile at her smile, relief settling into my belly.

We go through all the photos together, and Isa giggles at some of the crazy outfits I chose from the catalogs.

"Now when you see a G you don't have to try to remember what sound it makes. Just remember GUCCI. And when you see a V and forget that it makes a vvvv sound, think of Versace."

"This is way better than the one we have at school," Isa declares. "R for rocket? How relevant are rockets to our everyday life? I can remember these a lot better."

Her words fill me up.

Okay, maybe I did care about her opinion a little.

I hope the poster helps. And at the very least, I hope she feels like she has an adult she can talk to on bad days.

Sofia bribes Isa into taking a bath, and I head to a café near the apartment to sketch. Ideas for a new ensemble haunted my dreams all night, but nothing stuck.

There's a booth in the back corner, and I order an espresso, letting the aroma wake up all my senses.

Come on brain, you just need to come up with a showstopping ensemble for Marco to win him over so you can stay at the studio forever. It's not that hard.

I press my pencil to the page, its tip scratching faintly as I sketch, but every stroke feels wrong. It's like beating my head against a wall. Linen is the only material we have enough of to do pants. But if we stick with linen pants, it won't be different enough from the original.

When I return to the apartment, Marco has already left for the studio, and Sofia and Isa are getting ready for the park.

I settle onto the couch and flip to a fresh page.

Think, Lydia, you gorgeous genius. Cashmere. Cotton. Leather. Linen. What can we do? Maybe stitch them together like a quilt?

I sketch out a quilt suit. It's an abomination.

Isa careens through the living room shrieking like a banshee in nothing but her underwear. Sofia chases after her with a pair of leggings.

"You can't go outside in your underwear," Sofia says. "It's too cold."

"Then I'll wear a jacket," Isa replies.

"That'll look great," I mumble. Then I pause, pencil hanging in the air.

Hold on. Would that look great?

My heart kicks up a notch. I pull the sketchbook closer, fingers tingling, and flip to a fresh page. What if we use the leather for shortie briefs? Then we could use the linen for a loose, oversize blazer. I barely breathe as I sketch, the lead scraping hurried lines onto the paper.

The cashmere scarf is pashmina size, enough for a fitted shirt...

If we cut the cotton strips from the T-shirt...

My pen is flying across the page now. Leather shorts, a big linen jacket with a cashmere shirt, and a chunky scarf of braided cotton.

I add a fur hat to match the fur lined boots for this outfit. We don't have a hat like that, but it ties it all together and makes it feel like a cold weather outfit, despite the shorts. It's eclectic, but so is this collection.

It just might work.

Carefully, I color in the dark blue of the shirt, light tan of the jacket, and chestnut brown of the shorts.

"What are you working on?" Isabella is fully clothed next to me on the couch.

How long has she been there?

"Just an idea."

"For Dad's show?"

"Yeah, maybe."

Isa and Sofia head off to the park, and I color in the hat and boots. This is my big chance. I'll present it to Marco tomorrow, and he'll see what I can do. He'll see what an asset I am to the studio. I head to my room, rehearsing exactly what I'll say.

Sweat springs up along my hairline. It's been a long time since I cared this much about something.

Without warning, my sixth-grade teacher pops into my head.

The classroom is too bright, the fluorescent lights humming overhead. My fingers tighten around the edges of my Star Wars poster, soft from too much handling. The teacher's puzzled expression makes my stomach twist.

"The project was supposed to be about Warsaw," she says, voice kind and pitying.

Whispers break into laughter and my shoes squeak on the linoleum as I slink back to my desk.

I'd been excited. I'd thought I'd done a great job. And I became the class joke.

I drop onto the bed, mattress creaking beneath me, sketchpad pressing into my palm. The design looked brilliant minutes ago, but now, it feels ridiculous.

The collection is Midnight Garden. Who wears leather shorts at midnight?

And Marco's not looking for ideas from his nanny. He gave this task to Clara and Danilo.

The pad falls from my fingers to the floor with a thunk. It's better this way. Just thinking about sharing this with Marco makes my stomach knot. Getting Ds and Fs in college didn't bother me because I didn't care about my professors or the work.

Marco's rejection would destroy me.

Chapter Sixteen

Late morning sunshine filters through my window, and I pull the blanket over my head. Between the lumpy mattress that doubles as a torture device, and my anxiety at the mere thought of showing Marco my design, I did not sleep well.

I check my phone and Nico's sent me a pic of a bridge. He's hanging off the side of it with a bunch of guys his age. They're all cute in that dark-haired Italian way, but I can't take my eyes off Nico.

Check out this cool bridge!

You're gorgeous, I type into my phone. I want to smooch your beautiful dimples. Then I delete each word, write,

super cool bridge

I hit send.

He replies immediately.

It's by the Navigli canals. Have you been down there yet?

If it's outside downtown, I haven't been there.

No.

Bubbles wiggle on my phone, letting me know he's typing. Then his message comes through.

You should go.

I squash my disappointment.

Did you want him to offer to take you? He already asked you on a date. And you said no. Because he has a girlfriend.

Right. All true. I'm not getting tangled up in that drama.

I look at my phone.

But I could take a quick peek at that drama.

I Google "Nico Moretti's girlfriend", and am flooded with images of a tall, gorgeous blonde hanging off his arm at a number of glamorous events. Britta Larsson. The Swedish supermodel.

Ugh.

I bury my face in my pillow and scream.

My phone buzzes, and I snatch it up, but it's a text from Carmen.

What do you think?

She's wearing a long blue dress with a high collar and long sleeves. She looks like a pilgrim.

Are you churning butter? It's perfect.

After a moment, her text comes through.

I have a date.

Please don't wear that.

Then I return to the picture of Nico on the bridge and ogle the way his shoulder muscles bulge under his shirt. There's a sliver of exposed stomach, and I zoom in to get a better look at his abs, imagining what they would feel like under my fingertips. I want to spend the rest of the day snuggled in bed, looking at those two inches of skin. Instead, I throw my pillow across my room and text Carmen.

> Why don't you come over, and we'll find you something to wear for your date?

Carmen is the perfect distraction. Instead of pining after someone I can't have, I focus all my energy on dressing the woman in front of me.

"It's just a coffee date," Carmen says standing by my mirror. She's wearing my Armani blazer, and it looks great on her, like I knew it would.

It would look even better with my Chanel straight leg pants, but they'll be too small for her, and I won't put her through the embarrassment of trying on too-small pants.

"The guy is the brother of one of the secretaries at the school," Carmen says, "I don't have high hopes."

I rifle through my closet looking for an A-line skirt.

"Try this on," I say, handing her a bright pink Kate Spade. If she wears it high on her waist it should fit okay. I dive back into the closet for a loose blouse.

"I haven't been on a date in a while. What if I order pickles again?"

I pull my head out of the wardrobe and tune in to what she's saying.

"Could you maybe give me some pointers?" Her cheeks turn pink, and she drops her gaze. "On how to flirt without looking like a lunatic?" Her face is a tapestry of embarrassment and insecurity.

Oh, Carmen.

"Sure," I say, taking a moment to figure out where to begin. Carmen chews on a fingernail, growing more nervous by the second.

"I want to get better at this," she says, "but I don't want it to be like in a movie where I have to make a fool of myself in front of a bunch of different men before I figure out how to talk to the one I like."

"You don't have to make a fool out of yourself in front of anyone," I tell her. "In fact, you don't have to practice talking to any men at all."

Carmen's eyes narrow. "Who do I have to practice talking to?"

"Yourself," I reply.

Her brow furrows.

"I want you to practice talking to yourself—inside your head, or at home in front of the mirror—and reminding yourself how wonderful you are."

Carmen snorts and shakes her head, but I grab her wrist and her body goes still.

"Tell yourself how smart you are. How funny. How kind. How beautiful."

She licks her lips nervously.

"And it's not just talking," I continue. "I want you to treat yourself like you are head over heels in love with Carmen the Magnificent. Buy yourself flowers. Take yourself out to dinner. Wear a new shade of lipstick because you love how it looks on you." I lock eyes with Carmen. "Start loving yourself the way you deserve, and you won't have to do anything else. The men will come to you, begging for your time and attention."

Carmen lets out a shaky breath. "You really think so?"

I nod once. "I know it."

I slip into the conference room at 9:28 on Monday morning and take a seat at the back. I'm not exactly invited to this meeting, but no one said I couldn't come.

Danilo and Clara huddle together whispering, and Chelsie passes out coffees. I take one and sip it gratefully. Bianca stands next to Marco, wearing a dress that makes her look like the teapot from Beauty and the Beast. She points to things on her clipboard while Marco nods. The whiteboard at the front of the room is filled with Marco's scribbles, and pinned to the top is the sketch I drew on Saturday.

My stomach drops and my pulse pounds in my ears, drowning out the murmur of conversation around me.

What? How did that—? I didn't—

"Morning," Marco says, drawing all eyes to him.

My hands sweat, and my brain keeps firing unanswerable questions at me.

"We've got a lot to cover, so I'm going to jump right into it. I appreciate

Danilo and Clara working over the weekend to come up with a creative solution to our final ensemble. You both turned in great efforts this morning, and based on the things we discussed in our individual meetings, I'm confident we'll see your designs on the runway in the near future. For this show, however, I'm using a design from Lydia St. Clair."

Oh my gosh oh my gosh oh my gosh. What is going on?

I breathe in through my nose and out through my mouth. There's not enough oxygen. It's too hot in here, and I'm suddenly lightheaded.

"I'm sorry I didn't have a chance to talk to you about this," Marco says, looking at me.

If he's alarmed that his nanny is about to faint in the middle of the conference room, he doesn't show it.

"I was struck by your idea as soon as I saw it yesterday, but I thought it only fair to speak with our junior designers before making a decision. Unfortunately, those meetings ran long, and I didn't get a chance to meet with you beforehand. Forgive me. It won't be the last time things get rushed this week. Let's give a big hand to Lydia for her design."

Chelsie and Bianca clap next to Marco and look genuinely happy for me. The smiles on Clara's and Danilo's faces are about as real as the Prada boots at Sant'Ambrogio market.

"I'm going to focus my attention on bringing this design to life," Marco continues. "Here's what I'd like the team to work on..."

The rest of Marco's words are lost in my swirling brain.

He's using MY design for the ensemble!? How did he even get it?

My heart hammers, and I fold my arms across my chest to muffle the sound.

A runway show is going to include something I designed. And the catalog! Oh, sweet glory, what if people buy it? People could actually buy an outfit I designed.

My head spins, and I take another grounding breath.

"Okay team. Let's get to it."

Everyone shuffles out, but I remain seated. Partly because I missed all of Marco's instructions and partly because I don't trust my legs to support me.

"Sorry for the surprise," Marco says, but the grin on his face doesn't look sorry.

"No, it's okay. I mean thank you." My voice is faint and squeaky, and I swallow hard. "How did you get that sketch? I didn't mean for you to have it."

Marco raises an eyebrow.

"I mean, yes, I made it thinking about the ensemble, but I didn't think..."

"Isa gave it to me," Marco says.

Isa showed him my sketch? Why would she do that? Did she know what would happen?

Marco stands there, amusement flickering across his face as I pull myself together. "I'm sorry, I know you have a million things to do. I missed my assignment for this morning."

Marco chuckles. "It's okay. Your first design is a big deal. Enjoy this feeling. And keep chasing it. For today, I'd like you to work on organizing the accessories with Danilo and Clara. They've done this before. They can talk you through the details."

He turns to leave but pauses. "Isa also showed me your fashion alphabet." His eyes crinkle. "Very clever."

"*Grazie*," I say.

"Thank *you*," he says. "We're lucky to have you."

I'm not sure if he means as a nanny, or at the studio, but I exit the conference room on a designer cloud made of quality cashmere.

My design is going to be in Marco's show. All my dreams are coming true.

"So, the nanny gets her design in the show," Clara says when I arrive at the accessories table. Her eyes are narrowed in resentment, which makes her nose look even bigger than normal somehow. "What a surprise."

For a split second, I consider defending myself. Letting them know I didn't pitch my design to Marco. But instead, I simply smile.

"Marco says we're organizing accessories today. Where do we start?"

Clara looks at Danilo, and he gives her a resigned look, then turns to me. "Come over here, I'll show you how to do it."

I spend the rest of the day bagging scarves, earrings, necklaces, and hats and matching them to the bin with the correct photo on it. Danilo and Clara have a lot of snarky comments to say, all of them making it clear they don't think my design deserves to be in the show.

At first, I ignore their words, too happy to care about their silly opinions. But when Clara says there's no way I came up with the idea on my own and probably found the design online, I've had enough.

The blood in my veins runs hot and angry, but when I turn to Clara, my face is a smooth mask of calm.

"Just like those skinny jeans you wear, jealousy doesn't look good on you." I flick my gaze over to include Danilo. "And if you're worried what people will think of you getting passed over for the intern, don't be." I give them each a reassuring smile. "No one will be thinking about you at all."

I take a moment to enjoy their furious expressions, then I go back to organizing accessories for the runway show that will include my debut ensemble.

The wind is howling, blowing leaves off the trees like the branches owe her money, but I skip to Isa's school like it's the first day of spring. She's one of the last ones to walk out the door, and when she does, I scoop her up and swing her around.

"You devious, delightful, diabolical child," I say over her giggling.

"Do you know what happened when I got to the studio today?" I ask, giving her another spin.

"Maybe." Her eyes spark with hope and excitement. I put her down and pull her into a hug.

"Your dad announced that he's using my design in the spring collection. Mine!"

"Woohoo!" Isa says, only it's muffled because she's squashed against my stomach. I release her and squat down so we're at eye level.

"Thank you, thank you, thank you," I say, kissing her cheeks.

Isa giggles and pumps two skinny fists into the air. "I knew it was a good idea!"

"How can I repay you?"

"I accept gelato," she says cheekily.

So, we head to the gelateria on the corner. I don't care that it's a cold day or that my Gucci slacks are starting to feel tight around my waist. Gelato is a fantastic idea. Isabella gets stracciatella, and I get mango. We sit at a table inside and enjoy our cold scoops of heaven.

"So how did school go today?" I ask. "Throw any more punches?"

Isa manages to look offended and sheepish at the same time. "No. Um... actually, I apologized."

My mouth falls open, and I spoon some gelato in to cover it. Nothing I've seen from this child over the past month would lead me to believe she would apologize to a kid her age. Or anyone.

"How did it go?" I ask, keeping my voice neutral.

Isa shrugs. "He was kind of surprised."

I'll bet.

"His friend still makes rude faces at me, but he smiled at me at recess."

"Well, I'm impressed," I say. "That was very mature."

Isa nods, pleased with herself.

"Speaking of mature, do you think I should still be doing your homework?" It's a risky move bringing this up, but confidence and adrenaline are pulsing through me. If I can create a runway-worthy ensemble, surely I can find a way to stop doing a first grader's homework.

Isa's shoulder's slump and a drop of gelato falls from her cone and splatters on the table. "It's the worst."

I nod. "That's what I thought too. But in the two weeks I've been doing it, I've learned some things. I can help you figure it out super-fast."

"I know all the shapes and colors," she says. "I just get tripped up on the words."

"That's okay. We'll work through it together."

We finish our ice cream and get started on Isa's homework as soon as we get back to the apartment. She knocks out a shape coloring sheet and a counting activity in the first five minutes. With a little bit of guidance, she completes a sight word matching sheet.

"Not so bad, right?" I say.

She gives me a look that says "*I did the homework, but don't push it,*" so I leave it at that.

When Sofia gets home, Isa shows her the work she's done, and Sofia raves like her daughter painted the Sistine Chapel. Isa glows with pride.

"I hear there was some exciting news at the studio today," Sofia says with a smile.

"Dad's using Lydia's design!" Isa shouts. "And it was my idea. I gave him her sketch."

"Well, it was a very clever idea," Sofia says. She looks at me. "And from what I hear, a brilliant design."

Brilliant? Is that what Marco told her?

I can't keep the proud grin off my face.

Nico calls, and my already jumpy heart starts galloping.

"*Pronto*?" I say, slipping down the hall to my bedroom.

"Yes, I'm looking for the extremely talented intern whose design got chosen for the runway show?" Nico's voice is serious and formal like a reporter.

"That's me," I say with a giggle. I slap a hand over my mouth. I am *not* a giggler.

I settle onto the bed and hug a pillow to my chest.

"Congratulations, Lydia." His voice is back to regular now, and I want to scoop up the way he says my name and save it in a box so I can listen to it whenever I want. "I just stopped by the studio and heard the news."

"I still can't believe it," I say.

"Neither can I! Imagine my surprise when I discovered that my friend Lydia, with whom I have taken the sacred oath of elbow tassels, is a fashion prodigy and didn't tell me!"

I giggle again.

What is happening to me? I sound like a tipsy sorority sister.

"I'm not a prodigy. But Marco did tell Sofia that my design is brilliant."

"I am so excited for you." The happiness in his voice comes through even over the phone.

"Clara and Danilo were less than thrilled at Marco's choice."

Nico lowers his voice. "Did you see their designs?"

"No! Did you?"

"Hold on, I snapped pics when I snuck into Marco's office. I'll send them to you."

There's a buzz and two pics come through.

"The first one's Clara's."

I stare at it confused. "This looks exactly like the original ensemble."

Nico laughs. "Yep. She added leather braids to the vest and changed the scarf, but that's it."

I shake my head in disbelief. This was her opportunity, and she blew it.

"Danilo did a little better," Nico says, and I pull up his photo.

He kept the pants and shirt the same but turned the vest into a leather fanny pack. And left out the scarf.

All this time I assumed Danilo and Clara were brilliant designers. To see how uninspired and derivative their designs are is eye-opening.

"No wonder Marco chose mine."

"He didn't choose yours because the others were bad," Nico says. "I talked to him. He decided on your design before he'd even seen theirs. That's how good it was."

"Well, either way. I can't believe my design is going to debut on a runway in less than a week."

"And guess who's wearing it?"

My jaw drops.

No way.

"You already have your ensembles," I say. "This is for the model replacing Giovanni."

"The fill-in model is too tall for your design. Marco's going to lengthen the hem on my corduroy pants ensemble and have him walk it instead."

I imagine Nico in the design I created, and my heart thumps an irregular rhythm.

"What?" Nico says to my silence. "You don't think I'll do it justice?" He's teasing, but there's a note of uncertainty in his voice.

"Nico. Have you seen my design?"

"No. Your sketch wasn't in Marco's office. But I'm doing a first fitting tomorrow."

Laughter bubbles out of me, uncontainable.

"What?"

I shake my head, giggling helplessly. "You'll see tomorrow."

Chapter Seventeen

"Wow," Nico says, standing on a pedestal in the middle of the studio. Fabric scraps litter the floor like fallen leaves.

"Wow," I echo, unable to look away.

He's wearing nothing but small leather shorts. My gaze flickers over his long, toned legs, skims past the leather briefs, and lingers on his sculpted abs and bare chest. Light from the skylight makes his skin glow, and I clench my hands together to keep from running them over his shoulders.

Designers rush from model to model as Bianca barks orders and Marco sews furiously at a machine by the window. I'm supposed to be organizing accessories, but I can't pull myself away from Nico.

"Was this all part of your diabolical plan?" Nico asks, expression bemused.

"From the moment I met you."

He nods like he suspected as much. "Well congratulations on your double victory. Is this the type of thing you sewed with your sweet grandmother in her little cottage?"

"It is not."

But I can't help thinking Grandma Lottie would be tickled to see this particular outfit. Especially on Nico.

I try to focus on his face, but my eyes keep betraying me, drifting downward to his six-pack stomach.

Nico smirks. "You planning to work today or just check me out?"

Option two. Definitely option two.

I give an exaggerated scoff, then shove him off the pedestal, pretending I don't notice how hard his chest feels under my hand. He falls, wrapping an arm around me as he does. The studio's chilly, but Nico's arm is warm against mine. His breath on the back of my neck makes goose bumps break out along my arms.

"Thanks for waiting, Nico," Marco says, striding over, shirt in hand. "I adjusted the neckline, and I think this will work better.

Nico removes his arm from around my shoulder and steps back onto the pedestal. I sneak over to the accessories table, hoping Marco was too distracted to notice me snuggling one of his models.

"Those shorts are amazing," Danilo says when I come over.

I pause mid-step.

"Thanks?" The table is filled with jewelry, scarves, belts, and shoes. I pick a photo from the stack and begin searching for the accessories that go with it.

"And I really like the way you paired them with a blazer," Clara adds. "Bold move." I scan their faces for sarcasm or envy, but there's none to be found. Instead, they wear expressions I've seen my whole life—suck-ups looking to score points.

"That's kind of you to say." I select a gold bracelet from the pile, but it's not the one for my outfit, and I put it back.

"Well, it's only the truth," Danilo gushes, light reflecting off his gelled hair.

My shoulders straighten, and I look Danilo in the eyes. "I could have used some of that kindness, truth or not, when I showed up here a month ago."

Danilo looks at Clara, and she speaks for both of them. "About the way we treated you—we are so sorry. We didn't know—"

"That one day it might benefit you to be on my good side?"

Clara flinches, and Danilo's cheeks turn red. She opens her mouth, then closes it and shrugs.

"We will not be friends," I tell them both. "That ship has sailed. But we will treat each other with professional courtesy."

"Of course," Clara enthuses.

"Courtesy. Such a good idea," Danilo says.

I shake my head. They are ridiculous.

We tackle the task in front of us, organizing everything the models will wear with their ensembles. As we work, I sneak glances at Nico. He sees me looking and breaks into an off-key version of Taylor Swift's "Shake it Off." Marco smiles and shakes his head as he pins the hem of the linen blazer. Marco has quick-stitched all the pieces, and I get to see how my design looks on a real person. It's incredible.

"Looking good," I tell Nico as I get ready to leave.

He flashes a grin, but I can tell he's tired. He's been on his feet for hours with Marco poking and prodding, measuring and re-measuring.

"How'd you like my singing today? The last one was just for you."

The last song he belted out was Lady Gaga's "Poker Face."

"It was the dance moves I liked best," I say, slipping into my Burberry trench.

"This outfit is too restrictive to show off my best moves." He lifts his legs like an Olympic athlete stretching before a sprint.

"You should come dancing with us tomorrow night," I say.

"Yeah?" Nico's eyes widen in surprise.

Dang. I didn't mean to say that out loud. But I can't un-invite him, that will make this seem like a big deal. Which it isn't.

"Yeah. We go to this place, Calypso by Parco Sempione. I'll text you the details."

"Okay, count me in."

This is a terrible idea, my brain tells me. But my eyes have spent hours gazing at Nico's chiseled body and my ears have listened to his goofy singing and my heart thinks that seeing him tomorrow night is an excellent idea.

There's a smudge on my water glass, and I wipe it off with my napkin. It still looks smudgy. I dip my napkin in the water and rub some more.

"You okay?" Valentina asks, and I jump.

"Fine." I put the napkin down and drum my fingers on the table.

"Your hair looks gorgeous tonight," Carmen says, reaching out a hand to touch my curls. From the look on her face, it's like she's fingering prayer beads.

"Thanks," I say and start shredding the paper on my straw.

It's dumb to feel this nervous. Nico meeting the gang is no big deal. It's not like I'm introducing them to my boyfriend.

And besides, they're going to love Nico. Everyone loves Nico. If I were introducing Chad to them, that would be a problem. I touch a hand to my forehead wondering how in the world I dated that guy.

Nico walks through the door right on time, and I nearly leap from the booth to meet him.

Play it cool, St. Clair.

"You made it!" I say, trying to keep my voice chill.

"Of course."

His lips brush my cheek, and every nerve in my body goes still. *Could we just stay here, cheeks almost touching, breathing in each other's smell?* I pull away.

He runs a hand through his hair then shoves his hands into his pockets.

"Come meet the gang."

He follows me through a sea of dancing bodies to get to our back booth.

"Nico, this is Carmen, Valentina, and Paolo." I slide in next to Carmen, expecting her to squish over and make room for Nico. She doesn't. Nico squishes in next to me, his leg touching mine from hip to knee, and I forget to breathe.

"*Ragazzi*, this is Nico." My voice comes out shaky, and I take a sip of water. If Carmen were a cartoon character, there would be hearts bulging out of her eyes, and Valentina looks like she wants to break into applause.

I thought about texting them beforehand to let them know I was bringing Nico, but I didn't want them to think this was a big deal. Because it's not.

"The guy from work?" Carmen asks. I kick her under the table, then cough loudly to muffle her yelp.

"Aw, you've been talking about me?" Nico's eyes crinkle, and his dimples pop out.

"I was telling these guys about the poor model who has to wear my outfit."

"The one with tiny leather shorts?" Carmen squeaks. Her cheeks match my Royal Red lipstick, and I can tell she's visualizing it.

"That's the one," Nico says. "I'm about to be part of history. Lydia St. Clair's fashion debut." There's a note of pride in his voice, and I realize it's for me. He's proud of me.

"Hey, how was your coffee date on Sunday?" I ask Carmen, feeling bad I didn't text her Monday.

"Ugh. A disaster. He talked about himself in the third person and didn't ask a single question about me."

"I'm sorry."

She shrugs. "It's okay. The old me would have accepted his offer for a second date, but new me knows I deserve better, so I declined."

"Yes!" I throw an arm around her. "Well done."

A salsa song plays, and Nico offers me his hand. "Would you like to dance?"

"Are you a salsa dancer?" I ask.

"You better believe it."

I place my hand in his, noting the warm strength there, and follow him onto the dance floor. He pulls me into his arms and leads us in a flurry of dramatic dips and fancy twirls.

"I told you I had the moves," he says.

"I'm very impressed."

"Then my plan is working."

I smile, but my brain is racing.

Why does he want to impress me? Why did he even come out with me tonight? This is not the way you behave when you're dating a Swedish model.

Or maybe it is? This isn't Connecticut.

"Your friends seem really cool," Nico says.

"Oh, they're not my—" I stop myself. *Who am I kidding?* "Yep. They're my friends. And they're cool."

The five of us spend the next two hours dancing, laughing, and singing along to the music. At some point, Paolo and Nico head back to the booth, talking and laughing like old friends. It means something that Paolo likes him. Paolo wears a vintage Cartier watch. I trust his judgment.

"So, you and Nico, huh?" Carmen says, shimmying her shoulders toward me.

I shake my head. "We're just friends."

"Valentina, when you saw Nico and Lydia dancing earlier, did they look like they were just friends or like they were too people who wanted to smooch?"

"Definitely smoochy vibes," Valentina says.

"Let's talk about Lorenzo," I say. "Have you talked to him tonight?"

Carmen shakes her head looking proud. "Nope. I'm loving myself, and I'm going to let him come to me."

"Yes!" I say and high five her.

"I think it's already working," Valentina says. "I've seen him looking at you a bunch tonight."

Carmen shrugs like it's of no consequence to her, but her smile stretches across her whole face.

I glance over at the bar, and Lorenzo is definitely looking over here. They just announced last call, and there are only two people left at the bar. The music changes, morphing from a fast techno song to the opening chords of "You're Beautiful."

Paolo comes over to dance with Valentina, and Carmen starts heading back to the booth.

"Wait," I tell her.

"What? Why?"

"Trust me. I'm going to walk away, and I want you to count to ten before you follow me."

She looks at my gaze, locked on the bar behind her, and I can see her fighting the urge to look behind her.

"Don't look," I murmur. "Let him come to you."

Her face goes white. "What do I do?" She looks really and truly terrified.

"That depends. If you want to make this guy's night, you say yes when he asks you to dance. If you'd rather hang with friends, you come back to the booth with me."

Her lips curl into a tiny smile, and her shoulders straighten. "I could make his night."

I nod and walk slowly toward the booth. Over James Blunt's crooning, I can just make out their conversation.

"*Ciao,*" Lorenzo says.

"*Ciao,*" Carmen replies.

"You didn't come to the bar tonight."

"I didn't need any pickles," she says.

I clap a hand to my mouth to keep from laughing out loud. I'm too far away now to hear any more, but I think she's going to be okay.

My thoughts are so focused on Carmen and Lorenzo, I bump into Nico standing right in front of me.

"Oof. Sorry," I say. "I didn't see you."

"Standing right in front of you? Ouch."

I swat his shoulder and smile. "I was distracted. Carmen's been trying to get that bartender's attention for ages, and he just asked her to slow dance."

"Best way to let someone know you like them," Nico says. Then he looks me straight in the eyes and asks, "Want to slow dance?"

As if my body has taken over my brain, I nod and follow Nico to the dance floor. He slips one arm around my waist and takes my hand with the other. As he pulls me close, I catch a whiff of woodsy, spicy cologne. It's not his usual scent, and I wonder if he put it on just for tonight.

"Your hair looks especially lovely tonight." He reaches a tentative hand toward my face and into my hair, cradling the back of my head.

When we were salsa dancing, I could pretend it was casual fun, but this is different. My heart pounds, and I'm close enough to feel his heartbeat through the thin fabric of his T-shirt. His hand on the small of my back pulls me closer to him, and his thumb under my hair caresses the nape of my neck. We're in a tiny bubble, breathing the same air, our faces close enough that if I tilt my head to the side...

My whole body heats up with anticipation, but my brain pours water over the embers sending them sizzling.

What are we doing?

"What are we doing?" I ask out loud.

Emotions flash quickly across Nico's face. Surprise, embarrassment, possibly guilt. He leans back an inch.

"Dancing."

"I like dancing with you," I tell him honestly. "But it's not fair to the other people involved."

Nico's cheeks color. He doesn't meet my gaze. "You're right."

"I'm glad you came tonight. And I'm glad you met my friends. But I'm going to call it a night."

Nico shakes his head. "No, stay. I'll go."

I think about arguing with him, or at least walking him to the door, but I don't trust myself. Thirty seconds from now I'm going to say yes to everything I've been saying no to.

Nico walks out of the club, and I'm torn between congratulating myself and poking myself in the eye.

Would one kiss be so terrible?

Yes!

And it's not just my summer camp vow of not stealing people's boyfriends, its self-preservation. If I let things go further with Nico, *I'm* the one who will get hurt.

Despite my best efforts, I have feelings for him. And getting involved with someone who's not available would suck even worse than the time I walked in on my dad and his campaign manager making out on our couch.

I return to the booth, and Paolo, Valentina, and Carmen join me when the song finishes.

"Where's Nico?" Paolo asks.

"He went home. Early morning tomorrow." I keep my voice cheerful and meet Paolo's eyes like my heart isn't swirling in confusion.

"How was your dance with Lorenzo?" I ask, turning my attention to Carmen.

Her eyes light up, and she wipes sweat off the back of her neck "He's the dreamiest. He smells like peppermint, and I would have slipped the DJ everything in my purse to play the song on repeat."

The smitten look on her face is adorable. It's almost enough to erase the image of Nico's sad eyes just before he left.

It's for the best, I remind myself. *Any man who would cheat on his girlfriend is not worth dating. Better to avoid all the drama and focus on work.*

Chapter Eighteen

The studio feels like NASA readying a rocket launch. If the astronauts were sleep-deprived, running on espresso fumes, and arguing over accessories.

Steam hisses from irons and sewing machines rattle like caffeinated hummingbirds. The air smells of freshly pressed fabric and the cigarettes Marco smokes when he's nervous. The runway show is tomorrow and even though everything's ready to go, Marco insists on triple checking measurements and creating contingency plans.

I iron clothes, organize accessories, and match shoes, trying to forget that after tomorrow Marco won't need me anymore. A hollow ache settles in my chest as I survey the beautifully dressed mannequins, rows of sewing machines, and piles of fabric. *I'm not ready to leave all this.*

"You ready?" Nico asks, making me jump.

It's been so busy I haven't had the chance to talk to him today.

Okay, fine, I've been avoiding him.

Last night made it clear I can't be his friend. The feelings I feel for him are not friendly feelings. I want to snuggle with him on a cold day. I want to run my hands through his hair while he talks about bridges. I want him to be mine.

But he isn't. And I am a terrible sport when I don't get the things I want.

"For?" I ask.

Nico tilts his head, and a lock of hair falls into his eyes. "The show tomorrow."

"Show. Yes. Ready." Apparently, I can only talk to Nico in one-word sentences now.

Bianca rushes over and thrusts a strappy high heel at me.

"The strap is broken."

I take it from her and examine it. "Yes. It is," I say, as though all she needed was confirmation.

"I need you to sew it!" Exasperation oozes from her.

"Right! I'm on it." I head to a work station and spend the next thirty minutes punishing that strap for its audacity and making sure it will never fall off again.

I wave to Nico before I leave to get Isa. "I'll see you at the show."

A dozen emotions flicker across his face before he gives me a strained smile. "See you at the show."

Tears prick in my eyes as I step onto the sidewalk.

What is wrong with me?

I button my coat and straighten my shoulders.

Yes, I really like him, but I can't have him, and I will not have an emotional breakdown in public like some kind of Love Island reject.

Isa is grinning from ear to ear when she comes out and throws her arms around me in a hug.

"Good day?" I take her backpack and slide it onto my shoulder.

"The best! *Signora* Macaluso gave me back my homework, and I got all stars!"

She's jumping around like stars are actually diamond tennis bracelets, and I high five her, letting her happiness rub off on me. She worked hard on that homework. She deserves this.

"Well done!"

"Thank you." She looks at me. "You look sad."

"Just tired. It was a busy day at work. We've got the big show tomorrow."

"Ooh, what are you going to wear?"

I stop dead in my tracks. With all the excitement of my design getting chosen, I never stopped to think about what I would wear. I have nothing. I barely packed half my wardrobe and besides the ridiculous dumpster market, I haven't done any shopping.

"I have no idea. Will you come shopping with me? Help me find something great?"

Isa's face lights up like she's been crowned Queen of Italy. "Yes!" she squeals. "I would love to go shopping with you!"

We spend the next two hours enjoying the luxury of Dolce & Gabbana, Versace, Armani, and Prada. As we move from shop-to-shop, Isa practices her Fashion Alphabet. I stock up on quality staples that I don't have here in Milan and splurge on some new additions I could never find back in America.

The designers at shows usually wear something black and simple, so as not to detract from the collections. At Versace, I spot a knee-length silk dress and know it's the one.

"You look amazing," Isabella breathes.

She's not wrong. The cut is flattering, and the light catches the sheen of the silk making it shine with each movement.

Nico will love it.

Which is irrelevant. Because nothing is happening with Nico. I just need to make it through one more night. Surely, I can do that.

I can't do that. The venue is a swirl of color and movement, but my gaze locks onto Nico like he's a lighthouse and I'm lost at sea. His forest green shirt clings to his chest, as he wipes his hands on his burgundy suede pants. The hair and makeup team have gotten to him, and he looks like an Instagram-filtered version of himself.

I sneak into a dressing room and give myself a pep talk.

You can do this. One more night. Be a professional.

I apply another coat of Red Royalty for bravery. When I leave the dressing room, Nico is right there, like he was waiting for me.

"How are you feeling?" I ask.

"Terrible." He rubs the back of his neck with one hand, and under all the makeup and hair gel, his expression is one of misery. Worry shoots through me.

"What's wrong? What happened?" I want to reach out and touch him, but I clasp my hands tightly behind my back.

Professional boundaries, I remind myself.

Nico smiles but it doesn't reach his eyes. "Nothing happened. I always feel this way at shows."

"Really?"

"Really. All those faces staring at me, analyzing the slope of my shoulders and the curve of my butt." He clenches and unclenches his hands. "It's a nightmare every time."

He's always so happy at the studio, I assumed he loved modeling.

"Nico, I had no idea."

"I like the studio stuff, I just hate runway shows." His voice shakes, and my heart shakes with it, desperate for some way to cheer him up.

Before I know what I'm doing, I blurt, "My brother calls me Eggplant."

The misery in Nico's eyes is replaced with confusion, and my whole body is filled with horror.

Why in the world did I just tell him that?

"Your brother calls you—Wait! It's your embarrassing childhood nickname!" His eyes light up, and he breaks into a grin, dimples popping. "Why Eggplant? Because you're good for the heart? I can see that."

I smile, my regret fading at his happy expression.

"He calls me Eggplant because I got a black eye during an archery lesson and my whole face turned purple like an eggplant."

This has to be the least attractive thing I've ever told a man, but Nico scoops me into his arms.

"Thank you," he says into my hair. "For making me feel better."

"You've got this," I tell him. "You're going to go out there and walk that runway like you're John A. Roebling and it's the Brooklyn Bridge."

Nico pulls away, eyes wide. "You were listening!"

Nico has mentioned the guy who designed the Brooklyn Bridge a dozen times in the last month. And yes, I was listening.

He pulls me in tighter, and I nestle my head into the crook of his neck, where the warmth of his skin meets the faint scratch of stubble. His citrus smell is mixed with sweat, and I take a grounding breath.

"Are you sniffing me?" he murmurs.

"No. Maybe. You smell like grapefruit and dread."

His laugh rumbles through me, and I tighten my grip. Eventually the tension leaves his body, and his breathing slows. I don't know how long we stay that way, breathing in each other's scent, holding onto each other's warmth, but I never want it to end.

Nico releases me and runs a hand through his hair, breaking up the carefully coifed style.

A stylist zips to his side to fix it while Nico apologizes. When the stylist finishes, she turns hungry eyes to me.

"May I?" she asks, gesturing to my hair. I've worn it down and straight tonight.

"Sure," I say, and smooth my expression into something more pleasant than what I'm feeling as she touches my hair, oohing and ahhing.

Bianca rushes over, clipboard in hand. "They're ready for you backstage," she tells Nico.

"Okay." He follows her with heavy steps.

"Break a leg," I call after him.

He turns back, an appalled expression on his face. "I'm walking the runway! Why would you wish that for me?!"

"It's an expression. It means good luck."

"Then say good luck!" He gives me another scowl, but the right corner of his lip tilts up.

Once he's gone, I focus. Bianca is barking orders into a headpiece like this is the battle that will save the world from the zombie apocalypse, and she is the general.

"Reporting for duty," I say. "How can I help?"

"The first model walks in fifteen minutes, and I can't find Marco. Danilo just discovered an open seam in the gray corduroy pants, and I need to track down the right color thread to repair it." She looks ready to call in the nukes.

"I'll find Marco," I promise and dash through the throng of stylists, models, and assistants. Marco is nowhere to be found. I slip through the side exit to the seating area. Every seat is filled and the gentleman in the front row may or may not be Beckham. Unsurprisingly, Marco is not seated with the audience.

Worry squeezes my chest like poorly designed shapewear, and I sprint to the dressing rooms backstage, checking each one. Marco is in the third room. His eyes are watery, and his face looks pale and sweaty. There's a strong, sour smell in the air.

"Marco, are you okay?"

He nods. "Perfectly fine." Then he picks up the metal trash can and pukes into it. I turn and cover my mouth. I wish I could cover my ears. When I turn back, he's wiping his face with a handkerchief.

"Can I get you something? A doctor?"

Marco waves me away. "Unfortunately, this is just part of it for me." He opens a bottle of water, takes a drink, then spits it into the trash can. "I'll be fine when it's over." He grabs a piece of gum from a packet on the table and starts chewing vigorously.

"How do things look out there?"

"The place is packed, and Bianca has everything ready to go."

"Perfect." He takes a long drink of water then drops the bottle into the trash can. I make a note to find a janitor to take care of that. For now, I escort Marco back into the chaos.

The next thirty minutes go by in a blur. I help Danilo, Clara, and Marco dress each model before they go out. What felt like chaos is actually a well-organized show. There are no missing accessories, or broken shoes, or wardrobe malfunctions. Everything goes as smooth as satin.

I talk to Nico in snatches. "You look like you're about to make a run for it," I whisper as I straighten his collar.

"I'm counting down the minutes until I can," Nico says.

My design is one of the last ensembles to go out, and I slip out the side entrance to watch. A slow crescendo of applause rises as Nico strides onto the runway. Camera flashes flicker like fireflies, reflecting off the leather of his shorts. Somewhere in the audience, someone gasps. Honestly? Fair.

Nico's boots thud softly against the polished runway, barely audible over the chatter of the crowd. Light glints off his toned thighs, and his face is the same mask of aloof detachment all the models wear.

If you didn't know Nico, it would be easy to miss the anxiety etched into the set of his jaw. But I do know him, and I see how deeply uncomfortable he is at this moment. Without thinking, I bring my fingers to my lips and let out a loud whistle. Nico blinks and the right corner of his mouth twitches up in a smile. Then he turns and walks back down the catwalk while a hundred people take pictures of his butt.

I dart back inside as he's slipping off the linen blazer.

"Cat calling? At a runway show?" he shakes his head. "You Americans." But his shoulders look more relaxed, and his eyes have lost that glassy quality. "They loved your design," he tells me, leaning in close.

"Did they? I mean there *was* a lot of applause..."

"It killed. You're going to be a star." He kisses my cheek, and a burst of happiness shivers through me.

I want to savor this moment, but there's no time. We have four more models to dress, accessorize, and send on their way. By the time they've returned, my nerves are shot, and I'm ready to collapse into a heap in the corner.

Marco calls all the models to the stage. Then he calls Danilo and Clara and me to the stage.

I squint in the bright lights and squeeze my hands together. The applause is thunderous. I imagine that a small portion of it is for my design, and a feeling of pure joy starts in my toes and shimmies up to my scalp. Gratitude like I've never felt before overwhelms me. To be here. To be a part of this.

Marco thanks a few people but keeps things mercifully short. And then we're all backstage helping the models get out of their last ensembles.

The energy rippling through the group is electric. We did good, and we know it. I'm smiling so big my cheeks will be sore tomorrow, and someone is pouring Marco a glass of champagne. There's an afterparty, and even though adrenaline is coursing through me, and it will be hours before I sleep, I'm ready for a quiet room. I need some time on my own to process everything.

Danilo and Clara have already left for the party, so it's me and Bianca who put away the last of the ensembles. We're both giddy with relief, and Bianca smiles more in fifteen minutes than the whole month I've known her.

I track down my purse and jacket and head to the exit. Marco's spent the last thirty minutes at the door, thanking people and accepting congratulations, but now the crowds are gone and it's just us.

"Congratulations," I tell him, feeling drunk with happiness.

"Thank you," Marco says. "The show exceeded all my expectations. Which as you know, were extremely high." His eyes are shining, and even though he's sleep deprived and exhausted, there's no mistaking the satisfaction in his eyes.

I was going to talk to him about this on Monday, but I'm feeling so good, why wait?

"I appreciate the opportunity to have my design included in the show."

"It was well earned," Marco says, eyes crinkling.

"I'd like the chance to create more things for Rossi Designs, and I'm hoping you will consider me for the vacant junior designer position."

Marco's eyebrows furrow. "To replace Luigi?"

"Yes. I know it would only be part-time, because obviously I'm still Isabella's nanny, but I think I'm up for the job."

Marco's eyes soften, and his voice turns consoling. "Lydia, you have a real gift for design. But you don't have the education or experience for the junior designer position."

Heat floods my cheeks. "But—"

"Clara and Danilo both have four-year degrees from design school and five years experience. The leap from part-time intern to junior designer is a big one."

His words wash over me on a wave of embarrassment. Of course, they have degrees and experience. They're a million times more qualified than I am.

Why did I think I could get that position? Because I sketched one design?

Tears prick my eyes, but I've mastered the art of pushing them back in public.

"I know you enjoy working in the studio," Marco continues. "And as I said, you have a real talent for it. If you'd like, you can continue as a part-time intern while you're here in Milan." His eyes are full of pity, and I want nothing more than to fold myself up like a silk scarf and hide in someone's pocket. "Of course, if you'd rather not continue as an intern I understand."

With effort I switch on the senator's daughter and push down everything I'm feeling inside. I make eye contact. I smile. I say, "I would very much like to continue at the studio as an intern. I know I have a lot to learn, and I appreciate the opportunity. Congratulations again on the show."

And then I walk out, shoulders back, head high.

The tears are coming—I can't keep them at bay any longer—so I circle the building and slip into a side entrance. Legs trembling, I find an empty dressing room and curl into a ball, letting all my hopes and dreams drown in a flood of tears.

Chapter Nineteen

Sobs tear from my throat, raw and jagged, like waves crashing on a rocky shore. I scold myself for my dramatics even as my heart breaks.

Really Lydia? Sobs? Who cares that much about a stupid job?

But I clutch my knees, tears dripping down my cheeks because *I* do. It's not some stupid job, it's my dream job. And I was foolish enough to believe I could do it.

The sadness of watching my dream die mixes with the mortification of my conversation with Marco. I close my eyes and see the confusion on his face, followed by the pity in his eyes.

How could I have been so ignorant? Of course, it requires a four-year degree. It's a real job.

I know he offered to keep me on as an intern, but I'm too embarrassed to show my face in the studio again. It will be bad enough living with him, I won't shame myself further by clinging to the breadcrumb he threw me.

People talk about going after your dreams. They write songs and movies and books about it. But the truth is, going after your dream sucks. Caring about something so much that you work obsessively for it, only to discover you're never going to have it *sucks.*

I wipe my snotty nose on my silk sleeve, officially reaching peak-pathetic.

"Lydia?"

I freeze mid-wipe. *Is that?*

The door to the dressing room swings open, and Nico stands in the doorway grinning.

No. This cannot be happening. I am having a hallucination brought on by intense embarrassment and disappointment.

His gaze finds me huddled on the floor and the light in his eyes dims like a sun slipping behind storm clouds.

"Lydia, what's wrong?" Nico rushes toward me, panic in his eyes.

I must look like a deranged lemur—puffy eyes, tangled hair, and probably remnants of mascara running down my cheeks.

I stand on shaky legs, but my throat is too tight to speak.

Nico wraps his arms around me, firm and warm, unraveling the last of my composure, and the tears fall faster.

"What happened?" His voice is sharp with concern as he smooths my hair along the back of my head. "Did someone hurt you?"

I shake my head. *Only myself.*

Nico holds me for a long time, and I ugly cry into his shoulder, letting the sadness and embarrassment and disappointment flow out of me. My mother would be horrified if she saw me sobbing like this in front of an attractive man, but I simply can't hold it in.

When I'm really and truly cried out, I take a step back. A chill creeps over my skin as the warmth of Nico's body is replaced by cool air. I shiver. There's a discarded shawl on the bench and Nico picks it up and wraps it around me.

"What are you still doing here?" My voice sounds wobbly and pathetic.

"I was looking for you. I wanted to congratulate you on your first runway show."

"First and last," I say, bitterness flooding my words.

Nico takes my hand and warmth travels up my arm at his touch. "Why last?"

"I made a fool out of myself." It physically hurts to say the words out loud.

"Did you also parade in front of hundreds of people in tiny leather shorts?"

My lips turn up slightly, and I shake my head. "No. I just humiliated myself in front of one person. And realized my dream of working in fashion is dead."

Nico leads me to the bench and sits down next to me, waiting for me to continue.

"Everything was going so well, Marco looked so happy. And I just thought..." I take a breath. "I asked Marco if I could have the junior designer position that Luigi left open."

Nico's eyebrows raise, and I feel stupid all over again.

"Marco reminded me that I don't have a four-year degree in fashion. Or any experience." The tears threaten to come once more, but I push them back. "He was really gracious about it, but he made it clear I'm not qualified to be a junior designer."

Nico pulls me closer to him, and I drop my head onto his shoulder.

"Lydia, I'm so sorry."

"It's my own fault. I misread the situation. Of course, he wasn't going to hire me as a designer. I feel really stupid." It's a feeling I'm familiar with, and one I hate.

"You're not stupid, Lydia," Nico says into my hair. "You're brilliant. You just haven't had the training you need. Once you go to design school, and get a few years working, you'll be unstoppable."

I can't make it through four years of school. I couldn't even make it through one. And I tried twice. I shake my head against his chest, but I don't have it in me to explain. Plus, I don't want to see the look on Nico's face when he learns the woman he thinks is brilliant has already failed out of two schools. It's bad enough he found me sobbing like a maniac.

I sit up and use the shawl to wipe my face. Then I grab a hairband from my wrist and pile my hair into a messy bun.

"Anyway," I say, brushing everything aside with that one word, "you did amazing tonight."

"Lydia." His voice is low and patient. I can tell he wants to dig deeper into my woes, but I just can't.

"You didn't want to go to the after-party?" I ask.

"No." His eyes lock on mine then flick briefly to my lips. "I wanted to see you."

A floaty feeling fills my stomach, like when Robby and I sucked the helium out of balloons at my tenth birthday party. Nico reaches for my face and brushes away some hair that's escaped my bun. My breath catches, and the air between us feels thick—like the charged scent of rain just before a storm.

Nico starts to move away, but I don't let him. Quick as a flash I slide a hand behind his head and bring his lips to mine. They're soft and firm and send a delicious shock through me as we kiss. His fingers slide into my hair, threading through the strands before tightening, pulling me closer. All the sadness and embarrassment and disappointment slide off me as he kisses me.

I make a humming sound in my throat and wrap my arms around his back, feeling the edges of his taut muscles. I have kissed my share of men, but not like this. It's never been like this. When we pull away, his eyes are unfocused and his breathing uneven.

"I'm sorry," he says.

His words hit me like cold water.

"Sorry?"

"I shouldn't have kissed you."

In a flash, I'm off the bench and on the other side of the tiny room. This is more humiliation than one person should have to endure in a night.

"You didn't kiss me." I try to keep the hurt out of my voice. "I kissed you."

"But I kissed you back."

"Well, you can tell her I was the one who initiated it."

Nico brow furrows. "Tell who?"

"The Swiss model you're dating."

This whole night is a disaster. I've got to stop doing things without thinking.

"I'm not dating a Swiss model," Nico says.

I ball up the stupid shawl and toss it onto the chair in the corner.

"Swedish. Whatever."

"I'm not dating anyone," Nico says.

I analyze his face for signs of trickery, but as always, he's an open book.

"But Clara and Chelsie said you were." I stop short of telling him the internet confirmed it. I don't need to add stalker vibes to this already embarrassing conversation.

Nico shakes his head. "That was last year. It fizzled out, but I realized women bothered me less when they thought I had a girlfriend." His tone isn't arrogant, just practical. "So, when people assumed I was unavailable, I didn't correct them."

He takes a step closer to me. "But I never wanted you to think I was dating someone. I tried to make it clear when I asked you out that I was interested."

"Then why are you sorry you kissed me?" It's a pathetic question to ask, but it's out of my mouth before I can stop it.

What has happened to my impulse control tonight?

"Technically speaking, I'm not sorry I kissed you, because that was the best kiss of my life."

My heart pounds at his words, but I cross my arms, a protective shield I'm putting up too late.

"But I'm sorry I took advantage of you in a vulnerable moment instead of being a good friend."

"Maybe I don't want you to be my friend," I say. "Maybe that's why I kissed you."

Nico's eyes search my face looking for who knows what.

"This might be a fun distraction for you while you're away from your boyfriend," he drags a hand through his hair, "but for me it's more than that. I can't—"

"I don't have a boyfriend."

Nico stops, hand in hair. "Danilo and Clara said you had an American boyfriend."

"I broke up with him a month ago." I step out of my corner.

A smile breaks across his face, and his eyes fill with hope. "So, if you're not dating anyone..." He takes a step toward me. "And I'm not dating anyone..." Another step and he closes the distance between us. "Then maybe we could date?"

"That's a really good idea," I say, wrapping my arms around him.

"I'm almost as brilliant as you," he whispers.

And then he's kissing me and nothing else matters. Not jobs, or ex-boyfriends, or dumb mistakes I've made. Because whatever happened in the past, it somehow led me to this miraculous moment.

I wrap my arms around him tighter, savoring the solid warmth of his body against mine, the velvet softness of his lips. For the first time in a long time, everything feels exactly right.

Chapter Twenty

The weekend goes by in a blur because I spend every second with Nico. We walk around Milan holding hands. He takes me to four different bridges and tells me why they're awesome. He's so smart, but it doesn't make me feel stupid in comparison like I always feared it would. He talks to me like I'm brilliant too, and when I tell him about some of my fashion ideas, he listens like it's the most interesting thing he's ever heard.

Now it's Sunday night and we're snuggling in the back booth of a café near the Rossi house. The golden glow of wall sconces reflects off tiny marble tables, and the warm, pastry-scented air is a welcome relief from the cold outside. Nico's arms wrap around me, and I snuggle closer.

This is my new favorite spot to be, and I'm hoping if I play my cards right, I can come back in the next life as Nico's sweatshirt.

"You ready to go back to the studio tomorrow?" Nico asks, and I shake my head.

Every time I remember my conversation with Marco, a new wave of embarrassment washes over me. I've managed to avoid him all weekend. Surely, I can make it eight more months until I go home.

"Did you hear what happened after the spring show last year?" Nico asks.

I shake my head, and my hands curl around my tiny glass of hot chocolate.

"The whole crew went to this warehouse party outside Milan." Nico plays with a strand of my hair, winding it between his fingers. "Danilo was going through a breakup and drank way too many peach Bellinis. At the end of the night, he stumbled over to Marco like a drunk ballerina and—splak. Vomited all over him."

I gasp and put a hand to my mouth.

"And Marco was wearing a vintage Valentino sports jacket."

"No." *I knew Danilo was the worst.*

"It was terrible. But guess who was at work on Monday? Mortified, but there?"

"Danilo," I mumble.

"Exactly. If he can come into work after projectile vomiting on the boss, you can get past an embarrassing conversation. Besides, it wasn't that embarrassing. You asked for something, he said no. It happens."

Not to me.

"You weren't there," I say. "I came across as so entitled. Like I'd done one good thing and deserved a designer position."

"So, show him that's not really you," Nico says. "Show up as a teachable and hardworking intern." He kisses my cheek.

Yeah, but then what?

"It doesn't make sense to continue as an intern if I'm never going to become a designer," I say.

"Of course you'll become a designer," Nico says. "Finish the year as an intern, then enroll at one of Milan's amazing design schools. Your work is so good, Marco may even hire you right out of college."

There's no way I'm going back to school.

He frowns, and his full lips get even poutier. "Why are you shaking your head? It's a great plan. And it has the added benefit of keeping you here in Milan." He waggles his eyebrows and I smile, then sigh.

"I can't do it."

"Look, I'm not trying to put a lot of pressure on this relationship, I know it's still new. I just hate the idea of you going back to America."

I turn and give him a kiss. It starts sweet but heats up fast, and I break away flushed.

Man, I love kissing this guy.

"That's not the part I can't do."

"Then which part is?"

Ugh. I really don't want to have this conversation.

"I can't do the school."

"Why not?"

I try to find a way to explain without having to say the words. "I just can't. I tried it before and it didn't, uh, work out."

His brow furrows. "Why didn't it work out?"

My stomach tightens, and I sit up to put some space between us. Expectant silence swirls around us, and I force the words out, staring into my mug. "I have dyslexia."

The words feel heavy and bulky, unfamiliar in my mouth. I exhale sharply. "School was like trying to run through quicksand."

My face floods with heat and my body tenses, waiting for his reaction.

Nico takes my hand in his and traces lines down each finger to the tip. He doesn't say anything for a moment, and then, "That sounds tough." He looks at me like he'd take away every hard thing in my life if he could.

"It was tough."

"Tell me about it." Nico's soft voice and tender gaze crack my defensive walls. Before I know it, I'm spilling everything, even the stuff I've never told my friends back home.

"My first year was at Cornell. It didn't matter how much I studied; I couldn't pass any of the exams. It took so long to figure out the questions I ran out of time before I could write down my answers."

I want to leave it at that, but there's a rising urge to come clean, and I give into it. I disentangle my hand from Nico's and grab the napkin off the table.

"I bribed a TA for a copy of the final exam. I thought if I had a chance to look at it beforehand, I might be able to get through it all on test day. Even do well, since I knew the material."

I shred the napkin into tiny pieces until it's nothing but confetti.

"Did it work?"

I shake my head. "I got caught. My RA found the exam in my room. I think my roommate Heidi tipped her off." I've never voiced that suspicion out loud, but I've thought about it a lot. "The dean had a meeting with my father, and I'm not sure what favors were promised, but they let me stay until the end of the year with the understanding that I wouldn't return in the fall."

"Lydia, I'm so sorry."

I shrug. "It was my own fault for cheating. The next year my father got me into Engleman, and I was on academic probation by the end of the first semester. By spring, I knew there was nothing I could do to pass. So I went out in style."

Nico's eyebrows raise. "How stylish?"

"I convinced the Phi Beta Kappa fraternity bros to help me unleash a dozen chickens in the dean's office."

Shock flashes across Nico's face, but it's gone just as quickly and then he's nodding his head. "That seems like the only logical course of action."

I smile and squeeze his hand. "The dean was a creep—always standing too close and touching me when he didn't have to. Besides, I had to do something big enough that my dad couldn't fix it. Otherwise, I'd just start the whole thing over at a third school."

I let out a huffy breath, both relieved and embarrassed to have shared so much.

"Come here," Nico says, pulling me into his arms again. He rests his head on the top of my head, and I snuggle into the curve of his neck. We sit curled up for a while and then Nico asks, "What classes did you take at Cornell and Engleman?"

"Horrible ones. Law. History. Political science."

"Do you think it might be different if you studied something you love?"

I think about it. "I don't know."

"I won't pretend to know what it's like to go to school with dyslexia." He plants a kiss on my head. "I will say, when you love something, it makes the hard a little easier. And I'll be here to help whenever you need me."

Wrapped in his safe warmth, it's easy to believe him. Maybe it could be different this time. But the old panic lingers, curling at the edges of my hope like burned paper.

"How many people came to my dad's show?" Isa asks on our way to school the next morning. "Did they like the clothes? How could you tell? Did any of the models trip? What did they look like?"

I wasn't around all weekend, so I do my best to answer her questions now.

"A ton. Yes. They clapped. No. And the models looked like this."

I strike a dramatic pose, then glide down the sidewalk with slow, exaggerated steps, hips swaying just enough. I toss an imaginary scarf over my shoulder, chin tilted high, eyes fierce. Isa giggles as I spin, strike another pose, then walk back to her.

"You're really good at that," she says, eyes wide with admiration.

"Thank you." I pause and squat down so we're eye level. "And thank you for thinking my design was good enough to show your dad. You were the very first one to believe in me, and that is a big deal."

"I'll take fifty percent of all your profits," she says, holding out a hand.

"I work for free," I remind her. "But I did get you a little gift."

"What is it?"

"I'll show you when we get home," I say, handing over her backpack.

"I won't forget," she hollers over her shoulder, then joins the swarm of kids running into school.

At the studio, the mood is relaxed and celebratory. Chelsie, Clara, and Danilo drink coffee in the lobby and share stories from the party Friday night. It sounds like a wild one.

I hang my coat, imagine Danilo puking on Marco, and fight the smile on my face.

Sleep didn't come easy last night. Nico's words ran through my head on repeat, causing alternating jolts of panic and hope. When I left Engleman, escorted by security guards covered in chicken scratches, I vowed never to go back to school.

But maybe Nico's right. Maybe it would be different if I were studying fashion.

Whether I go back to school or not, I'm not ready to give up working in the studio. I love this place too much. Which means I need to stamp out any awkwardness that might be lingering after my misstep on Friday.

"*Buongiorno*, Marco," I say when he pops out of his office.

"Lydia!" He still looks tired, but it's a happier tired than last week. "I was hoping to talk to you all weekend. But maybe it's better to have this conversation at the office."

"I want to talk to you too," I say. "I need to apologize."

Marco raises an eyebrow and lets me continue.

"I should have never asked about being a junior designer. I didn't understand the requirements for the position, and I made assumptions without doing my homework. I'm sorry I put you on the spot Friday night. It was unprofessional of me."

"Well, I don't know that we need to maintain a strict professionalism between us, since you've seen me in my pajamas." He pauses. "But I appreciate your understanding of the situation, and I'm relieved there are no hard feelings."

"None at all," I say, like I didn't sob for thirty minutes on the floor of a dressing room. "And I'm grateful for the opportunity to continue in the studio and learn as much as I can."

"Good. Because there's a lot of work to do to get ready for the photo shoot on Friday."

And just like what we've moved forward.

I let out a relieved sigh. The truth is, I'm not well-practiced in the art of apologies and that went even better than I'd hoped.

The whole team meets in the conference room, and Marco congratulates us on a successful show. There's whooping and cheering, and Marco lets us carry on for a moment before motioning for quiet. He outlines the tasks that need to be completed before the shoot on Friday, and we all jump in. I work with Danilo and Clara to evaluate each of the ensembles. They're cleaned and pressed from the dry cleaners, but Marco wants us to check for loose buttons, torn seams, or anything less than perfection. Before I leave, we manage to make it through all twenty-one outfits and only find one semi-loose button.

Then it's off to pick up Isa who chants, "*Regalo, regalo, regalo,*" gift, gift, gift, all the way home.

When we get to the apartment, I make a big deal of looking under my bed, checking the closet, and peering inside the oven to find Isa's gift. She follows like a shadow.

"Oh, here it is!" I say, pulling my phone out of my purse.

"Um. That's your phone," Isa says.

"Yep." I pull up the newly downloaded Audible app and click onto the *Glitter the Mermaid's Magical Adventure in Rainbow Land* audiobook.

"I know you and Juliet read the first *Glitter the Mermaid* book. I thought you and I could listen to the second one together."

"Listen to it?"

"Yeah. The narrator who reads the story can do like twenty different voices." I swipe a piece of hair out of her eyes. "What do you think, are you in?"

"I'm in!" She wiggles her hips in excitement, and it reminds me of a wiggly caterpillar on a branch.

"Okay, what happened in the first book?"

Isa chatters excitedly, reliving every detail of Glitter's first adventure, hands waving, eyes bright. I stir cocoa powder into steaming milk, the rich scent curling into the air, then we settle onto the couch with our hot mugs. I hit play and the Minky throw makes a soft cocoon around us as the narrator's voice fills the living room.

Some time later, just as we're following Glitter and her friends into a creepy underwater forest, Sofia opens the door, scaring both of us out of our skin.

"We thought you were a giant sea-spider," Isa says, scowling.

"I'm not," Sofia says, shooting me a puzzled look.

"We're listening to the audiobook of the second *Glitter the Mermaid*," I tell her.

"It's more fun this way," Isa says. "The narrator does all the voices."

"Sorry for interrupting," Sofia says, slipping off her shoes and hanging her coat up.

"This is a good place to stop anyway." I gather our hot chocolate mugs and bring them to the kitchen.

"Do we have to?" Isa whines, following me into the kitchen.

"Yes. Because I'm going out and if you listen to it without me, I'll send you into the Forbidden Seaforest all by yourself."

"Fine." Isa pouts. "Where are you going?"

"On a date."

"Ooh, where? With who?"

"Isa," Sofia calls from the living room. "We don't pry into people's personal lives."

"It's okay. I don't know where we're going actually. Nico planned it."

"You're going out with Nico?" Sofia says, walking into the living room and breaking her own rule.

"Yes..."

Is it unprofessional for someone on the team to date one of the models? I didn't even think of that.

"Will Marco be okay with that?" I ask.

Sofia smiles. "Marco will be thrilled. Nico's his favorite."

"He's a lot better than Stormy the evil octopus.," Isa says sagely, and I nod my head in agreement.

Chapter Twenty-One

Nico's waiting for me at the entrance to Parco Sempione, a picnic basket in his hand. The last rays of sunlight filter through the trees casting shadows on the cobblestone path. A crisp breeze carries the scent of pine.

"Ooh, what's in the basket?" I ask.

Instead of responding, he scoops me into his arms and kisses me, sending a slow, melting warmth down my spine. I take a deep breath, letting his warm citrus smell envelop me. Turns out, I don't care what's in the basket, all I want to do tonight is this.

"I missed you," he says into my neck.

"You're absurd. You saw me yesterday."

Still, I don't let go either.

"It was too long ago," he says.

I laugh, and he squeezes me tighter.

"You should probably know, I have zero chill." He smooths my hair out of my face. "When I like someone, I can't play it cool."

"So, you like me, huh?"

"A lot." He lowers his hands to my hips and squeezes them gently.

"Good." I stand on tip toe to kiss his smooth, full lips. "I like you too," I whisper in his ear.

"Follow me," he says softly, taking my arm in his and leading me into the park. Apart from the occasional rustle of birds settling in the trees, the only sound is the leaves crunching beneath our feet. The farther we walk, the darker it gets until the trees are just silhouettes. Nico leads me off the path to a tall pine tree and lays a blanket on the grass. The cool night air pricks at my skin as I settle onto the blanket, the fabric slightly scratchy against my hands. Nico hums as he pulls items from his basket.

I was expecting gourmet cheeses, breads, and fruits. Instead, Nico pulls out chips, candy bars, pretzels, and cans of soda.

"This is quite an assortment," I say, and he smiles sheepishly.

"I wanted to cook you a feast, but Julia got an ear infection, and my mom was working so I had to take her to the doctor. These were the finest selections from their vending machine."

I lean over a packet of crackers and kiss him soft and slow. "This is wonderful."

"Nothing but the best for you." He tucks a strand of hair behind my ear. "How did work go?"

"Better than I thought," I reply. "I apologized to Marco, and he was cool about it."

"So, you're staying at the studio?"

"I am."

"And you're going to go to design school and stay in Milan for the next four years?" He doesn't hide the hope in his voice.

"Still thinking about that one."

"Well, let me see if I can persuade you." His lips go to my neck just below my ear, and his hands slip through my hair. A delicious shiver spreads through me, like a spark igniting under my skin. Then his lips are on mine, warm and delicious. My body melts into his, and my thoughts tangle like thread caught in a sewing machine.

I wouldn't mind four more years of this, I think blearily. Then I run my hands down the taut muscles of his back and give up thinking entirely.

"Nico!" the gang cheers when we walk into Calypso holding hands on Wednesday night. The place is packed, and their excited yells are barely audible over the pulsing music and loud chatter. We slip into the back booth, and Valentina and Carmen, like the true dorks that they are, make excited smoochy faces behind Nico's back.

"How was the show?" Paolo asks.

"Show us pics," Carmen demands.

I pull out my phone and show the gang the photos I took at the show. Nico in his first outfit. Nico in his second outfit. Nico getting his hair touched up by a stylist.

"You took a lot of pictures of me." Nico grins and slides an arm over my shoulders pulling me close.

"Is this the outfit you designed?" Carmen exclaims when she gets to Nico in the shorts.

"It is."

"It's amazing," Valentina says, leaning over Carmen to see the picture.

"Well, I think the model is what really sells it," I say.

"That outfit could make anyone look good," Nico replies.

"You two are disgusting," Carmen says, but she's smiling.

"Should I grab some snacks for us?" I ask. "Tonight's on me. To celebrate surviving my first runway show." I didn't tell Carmen or Valentina about making a fool out of myself in front of Marco or bawling my eyes out afterward. Let them think the whole night was a success.

"Cheers to Lydia!" Valentina says.

"Cheers to leather shorts!" Carmen says.

"Cheers to free food!" Paolo adds.

The bar is crowded, but Lorenzo sees me and comes over immediately.

"*Ciao, bella*," he says. I can see why Carmen has a crush on him. He's got a decent body and a symmetrical face. But there's too much arrogance in his smile, and based on the sandalwood fumes coming off him, he's one of those men that mistake cologne for charm.

"Can I get five virgin daiquiris, bruschetta, caprese salad, and a cheese plate?"

"Of course, love. Anything else?"

"That's all."

"I'll have it ready for you in just a moment." Another smile.

"*Grazie*."

I turn to go but he puts a moist hand over mine. "No need to hurry off."

I remove his hand. "My friends are waiting."

"Well maybe we get together sometime without your friends." He gives me a wink.

Ugh. Gross.

"No thanks," I say, no smile, making it clear I'm not interested.

Poor Carmen. She's completely smitten by this tool.

"Food and drinks are on their way." I say, joining the group, smile in place.

"I saw you talking to Lorenzo," Carmen says giddily. "How did he sound? Did he ask about me?" She leans in, waiting for my answer.

"The bar was pretty loud."

"I can't stop thinking about our slow dance last week," Carmen says, a dreamy look on her face.

How do you tell someone the guy they're crushing on is worse than polyester?

"Has anyone heard from Juliet?" Valentina asks.

Carmen and Paolo shake their heads.

"She and Jake broke up," Valentina tells me.

I shrug.

"That's terrible!" Nico says. "Why did they break up? Also, who are Juliet and Jake?"

The gang fills Nico in on the last nanny's love life, concluding with "I guess the long distance was just too hard."

"Interesting," Nico says. "Has Lydia mentioned her plans to stay in Milan next year?"

"What?" Carmen says, eyes bulging.

"Really?" Valentina asks excitedly.

They both grin at me, and I can't help thinking of my friends back home who don't seem to have noticed I'm gone.

"I'm thinking about it," I say. "I might look into a design school here in Milan."

"That would be awesome!" Valentina says, and Nico nods his head vigorously.

"I don't even know if I can get in," I say, wanting to slow this train down.

"You'll get in," Carmen says, eyes shining with excitement. "You're an amazing designer! You can do anything!"

The compliment is so genuine and so encouraging, my throat tightens.

"Thanks, Carmen," I say. Then silently curse her for making me emotional in public.

It's so easy to let Nico and Carmen convince me that I could go back to school. But they weren't there when I stayed up until 2am trying to finish the reading before class. They didn't see me get back essay after essay covered in red ink. They don't know the shame and embarrassment I felt, or the energy it took to pretend like none of it mattered to me. School is my personal hell, and I would be crazy to go back.

Nico is pointing out the pockets I designed on the blazer, his gorgeous face glowing with pride.

I look at the ensemble I created. I look at the man I'm dating.

Maybe crazy is underrated.

Chapter Twenty-Two

A sea of long limbs and designer clothes stretches across the studio, laughter rippling through the air as trendy beats pulse from the studio's overhead speakers. The scene is like a house party in the Hamptons but instead of lounging with a drink in my hand, I'm hustling.

I line up ensembles in the order they'll be photographed, find the right shoes and accessories for each model, and avoid the stylist who keeps trying to brush my hair. I help the photographer, Antonio, set up a zillion lights and re-hang the black backdrop curtain that keeps falling. Marco's so focused on the shoot he's oblivious to everyone else in the studio. But if he does notice me, I want him to see me working.

Once the lighting is exactly right, Antonio starts shooting. It's not like the movies where the photographer calls out random things like "You're a hedgehog on ice skates" and the models respond with preening poses. Vangarten is first, and Antonio instructs him on the exact pose and facial expression he wants. "Shoulders toward me, lean in, chin tilted left, no smile."

Instead of "You're a magnificent butterfly! The camera loves you!" Antonio says "*Sí*" when they get it right, and "No" when they get it wrong. All the while Marco hovers like an expectant father, trying to gauge how everything looks.

Most of the shots are individuals so there's a lot of sitting around for the other models. Except they can't actually sit because Bianca will poke them back to a standing position so they don't wrinkle the clothing.

Nico is leaning against a table chatting with some other models. I tied the scarf around his neck myself and it was embarrassingly difficult to keep my lips off him. But I'm determined to remain professional. Marco's not going to write me a letter of recommendation if I spend my time smooching instead of working.

But after work...

"Want to come with me to pick up the food?" Chelsie asks, snapping me out of my inappropriate daydream. She adjusts her oversized glasses. "Or do you want to stay here and ogle the models?"

"There are models here today?" I ask. "I hadn't even noticed."

Chelsie gives me a smirk, and we grab our coats and head for the door. Marco ordered so much food from the restaurant across the street it takes us three trips to bring it all in.

"Are they going to eat all this pasta and bread?" I ask Chelsie, as I arrange plates and forks.

"Some of these models haven't had carbs in months and won't work again until the spring collection in February. Last time, we ran out of food, and I watched two models circle each other with plastic forks like they were in the *Hunger Games*."

The scent of garlic and oregano makes its way across the studio and the models who have finished their shots rush the table. Chelsie and I back away to safety.

Across the studio, Antonio is directing Nico who's wearing my ensemble. I walk over to get a better look, my eyes running over his tan legs and sculpted shoulders. Once I finish my shameless ogling, I take in the outfit.

The leather shorts demand your attention, so it's easy to miss how beautifully the oversized jacket hangs on his shoulders and the details in the braided scarf. Each individual piece is perfect and together they make something magnificent.

I did this.

Excitement and pride flow through me, effervescent and tingling, like the first sip of San Pellegrino.

Back at the Rossi's apartment, I tell Isa all about the photo shoot, describing every outfit in the catalog.

"Why would anyone ever want to be a teacher or a policewoman when they could be a designer?" she asks, bewildered.

"I honestly don't know." The thought of going to work every day at a studio like Marco's, creating beautiful things, and then sharing them with the world...It feels too good to be true. And yet people do it. And if I play my cards right, maybe I can too.

Isa and I settle onto the couch for more *Glitter the Mermaid* and just as we get to the exciting part with a giant sea-spider about to eat everyone, I get a text from Sofia.

Marco finished the photo shoot and would like to take me out to dinner to celebrate. Are you able to babysit Isa tonight?

Ugh. It's a Friday night, and I want to go out with Nico, not stay home and babysit.

On the other hand, Marco and Sofia have barely seen each other this month and hanging out with Isa isn't as bad as it used to be.

Sure.

I type. Then pause.

Would it be okay if Nico came over too?

Her response is immediate.

Of course. There's a credit card in the drawer of the coffee table. You can order some pizza if you want.

Will do! Have fun!

"What's up?" Isa demands.

"Your mom and dad are going out to a fancy dinner tonight."

Her face turns scowly immediately. "Why don't I get to go?"

"They're going to one of those restaurants that only serves things adults eat, like escargot and calamari."

She looks even more offended. "I love escargot!"

Of course she does.

"We get to order pizza. And we could watch the first *Glitter the Mermaid* movie."

"Fine. But I get to choose my own pizza."

"Of course. Also, I thought it would be fun to have my friend Nico over. What do you think?"

"Are you going to kiss?" Isa asks, eyes narrowed. "Because I once saw Juliet and Jake kissing when they thought I was sleeping, and it was gross. Like two fish fighting over the same worm."

I bite back a laugh. "I promise no kissing. But how about I get to hold his hand?"

Isa thinks and then says, "I'll allow it."

How did I end up negotiating with a seven-year-old for how much action I'm getting tonight?

I text Nico about our change of plans, and in true Nico fashion, he's up for anything. He shows up just after the pizza and pulls me into a hug.

Babysitting on a Friday night should feel like a tragedy. But wrapped up in Nico's arms, his scent mingling with the smell of fresh pizza, it feels perfect in a way that makes my chest ache.

He gives me a kiss and Isa squawks from the couch. "No kissing! You promised!"

"He didn't know," I tell Isa. "Give us another chance."

Isa sizes Nico up, suspicion written all over her face.

"You get one more chance," she declares.

"What's going to happen if we kiss again?" Nico whispers in my ear.

"I don't know, but we definitely don't want to find out," I whisper back.

Isa settles on the couch, and Nico sits next to her.

"Sorry about the kissing," he says. "I didn't know the rules."

Isa gives a single nod to acknowledge his apology but doesn't turn her head to look at him.

"I brought something for you," he says. Now Isa turns her whole body to face him.

"Is it something dumb?" she asks.

"Isa!" I'm embarrassed, even though I shouldn't be. It's not my fault she has terrible manners.

"You might think it's dumb," Nico says. "My sister Julia is your age, and she thinks it's really cool. When I told her I was coming over here, she said I could bring it for you to play with tonight."

Nico pulls a six-inch plastic toy from his pocket. It looks like a witch with wings and a tail.

Isa's eyes light up. "A dragon witch! I don't have this one! Can I keep it?"

Nico shakes his head. "It's just on loan for tonight. Julia would be super sad if I didn't bring it back home to her."

"O...kay," Isa says, taking it from him. She looks sadder about having to return it than happy she gets to play with it.

"Why is that dragon a witch?" I ask, snuggling onto the couch next to Nico.

"I honestly have no idea. But there's a whole set of mythical creatures that are also terrifying. There's a vampire unicorn."

"And a skeleton fairy," Isa adds. She's already brushing the dragon witch's creepy gray hair.

"Who is making horrifying toys for children?" I ask. "And why?"

"Mattel," Nico says. "Because the little weirdos love them."

Isa sits on the couch like a queen on her throne, while I dish out pizza like a humble servant. The pizza is delicious—tangy sauce and a crispy chewy crust—and the movie is probably good too, but I'm only half-watching. My senses are focused on the warmth of Nico's hand in mine, and the way the muscles in his leg tense and relax.

"Time for bed," I say when the movie finishes. I have no idea what her bedtime routine is, but it probably starts around now. "Put on pajamas and brush your teeth and do the stuff you normally do before bed."

Isa raises an eyebrow but heads down the hall to her room. No arguing. No whining. *I'm getting really good at this nannying thing.*

"How did the photo shoot finish up?" I ask.

"Fine. It's five hours of getting posed like a puppet and bossed around like a child, but we made it through."

"I'm sorry you got bossed around," I say, sneaking a kiss. "That doesn't sound fun."

"It might be fun if you were bossing me," Nico says, lips curved in a wicked smile. He pulls me in for another kiss, and I wrap my arms around him.

There's a crash and a yelp, and I go to Isa's room to investigate. She's sitting on the floor, fully clothed, building a gigantic tower out of blocks. Half of it lies in a pile next to the dragon witch.

"It's bedtime," I tell her. "What are you doing?"

Isa turns big eyes on me. "I always build with blocks before bed. It relaxes me."

I narrow my eyes, but don't call her bluff. "Block time is over. Please put on your pajamas and brush your teeth."

"Sure thing," she says and moves to her dresser and pulls out pajamas. I leave to give her some privacy.

Nico's looking at the books on the Rossi's shelf, and I take a moment to admire his profile. He really does look like a model from a catalog. Until he turns to me and smiles, and then he looks like my Nico.

I close the distance between us, my body drawn to his in a way I can't explain. As he reaches for me, Isa wanders into the kitchen, flinging open cupboards and pulling things out.

"What are you doing?" I call from the living room. I don't even try to hide my exasperation.

"Making hot chocolate." Her tone suggests I'm a little slow to miss something so obvious.

"It's bedtime!" I stomp toward her.

"The warm milk settles my stomach."

I cross my arms. "What else do you normally do before bed?"

"A bubble bath. Thirty minutes of reading. A foot massage. And then you sing me three songs."

I look at my watch. It's already 9pm. There's no way we're doing all that. I stare her down, and she holds my gaze.

"No bath. No foot massage. We listen to ten minutes of our book, and I sing you one song."

"Will you scratch my back while you sing?"

"Fine!'

"Deal!" She takes a big slurp of her hot chocolate. "After I finish my hot chocolate of course."

I throw my hands in the air and stomp back to the living room.

"How do parents do this?" I ask Nico.

He smiles. "They hire nannies."

I get Isa's teeth brushed and tuck her into bed. Nico and I sit on the floor while we all listen to a chapter of *Glitter the Mermaid's Magical Adventure in Rainbow Land.* Nico gets sucked in quickly and looks genuinely disappointed when I turn it off.

"Now a song," Isa says. "And a back scratch."

"Alright, flip," I say and crawl onto the bed next to her. She's wearing a soft nightie with little kittens on it, and I make big circles with my fingernails on her back. "What song do you want?"

"Elvis," she mumbles, face in her pillow.

I know zero songs by Elvis, and I start to tell her so when Nico opens his mouth and sings the opening line of "Can't help falling in love." Unlike his goofy squawking at the studio, he sounds beautiful tonight, his voice low and rich.

I have a sudden memory of my parents playing this song and dancing in the kitchen. I must have been about five, because it was when we lived in the small house outside of town. Before my dad's law career took off. Before all the affairs began.

I scratch Isa's back and listen to Nico's voice and think about the way my father held my mom like she was his whole world. And how she believed it.

She probably felt all the same things I'm feeling now, that intoxicating blend of attraction and excitement. She probably never imagined it would lead to all the heartache she's been through. She's a cautionary tale, and I need to keep my head on straight, or I'll end up just like her.

By the time Nico finishes, Isa's eyes are closed, and I'm feeling like a fool for rushing in.

Chapter Twenty-Three

The Duomo's spires glint in the fading light, and the glow of streetlamps reflects off the damp cobblestones. I'm early for my date with Nico and grab a seat at one of the outdoor tables off the piazza. October cold nips at my cheeks, but the warmth of nearby space heaters wraps around me like a wool coat. I order a cappuccino to sip while I wait.

The studio was slow today, but Marco announced that the theme for the Winter show in February is Frosted Fairytale. He didn't show us any designs yet, but he mentioned capes. I slip my sketchpad out of my bag and flip to a fresh page. My pencil flies across the paper as I sketch a riding cape in luxurious red velvet. Next, I design a double-breasted suit in dark gray velour, like wolf fur.

Can I design a granny chic gown?

The scratch of pencil on paper mingles with the clinking of mugs in saucers and the occasional car horn. I'm deep into a sketching trance but vaguely notice when someone sits down next to me.

"*No, grazie,*" I say without looking up.

"Lydia." Nico's voice, low and sweet, breaks through my haze. From the smile on his face, it's not the first time he's said my name.

"Oh! It's you!"

"What are you drawing?" he asks, leaning over and kissing my cheeks.

"Just some ideas for the next show." I slip my pad back into my bag and turn to give Nico a proper kiss. The tip of his nose is cold, but his breath is warm and my heart races as his lips press into mine.

Since the show is over, the models aren't coming into the studio for fittings, and Nico and I don't get to hang out during the day anymore. It's for the best. Every time he gets near me, I go from rational human to starving woman at an all-you-can-eat buffet. We're *this close* to what HR would likely call "an inappropriate workplace incident."

Nico takes my hand and kisses my knuckles. "I'm glad you're in design mode because..." He drums his fingers on his legs to build suspense. "I'm taking you to the Milan Institute of Design. They're having an open house tonight, and I thought it might be good for you to see it in person."

My stomach sinks. We're going to a school. For a date.

Nothing says romance like higher education and revisiting trauma.

I'm not convinced school is the right path for me, and I follow Nico with heavy steps. It's only a ten-minute taxi ride, but by the time we get there, my palms are slick with sweat. I press them against my thighs, but the wool fabric of my trousers does nothing to soak up the anxiety clinging to my skin.

"You got this," Nico murmurs as we step through the main entrance. I nod, mustering as much bravery as I can. "And we can leave anytime you want."

Prospective students wander through the hallways, and I size up each person we pass.

I bet they haven't been kicked out of two different colleges. I bet they don't break into a sweat thinking about a teacher calling on them to read in class.

My heart races, and I brainstorm plans for getting out of this.

Can I convince Nico there's a bridge in Milan he hasn't visited yet?

Professors are holding mini lectures in classrooms all over campus, and Nico stops at a door marked Intro to Fashion Design. "Want to take a look?"

I don't. I feel small and stupid, and I want to get out of here. But I allow him to lead me into a large auditorium. The lecture has already started, and we take seats in the back.

"Fashion is an essential means of self-expression," the professor says.

He's younger than any of the professors I had and dressed substantially better, in fitted jeans and a wine-colored blazer.

"When we choose what we want to wear each day, we are choosing who we want to be. Are we an athlete? An academic? A working professional?" The professor's voice carries with effortless charisma, rising and falling like a conductor leading an orchestra of ideas. The room is silent except for the sounds of pens scribbling and the occasional rustle of someone shifting in their chair.

"Our clothes tell the world what we think of ourselves. In fact, they *shape* the way we think of ourselves. As designers, it is our job to create clothing that resonates with those who wear it; that helps them feel their best and become their truest selves. And yes, fashion is often aspirational, but that's not always a bad thing, let's look at the Francini model on consumer behavior with regard to clothing..."

I hang on his every word. Thirty minutes go by in the blink of an eye, and he finishes his lecture well before I'm done listening.

I turn to Nico, wide-eyed. "Wasn't that spectacular?"

He smiles. "I don't know, I dozed off around the time he mentioned the Carrie Bradshaw effect on consumption patterns." He yawns and stretches, his smile sleepy and playful. "But you loved it."

"I did. I knew what he was talking about the whole time, and he didn't make anyone read out loud in front of the class."

We tour the whole campus, peeking into classrooms and admiring colorful displays of student work. A feeling takes hold of me, like the first time my mom took me to Fashion Week when I was sixteen.

I want this. I may be out of my beautiful brunette head, but I want to go to this school.

Nico and I walk through the doors back to the regular world, and my mind starts listing all the things I need to do to make this happen.

"So, what do you think?" Nico asks.

"I love it," I admit, uncomfortable with sharing my true feelings.

"I thought hearts were going to jump out of your eyes, like a cartoon character."

"I wasn't that bad."

"You were," Nico says in delight.

I've always had such a good poker face. I must be losing my edge.

Or maybe I don't always have to hide how I feel.

"Should we work on your application tonight?" Nico asks, squeezing my hand.

"I still need some time to think about it."

"What's to think about? You want to be a designer. You love the school. Let's do it."

"It's not that simple."

"What's complicated about it?"

I let out a breath, trying to think of the best way to explain it.

"It's like you're out to dinner at a restaurant that's famous for steak, and everyone is ordering steak, and the person who's paying for your dinner says, 'You should really get the steak.'" We cross the street and stroll in the direction of downtown. "But you don't want steak. You want a ham sandwich. Only when you tell the person who's paying for dinner, he says, 'Don't be ridiculous, you're not going to fashion school. You're going to be a lawyer.'"

Nico barks out a laugh. "I see."

We walk in silence for half a block, listening to the sound of Milan traffic, and then Nico says, "How bad do you want that ham sandwich?"

"Really bad."

"Then leave the restaurant, go to the best deli in town, and buy yourself a ham sandwich."

I nod. "Yes. But ham sandwiches cost money I don't have. Not until I turn twenty-five. I have money for clothes and trips, but no ham sandwich money."

"Maybe you can work while you go to school. That's what I did."

Well, there's a new concept.

I mull that over for a moment, then squeeze his hand. "How were your classes today?"

"Amazing. Let me tell you why engineering is the salmon filet of careers."

I smile and listen, and even with the obstacles ahead of me, my future feels like a fresh page in my sketchbook, ready for me to create something beautiful.

Chapter Twenty-Four

Design school consumes my thoughts for the next week, and I come to three certain conclusions:

1. I want to go. I want to learn about fashion and be surrounded by people who love fashion and get the degree I need to as a designer.
2. Getting a job to pay tuition is out of the question. I can't sail effortlessly through homework and exams like Nico does. Passing classes will take all my time and energy. There's no way I can juggle school and a job.
3. Which means, if I want to go to design school, I need to get my father on board.

Monday night after Isa's gone to bed, I call my father for the dreaded conversational chess match.

"Lydia!" My father's voice bursts through the phone, strong and confident. We haven't spoken since I got here, and on the surface, he sounds like a father delighted to hear from his daughter. But underneath there's apprehension. He's waiting to hear what I've screwed up now.

"Hello, Father, I'm just calling to check in." It's the first pawn advancing.

"Wonderful! Tell me about Milan."

He makes it sound like it's a destination I chose and not punishment for making him look bad. It's a bold move, but like a true politician, he rewrites history.

"I'm really enjoying it."

"I saw from your credit card statement how much you enjoyed it last week." He's putting me in check.

"Yes, I left so quickly, I didn't have a chance to pack properly and most of my clothes are still back home." My king has moved out of danger and now my queen is on the offensive. "I've been so busy, I'm just now picking up some essentials."

"Nannying taking up all of your time?" He has the audacity to sound condescending, when he's the one who chose this for me. I prepare for attack.

"Actually, I've managed to secure an internship for my time here. I thought it would look good on college applications."

There's stunned silence on the other end of the phone, like a key player has been taken unexpectedly. Then, "Tell me more."

"I'm working at the Rossi Design studio. Marco Rossi is an up-and-coming fashion designer. His spring collection came out three weeks ago."

"Fashion huh?" The skepticism in his voice is clear. "I don't know how helpful an internship like that will be on a college application."

The king is right where I want him, and I go for the attack. "It is if I'm applying to the Milan Institute of Design."

Another pause. "Honey."

I wait. If he wants out of check, he'll have to get there himself.

"I know you like clothes, but fashion is not a viable career option."

"It is," I counter. "There are plenty of designers here in Milan that have made successful careers out of it."

He clears his throat. "I'm sure that's true. However, I don't think it's the right path for you, sweetheart."

"Believe it or not, I'm good at it. Marco, my boss, even used one of my designs in his collection."

"Now, I didn't say you weren't good at it," he says. "I'm sure you're a great little designer. I remember those sketch pads you had around the house, and I think that's a great little hobby for you."

My grip tightens on the phone, knuckles sharp, white peaks.

Say "little" one more time, and I will end you.

"Now, the St. Clairs have a legacy of strong careers in law or medicine. But I understand that may not be the best fit for you."

He's putting a piece out there for a trade, but I can't tell yet what he's getting.

"College isn't just about choosing a career. It's about forming relationships that will define you. I don't see you making those connections in fashion school."

When he says connections, he means a husband. If I can't become a lawyer, the least I can do is marry one. He's given up hope of me earning a respectable degree, which means I must earn a degree in Landing a Wealthy Husband, with a minor in Looking Pretty At Events. And perhaps a graduate program in Smiling Supportively While My Husband Talks Over Me.

Fury has made me mute, and my dad takes advantage of my silence to pick off the remaining pieces on my board.

"Don't you worry about school. I'm putting something together right here; a place where you can make those important connections. And with an easier courseload, you'll have plenty of time to color on your notepads."

"I've got to go," I say.

"Of course." He sounds relieved. "So glad we could have this chat. Take care of yourself."

What's it called in chess when the king abdicates the throne because the opponent is insufferable? That's what happened tonight.

It doesn't matter what I say. There's no winning this game.

Clouds gather like purple mountains in the sky and unleash a torrential rain over the city. Nico and I were supposed to take an electric bike tour around Milan, but that's not happening.

"Want to head to my place and watch a movie?" Nico asks.

"That sounds wonderful." I'm hoping "watch a movie" is code for smooching.

It's not. Nico doesn't have his own place, so instead of spending the evening tangled up in his arms, I'm meeting his mom and three sisters. It's like ordering a silk evening gown and receiving a cotton T-shirt.

The door swings open, and laughter and overlapping voices flood my ears before I even step inside.

"Nico! Lydia!" A short, chubby woman with Nico's dimples pulls us into the apartment with the enthusiasm of a long-lost friend. "You're soaking wet! Let me warm up some soup for you."

For the record, we're barely damp, and we've already eaten, but the futility of mentioning this is obvious.

A little girl who looks about Isa's age grabs my hand and pulls me toward the couch. "Lydia, sit by me."

"You don't have to hog her," says a scowly-looking girl with a short bob.

A tall girl with long dark hair hovers next to me. She's clearly the oldest of the sisters and doesn't seem to know what to do with her hands. They keep fluttering at her side, then coming up to her face to cover her mouth. "I, like, really love your hair," she says.

"*Grazie.*" I give her a reassuring smile.

There are six of us in the living room, and we fill it up. I can see a kitchen and bathroom from where I'm standing, and a short hallway with three doors.

"Alright girls," Nico says, putting an arm around my waist. "Let's give Lydia some space."

He sits on the lumpy brown sofa and pulls me down next to him. The littlest girl snuggles in next to me.

"This is Julia," Nico says, ruffling her hair. "She's seven, like Isabella." He gestures to the girl with short hair sitting on the other side of him. "This is Camilla. She's twelve. And lastly Benedetta, who is seventeen."

Benedetta is the only one still standing and as though she realizes it the same time I do, she sits down fast like she's playing a game of musical chairs. She tucks her hair behind her ears and gives a little wave.

"Girls this is Lydia," Nico says.

"We know that," Camilla says.

"It's nice to meet you," I say. "Nico's told me a lot about you."

Nico's mom comes into the living room carrying two bowls and sets them down on the battered coffee table.

"And this is my mom, Gloria," Nico says. "The greatest cook in Milan."

She waves off his praise with a dish towel, but her lips press together in a barely contained smile, basking in Nico's praise.

"Welcome to our home, Lydia."

She hands me my bowl and waits expectantly while I take a bite. It's a vegetable soup with a savory broth and bright chunks of carrots and zucchini. I take a small bite and then another bigger bite. It might be the best thing I've eaten all week.

"This is delicious," I tell Gloria, and she beams.

"All right, all right, let's give Nico and Lydia some space," Gloria says. "Camilla and Benedetta, you've got homework to do. Julia, why don't you help me in the kitchen."

Camilla grumbles and trudges to her room. Benedetta gives me another little wave, then follows Camilla.

Julia stays exactly where she is, snuggled next to me, and says, "You don't mind if I watch the movie with you, do you Lydia?"

Her face is sweet and hopeful, and I let my plans for making out with Nico die a sad death. "Of course I don't mind. What should we watch?"

So that's how we end up watching *The Fairy Princess and the Unicorn Surprise*. Except ten minutes in, Camilla comes out of her room and asks if I'll play cards with her, and ten minutes after that, Benedetta comes out to see if I'll teach her how to do her eye makeup. The movie plays in the background while we all hang out.

Halfway through the movie, Carmen calls. I let it go to voicemail, but she calls two more times, so I slip out of the apartment to take her call.

"It happened! He asked me out last night! I think it's because I've been taking your advice. Where were you and Nico, by the way?"

"*Ciao, Carmen*. I'm doing well. Thank you for asking."

"Sorry. *Ciao*. I'm freaking out. Lorenzo got my number last night and said he wants to take me out."

"Wow."

That guy is the worst. He is definitely going to break her heart. And probably also steal her wallet.

"I told him yes. Of course. I would love to. I'm available anytime."

Oh, Carmen.

As though reading my mind she asks, "Should I have pretended to think about it first? Or played hard to get?"

What's done is done and offering feedback now will only feed her insecurity.

"You did great, Carmen," I tell her.

"I thought maybe you could help me choose the right outfit. You know, when he tells me where we're going on our date." She gives a squeal like she can't believe her good luck.

"Of course. Just let me know the details, and we'll find something great."

"Okay! I'm not sure if he was thinking Friday or Saturday, so I'm going to get my hair done tonight. That way I'll be ready either way."

"Great plan." And maybe I was too harsh on Lorenzo. It's not like he was dating Carmen when he asked me out. He's probably no worse than any other bartender in this city.

Carmen gives one more happy squeak, then hangs up to make a hair appointment.

When I slip back into the Moretti's living room, Gloria has joined the group for cards. She motions for me to take a seat next to her.

I've met a lot of mothers, and even though I come from one of the best families on the East Coast, there's always coldness; skepticism that no matter how beautiful or well-connected I am, I couldn't possibly be good enough for their son. Chad's mom was the worst, grilling me on my career path and political views.

I settle in next to Gloria, prepared to give her the full genealogy of my family and explain how I voted in the last election.

"So, what are your favorite foods?" she asks, catching me off guard. Her face is bright and expectant.

"Oh, um. I love tortellini. And lasagna."

"How about ravioli?" she asks. She's holding her breath like we're on a game show and everything hangs on getting this question right.

"I love it," I tell her truthfully, and the woman claps her hands like we just won a new car.

"That's my specialty! I'll make it for you the next time you come."

And then the interview's over. We play cards. We laugh at Julia's shameless cheating. And I don't have to name drop or perform conversational gymnastics to win these people over.

Apparently, the fact that Nico likes me is enough to convince them I'm good enough.

As the city slips past my taxi window on the way home, I mull over this easy acceptance. And wonder how in the world five people live in that tiny apartment.

It's 4am when my brother calls. Apparently, he has as little regard for my sleep schedule as I do for his.

"It's the middle of the night—what do you want?" My voice is somewhere between a growl and a yawn, like an annoyed bear cub woken from hibernation.

"Hey, Eggplant," Robert says. "Just calling to catch up. Sorry it's been so long, I've been wanting to check in, I'm just slammed at work."

"I'm doing great. Now let me go back to bed."

"Really?"

I snort. "Is that so hard to believe?"

"No, of course not. I just...wasn't sure. What have you been up to?"

Ugh. I guess we're doing this.

I sit up in bed and flick on the bedside lamp, squinting in the sudden light. Yawning, I fill him in on the studio and Marco. I tell him about Nico but make it sound more casual than it is.

"I think I want to stay here," I say.

"For the rest of the year?"

"Past that. I want to live in Milan after this nanny job is over. They have an amazing design school here. I went to the open house, and this professor was so cool."

There's silence on the other line, and I think I've lost him but then he says, "I've literally never heard you describe a professor as so cool." He chuckles. "I've never heard you excited about school at all. Dad will be thrilled."

"Nope." The blanket bunches in my closed fists. "I already talked to him. I won't find a respectable husband at design school, so what's the point?"

"Oh, Egg. What does Mom think?"

"Does it matter? She'll do whatever Dad says."

I can almost feel Robby nodding on the other end of the phone.

"Well, you still have some time. I'm sure everything will get sorted out."

I appreciate the encouragement, but we both know our dad. He doesn't change his mind about this sort of thing.

I ask Robby about his life, and he tells me of sleep deprivation and assisting an open-heart surgery. To me those things shouldn't go together, but medicine is crazy.

Chapter Twenty-Five

I want to slow down time and savor every gorgeous moment of this life. My days are filled with fashion design, and my nights are filled with Nico. I can't get enough of either.

Against my wishes, the weeks go by at an alarming rate.

On Halloween, Nico helps me throw a small party for Isa and her first-grade friends. He dresses up like an American baseball player, which may have something to do with the fact that I mentioned baseball was my favorite sport, and Julia comes as a fairy. She gasps when she sees Isa's costume and says, "You are the most beautiful mermaid I've ever seen." Isa takes an instant liking to her.

Carmen comes as an angry witch. She was supposed to go out with Lorenzo, but just like every other time, he canceled at the last minute. They have yet to go on a single date, and even though I tell her to move on, she clearly can't. She eats chocolate Baci on the Rossi's couch and hisses at any children who get too close to her.

November arrives, and I convince Paolo to host a Friendsgiving dinner, which I have catered by a nearby restaurant. Gone is the bland, overcooked turkey and weird stuffing. Instead, our table overflows with buttery risotto, rosemary-infused lamb, and golden focaccia still warm from the oven. Afterward, Nico tricks us into playing a terrible and hilarious game that involves getting blindfolded and then dodging water bottles hanging from the ceiling fan.

"It's a game of skill and strategy," he claims.

It's a game of chaos and betrayal, and I go down in the first five seconds.

The last days of November drift away like golden leaves in the wind, and before I know it, December has wrapped the city in twinkling lights. We're two weeks from Christmas, and I'm navigating the cheerful mob of shoppers downtown. Store windows glow with dazzling displays of silk scarves, sparkling jewelry, and stylish handbags.

Prada, Gucci, and Versace offer expensive colognes and impressive gifts, but none of it seems right for Nico. I want to get him something unique, that only he would like.

My phone vibrates, Karen's name flashing on my screen, and I mutter a curse.

"Merry Christmas Karen!" I say. "Calling to ask my dress size? I'm a French 34, as always. For you I'm picking up some quality lip balm. I know your lips must be chapped from kissing my dad's—"

"I'm calling about holiday travel plans," Karen cuts me off.

"What travel plans?" If my father thinks I'm flying home to make a family appearance at some holiday fundraiser, he can think again. He's the one who shipped me here, and I won't be at his beck and call.

"While Christmas is usually spent with family," Karen says, "the senator's schedule is extremely busy this year, and I'm afraid there won't be much time for outside activities."

Her words sink in like a cold wind through a cheap coat. She's not telling me to come home. She's telling me not to bother.

Way to embrace the holiday spirit, Karen.

"Don't worry, Karen, you can have my father all to yourself, no pesky family to distract him."

I hang up without another word.

I'm not sure if Karen is sleeping with my father. She's certainly older than most of the women he goes for. I picture the two of them exchanging romantic Christmas gifts while my mom spends the day at the spa.

I wasn't planning to go home anyway. I'm going to spend a wonderful Christmas with the Rossi family.

Tiffany beckons like an old friend, and I slip inside. The glass counter gleams under the soft glow of the boutique's chandeliers. Silver charms catch the light, each one delicate and shining. A tiny fish charm makes me think of Isa.

"*Scusi, Signora,*" I call to the woman behind the counter. "Can you show me your selection of tree charms?"

"Will we see the Statue of Liberty?" Isa is asking Marco when I get back to the apartment. The turquoise Tiffany box is nestled in my purse, and I zip to my room and tuck it under my bed. I don't want Isa to see it until Christmas.

When I come back to the living room, Marco is showing Isa something on his phone.

"That's Las Vegas. And look, they have a miniature Statue of Liberty right there."

"Is that a rollercoaster on the top?" Isa asks, brows furrowed.

Marco looks closer. "It might be. *Che cavolo*, that looks terrifying."

"And that's where Juliet lives?" Isa asks.

"She lives close by," Marco says. "I think. I'll give her a call and confirm. But I know she's going to be so excited to see you."

My fingers tighten around the back of the armchair as their words settle in.

"We're going to America!" Isa says, grinning up at me. "And Disneyland!" She looks at Marco. "Right?"

"*Si, principessa*, we'll take you to Disneyland after the show." Marco kisses the top of her head.

"When are you going?" I ask, making my voice sound normal.

"Next week," Marco says. "There's a Fashion Expo in Las Vegas. Bianca's been trying to convince me to dip a toe into the American market for years. And it looks like this year we're doing it."

"And he's taking me and Mom!" Isa yells gleefully. "And we're going to see Juliet."

Oh.

"We'll get back the day before school starts on January fifth."

"Wow. I had no idea."

My feelings are not hurt. My feelings are not hurt.

"I'm sorry for the short notice. It didn't look like it was going to work out this year, and then a spot opened up and Bianca got us in."

"What collection are you bringing?"

"The Las Vegas show is different than a runway show. Each designer shares seven ensembles from their last four collections. Which reminds me, I need to ask Bianca..." and then Marco wanders out of the room scratching his head.

"Lydia, do you want to see the necklace I made for Juliet?" Isa asks me. "I put the beads on all by myself. Except the hard ones. Mom did those."

Without waiting for an answer, she grabs my hand and drags me to her room, where an aggressively neon bead necklace sits on her chair like a radioactive snake.

"Ta-da! She's going to love it, right?"

"Of course she is," I tell her. I'd rather light myself on fire than wear something like that. But that knowledge doesn't keep a ridiculous feeling of jealousy from slinking into my belly.

I will not *be jealous of the fat nanny.*

Isa brushes her teeth while I lay out her pajamas. As soon as she's tucked under the covers, I get myself ready for bed, washing my face and ignoring the heavy feeling pressing against my ribs.

My father doesn't want me home. The Rossi's are going to America for Christmas.

I brush my teeth then head to my room and pull on my favorite silk pajamas.

My phone vibrates, and Nico's name lights up my screen.

"*Ciao, bella*!"

The muscles in my shoulders relax at the sound of his voice. "*Ciao,* Nico."

"So, my mom is planning a big Christmas dinner, and she told me to ask if you prefer lasagna or ravioli. I'm going to tell you right now, whichever you choose will be amazing."

I pause to process his words. "You want me to have Christmas dinner with your family?" My voice breaks unexpectedly on the last word, and I cough to cover it.

Apparently, it's not convincing, because Nico picks up on the weird vibe immediately.

"Unless you don't want to. I mean, I just assumed you'd spend all day with us on Christmas. Julia has already made you several terrifying drawings of snowmen. But I should have talked to you about it earlier. If it makes you uncomfortable or you think things are moving too fast, you don't have to do Christmas stuff. You and I can just hang out later."

"I'd love to do Christmas with your family," I say, swallowing the lump in my throat.

"Really?"

The excitement in his voice is a balm to my wounded heart. "Really."

"Perfect because my sisters are already arguing over who gets to sit next to you at dinner. I'm pretty sure they like you more than me. Which is fair since they've known you for two months, and I've only been their big brother *their whole lives*."

I laugh at his fake annoyance and sink into bed, wrapping the blanket around me.

"Let me give you the rundown of all the weird Christmas traditions we do, so you're not alarmed. First, my mom's going to hide a marble somewhere in the pasta, which sounds like a choking hazard, and it is, but if you find it, and you don't choke, you get good luck for the next year. Then there's singing Christmas carols, as you know I'm a fantastic singer, but my mom and sisters, not so much..."

Nico's voice is warm, like a fire crackling on a cold night, and I let his words settle around me, soft and safe. As Nico explains the overly complicated rules of their Christmas BINGO, I'm filled with so much gratitude and affection, I want to buy him the Brooklyn Bridge for Christmas.

Chapter Twenty-Six

"What if the plane falls?" Isa demands, her small hands digging into her hips, one bare foot tapping against the carpet. "*Then* what will we do?"

The Rossis are heading to the airport in a couple of hours, and Isa, who has talked about this trip nonstop for the past week, now refuses to get on the plane.

"The plane won't fall," Sophie says. Her voice carries the strain that comes with answering a question for the fourteenth time.

The family is packed and ready, leaving Isa with nothing to do but ask a million unnerving questions.

"What if the pilot falls asleep? What if one of the wings falls off? What if one of the flight attendants is actually working for an evil genius who wants to crash the plane into the volcano lair of his arch nemesis?"

I tilt my head. "Is that a thing that happens?"

Isa nods. "I saw it in a movie."

"I think it's time for *Glitter the Mermaid*," I tell her. Isa bounces after me to her room, where we squish onto her bed, and I turn on my phone. We get lost in the magic and drama of the ocean's magical worlds until Sofia knocks on the door an hour later.

"It's time to have a snack and then off to the airport."

"But this is a good spot," Isa whines.

"Well, maybe Daddy can put it on his phone, and you can listen to it on the plane."

I give Sofia a pleasant smile while silently cursing her for suggesting Isa listen to *Glitter the Mermaid* without me.

"Nah, I'll wait until we get back so I can keep listening with Lydia."

I give Isa a squeeze. *Thatta girl.*

"I have a Christmas gift for you," I tell her once Sofia's gone back to the kitchen.

"Ooh! I was hoping you would!" Isa says shamelessly.

She zips in front of me to my bedroom and starts yanking open drawers and tossing aside shoes.

I pull the turquoise Chelsie box from my nightstand and hand it to her.

"Ooh, Tiffany," she breathes, eyes widening as she cradles the box in her hands like it contains the source of all happiness. She's seven, but she's wise beyond her years. After carefully untying the bow, she takes off the lid and sets it on my bed then pulls out the white tissue paper.

"A charm bracelet!" she says, pulling it out. Her eyebrows dip. "A fish? I don't even know how to fish."

She hates it. I should have gotten her a toy.

"And a tree..." She fingers the delicate silver charm. "A fish in a tree! Like us!"

A jolt of happiness shoots through me. She does remember.

"It's to remind you how smart and talented you are." I pull up my sleeve to show her the matching one on my wrist. "I even got one for myself."

"I love it!" she says. "Will you put it on me?"

She wiggles when I tickle her arm, and I fasten the bracelet around her wrist.

"I didn't make you a bead necklace like I did for Juliet," she tells me.

"It's okay. You didn't have to get me anything." I know she and Juliet are very close. They spent a whole year together, and I've only been here a few months.

Isa scrunches her nose. "Of course I got you something. I just didn't make you a necklace. Juliet will wear anything no matter how ugly it is, but you're not like that."

"Oh."

She is right about that.

"Stay right here, I'll get it for you."

She dashes out and returns with a big sketchpad. "I noticed you filled up almost all the pages in your design book, so I told Mom we should get you a new one."

She hands it to me, and my heart squeezes. It's not a big deal. But no one has ever gotten me such a thoughtful gift before. My parents always give me gifts they want me to want, and my friends and boyfriends get me things that make them look cool but have nothing to do with me.

"What a perfect gift," I tell Isa and scoop her into a hug.

Italy is doing weird things to me, like turning me into a hugger.

I spend a good chunk of the next day tracking down the gift I have in mind for Nico. It's 50/50 if it will work out, but if I can pull this off, he's going to love it.

Right? Maybe. I'm not quite sure.

After a trip downtown for more shopping I meet Nico, Carmen, and Valentina at Paolo's apartment for a white elephant gift exchange. His place is decorated tastefully with twinkling lights and boughs of greenery. The aroma of hot apple cider wafts in from the kitchen.

We settle onto soft leather couches in the living room, and Valentina goes first, unwrapping a gift box and pulling out an exceptionally ugly Christmas sweater. It's red plaid with flashing green lights and actual tinsel dangling off the front.

"Oh!" Her face is losing the battle to look happy about this new gift.

When it's my turn, I heft a giant box onto my lap and remove a mountain of white tissue paper to reveal a used bowling ball, smooth and cool against my fingers. Carmen claps a hand over her mouth, giggling uncontrollably.

This has her name written all over it. And I'm guessing she got it at the market.

I dig around in my purse for some hand sanitizer.

Then Nico picks my gift. There was a twenty-euro limit, but I ignored it. Nico tugs off the wrapping, and the second the glossy black leather is visible Valentina sucks in a sharp breath.

Carmen lets out a shriek. "Is that Kate Spade?"

"I believe so," Nico says, glancing at me.

"It's my turn next, right?" Carmen asks without taking her eyes from the designer handbag.

"It is," Paolo confirms.

Carmen moves so fast, I don't even see her take the bag. One second, Nico is holding it, the next, Carmen is clutching the purse to her chest like it's a life preserver and she's drowning.

"I choose this!" Her cheeks are flushed with happiness, and her eyes shine brighter than Paolo's Christmas tree.

"So that means I choose a gift from the middle?" Nico asks.

"Yes, or you can steal a gift," Paolo says. Nico chooses a new gift, a rubber fish that sings Christmas carols.

"This is exactly what I needed." He grins in delight.

"All right, Paolo. You're the last one up," I say.

There's one gift bag left on the table, but Paolo doesn't reach for it. Instead, he reaches for Valentina's hideous sweater.

"Are you really going to wear that?" she asks. The idea of Paolo wearing a plaid sweater with Christmas tinsel dangling off the front is absurd.

"What can I say? I don't have any sweaters like this."

"O...kay." Valentina reaches for the last gift, then stops. "Wait a minute. I can choose any gift, can't I?"

"Yes, you can," Paolo says at the same time Carmen says, "No no no no," and hides the Kate Spade bag behind her.

"I'm sorry, Carmen," Valentina says, and it's obvious she really is. "I know you love it, but I also really love it."

Carmen looks at Valentina and nods slowly. "I understand," she whispers.

With shiny eyes, she passes the handbag to Valentina and chooses the last gift. It's a mug shaped like *Babo Natale* and filled with Baci chocolates. Carmen presses her lips together in an almost-smile, but there's heartbreak in her eyes. I can't wait any longer.

"I have two more gifts," I announce, pulling them from behind the couch.

"For you," I say to Carmen, handing her a large gift bag.

"Thanks," she says, pulling the tissue paper out. "I didn't mean to—"

She stops mid-sentence, eyes locking on mine. Tears spill onto her cheeks, but she's grinning.

"She's crying," Nico whispers, shifting in his chair. "Why is she crying?"

"You'll see," I say.

Carmen lifts the handbag from the tissue paper like it's something sacred, her fingers grazing the smooth leather. It's identical to Valentina's, and she places it carefully over her arm, then comes around the table and hugs me tight, her breath hitching in my ear. "Thank you."

"You're welcome," I say.

I hand the box to Paolo. "And this is for the host."

Paolo lifts a silk Versace tie from the box. "Wow. This is beautiful."

"I thought it would go well with your wardrobe," I tell him. "With the exception of your new sweater."

"Thank you, Lydia. You spoil us."

"You're the best!" Valentina says.

"My favorite person in the world!" Carmen says.

The two of them clutch their matching handbags grinning like children. Valentina strokes hers like it's a Persian cat and Carmen slips hers over her arm and grips the straps as though a horde of purse snatchers might leap out from behind Paolo's couch.

This is so much better than giving gifts to my friends back home.

"What about Nico's gift?" Valentina says.

"I got a singing fish," he says, looking as happy as the rest of them.

"I'm still working on your Christmas gift," I tell him. "But I promise it will be here by Christmas. And you're going to love it."

I think.

"Oh no. Are we one of those couples who buy each other presents?" Nico makes a panicked face, and I swat his arm. He catches my wrist, his fingers warm against my skin, mischief dancing in his eyes. Then, somehow, we're kissing, the world narrowing down to the press of his lips and the pounding of my heart.

Paolo coughs loudly, but Carmen says, "She bought us the most glorious handbags ever made, she can kiss as much as she wants."

Chapter Twenty-Seven

Flurries of snow drift down from a gray sky, coating Milan's deserted streets in a thin layer of white. I've never liked Christmas Day. It's not something I tell people because they would think I'm a monster. But it always feels phony. Carefully staged photos. Pretending to love presents that are usually terrible.

So, I'm surprised by the unexpected flutter of excitement in my chest as I catch a taxi to Nico's. Spending time with his family is so much simpler than spending time with mine. There's no pretense, no competition, no insults disguised as compliments.

Last year's Christmas dinner pops into my head. Halfway through the meal, my mom noticed one of our dinner guests wearing the same gold necklace she'd received from my father that morning. She "accidentally" dumped a tureen of gravy into my father's lap.

What kind of idiot gets his wife and his mistress the exact same Christmas gift?

Of course, my father hadn't known my mom invited her new tennis partner to Christmas dinner.

So yes, I'm looking forward to a drama-free day with the Moretti's. Plus, my contacts came through and my gift for Nico arrived last night. I can't wait to give it to him. Mostly.

By the time I get to Nico's apartment, I'm humming like a Christmas caroler drunk on eggnog and Mariah Carey.

Nico opens the door before I can even knock.

"Merry Christmas!" I say, enjoying the gust of warm air from the apartment.

Nico steps outside, closes the door behind him, and slips my heavy Marc Jacobs tote off my shoulder, lowering it to the ground.

"Merry Christmas," he says softly, voice low and warm. He puts a hand to my cheek cradling my face and sending my heart rate spiking. The other hand wraps around to my lower back. The air is cold, and there's a stiff breeze blowing, but Nico is all warmth.

"You look gorgeous this morning," he whispers, kissing just below my ear.

"*Grazie*," I respond, breathless. "You too." His hands are in my hair, then at my hips, pulling me closer to him. I stand on tiptoe to erase the last shred of space between us. This is exactly how I want to spend this day.

"Merry Christmas!" Julia says, leaping out the front door.

Nico groans and rests his forehead against mine.

"Julia," he growls, eyes closed, breathing fast.

"Why are you guys out here?" she asks, looking down the street. "It's freezing." She's grinning like a maniac, and there's reddish-pink all around her mouth. Could be a candy cane, could be poorly applied lipstick. With a seven-year-old, you never know.

"Merry Christmas," I tell her. "You're right, it is cold out here."

"But private," Nico says, so low only I can hear. "Almost private."

Julia tugs on my hand to pull me inside as I whisper to Nico, "Why don't you come over to the Rossi's tomorrow? We'll have the place to ourselves..."

Nico swallows, then nods, then starts kissing me again.

"Come on!" Julia says, and with a sudden yank, I'm pulled away from Nico's mouth and into the Moretti home. It's warm and filled with the buttery smell of fresh baked goods.

"Lydia!" Gloria calls from the kitchen. "Merry Christmas! Have you had breakfast yet? I've made scones with fresh cream."

"Lydia! Look what I got!" Benedetta says holding up a makeup palette. It's one of the cheap ones with weird colors that smear easily, but she's grinning like it's Chanel. "Can you show me how to do that eye thing again?"

"Merry Christmas, Lydia," Camilla says coming down the hall. "I got you something, but you'll probably hate it."

I take a breath. The last sixty seconds have been a lot.

Nico wraps his arms around me from behind and nuzzles my neck. Or maybe it just feels like a lot compared to my own family gatherings that never felt like enough.

"Merry Christmas!" I say.

Gloria insists on feeding me before she'll allow any gift giving. When I've cleaned my plate, she squishes next to Benedetta and Camilla on the couch, while Nico and I share the armchair. Julia bounces around like a reindeer on its third Red Bull then finally settles onto the floor at my feet.

"Me first!" she says, and Nico gives her a soft swat.

"Of course," I say, and reach into my large Marc Jacobs tote. I didn't have time to wrap anything. Or rather, wrapping a bunch of presents felt tedious after a day of shopping, so I didn't.

"This is for you," I tell Julia and hand her a mermaid zombie doll with rainbow hair.

"It's a Mermombie doll! Look at her hair! Just like the commercials!"

"Where did you find that?" Nico asks. "We looked everywhere, and they were sold out."

"I guess I'm just lucky," I say. Nico narrows his eyes. The truth is they were sold out everywhere, but I found one on display at a store downtown and charmingly bullied the store manager into selling it to me.

"And this is for Camilla," I say, pulling a black leather jacket from my bag. If I remember correctly, being twelve sucks. It's a confusing spot between child and teenager where no one takes you seriously and all you want is to feel cool. Robert got me a leather jacket for my twelfth birthday, and I loved it with all my heart.

"That's for me?" Camilla asks, then glances at Benedetta, like maybe I meant her older sister.

"It's for you," I confirm. "A jacket like this needs a cool girl to wear it, and I thought you'd be perfect for it."

She slips it on, and a shy smile fills her face. "Thank you."

"You are very welcome. Now for Benedetta."

It took me a while to come up with this one. I pull out large bottles of Pureology Hydrate shampoo and conditioner. Benedetta sees the name on the bottles and gives a little gasp.

"It's the hair care system you use!" she says.

It was one of the questions Benedetta asked me the first night I came over. And I saw the expression on her face when she looked them up online to see how much they cost. Even I can admit they're stupidly expensive.

She takes the bottles from me like she's accepting an Oscar, eyes wide in thrilled disbelief.

"Thank you," she says, hugging them to her chest.

For Gloria I pull out an envelope and hand it to her.

"You didn't have to get anything for me," she says.

"Open it. And if you don't want it, I'll take it back."

She opens the envelope and pulls out a certificate. "A spa day!"

"I know how hard you work at your job and as a mom to these crazies. I thought you could use some pampering."

"I've never done a spa day before!" She reads through the lists of services included and looks at me wide-eyed. "A hot stone massage! A seaweed wrap!"

"I haven't been to this spa," I say, "but the reviews are good." I think of the spa I go to back home, how many self-care treatments I enjoy without a second thought. And Gloria, who works harder than any woman I've ever met, has never gone once.

"You are spoiling my family," Nico says, giving me a kiss. It feels good spoiling people you care about. And turns out it's a lot more fun to give gifts to people who couldn't get those things for themselves.

"Now Nico's gift!" Julia shouts. She's making her Mermombie prance up and down the arm of the couch.

A wave of nerves hits me. I didn't think that I'd be giving Nico his gift in front of his whole family.

Is it going to seem stupid? Did I go through a lot of time and expense for a stupid gift?

Before I can pull it out, Nico wraps his arms around me. "Hold on, I want to give you my gift first."

He slips out of the chair and retrieves a wrapped gift from under the tree. Anticipation lights up his face as he hands it to me. The wrapping paper is red and there are at least seven bows on it.

"Nico wrapped it, but I added the bows," Julia tells me.

I pull back the wrapping paper to reveal a black satin Vera Wang skirt. I subtly check to see if there's something else, but it's just the skirt. All four women in the Moretti family lean forward to see my reaction, and Nico shifts his weight from his left foot to his right and then back again.

Honestly, I'm underwhelmed. It's a lovely black skirt, but it looks like something every other boyfriend has given me. Things with Nico are so different from my other relationships, I was hoping for something...more personal.

Thankfully, every Christmas since I was a child has trained me to be an excellent gift receiver, and I ooh and aah and tell Nico what a perfect gift it is.

"Vera Wang is a fancy designer," Julia says from the floor.

"She knows that," Camilla says, annoyed.

But Nico beams with pride. "Do you want to try it on? I wasn't sure about the size."

I slip into their bathroom and try the skirt on. It's a little big in the waist, but I pleat the top and grab a bobby pin lying near the sink to hold it in place. Then I pull my sweater down to cover it.

"Wow!" Benedetta says when I walk out. "You look amazing!"

Julia and Gloria clap, and Nico whistles. I smile and give a dramatic spin.

"It fits you perfectly," Nico says.

"I love it," I tell him. "Thank you for the lovely gift."

And it really is lovely. It just feels a little generic. And it makes me feel silly that I spent so much time and effort on Nico's gift, when he just bought mine off the rack.

But it's fine. Everyone does gifts differently. It's no big deal.

"I don't want to get anything on this," I tell them. "Let me just change back into my pants."

The Morettis don't have a full-length mirror in their bathroom, so I can't see the whole thing, but it does look nice on me. I'll sneak it into the studio and take in the waist so it fits perfectly.

I change into my pants and nearly smack Gloria with the door as I leave the bathroom. This apartment is ridiculously small.

"I'm so sorry!" I say.

"It's fine," she says, waving me off. "Happens all the time." She looks at the skirt in my hands.

"You like the skirt?"

"I do."

She nods, but she's looking at my face like she can see into my head.

"Nico's not working at the studio right now, because it's the slow season," she says, "but he saw that skirt, and he was determined to get it for you."

From the living room, Julia shrieks, "No, Mermombie! You can't eat your own tail!" followed by Nico's deep, monstrous growl.

"You may have noticed," Gloria continues, lowering her voice, "we don't have a lot of extra cash in this house."

Heat creeps up my cheeks, and I'm not sure how to respond to her statement.

"I suggested Nico buy you a nice black skirt from the market, but he told me, 'Lydia, is the real deal. She deserves the best.' So, he called my boss to see if he could pick up shifts at the restaurant. Of course, around the holidays everyone wants to take time off, so my boss agreed." She looks at me, gaze level, expression serious. "I know a girl like you buys yourself a skirt like this on a whim, but Nico worked seven dinner shifts to get that for you."

Her tone is matter-of-fact. She's not judging, but she wants me to know the cost of what I'm holding.

Tears prick behind my eyes, and I nod.

"I understand," I tell her. "Thank you for telling me."

She gives one more nod, then heads back to the living room. A lump rises in my throat, hot and stubborn, but I blink hard and bully my tears back into their ducts. Then I join Nico on the armchair, snuggling into his warmth.

"*Grazie*," I whisper in his ear. "The skirt is gorgeous, and you did *so good* getting it. I can't wait to wear it everywhere."

"I'm so glad," he whispers back, kissing my cheek.

"Are you ready for your gift?" I ask.

"Bring it on."

The red ribbon crinkles under my fingers as I smooth it over the package and my stomach flips. I hand him the box and hold my breath.

"Whoa, this is heavy." He carefully takes off the bow, then lifts the lid.

"What is it?" Julia calls.

Nico lifts out a brick of white granite, flecked with black and shows his mom and sisters.

"A brick?" Camilla asks, puzzled.

Nico's lips quirk in amusement as he waits for my explanation.

"That is one of the original bricks used in the construction of the Brooklyn Bridge."

His smile drops. The brick drops in his lap with a thunk, and he turns to me, eyes wide. "This is from the Brooklyn Bridge?"

"Yes."

"Do they know you took it?"

I laugh. "Yes. They did a rehabilitation project on the Brooklyn Bridge last year, and—"

"I read about that!" Nico says, picking up the brick again. "But how did you—?"

"A family friend oversees the Department of Transportation. He got in touch with one of the project directors and asked for one of the bricks they removed."

Nico and his family stare at me speechless, and I awkwardly fill the silence. "You were talking about how much you love the Brooklyn Bridge and were going on and on about the arches and the masonry work."

Gloria smiles. "He does that."

"I thought it might be a neat gift, you know, something you couldn't get anywhere else." The longer I stare at the side of Nico's face, the greater my doubts.

Who gives a brick as a Christmas gift?

Finally, Nico turns to me, his face glowing with happiness. "This is the greatest gift anyone has ever gotten in the history of gift giving." He leans in and kisses me.

"No offense, Mom," he adds. "The roller skates I got when I was ten were really great. But this is the *Brooklyn Bridge*." He holds the brick above his head. "Did you know that UNESCO is considering the Brooklyn Bridge as an official World Heritage Site?"

"Oh no," Camilla says, "he's doing that thing."

"Oh yes!" Nico says, leaping off the armchair. "Did you know that when it was built, the Brooklyn Bridge was the longest suspension bridge in the world? It's over a mile long."

"Cool." Camilla says, in a bored voice.

"It was the first suspension bridge to use steel cables. That was a big deal."

"Should we move on to the gifts we got Lydia?" Benedetta asks, but Nico's not finished.

"More than 100,000 vehicles cross it every day!" Nico continues waving the brick around for effect. "But it's not just functional, it's beautiful!"

Julia starts giggling at this point and so do I.

"Those gothic masonry arches?" Nico puts his fingers to his mouth and does a chef's kiss.

"We get it, we get it," Camilla calls. "The Brooklyn Bridge is awesome, and you're a weirdo. Now can we give Lydia our gifts?"

"Yes!" Nico practically yells. "Give her all your gifts! All the gifts in the world for this amazing woman who has given me a piece of architectural history." He carefully lays the brick back in the box and then pulls me out of the chair and starts dancing me around the small living room in what I think is the polka.

It's silly and over the top and makes me feel so good.

He finally stops and pulls me into his arms for a long kiss. Applause fills the small space, along with whistles and cheers. Heat prickles up my neck, but instead of embarrassment, something warm and euphoric spreads through me. Something that feels a lot like love.

Chapter Twenty-Eight

The next week is perfection. Not because I'm on a yacht in St. Tropez or shopping in Paris. I'm in an apartment with Nico, eating food he cooks, kissing him every chance I get, and engaging in deep discussions about bridges. Who knew infrastructure could be so sexy?

We've just spent the day ice skating in Piazza Duomo, and the warmth of the Rossis' apartment feels divine to my still-numb toes. Nico settles onto the couch with a book, and I pull out my laptop and open the application for the Milan Institute of Design.

The application and I have been in a staring contest for a week now. So far, the application is winning.

The glow of my laptop screen glares back at me, the cursor blinking impatiently. My fingers hover uselessly over the keyboard as the words on the application shift like waves, refusing to settle into meaning. A lump rises in my throat, heavy and familiar.

"Just a few pages left," Nico says beside me.

"*Sì.*" I make it sound like a few pages is no big deal, but trying to complete this feels like wearing a corset that's two sizes too small.

If I can't even fill out the application, how am I going to survive at school?

"What's the next question?" Nico asks.

I look at the next question. It takes me a solid minute to understand what it's saying, and heat rises up the back of my neck.

"I need a snack." My voice comes out too high, and I disentangle myself from Nico and head to the kitchen.

What was I thinking? I can't read all those questions and write all those answers. This is exactly why I didn't make it at college before.

"You okay?" Nico calls from the living room.

"*Sí.* Just hungry. Want anything?"

His response comes slowly. "No, I don't need anything."

The tile floor is cool beneath my bare feet, a stark contrast to the heat prickling at my neck. I yank open a cupboard and scan the shelves, but nothing calls to me. Crackers. Pasta. A forgotten bag of cookies. Blegh.

"Lydia." Nico's voice startles me.

How did he get into the kitchen so fast?

"How's the application going?" He pulls me into a hug, his arms wrapping around me before I can pull away. His heartbeat is steady against mine, and his familiar scent envelops me.

"Great."

"Do you need any help?"

"I got it."

Nico takes a step back and looks into my eyes. "You don't have to do this, Lydia."

I turn and grab a bottle of water from the fridge. "Do what?"

"Keep up this façade." He rests against the kitchen table facing me.

"I don't know what you're talking about." I take a long sip of water.

"And I don't know what you're thinking."

"What's that supposed to mean?"

"It means you never tell me stuff," Nico says with a sigh. "You act fine when you're not. You say you don't need help when I think you might. For the first month after I met you, I didn't even know you liked fashion. You pretended you were working at the studio out of boredom."

I take another sip of water, unsure how to respond.

Nico runs a hand down his face. "I'm crazy about you, Lydia. You know I am. And I think the feeling's mutual. But if we want this to work, you've got to let me in. Share stuff with me. Let me get to know you."

"I'm tired."

It's true. I'm also discouraged, embarrassed, nervous, and disappointed. And if I choose not to tell him those other things, well, that's my choice.

Nico nods slowly, disappointment filling his eyes. "Then I'll head home and let you get some rest."

Nico's been staying late every night and leaving this early feels like he's punishing me for not baring my soul.

Fine.

My stubbornness flares. I walk him to the door and kiss his cheek, his stubble scratchy against my lips. Then I step out of reach before he can pull me into his arms.

He sighs and walks out the door, and I wallow in a victory that feels like defeat.

What does he want from me?

I grab my computer and head to my bedroom, closing my door harder than necessary.

Maybe I don't share every thought that comes into my head or go running to him every time I have a problem. It's called being low maintenance. Most guys would love a girlfriend like that.

It's too early for bed, so I call Carmen and she answers on the first ring.

"Lydia."

"*Ciao*, Carmen. *Come va*?" What's up?

"Nothing. Are you okay?" Her voice sounds worried.

"I'm fine. Just calling to chat." I wander my room, nudging a pair of shoes I left out.

"You never call to chat."

"Sure I do."

"No...I always call you."

"Well, I pick up, so that's pretty much the same thing."

"Not at all the same, but whatever. What do you want to talk about? My job is still terrible. Lorenzo keeps asking me out and then canceling because of some emergency. This week it was his sick grandmother."

"I actually wanted to talk about Nico." The words sound ridiculous coming out of my mouth.

"Oh."

"It's not a big deal. He said something tonight about me never sharing anything with him or letting him know me. Which is ridiculous, right?"

Carmen bursts out laughing.

I'm beginning to remember why I don't call her.

"Lydia, we've been friends for three months, and I just found out last week you have a brother. Nico's right, you don't share."

"Because oversharing is lame."

And information is currency, traded for favors and used for leverage.

"It's not oversharing when you mention that you have a sibling. Or that you love fashion. Or when you explain why you filled the dean's office with chickens."

I smile. That's clearly been haunting her.

"What difference does that stuff make?"

"It makes a difference! It helps us get to know you. And it makes us feel like you trust us."

I don't trust them.

The realization stops me in my tracks, and I settle onto the bed.

Why don't I trust them?

Carmen talks about how she's an open book, happy to share anything, while my mind wanders. I learned not to share information or show vulnerability because it ended badly for me. But like a lot of coping mechanisms, it works until it doesn't.

The gang in Milan isn't part of the Connecticut gossip chain. They've never done anything to hurt me. And keeping these walls up is no longer serving me.

Once I see it, it feels obvious. And whatever my other weaknesses are, I've always been good at adapting.

"My brother's name is Robert," I say, interrupting Carmen. "He's the only good thing about my family. My father is a senator, and my mother is a senator's wife." My feet tap nervously on the carpet, but I keep going. "I've loved fashion since my grandma first handed me a needle, but my parents made it clear it was an unsuitable career for a St. Clair." I squeeze my blanket. "I filled the dean's office with chickens because he was a creep, and because I was failing all my classes and needed to get kicked out before my father convinced them to let me stay."

Carmen's breath on the other end of the line is the only indication that she hasn't hung up.

"I'm dating an amazing guy," I continue, "and I've never felt this way before, and I'm afraid I'm going to screw it up."

After a pause she says, "Nice to meet you, Lydia St. Clair. We're going to be great friends."

Chapter Twenty-Nine

Early the next morning, I send Nico a message.

> Hey, I could use some help on my application.
> Want to come over?

Thirty minutes later, he's at my door. He pulls me close, his arms firm and steady. His cheeks are ice-cold, making my own skin prickle, and I kiss him until we're both warm.

"Good morning," he says, breaking away.

"Good morning." I press another kiss to his lips, an apology for my pettiness last night and a thank you for coming over this morning.

We move to the couch, and I open my computer, nerves bouncing through me.

How will this work? Is he going to read to me like I'm a Victorian orphan who's never seen a book before? Is he going to sit in excruciating silence as I struggle to put the words together?

"I skipped breakfast when I saw your text," Nico says. "Do you have any toast or anything?"

"Lucky for you, toast is my one and only culinary specialty."

I head to the kitchen and grab two slices of bread from the package.

"I don't think I've asked you before," Nico says from the living room. "Why do you want to go into fashion design?"

I drop the bread into the toaster and press the button. It sinks with a soft thunk.

"I guess it's kind of like you and your bridges. I like fashion because it's functional and beautiful at the same time. Clothes serve a purpose, and they can also be stunning while they serve a purpose." I think about it and add. "Just like bridges, fashion connects us. It can connect us to other people. It can connect us to the person we want to become."

"Interesting," Nico says. There's a pause. "You wear a lot of Versace. What do you like about them?"

The toast pops up, and the scent of warm bread drifts through the air as I spread the butter, pale yellow melting into toasted brown.

"Versace is my fave because their use of colors and textures is distinctive and fun while still being classic." I pause to collect my thoughts, and the clatter of the keyboard fills the silence.

I step into the living room. "Are you writing down my words?"

Nico's head snaps up, guilt flickering across his face. "Maybe." He runs a hand through his hair. "I thought it might help. Me reading the questions and you answering them out loud."

Heat floods my face, embarrassment curling low in my stomach. But beneath it, gratitude rises. Because it does help.

I swallow the lump in my throat. "That's a good idea."

I hand him the plate of toast, and he places it on the coffee table, confirming my suspicions that it was just a distraction. He reaches out a hand, and I let him pull me onto the couch next to him.

"I also think it will be good practice for the future, when you're a famous designer and reporters ask you deeply insightful questions like, 'What's your favorite color?'"

My lips curl into a smile. "Well then, please continue the interview."

Nico straightens his back, grabs a hairbrush off the coffee table, and tilts it toward me. "Now, Ms. St. Clair, you've obviously had a ridiculously successful career, but tell me about your first experience in a fashion studio. What did you learn?"

I take the hairbrush/microphone from him and give him a smile. "Well

Mr. Moretti, that is an excellent question. I had the privilege of working at Rossi Designs, and I learned a lot."

Nico types as I talk and it's so much easier this way. With each question, he gets more ridiculous as an interviewer, and I give dramatic waves to the imaginary paparazzi filming our conversation. Before I know it, we've covered all the application questions, debated the ethical implications of skinny jeans, and survived one dramatic reenactment of a runway walk.

"Just one more question to finish this up," Nico says. "Who would you say is the most charming and delightful man in all of Milan?"

I take the brush from him and give him a long slow kiss. "Nico Moretti. Hands down."

He smiles. "Good answer."

I lean in for another kiss, but he pulls away. "This is a masterpiece," he says pointing at the open application. "I'm submitting it now."

I watch him click the green button, and then he closes the laptop, moves it onto the coffee table, and pulls me onto his lap.

"Well done," he says, staring into my eyes like he could do it all day.

"How should we celebrate?" I ask.

His lips meet mine in a slow, deep kiss, stealing my breath. My arms wind around his neck, fingers threading into his hair as warmth unfurls inside me. My heart pounds against his chest, fashion and deadlines forgotten.

The Rossis make it home the next day, and I'm surprised that I might have actually missed that tiny monster. She tells me about all the things she saw in Las Vegas and about getting to see Juliet.

A pang of jealousy leaps inside me, but it's squashed seconds later when she says, "I told her all about you. And your hair. And your amazing clothes. And how you're working for my dad, and he chose your design for the show."

It's nice to have a seven-year-old bragging about me. Honestly, it's more than my parents do.

Benedetta got my number from Nico, and texts me pictures of her attempts at smoky eyes and contouring. I make a note to ask Nico when her birthday is so I can buy her some decent makeup.

The first week back in the studio is low-key. I help out where I can but have a lot of time to draw and daydream.

I sit at my favorite table by the window and think about a fun idea for the spring collection Marco will debut in September. I'm looking for a unifying thread that ties all the ensembles together, but my thoughts keep coming back to Nico.

Could I convince Marco to do a Nico-themed collection? Probably not.

Nico mentioned taking a trip to Venice to see *il Ponte dei Sospiri.* I'll have to ask Sofia and Marco if I can take a weekend off after the winter collection debuts in February. It shouldn't be a problem since I don't do any nannying on the weekends.

There are always cheap flights from Venice to Paris, and I wonder if we could do both cities in one weekend. Paris has some beautiful bridges spanning the Seine.

Ooh, I bet Nico would love to add London to the list so we could see the Tower Bridge.

Of course, London in February is dreadful. Better to visit in late spring, when the weather's nice.

I sketch out a cute little trench coat with dark skinny jeans. And if we're going to Paris, I'll need a beret. Before I know it, I've sketched out seven different outfits for traveling Europe in the spring.

Spring Travel is a funny idea for a collection, but now that it's in my head, accessories and footwear flood my brain. A delicate gold sandal from Greece, a sturdy black heel, like a Spanish Flamenco dancer...

This could be something fun.

Within days, the studio transforms from a peaceful haven for daydreaming to a crowded hive of activity. Machines whir, fabric rustles, and voices rise and fall in a symphony of creative chaos.

On January tenth, the whole team meets in the conference room to discuss the Winter show. Marco scribbles on his notepad like a man possessed. Bianca paces the floor behind him, and Chelsie brings in coffee for everyone.

Danilo and Clara sit across from me. There's an uneasy peace between us. They've dropped the obsequious groveling, but they haven't gone back to the condescending disdain from my first month. It's not a bad spot to be in. I still hope they fall into a mud puddle while wearing white, but I'm not going to be the one to push them.

"All right, team," Marco says, "The winter show is one month from today. You've all seen the designs for our Frosted Fairytale collection. Do you have any questions?"

No one raises a hand.

"Perfect. Then let's jump into the work that needs to be done."

Marco hands out assignments, and I remember my first task here: snipping beads off a string. This morning, I'm cutting out a dress, the smooth glide of scissors through silk reminding me how far I've come. Clara and Danilo work next to me, the rustle of paper patterns and the clack of scissors filling the air.

One month out means the models come in for weekly fittings, and Nico picks up extra shifts to help out. We haven't worked together since we started dating, and I'm a little nervous.

You're a professional, I remind myself. *So, behave like a professional.*

The door to the studio swings open, and a wave of cologne, laughter, and booted footsteps announces the arrival of the male models. Nico is third in the studio, and his face breaks into a grin when he sees me. He walks toward our table, and Clara stands up straighter next to me.

"Danilo," Nico says, with a nod, "Clara."

They both nod back at him. Then he pulls me into his arms and kisses me. Not a polite peck, but a full blown, cover-of-a-romance-novel kiss.

"You look gorgeous today," he tells me, then walks to the space set up for him with a chair and a stool.

It takes me a moment to tear my eyes away from him, and when I do, Danilo and Clara arc gaping at me.

Clara opens and closes her mouth while blinking several times. I've never seen a goldfish try to explain theoretical physics, but I imagine it would look like this.

"So...you and Nico...that's a thing that's happening?" she croaks.

"*Sì*, it's happening." I watch Nico chatting with Marco, hands waving, laugh bubbling out of him. "And yes, it's every bit as good as you're imagining."

The lead up to the winter collection is significantly less stressful than the spring show. Maybe it's because I've learned so much since fall, I'm able to lighten the workload for the team. (Marco tells me so twice.) And maybe it's because nobody posts videos of their ensemble, forcing us to create a new design from scratch.

We spend the month fitting models, sewing Marco's designs, and organizing accessories. The pressure to top last year's show is intense but gazing at the models on our last day of fittings, I think Marco's done it.

There's fur as white as untouched alpine snow—a stark contrast to the gray mounds that currently fill Milan's streets. And velvet in jewel-toned blues and rich reds that beg to be touched. Marco embraced the fairy tale aesthetic, weaving in glistening tiaras and delicate wands that catch the light with every movement.

I overheard him ask Bianca if they could send models down the runway on horseback. Bianca stared at him for a full ten seconds before responding, "Unless you want horse poop to be part of your couture line, absolutely not."

"*Ciao, bella,*" Nico says, coming up behind me and nuzzling my neck.

There may be another reason this month has gone so well. Having Nico in the studio two days a week is heaven. All attempts at professionalism fell apart after the first day, but nobody seems to mind.

"Just don't break up with him until after the show," Bianca whispered to me at one point, and I laughed.

Nico is the best thing in my life. Which is saying something because my life has turned very good recently. The Milan Institute of Design received my application and called last week to schedule an interview.

I turn and give Nico a kiss. "How are you feeling? Sad about the last runway show of your career?"

The relief on Nico's face is more in line with a man who's escaped a burning building than a man whose walk inspires applause. He pulls me into his arms. "How could I be sad about anything?"

I feel the same way. We've been dating for four months, and I'm waiting for something to go wrong. Instead, it keeps getting better. I can't stop thinking about him. I want to be with him all the time. Somewhere along the way, this thing between us got real and big.

His lips brush mine, and I'm seconds away from dragging him into the supply closet. Instead, Bianca asks us to hang all the ensembles in their labeled bags, and we do as we're told.

The show is at a different, bigger venue than last September, and the place is already packed thirty minutes before the show is due to begin.

Isa spent the last week begging and pleading to go to the runway show, insisting she was old enough, and on Friday afternoon, Marco finally relented. She and Sofia are seated in the front row, and she gives me a big smile and thumbs up when she sees me peeking at the audience.

Backstage pulses with nervous energy. Heels click against the floor, fabric rustles as last-minute adjustments are made, and the air smells of hairspray and anticipation. I help Bianca find a scarf a model dropped while simultaneously playing hide-and-seek with the stylist who keeps trying to touch my hair.

Once the models start walking, the night turns into a blur. Partly because the lights backstage are so bright I have to squint, and partly because my head pounds like it's a bowling ball being hit with a hammer.

I don't get sick often, but when I do it takes me down hard and fast. I'm grateful this started tonight instead of yesterday, or I would have missed the whole show.

When Marco steps onto the stage at the end of the night, the room erupts into applause. Models surround him, shimmering in velvet and crystal, like storybook royalty. Nico places a glittering crown on Marco's head, and the crowd's cheers swell. Within minutes, the press is calling him Marco Rossi, King of Fashion. I suspect Marco will pretend to hate the nickname while secretly loving it.

The scene backstage is euphoric exhaustion. Marco is beaming and even Bianca looks happy. But Nico's smile shines the brightest.

"You never have to walk a runway again," I murmur. "Just bridges from here on out." He pulls me into a sweaty hug and happiness spreads through me like warm honey.

Isabella comes bounding into the backstage area and throws herself into Marco's arms.

"That was amazing! The outfit with the white cape was my favorite! Where did you get those crowns? Can I have one?"

Sofia gives Marco a kiss and collects Isa, leading her from the building as she continues to shout questions and comments.

Most models and stylists have left to go to the after-party at the Four Seasons, but Nico stays and helps me and Bianca and Marco pack the ensembles so they're ready for the catalog shoot. When everything's accounted for, the four of us head to the exit.

"You two coming to the party?" Marco asks. The slope of his shoulders is relaxed, and his smile is easy.

"Absolutely," Nico says. He holds the door open, and we walk into the February cold.

The night air is sharp, biting against my flushed skin as I slow my steps, letting Marco and Bianca get ahead of us. Nico matches my pace, tucking me into his side.

"I'm going to call it a night," I tell him. "I'm exhausted."

"Oh. Okay, no worries, we can relax at your house."

I shake my head, and it hurts so I stop. "I don't want you to miss the party."

"It's no big deal, I'd rather hang out with you."

"It is a big deal. This was your last show. And you've been working with some of these models for five years. Go celebrate. Besides, I'm going to go straight to bed when I get home."

"How about I come over and take care of you?"

In the movies, this would be the part where he wipes my forehead with a cool cloth, and we share a dozen tender moments. In reality, I will go into goblin mode: blanket nest, dramatic groaning, and So Much Snot.

Definitely don't need Nico to witness that.

"Let's catch up tomorrow, and you can tell me all about the party," I tell him.

"I'm sorry you're not feeling well."

A dull ache has pressed behind my eyes all day and my limbs feel like cement, but I also feel...amazing. Maybe it's the extra strength Tylenol I chugged an hour ago, or maybe it's this man in front of me who makes everything feel wonderful. I've been working on sharing my feelings with Nico, but I don't even know where to start with something like this.

"Nico—" I stop walking and stare up at him. "The last four months have been amazing and I...the thing is..."

Ugh, how do people do this?

"This thing between us—it's gotten big. At least to me it feels big. Like, bigger-than-Versace big."

What am I even saying? How can I be so bad at this?

Nico smiles, eyes shining in the moonlight. "That 'bigger-than-Versace' feeling? We call that love."

A rush of warmth spreads through my chest, battling the cold that nips at my cheeks.

"Oh, yeah?"

The air between us crackles with anticipation.

"Yeah." Nico's eyes lock on mine, a slow smile spreading across his face. "I love you, Lydia."

My response is immediate, like the words have been waiting anxiously to come out. "I love you too, Nico."

He reaches for me, and I crash into him, all my pent-up emotions bursting like fireworks as his lips meet mine. Electricity shoots from my scalp to my toes, and I pull him closer to me, wrapping my arms around his neck. The world narrows to this moment—his touch, his scent, the press of his body against mine, grounding and exhilarating all at once. I can't get enough. I want to kiss him on this cold street forever. I want to—

Wait. Oh no.

I break away just as a sneeze explodes out of me, rattling my head so painfully I wince.

Nico bursts out laughing, and I scowl.

"You're sick."

"I'm fine, come here." I grab his face for more passionate kissing, but he turns the kisses soft and gentle.

"Let's get you home," he whispers.

"Now you're talking." I raise my eyebrows suggestively.

Nico smiles against my mouth. "I mean to bed."

"That's exactly what I'm thinking."

Warm breath tickles my neck as he chuckles.

The thought of snuggling into a nice soft bed with Nico's arms around me is so enticing, I almost ask him to skip the party and come home with me. Then I remember how I nearly blew snot all over him while we were kissing, and I reconsider.

Nico waits with me for a cab, pressing a lingering kiss to my temple, his breath warm against my chilled skin. I take a breath, and my clogged nose honks like an angry goose.

"So sexy," Nico says, grinning.

I groan and shoo him off to the party. As I slide into the cab, exhaustion settles over me, my limbs weighted and achy.

But beneath that, my heart feels impossibly light, like chiffon caught in a summer breeze.

Chapter Thirty-One

Saturday morning finds me laying in a nest of blankets on my bedroom floor. My flu-addled brain must have decided the lumpy mattress with broken springs was too comfortable and crawled out of bed.

Late morning sun filters through my window and Isa stomps around in her bedroom, floorboards creaking in protest. My muscles ache from a restless night, and my skin is clammy with fever sweat. A glance at my phone tells me it's 10:30am. I have a missed call and text from Nico.

Can I see you?

Flipping my phone to camera mode, I flinch at the reflection. Dark circles ring my swollen eyes, and my skin is pale, blotchy, dull, and shiny all at once. My hair looks like a family of squirrels tried to braid it, then gave up and built a nest on my head instead.

No you may not.

His reply comes quickly.

I'll bring you some of my mom's soup.

It's tempting. Gloria makes a vegetable soup I would trade my Louis Vuitton pumps for. But Nico and I said "I love you" last night—did that really happen?—and I can't have him coming over this morning, catching one look at the swamp monster I've become, and walking right back out.

Tomorrow.

Only Sunday is no better. My bones ache, my head is too heavy for my neck, and every swallow sends a scratchy burn down my throat.

"You look like my mermaid zombie," Isa tells me. "Minus the mermaid part. So, I guess just a zombie."

"Thanks a lot," I snuffle, then shoo her out of my room so I can sleep more.

Nico's been texting all day, and by Sunday night, I feel good enough to talk to him on the phone.

"How about I come over?" he says.

"It's already late, and I have to get up early tomorrow." *Plus, I've gone three days without a shower, and the fragrance coming off me is more Dumpster than Dior.*

"Let's do dinner tomorrow night," I suggest.

Silence from Nico. "Okay. There's some stuff I want to talk to you about."

"What stuff? Let's talk about it now."

Another pause. "I'd rather talk in person."

Tendrils of panic curl up my spine, but I shove them down. I refuse to be one of those insecure girls who worry about their boyfriends dumping them. *Nico told me he loved me. We're good. Besides, I'm Lydia St. Clair. I don't get dumped.*

"Okay, let's talk tomorrow at dinner." I smile to make my voice sound unconcerned. Then I hang up, take some Tylenol PM with lukewarm water and crawl into bed. It's mostly for the cold, but partly to keep me from overthinking whatever's going on with Nico.

By Monday morning, the evil forces of flu have released me from their clutches. I shower, wash my hair, and wear my favorite Jimmy Choos to the studio. The wintry air is cold and sharp, stinging my nose with each breath.

Bianca's at reception, her no-nonsense bob swinging as she juggles multiple calls. The sharp ring of the phones, and the rapid tapping of nails against the keyboard starts my head aching again.

"Chelsie's sick," she mouths, and I wonder if she got it from me.

I hang up my coat and bag, then walk through the lobby to the main studio. Marco's in his office, but his door is open and it sounds like he's going over the upcoming catalog shoot with Antonio.

We'll probably spend the morning checking the ensembles after their dry cleaning, like we did last time. I head toward the back of the studio where they're hanging, but Danilo and Clara block my path.

"How are you holding up?" Clara asks, her head tilted sympathetically.

"I'm doing okay."

They must have heard about my flu from Marco.

"We're so sorry." Danilo's eyes bore into mine, searching for... something.

"It's no big deal, I'm already over it."

Clara and Danilo share a surprised look.

"But I hear Chelsie may be next," I tell them.

Danilo gasps and Clara's eyes go wide. "No! I had no idea."

"Yeah, I think that's why she's not here today."

Danilo shakes his head. "Because she's with him? That tramp!"

And that's when I realize we are not talking about the same thing.

I cross my arms. "I don't have time for a TV sitcom misunderstanding. What are you guys talking about?"

"We're talking about you and Nico," Clara says.

My eyebrows furrow. "Why? Me and Nico are fine."

"Oh, *tesoro*," Danilo says, voice dripping with gossip-induced glee. "You're not."

Fast as a blink Clara passes me her phone, and I'm staring at the Metro paper's social column. There's a photo of Marco onstage with his crown and some photos from the after-party. Apparently, I'm not seeing whatever it is Clara and Danilo want me to see because Clara snatches the phone, zooms in on one photo, and hands it back to me.

It's Nico. Tangled up with a tall blonde.

No.

I want to shove the phone back at Clara, erase the image from my brain, but instead I look closer, taking in every detail. Her gold mini dress clings to every curve, shimmering under the party lights. Nico's arms coil around her waist, and his mouth is crushed against hers. My stomach twists, a sour taste rising in my mouth.

"You didn't know?" Danilo asks, eyes bright, like this keeps getting better.

I shake my head dumbly.

"It's his ex-girlfriend, Britta Larsson," Clara says. "They got back together at the after-party."

I stumble backward, as though the weight of her words has physically knocked me off balance.

Clara and Danilo hover, and by the look on Clara's face, she's itching to hit record on her phone and film my dramatic reaction. My father's words filter through the shock: The only thing that can make an incident worse is your reaction to the incident.

I take a grounding breath, force my expression into neutral and say calmly, "Thank you for letting me know."

Then I walk into the lobby, mouth "emergency" to Bianca, who's still on the phone, and grab my purse and coat and walk out.

An icy wind slices through my coat as I fumble with the buttons, my fingers shaky and uncoordinated.

So, this is what Nico wanted to talk about. He's back together with his ex-girlfriend. And he wanted to break up in person instead of over the phone, because only a jerk breaks up with their sick girlfriend over the phone. Nico won't want to be a jerk.

I, on the other hand, don't care about being a jerk. We will have this conversation over the phone because there's no way I'm seeing Nico again.

A gust of wind picks up a plastic bag and deposits it in the bare branches of a tree.

If Nico wanted out of our relationship, fine. But why tell me he loved me? It doesn't even make sense.

Then again, how many times has my father told my mother he loves her? Saying I love you doesn't mean anything.

I pace the sidewalk in front of Rossi's Designs, anger and confusion swirling inside me as frigid as the winter wind.

Maybe he didn't want out of our relationship. Maybe he just wanted something with Britta as well.

Rage courses through me, and I jab at my phone so hard I chip a nail.

The pain is enough to clear my head for a moment. I take a breath. I am not a Desperate Housewife. I'm not going to call Nico yelling and crying and threatening to slash his tires. I am a St. Clair, and that's not how we behave.

If I were my mother, I would pretend I didn't know anything about another woman and hold on to Nico any way I could. But I'm not my mother. And I have too much pride to be with someone who's cheating on me. I take one more breath, then hit Nico's number.

"Lydia, good morning! How are you feeling?" The warmth in Nico's voice is enough to transform my rage into tears, and I can't have that. I push all of it down—the anger, the sadness, the hurt—until I am numb and in control.

"We're done." My voice is the cool, clipped tone of a businesswoman checking things off her to-do list. "I know you wanted to do this in person, but I'm afraid that's not possible. Consider this our final call."

"What? What are you talking about? Why?" Confusion and panic fill his voice, but I keep mine calm.

"Because you've moved on to someone else. I would have appreciated a heads up beforehand, but nothing can be done about that now." We may as well be discussing company mergers and acquisitions for all the emotion in my voice.

"I haven't moved on! If you're talking about Britta, nothing happened."

Of course he's denying it. This is what men do.

"Nothing happened!?" My cool demeanor is precariously close to slipping. "The Metro social column disagrees. And their photo was pretty convincing."

"They ran a photo?"

"In color. Have you been dating her this whole time, or did you just hook up again this weekend? You know what, it doesn't matter. This is over."

"Hold on. It wasn't like that. Where are you? I'll skip my next class, and we can talk."

The part of me that is soft and stupid leaps at this opportunity.

Nico says it wasn't like that. He'll explain and it will all make sense.

And if I hadn't seen my parents have a dozen conversations where my dad "explained what really happened," I might fall for it. But I know how this plays out. I can let myself get sucked back in by his beautiful face and enticing words, or I can end this while I still have a shred of dignity.

"Sorry, Nico. I'm done with this."

There's a frustrated growl on Nico's end. "You're done, just like that?"

"*Sì.*"

"Lydia. Please. If you'll just listen to me, we can work through this."

If he thinks I'm the forgiving type, he clearly doesn't know me.

"I'm not interested in working through this. It's over for me." I can tell he's about to say more, but I hang up.

Then I drop onto a nearby bench, the metal slats cold and dirty. Nico calls twice, but I don't pick up. He sends me texts, but I delete them as quickly as I can, then block his number. Because I know if given the chance, I'll believe whatever flimsy excuse he offers me. I'll believe it because I want to believe it. I'll crawl back into his arms. And I will end up hurt again and again. Just like my mother.

Chapter Thirty-Two

I'm an exceptional actress, and Monday and Tuesday, I put on a convincing performance of "delightful young woman whose heart isn't smashed."

The mean part of my brain says, *I told you so. This is what happens when you trust people. They screw you over every time.*

The kinder part of my brain says, *It wasn't your fault. Nobody could resist those dimples and that goofy sweetness. But I hope you learned your lesson and never do something as stupid as falling in love again.*

There's a lot to do to get ready for the photo shoot on Friday, but somehow, mornings at the studio drag by. Chelsie is still out, and Clara and Danilo wisely keep their distance.

On Wednesday at 1pm, I take a taxi to the Milan Institute of Design. The carved stone columns glow in the afternoon light, and my heels click on the gray cobblestones as I make my way to the administrative building. Everything is just as beautiful as the last time I saw it, but it feels different without Nico.

I grind my teeth in frustration. This is my chance. This is the first step to getting everything I want. And I won't screw it up by thinking about Nico.

On the third floor, an older woman named Perla leads me to a conference room. My stomach should be twisting into knots, but instead, there's hollowness, as if all my feelings have drained out of me. The air in the conference room is too warm and my black silk dress clings uncomfortably to my skin.

Photos from various fashion shows hang on the wall. The Lydia with feelings, curiosity, and interest, would get up and look at them. But this Lydia, the lifeless robot, sits and waits. A delicate melody floats through the air, the sound so subtle I almost miss it beneath the quiet hum of the overhead lights. Then, recognition dawns in aching familiarity. "I Can Do It With A Broken Heart," by Taylor Swift. The soft violins swell, and a smile tugs at my mouth.

Yes, it sucks that when I imagined this moment, Nico was waiting outside for me. And it sucks that I won't be able to tell him about it. But I can do this. As splintered as my heart feels right now, I know what my goals are, and I can do this.

The personal pep talk comes just in time. The door opens with a quiet click, and in strides a woman with effortless confidence. Her tailored black trousers swish as she moves, and her silk blouse—deep emerald with delicate gold buttons—catches the light. The purple cat-eye glasses perched on her nose give her a sharp, discerning look, but her warm smile softens it.

"You must be Lydia. I'm Professora Lanna." She shakes my hand, her grip firm but not aggressive. It's the kind of handshake that says, "I run this place, but I'm not a tool."

"Please have a seat," she says.

The greeting triggers every social encounter I've had, and my charm comes back like muscle memory.

"It's a pleasure to meet you, Professora Lanna. Love your blouse. Is that Dolce & Gabbana?"

"It is." Professora Lanna beams. "And if I'm not mistaken, you've chosen Versace for this meeting."

"I like to stick to the classics for big moments," I say with a smile.

"We were very impressed with your application." She pulls it up on her tablet. "Do you have any real-world experience?"

"I've been working at Rossi Studios the last four months."

"Marco Rossi? He's very up-and-coming. His show last week was incredible."

"It was," I agree. "I had the privilege of seeing one of my designs included in his spring collection last fall."

Her eyebrows go up, impressed. "Tell me more."

I launch into the story of how the original ensemble got leaked, and we were frantic to create a replacement. I mention that I nanny Marco's seven-year-old daughter, and she showed him my design. I share how surprised I was when I saw my sketch on the whiteboard at the studio.

It's a good story, and I tell it well, playing up the funny parts, and maintaining an attitude of grateful humility throughout.

"That is really something. Do you have the sketch on you? Or is it framed back home?"

I laugh and pull out my sketch pad. "I have it here, along with my other sketches, as requested."

I hand it over, and her eyes go big. "The leather shorts ensemble was your idea? I heard about this one!"

I smile graciously and tell her once again how lucky I've been to work with Marco Rossi.

We look through the rest of the sketches I brought, and she makes happy humming sounds.

"Well, you certainly have the creativity and talent we're looking for," she says.

"Thank you."

She asks a few more questions about my previous schooling, and I gloss over my education in Connecticut, emphasizing my belief that one should pursue their chosen field in the best institution possible, and I believe that to be the Milan Institute of Design.

At the conclusion of the interview, she shakes my hand with a smile.

"It was an absolute pleasure to meet with you today, Lydia."

"Likewise, *Professora*."

"Now if you'll stay put, Lucia will be in with the written exam."

The smile freezes on my face. "Written exam?"

"Yes, we find it easier to administer it right after the interview, so candidates don't have to make another trip in."

"Of course," I say. As though the words "written exam" don't make me want to pull the fire alarm and escape in the chaos.

The woman who scheduled the interview said nothing about a written exam. My palms are damp, and I rub them discreetly against my dress as Lucia walks in.

"Professora Lanna told me you're the one who designed the leather shorts for the Rossi spring collection," she says with an impressed smile.

"*Si.*"

She hands me a pencil to go with the exam, oblivious to the fact that I'm seconds away from total and complete self-destruction.

"Congratulations, I heard they stole the show." She smiles again and hands me a stack of papers stapled in the top left corner. My throat tightens, a familiar panic clawing its way up my chest.

"I'll just be here in the corner if you need anything. You have an hour to complete the exam, but most finish well before then."

I'm not most.

I close my eyes and take a deep breath. Maybe it won't be so bad. Doctor Fineman's office gave me a little sheet of helpful tips for people with dyslexia. I will take my time and get through this.

But when I look at the first question, I can't remember any of the tips. I try to make the letters stay in their places, but I don't know how. They only get blurrier as my eyes fill with tears.

Curse you, Dr. Fineman, and your stupid sheet of un-memorable tips.

Suddenly I'm furious.

Why do I have to take this stupid exam? Professor Lanna saw my designs and loved them. She said my application was great. What else do I need to prove to these people? When will it ever be enough?

"Excuse me," I say to Lucia in the corner. "Could I use the bathroom?"

Her eyebrows dip but she says, "Of course. It's down the hall and to the left. You'll need to leave your exam here while you go."

I'm more than happy to leave that exam on the table. I never want to see that exam again.

I thank her and slip out the door, then walk quickly down the hall. The bathroom is empty, thank goodness, and I look at my reflection in the mirror. My eyes are a little red, but my makeup has stayed put.

Why did I think I'd be able to do this? I drew some fancy pictures so now all of the sudden I can go to college?

I feel a spike of anger toward Nico. He made me think I could do this. Well, he's an idiot. And so am I for listening to him.

I exit the bathroom and walk down the hall in the opposite direction of the conference room. After winding through a maze of hallways, I finally find a set of stairs that leads to the ground floor and a side exit.

I no longer feel furious—or disappointed. I don't feel anything.

As soon as I pick up Isa, she asks about the interview.

"They had to reschedule it," I tell her.

"Rude! You can't just cancel something important like that."

I shrug. "Some people are just rude I guess."

We go to the park, but it's too cold to play long. Back at home, we make hot chocolate and listen to *Glitter the Mermaid*. I don't hear a word.

My mind is trapped in that conference room, the panic still coursing through my system.

What could I have done differently?

Nothing. There is nothing that would have miraculously helped me complete that exam.

Sofia and Marco come home from work and make dinner, but I don't join them. Instead, I sit in bed, staring at the wall, wondering how all my dreams got wrecked so quickly. Wondering what in the world I'm going to do now.

"Aren't you going out dancing tonight?" Isa asks, appearing at my doorway. "It's Wednesday."

"I don't really feel like dancing."

Or telling my friends I blew my chance at being the brilliant designer they think I'm destined to be.

I can barely manage the weight of my own disappointment; I don't need theirs on top of it.

"Well, of course you don't feel like dancing when you're wearing that," Isa says.

My oversized Adidas sweatshirt is speckled with croissant crumbs, its sleeves stretched from too much tugging.

"Put on something nice," Isa continues. "You'll feel better."

I think about these wise words. She's right. I need to look good to feel good. This is what I do. I'm beautiful and charming.

"Thanks," I say. "You're right. I'm even going to shower first."

Isa throws her hands in the air like someone scored a touchdown, and I feel a spark of gratitude for this tiny cheerleader. I shower, blow dry my hair, and do my makeup. I put on my Dolce & Gabbana skinny jeans and the green sleeveless top that matches my eyes. I look good. And I feel like my old self. This is what I do.

By the time I make it to Calypso it's past 9pm. Valentina, Paolo, and Carmen are in our regular booth, but something in me won't let me go to them.

I can't face them. Can't tell them what happened at the interview. Can't explain why Nico's not here. I can't bear to see the pity in their eyes for their single friend who flunked out of two colleges and couldn't even get into the third.

I make a sharp turn and head to the bar. There's a wall of colorful glass cubes blocking this part of the bar from the dance floor, and I settle onto a stool, grateful for the shield. The croissant I ate hours ago has faded, leaving me hollow inside. I order a sandwich, but the first bite turns my stomach, and I leave the rest.

Lorenzo makes his way over, stupid grin on his stupid face, and I groan. I do not have the patience for this clown tonight.

"*Buona sera*," he says, stopping in front of me like he's presenting me with a gift.

"*Buona sera*," I reply, then spin away from him to look across the room. There's a group of guys at a table ten feet away, and a small smile sends one rushing over to me.

"*Ciao, bella*," he says when he reaches my side. "Is this seat available?"

I nod, and he sits and offers to buy me a drink. I decline. He tells me how beautiful I am and asks for my number and none of it feels as good as I was hoping it would, so I send him away.

Ten minutes later, the whole thing repeats with a different gentleman. It's the same generic flattery. My "eyes sparkle like stars," my "hair is a cascading waterfall." I want to scream, but I smile and laugh until I can't take it anymore, then I let him know I'm not interested. By the time I've sent away the third guy, I'm ready for a drink.

"Scotch, neat," I tell Lorenzo who's been hovering for the last hour.

"Sure thing," he says and pours me a double.

The glass is cool in my hand, condensation beading along the sides. I take a sip, and the scotch burns its way down my throat, leaving a smoky trail in its wake.

I don't usually drink. I got stupidly drunk on margaritas two years ago at a Cape Cod beach party and have avoided alcohol ever since. But desperate times call for questionable life choices.

"This one's on the house," Lorenzo says, bringing me a second.

I hadn't planned on another, but it is on the house. It goes down even quicker than the first. There's a song playing that I like, but I can't remember who sings it. I want to ask Carmen, she'd know, but I still don't want to go over there.

I'm not sure at what point Lorenzo steps out from behind the bar, but suddenly he's right next to me. "Want to dance?" he asks.

I shake my head but keep my eyes focused on his. Sensing an opportunity, he leans toward me. His lips are inches from mine when I close the distance between us.

I'm not drunk. I know exactly what I'm doing. But I can't explain why.

Lorenzo's lips are...fine. Not life-changing, no fireworks. More like a three-star Yelp review. "Pleasant but forgettable. Would not visit again." I close my eyes, trying to lose myself in the moment. But he's too tall and the hair on the back of his neck isn't soft like Nico's. Plus, his cologne smells like a car freshener. Still, I wrap my arms around his neck and squeeze my eyes tighter, trying to pretend that he's Nico and everything is okay between us.

Lorenzo's hands move down to my butt, and I break away. His grinning face triggers a disgust so deep I'm nauseated. I take a step away from him, hitting my back against my stool and almost losing my balance. Catching myself at the last second, I look down the bar to see Carmen staring right at me.

Her mouth is pinched closed, and her eyes are wide with shock and hurt. She shakes her head, then walks back to the booth, out of view. I step after her, but Lorenzo's hand clamps around mine.

"Where are you going? We were just getting started."

"This is not happening," I tell him. My brain feels slow. "I mean it happened already a little, but that was a mistake and that's the end of it."

I break away and run around the glass-cube wall to the booth. Carmen is crying with her head in her hands, and Valentina has her arms around her. Paolo looks at both of them, brow wrinkled in confusion.

I stumble a little before reaching their booth but stay on my feet.

"Carmen, I'm so sorry," I say. "I don't know what happened. I wasn't thinking."

"Sorry about what?" Valentina says, looking as confused as Paolo. "What happened?"

Carmen lifts her head and looks at me, eyes blazing. "She kissed Lorenzo."

"What?" Valentina looks even more confused, like she's sure she misheard, but Paolo's face goes serious and disappointed.

Valentina looks from me to crying Carmen, then back at the bar.

"You kissed Lorenzo?" she asks, still unsure.

"It was nothing." I'm a jerk for even trying to defend myself.

"You were all over each other," Carmen yells. "And of course it meant nothing to you. No one ever does."

Then she drops her head back into her hands and cries harder. Valentina rubs her back in circles, eyes on me.

"Oh, Lydia," she murmurs. I'm expecting anger in her eyes, but all I see is pity, and I feel a thousand times worse. She's right to pity me. *What kind of pathetic loser kisses her best friend's crush, just to feel better about herself?*

"I'm sorry," I whisper.

Carmen lifts her head and fixes me with a fiery glare. "You are dead to me."

Her words are a punch to the gut, and it takes me a moment to recover. When I'm sure my legs will support me, I turn and walk away before they can see the tears streaming down my cheeks.

Chapter Thirty-Three

The apartment is cloaked in silence when I step inside, the air thick with the scent of leftover dinner and the faint musk of people sleeping. I take another shower, trying to scrub away sweat, alcohol, and shame. Scalding water pelts my skin, turning it pink, but I don't feel any cleaner.

Back in my bedroom, I try to make a plan, but my brain is bombarded with so many terrible images of the last forty-eight hours I can't think straight. I've lost Nico. I've lost design school. I've lost my only real friends.

I need to get out of here.

The date on my phone catches my eye, and a vague idea pops into my head.

With trembling fingers, I dial Karen's number. Each ring pulses in my ear, the seconds stretching like hours.

"Lydia," she says, when she finally picks up. Her tone conveys how much she did not want to answer this call.

"I'd like to book a flight home tonight, for my dad's birthday tomorrow, but I wanted to check with you first." I know she'll appreciate humbly asking for permission. "I should have given you more notice, but it's been a crazy week."

There's silence on the other end, but she hasn't said no so I continue. "I can't be gone too long, I've got a lot going on here, so I was thinking of a roundtrip ticket returning next Monday."

There's no way I'm coming back on Monday. There is nothing left for me here. But the only way she'll let me come home is if she thinks I'm leaving again.

She huffs. We both know my father hates surprises.

"Since the senator didn't have any family time at Christmas," I continue, playing my final card, "I know he'll want to spend his birthday with family."

Now she can either book me a flight home or admit that Senator St. Clair is not a family man at all.

"What a lovely idea," she says, opting for the first choice. "I'll get that booked right away and send you the details."

"Wonderful. Thank you, Karen."

I hang up feeling empty. I finally have it. My ticket back home.

I wrestle my suitcase from under the bed, dust clinging to my fingers. The zipper rasps open, and I shove clothes inside, fabric wrinkling under my frantic hands. The carry-on is too small for all the new clothes I've bought, so I squeeze the rest of it into my oversized Marc Jacobs tote. The same one I brought to the Moretti house, filled with gifts for their family.

I dash to the bathroom to get my toiletries and come out to find Isa standing in the hall.

"What are you doing?" I whisper.

"I had a nightmare."

She doesn't whisper. Her voice echoes in the hallway, and I'm sure she's going to wake up Marco and Sofia, which would be catastrophic right now.

"What are you doing?" she practically yells.

"Shhh. I'm not doing anything."

She rubs her eyes and looks at the bag of toiletries in my hand. I slip back into my room, hoping she'll go back to hers, but she follows me.

Her eyes open wider as she takes in my packed suitcase. "You're leaving?"

I close the door behind her and give another "shhhhh."

Her small fists tremble at her sides, dark eyes glistening in the dim light. "You were just going to leave?"' Her voice cracks, slicing through the stillness. "Without saying goodbye? Why?"

The accusation in her voice pierces through me.

"It's complicated," I say.

"You only care about yourself! You are the worst nanny I've ever had!" With that, she opens the door and storms out.

I sink onto the bed. *She's right. I am the worst nanny. All the more reason to leave.*

My phone vibrates. Karen booked me a flight departing at 3am. It's almost midnight, and a taxi to Mal Pensa will take close to an hour. I've got to go now.

I drag my suitcase down the hall, its wheels groaning against the hardwood. Outside Isa's closed door, muffled sobs slip through the crack. My chest tightens. I ache to push open the door, and pull her into my arms, but there's no time.

Plus, I would only make it worse. I make everything worse. So, I grip my suitcase tighter and walk out the front door.

Fluorescent lights hum overhead, casting cold blue shadows across the empty terminal. My footsteps echo on the tiled floor, swallowed by the cavernous quiet. The security line is nonexistent, just a lone agent stifling a yawn as I hand over my passport. I make it to my gate and sink into a sticky vinyl chair. According to my boarding pass, Karen booked me a middle seat in coach.

She really does hate me.

It's turning into a large club.

Isa loathes me. Carmen, Valentina, and Paolo will never talk to me again.

Marco, a man I respect and admire, doesn't hate me yet, but he will when he wakes up and sees I've walked out on his family.

And leaving mid-interview definitely burned my bridge at the Milan Institute of Design.

Bridges makes me think of Nico, which makes the tears come. I don't even understand what happened between us. *Why would he tell me he loved me if he didn't mean it?*

Or did I tell him first, and he felt bad so he said it back? I try to remember exactly how it happened, but the memory is hazy.

I know better. I know what happens to women who let their guard down, and I fell into this trap anyway.

I slip on my headphones and pull up my favorite playlist, but it doesn't stop the hurricane of thoughts swirling through my brain.

I managed to get a flight home, but now what?

Like a movie on the big screen, I can see exactly how the next year will play out. My father will pretend he's happy to see me, and Karen will find me an out-of-the-way internship where I won't make trouble. When I see my friends, I'll share stories about the amazing things I did in Milan, leaving out everything I truly care about. At the first party of the season, I'll find the alpha male of the group and make him fall in love with me. When fall comes, I'll go to whatever overpriced institution my father got me into and find an ambitious man looking for a beautiful wife with no dreams of her own.

It's a bleak picture, made worse by the fact that I've gotten a taste of what real friendship is. What real love is. What it really feels like to live your dream. How can I go home and accept empty substitutes for those things?

For a moment in Milan, I caught a glimpse of who I can be when I'm not wasting time pretending away my weaknesses or building walls to keep people out. And now I can't un-see it.

As I stare at the dingy gray carpet the realization sinks in: No one can give me the life I want but me. I can keep hiding behind excuses, safe in the comfort of well-worn limitations, or I can chase what I want like my happiness depends on it.

I want to be a designer. I want to be a good friend and nanny. I want a relationship where I love and am loved.

It won't be easy. I've made a real mess of my life. But for the first time, I care about something enough to stay and fix it instead of running away. I'll have to swallow my pride and push myself. But the woman I glimpsed these past few months seemed like the kind of woman who could do anything. Maybe even hard things.

A sleepy-looking flight attendant announces boarding for group A. I look at her, then look down at the charm bracelet on my wrist.

I can't keep judging myself by someone else's standards. But I can't let myself off the hook either. Even if I'm not book smart, even if I don't have great experiences with relationships, there's a lot I can do. And I'm ready to try.

By the time the flight attendant calls for group B, I'm already heading to the taxi stand.

Chapter Thirty-Four

"Good morning, Isa," I say as she walks into the kitchen. I slept less than three hours last night, but I'm up and dressed, hoping my second cup of espresso will cut through the haze of exhaustion.

Isa's eyes go big, and her steps falter. "You—What—How did you?" Her tiny finger points at me accusingly. "I thought you left."

"It sounds like you had a bad dream last night."

She rubs her hair, and it sticks up like a porcupine. "I did have a bad dream..." Her brows knit together.

Marco walks into the kitchen and gives Isa a kiss.

"Morning, Lydia. Are you ready for some ironing today?"

The catalog photo shoot is tomorrow, and today will be spent banishing every wrinkle from every article of clothing we've created.

"Looking forward to it. But I have an appointment first, so I'll be a little late."

"No problem. I'm sure Danilo and Clara will leave plenty for you to do."

Isa keeps quiet until we step into the elevator, the smell of cigarettes and perfume filling the small space. Then she confronts me, arms crossed, eyes blazing.

"You left last night." Her voice drips with the betrayal of a soap opera heroine discovering her long-lost twin is evil.

"Why would I leave a glamorous life as Isa's nanny?"

"I don't know, but you did."

The elevator creaks, reluctantly bringing us down, and I level with her.

"I did. And I'm sorry. For leaving. And sneaking out like a coward without telling anyone."

Isa, who has never struck me as the forgiving type, presses her lips into a line.

"Leaving had nothing to do with you," I continue. "Believe it or not, I like being your nanny. I like doing our nails together and listening to *Glitter the Mermaid* together and going shopping together."

The elevator lurches to a stop on the ground floor, and we walk through the lobby and into the morning cold.

"So why did you leave?"

I adjust my scarf and make sure Isa's hat doesn't slip off. "Because things got hard. Because I was sad. Because I'm a sissy who runs away from things instead of staying to fix them."

"I don't think you're a sissy," Isa says loyally, and I squeeze her hand.

"Not anymore. From now on, I'm going to be my bravest self and do things even if they're hard or scary."

"Like eating bumble bees? That would be hard and scary."

"That would be," I agree. "I was thinking more grown up scary. Saying sorry. Asking for help. Trying again."

"Saying sorry is the worst," Isa says. "I'd rather eat bumble bees."

Our bus rumbles to a stop in front of us, and I find two seats near the back.

"But remember that time you apologized to the boy you punched, and now you're friends?"

"Yeah, that wasn't so bad."

The bus jolts forward, and I clutch the cold metal rail to keep my balance.

"I'm hoping I can do the same thing."

Isa's eyes go wide. "Who did you punch?"

I smile and it turns to a grimace. Carmen probably would have preferred a punch to what I did.

"I didn't punch anyone. But I have other stuff to apologize for."

I drop Isa at school and spend an extra moment looking at my reflection in the glass door. My hair flows down my shoulders, thick and shiny, my best feature among very good features. The nearest five-star hair salon is a short walk from here, and I think things over as I navigate the crowded sidewalk.

Showing up when things get hard matters. But how you show up matters too. I can't do things the old way.

Soft bells chime as I walk into Belli Capelli, and I breathe in the sweet scent of lavender. The rhythmic snip of scissors blends with the hum of the hairdryer, and I settle into a soft leather chair to wait. A few minutes later, a stylist offers me a San Pellegrino and leads me to a chair in the back.

"Gorgeous hair," she says, running her fingers through it. "What do you have in mind this morning?"

Maybe I'm being needlessly dramatic. Or maybe I need to see what I can do without relying on beauty and charm. Either way, I've made my decision.

"Cut it all off," I say.

Bianca gasps when I walk into the studio.

"Your hair!"

I smile at the horrified look on her face. It's not like I shaved my head. I have a cute little pixie cut. It's strange not having the weight on my shoulders, but the lightness feels good.

"Thanks," I tell her, pretending she complimented me. "Does Marco have a gap in his schedule I could sneak into this morning?"

She must put together that I'm going through something because she says, "He has a few minutes right now. If you're fast."

"Thanks. I will be."

I dash to Marco's office just as he's about to walk out.

"Good morning, Marco. I'd like a favor."

"Good morning, Lydia. I like the new look."

"Thank you. I'm wondering if you have any leftover material I could buy from you."

"I might. What do you have in mind?"

"I'd like to sew a dress for a friend of mine. I need three yards."

The sparkle in Marco's eye tells me he'd like to ask more, but the professional in him wins out. "I think we have a fair amount of material leftover from last year's winter collection. Bianca can show you. Take as much as you need."

"I'd like to pay you for it."

Marco smiles. "Let's take it out of your paycheck."

Bianca shows me the excess material available, and I choose three yards of silky satin in a dark green.

She eyes me folding the fabric and putting it in my bag and asks, "Did we have you sign a non-compete agreement with us?"

"I'm not competing. I'm just sewing a gift for a friend."

She narrows her eyes. "I'll print one up for you to sign anyway."

"Happy to." And even though I've worked in a fashion studio for barely six months, it's nice that Bianca sees me as competition. Maybe the hair is working already.

After several hours of my best ironing, I leave to pick up Isa. I call Valentina on the way, knots gathering in my stomach with each unanswered ring. If I can't even get Valentina to talk to me, I'll never get Carmen back. And I will have lost the best friend I've ever had.

Just as I'm about to hang up I hear, "*Pronto.*"

"Valentina. I'm so sorry. I know I messed up, and I want to try to make it right."

There's a long pause. "I'm not sure that's possible. Carmen spent the whole night crying. I won't repeat the names she called you, but they weren't good ones."

"I know. And I deserve it."

"I just...I don't understand why."

The instinct to keep everything to myself is strong, and my pace on the crowded sidewalk picks up, as though I'm trying to outrun my stupid mistakes. I take a breath. Slow down.

"Because I bombed the interview at design school," I tell Valentina, cringing as I say the words. "Because Nico and I broke up. Because I make terrible decisions when I drink whiskey." The exposed, vulnerable feeling coursing through me makes me pick up my pace again.

"Oh."

"Lorenzo happened to be there when I felt stupid and inadequate. I didn't mean to hurt Carmen. I wasn't even thinking about her." I let out a sigh. "Which is the problem."

Parents and nannies are gathered outside Isa's school, and I step off to the side and wait for the doors to open.

"I'm sorry you were feeling that way," Valentina says gently.

"Yeah." I clear my throat. "I know it will take Carmen a decade to forgive me, but I have to try."

"What do you have in mind?"

"I want to make something for her. Can you tell me the size of that blue dress she has? I know it's her favorite."

The rest of my conversation is cut short by Isa's scream.

"What did you do to your hair?" she shrieks.

"Valentina, I've got to go. Just text me her dress size when you get it."

Isa's mouth hangs open, her expression horrified, as though I've shown up to her school stark naked. I stand still as she circles me, seemingly searching for the twenty inches of missing hair.

"I cut it off," I tell her. My tone suggests she might have figured that out on her own. I run my hand up the back of my neck, newly exposed to the cold wind, and a thrill zips through me.

Isa is close to tears. "But you had the most beautiful hair I've ever seen! Why would you throw it all away?"

I take her backpack and slip it onto my shoulder. "Let's walk, and I'll tell you a story."

Isa's eyes tell me she has a dozen more questions, but her lips pinch shut. The city bustles around us—voices chattering in Italian, the scent of pizza drifting from the pizzeria on the corner—as I guide us down the crowded sidewalk.

"Once there was a little girl who had a blue nose. This was not in some far-off land where people have colorful noses, and everyone is okay with it. This was in this land, where a blue nose is not something you see every day. And even though this girl was funny and a very good juggler, all anyone saw was her blue nose. Pretty soon even she began to think it was the most special thing about her. She stopped juggling or telling jokes. She just wandered around letting people admire her blue nose."

Two moms with strollers pass in front of us on the sidewalk.

"And then one day, after a long time, she remembered that she was smart and funny and a good juggler. And she wanted other people to remember too. So, she went home and scrubbed and scrubbed her nose, until it turned a normal nose color."

"So, she wanted to be normal, like everyone else?" Isa asks.

"No." I stop on the sidewalk and wait until she looks at me. "She wanted to be exceptional. And she needed that distraction of a blue nose gone so that she could remember her true talents. She went on to be the most amazing juggler and joke-teller the world has ever seen."

"That's a weird story," Isa says.

I shrug and loop my arm through hers. "People are weird."

Chapter Thirty-Five

I wake up before my alarm and lay in bed staring at the ceiling. It's Friday. The day of the catalog shoot. The day I see Nico for the first time since he shattered my heart into confetti. The saddest confetti in the world.

I miss his face so much it hurts. Also, I can't bear the thought of seeing him. Will he try to talk to me? Do I want him to?

I push these thoughts aside and search through my closet for something to wear. Just a regular casual outfit, like I always wear to the studio. And if I look so amazing that Nico is punched in the face with regret, well that's just a bonus.

Forty-five minutes later, I'm standing in front of Rossi Designs in a Cristallini wool dress with a healthy dose of Red Royalty on my lips. For a moment, I miss my hair, it was a reliable showstopper. But I also like the idea of Nico seeing the new me. The kind of woman who doesn't have time for long hair or cheating boyfriends.

Time to go in there and show him what he's missing.

Only my feet, in their beautiful Tom Ford knee boots, refuse to move. The five steps leading to the studio might as well be Mount Everest. Sweat breaks out all over me, and I'm regretting the wool dress. I should have worn something with more ventilation.

"*Buon giorno*, Lydia," Bianca says, marching past and holding the door open for me. "You coming?"

"*Sì.*" But I stay where I am until Biana lets out an impatient sigh.

Ignoring the insistent throb of my pulse in my ears, I climb the steps and enter the studio.

Chelsie's still out, and Bianca races for the reception desk where three phones are ringing. Laughter and chatter drift through from the main area of the studio as I approach the closed door.

You can do this Lydia. You've seen exes before. You'll be friendly and gracious.

Bianca's on the phone but looking at me strangely, so I push the door open and walk into the studio. Nerves claw at my stomach and there's a sour taste in my mouth.

Don't puke. Don't puke.

All the models are here, and my eyes find Nico like magnets drawn to the North Pole. He's on the other side of the studio, looking at his phone. *Is he texting her?*

As though he can feel my gaze, he turns and we make eye contact. I try to force a smile onto my face but can't make my muscles move.

He takes a step toward me and panic races through me like a wildfire. *What is he doing? What do I do? Is he going to—*

"Lydia! Thank heavens you're here." Marco touches my shoulder breaking the spell. "Isa's school just called. She lost a tooth, and she's freaking out and wants to go home. Sofia's in a meeting, and I can't leave the shoot. Can you go pick her up?"

I'm slow to process his words, but when I do, relief breaks through me like water through a dam.

"Yes! I'll pick up Isa. I'll go right now."

And then like designer purses at a sample sale, I'm gone. I turn and sprint through the door, giddy at my escape.

Isa's waiting for me in the nurse's office, eyebrows furrowed in a scowl, hands clutching a clear bag.

"Isa! *Tanti auguri*!"

Her scowl gets scowlier. "Congratulations? This is a joke. I want my tooth back in my mouth."

I sign a form from the nurse, then we head toward home.

"Isn't it exciting to have a tooth fall out?"

"It's disgusting. There was blood everywhere." She thrusts the bag at me, and sure enough there's a bloody tooth in there.

"Do you have the tooth fairy in Italy? That leaves you money if you put your tooth under your pillow?"

"We have *Topolino dei denti*. He's a mouse that leaves gifts in exchange for teeth. Like a complete weirdo."

"Sounds like you've got some gifts to look forward to."

"I look like a clown, and I talk like an *imbecille*. Not worth it."

I smile. It was a top tooth and she is lisping a little.

"It wasn't even loose," she whines as we climb on the bus.

I think about that and lean close and lower my voice. "Do you know why you lost your tooth this morning?"

"*Signora Macaluso* says it's a perfectly normal part of our development."

"But why today? At this moment? When your tooth wasn't even loose?"

Isa shrugs.

"I think you lost your tooth because the universe was doing me a favor."

Isa's eyebrows scrunch together like a tiny caterpillar.

"I was about to talk to someone I really didn't want to. And then your dad asked me to come get you from school, and it saved me from the worst conversation ever."

"Who didn't you want to talk to?"

Dang. I should have expected that question.

"Nico."

"Why? I like Nico."

"Me too. But then he smashed my heart into a million pieces."

"Oh. I don't like Nico."

I give her a shoulder bump of appreciation. "So you see? Losing your tooth totally saved me."

"Lydia?"

"Yeah?"

"The next time the universe wants to rescue you from an ex-boyfriend, tell it to leave my teeth out of it."

Isa and I spend the day listening to the third *Glitter the Mermaid* and it's so much scarier than the second one. Once Marco and Sofia get home, they ooh and ahh over Isa's missing tooth, and I sneak off to my room to work on Carmen's dress.

Valentina sent me Carmen's dress size, and to be extra sure, I got the sizes of her three favorite skirts and three favorite tops. Women's sizing can be so wonky, and I want this to fit Carmen perfectly.

Once I have her measurements, I sketch the dress I have in mind. I start with a midi-length to elongate her legs. A full skirt will provide movement and complement her full butt, which I know she feels self-conscious about. A fitted waist will highlight her hourglass figure, but I'm stuck on the neckline and sleeves. A sweetheart neckline would be flattering, and she has the assets for it, but it doesn't fit her personality. She's not that sweet.

I think of a dress Grandma Lottie and I worked on together. I was fifteen and it wasn't for any special occasion. I think Lottie could tell I was having a hard time with my dad, so she came up with a project for the two of us. It was the first time I did a scalloped neckline, and I fell in love with it.

I sketch out a boat neckline with a scalloped edge for Carmen. Elegant and sophisticated. Three-quarter length sleeves make it versatile for dinner or a cocktail party. I create the pattern out of old cereal boxes and begin cutting the fabric, Grandma Lottie's voice in my head.

She'd be proud of me, I think. Not the Lydia I was last week, but the woman I'm trying to become this week, making amends the best I can.

"Whoa, what are you doing?" Isa asks on Sunday afternoon. I left the door open a smidge after my last bathroom break, and Isa stands in the hall, peeking through the crack.

"I'm making a dress." I open the door wide so she can come in.

"That fabric is amazing." She fingers a piece of the sleeve laid out on the floor.

"I got it from your dad." I bend over to straighten part of the bodice section. "He has very good taste."

"Thank you."

I look up, and Marco is standing in the hall next to Isa.

"Good to see you're putting the fabric to good use," he says.

"She's making a dress," Isa says.

"It might be easier for you to work on it at the studio," Marco says.

"I don't want to take away from the time I'm supposed to be helping you."

Marco shakes his head. "It's going to be dead for the next few weeks until we ramp up for the spring collection." His gaze takes in the collection of cereal boxes, and his lips twitch into a smile. "Bring that dress to work so you can sew it properly."

I planned on hand-sewing everything as penance, but using a workstation and sewing machine speeds up the project. As I work, I think of Carmen. Her bravery in putting her authentic self out there. The way she says what she thinks. Her genuine happiness when I told her about design school. She's the best friend I've ever had, and I miss her.

I finish the dress on Friday. Despite all the sketching and sewing I've done here, this is the first item I've created from scratch. It turned out well. Grandma Lottie would be proud. *I'm* proud. Which is a nice change from the self-loathing swirling through me.

I text Valentina.

"Can I see Carmen?"

"She won't want to see you."

"I know. Can you lure her to the market tomorrow?"

"She is easily lured to the market."

The next morning, I wait next to a table filled with shoes, trying to keep my pounding heart from giving me away. Valentina, Paolo, and Carmen stroll toward me, and sweat breaks out on my neck, despite the cold air. Paolo and Valentina spot me first, probably because they're looking for me. Valentina's mouth forms a little "O" of surprise. I've grown so accustomed to my hair I forgot the gang hasn't seen it yet.

Carmen continues walking, oblivious, while Valentina and Paolo subtly drop behind her, ready to block her path if she tries to run. I'm touched by their help. It's more than I deserve.

Carmen's taking forever to see me, and when I can't stand it anymore, I take a step toward her.

"*Ciao*, Carmen."

Her head snaps around to find me, eyes locking on mine. Anger radiates off her, making me immediately doubt the wisdom of this plan.

"What are you doing here?" She looks at me like I'm something gross she stepped in. I feel even lower.

"I came to see you."

"I don't want to see you."

"I know. That's why I had to ambush you at the market."

Carmen turns and glares at Valentina.

"Just hear her out," Valentina says.

Carmen turns to me, arms crossed, the expression on her face saying *this better be good*.

And I panic. Because I have no good explanation, no good speech. I'm just a terrible friend holding a beautiful dress.

I've never tried to apologize or make things right with someone. Most of my friendships just end when I'm done with that person. But I don't want to be done with Carmen. I want to fix what I've broken.

I thrust the gift bag with the dress at her.

"I'm sorry," I say. "I know it's not enough, but I don't know what else to say, because explaining why I did it will make it sound like I'm justifying my actions. And I know what I did was unjustifiable. You are the truest friend I've ever had. And I wish so badly I could undo the harm I've done to you." My eyes prick with tears, and heat floods my cheeks as I realize I'm about to cry in a crowded market.

"You don't have to forgive me," I say. "I wouldn't if I were you. I mean, I've been in lesser situations, and I have not forgiven people. I just want you do know how deeply sorry I am and how much I—"

"Can you wrap this up? Because I want to see what's in this bag." Carmen's lips are a straight line, but her eyes have softened.

"Oh! Um, yes. It's a dress."

Carmen pulls out the dress and holds it in front of her. "You made this for me?"

"I sewed every stitch for you."

Her eyes get shiny as she looks at it. "Because clothes are my love language."

"They are," I say.

"And you love me," she says, the corners of her lips turning up.

"I do. I'm a terrible friend, but I do love you." Now the tears are actually spilling out of my eyes, and I don't know what to do with myself. *Who is this weepy mess of a person? What has happened to the years of beautifully suppressing emotions in social situations?*

"Valentina told me about the interview," Carmen says. "And Nico. And the whiskey."

I shrug, letting the tears run down my cheeks all the way to my neck.

"Come here," Carmen says, and I step into her arms, relief flooding through me. She wraps me in a hug, and I marvel that I could be this lucky to have her friendship again.

"I'm sorry," I whisper into her hair.

"I know," she says. "And you probably did me a favor. I think Lorenzo was bound to break my heart."

"He did have that vibe about him."

She steps back and gives me a sharp look. "But you are wingmanning me big time when we go out."

"Absolutely," I say.

Her smile turns wicked. "It'll be easier now, without your magic hair getting in the way."

"I'm hoping the new look might help with a lot of things."

"Now let's try on this dress," Carmen says and strips off her coat and sweater until she's wearing a white tank top and leggings. She slides the dress on carefully, like she doesn't want to break it, and I zip up the back.

"Oh, Carmen," Valentina breathes. "You are a vision."

Carmen does a slow spin, and Paolo says, "Beautiful dress for a beautiful woman."

It fits her perfectly. Just like I hoped, the fitted waist and flared skirt flatter her figure, and the neckline and sleeves give the dress an air of elegance.

"No fair that everyone can see how great I look but me," she says, sounding like Isa.

"Let's find you a mirror."

Paolo carries her coat and sweater and Valentina carries her purse, and I track down a full-length mirror two tents over.

"You are right," Carmen says, grinning from ear to ear. "I look amazing."

"Agreed," I say. "I'm no expert, but it may look even better without the black leggings."

"You are an expert," Carmen says. She runs a hand down the front admiringly. "I can't believe you made this."

I can hardly believe it myself. It took six solid days and an obscene amount of work, but it was worth it.

The joy of making something beautiful feels almost as good as Carmen hugging me.

Chapter Thirty-Six

"All right, team," Marco says as we file into the conference room Monday morning. "We had a great winter collection, and I know it's not quite March, but I'd like to brainstorm ideas for the spring collection in September." Marco's marker squeaks against the whiteboard as he scrawls big letters across its glossy surface. BOLD. RISKS. SPRING. The scent of dry erase marker fills the air.

"We want to capitalize on our success and propel Rossi Designs even further. We're not playing it safe. This is a time to take risks." His eyes sparkle, and his energy is contagious. It makes me want to go skydiving. Or try a new shade of lipstick.

"I'm looking for a theme for the spring collection. Something bold, adventurous. No pastels. We've got a lot of creative minds in this room, and everyone's ideas have merit, so feel free to share anything that comes to mind."

The air is thick with hesitation. The overhead lights hum, and Clara's chair scrapes the floor as she shifts, but other than that, the room is silent. Ideas are bouncing inside my brain, and I want to shout them all out, but I wait, curious to see what Clara and Danilo will suggest.

"What are some words or feelings you associate with spring?" Marco asks, standing at the whiteboard, marker poised.

"Rain," Clara says.

"Okay," Marco's eyebrows dip, but he writes rain.

"Um flowers?" Danilo asks like it's a question and not the answer.

"Okay, florals can be fresh and innovative," Marco says. "What else?"

"Pastels!" Clara blurts out, her voice hopeful. "Oh wait. You said no pastels." Her shoulders droop.

"That's okay," Marco says. "Let's keep brainstorming."

After Danilo offers spring cleaning, and Clara mentions allergies, Marco looks at me with desperate eyes.

"Lydia? Any ideas you want to share?"

"Well," I begin. "I thought spring travel might provide some fun possibilities for a collection." I pull out my sketchpad and flip back to the designs I came up with a month ago. "French berets, British trench coats, Greek gold sandals and sundresses."

Marco's eyes light up. "Ooh, spring travel across the continent. I've been looking for an excuse to work lederhosen into a collection."

A laugh sneaks out of me. "There you go."

Marco nods and murmurs something about leather from Florence and French silk. When he remembers the rest of us are here, he snaps back to attention.

"Great ideas. All of you. Let's think about these over the next two weeks and start solidifying our plans at the end of the month."

We file out of the conference room, and Marco stops me. "Lydia, could I take a look at those sketches?"

"Of course." I hand over my pad. It doesn't mean he's going with my idea for the collection, but he likes it and that means something.

"Wow! Lydia! I love your hair!" Chelsie comes into the conference room as Marco heads back to his office.

"Thanks. Are you feeling better? I think I passed you the flu."

Chelsie shakes her head. "It turned out to be strep throat. That's why I was out so long."

"I'm so sorry."

"Yeah, I'm bummed I missed the after-party. My friend, who's an assistant to one of the stylists, said Britta Larsson showed up and started a bunch of drama."

My senses go on high alert. "What else did she say?"

Chelsie shrugs. "Just that Britta rolled in with her publicist and a swarm of paparazzi. Then there was some big drama, security stepped in, and she was kicked out."

What?

"Chelsie, I need more information."

"Sure, I'll ask my friend."

I stare at her.

"Oh, you mean right now." She grabs her phone, and I close the door to the conference room.

"*Ciao*, Katia." Chelsie perches on the edge of the table, tapping her nails against her phone. "I need the deets on the Rossi after-party. What happened with Britta Larsson?"

"Ooh. It was A Thing!" A dramatic nasal voice blares from Chelsie's phone, and I hang on Katia's every word. "Britta showed up about an hour into the party with her full entourage. She headed straight to Nico Moretti and started saying all this stuff about what a great couple they were, and how much she missed him and how they should get back together. It came off a little desperate. I mean, I get it, Nico is a God, and I would give my right arm to—"

"What did Nico say?" I interject.

"At first, he was cool about it. Told her they were just friends, and he was with someone else. Which I did not know. Who is this woman, and does she know every woman in Italy wishes they were her?"

"What happened next, Katia?" Chelsie says. I squeeze her hand in gratitude.

"So, Nico says he's not interested, she goes in for the classic goodbye hug—respectable, innocent—then BOOM, ambush kiss! Right on the mouth. That's when Nico lost it. Pushed her away and called for security."

"He pushed her away?" My voice comes out fast and sharp. "You saw it?"

"Yeah. He was having none of it. Plus get this—I heard from another assistant that Britta doesn't even like him. The whole thing was a publicity stunt. Britta's starting to fade, and after the spring collection, Nico took off. So of course, Britta's publicist wanted them to get back together. When that didn't work, she snapped a pic of them kissing and gave it to the press to get some media attention."

"No." I sit down hard trying to reconcile this new information with what I thought I knew.

"Thanks, Katia," Chelsie says. "Gotta go. *Ciao.*"

Chelsie sits beside me and squeezes my hand. "What happened with you and Nico?"

"I saw the picture in the newspaper, and I ended things with Nico. I thought..."

"Oh, Lydia. Didn't Nico explain?"

My mind pulls up our last conversation, frantically trying to remember what Nico said.

"He sent me a bunch of texts, but I deleted them. And I blocked his number."

Is it possible he really wasn't cheating? Why didn't I read his texts? Why didn't I let him explain?

Because I was so sure he was just like my father.

I try to call him and remember I deleted his number.

"Chelsie, can you look up Nico's number for me?"

Her expression turns pained. "I can't. He's an employee, and I can't release confidential information."

"But—you—we just!"

"I know. But I could lose my job. The last receptionist got fired for giving out the models' personal phone numbers." Her voice drops to a gossipy tone. "Apparently, she was selling them. I heard she made a good amount of money before Marco found out."

"I've got to talk to Nico."

"Maybe go to his house?"

I don't want to cause a scene in front of Gloria and his sisters.

"Thank you," I tell Chelsie. "For getting me more information."

I stumble into the studio, mind reeling, limbs shaking. I find a pile of clothes sitting by the ironing board and go to town. The iron hisses and steam rises in waves as I press them so fiercely they'll be terrified to ever wrinkle again.

I should have listened to Nico!

It's probably too late now. He probably moved on and found a new girlfriend who doesn't block his calls and delete his number.

"Lydia." Chelsie stands a few feet away, eyeing me and my iron warily.

"There's a runway show you might be interested in. It's at La Galleria this Friday night."

"Okay..."

"The designer is Fauci. If you look it up online you can get more info, like the list of collaborators and the names of the models." She looks at me a moment longer, then walks through the door back to her desk.

My intestines take up juggling as I grab my phone and look up the show. Sure enough, Nico is listed as one of the models walking.

What? He was so relieved to do his last runway show with Marco. Why is he doing another?

I think of him picking up shifts at his mom's work to pay for my Christmas gift and wonder if Camilla needs braces, or some other expense Nico's trying to pay for.

My heart squeezes thinking of this wonderful man I let slip through my fingers. But maybe it's not too late.

I give Chelsie a small salute as I leave, hope growing inside me like a desert flower.

"So, you're just going to show up at his show?" Carmen asks Wednesday night. We decided to give Calypso a break for a while, and we're spending the evening at a free art exhibit.

"Yeah. I mean, I'm not jumping out of a cake or anything. I'm just going to talk to him."

I try to decide if the abstract painting on the wall is hanging upside down on purpose.

"Do you think maybe you should jump out of a cake?" Paolo asks with a wicked gleam in his eye.

"I do not."

"People love grand romantic gestures," Valentina says.

"False. People like other people's grand romantic gestures."

I've been on the receiving end of several such gestures, and it's always awkward. How do you tell a man who commissioned an ice sculpture of you that you just want to be friends? With a kind smile and a pat on the arm, but still, I don't like doing it.

"Is that a banana duct taped to a canvas?" Valentina asks.

"I heard it's going to auction for five million dollars," Paolo says.

"Rich people are ridiculous," Carmen says.

"Agreed," I say. "I wouldn't pay more than four."

The three of them stare at me horrified.

"It was a joke!"

"I still think you should do something big for Nico," Carmen says.

"I don't need to do some big thing. I'll just go and talk to him. That will be enough."

Chapter Thirty-Seven

It doesn't feel like enough. Sitting in the back row of the venue waiting to catch a glimpse of Nico, I long for a flash mob, a juggler, or a cake to jump out of. Anything to increase my odds of winning him back. Because I know in my heart if I don't, I will be sad and miserable for the rest of my life.

A hush falls over the crowd as the lights dim, casting an ethereal glow over the runway. The first three models glide forward, their heels clicking against the glossy floor. But they're not Nico. And their ensembles, a visual cacophony of silk, leather, and metallics, are somehow both aggressively avant-garde and deeply boring.

And then Nico appears, emerging from the backstage shadows like a secret and striding down the runway with effortless grace. The overhead lights sculpt his sharp features, highlighting the cut of his cheekbones, the precision of his jawline. My eyes drink him in like he's a tall glass of water and I've crawled through the Sahara to get here.

His face is the closed off, aloof face all the models wear, and it's so different from his relaxed, goofy smile it makes me ache. I want to tickle him, yell his name, do something to break that stone face, but I stay quiet. I admire him as he walks down, turns, and walks back.

He walks three more times over the next thirty minutes. Each time, my heart hammers in time to his steps. It's like all the cells in my body know they're in the presence of the man who's stolen my heart. The show finishes with minimal applause, and I'm grateful I work for Marco and not this Fauci guy.

The crowd dissolves quickly, and I hover near the backstage door waiting for Nico. My palms are damp, my fingers clumsy as I swipe them against my dress. Every second stretches, slow and thick, like honey dripping from a spoon.

Memories of my first show with Marco flood back: crying in the dressing room, Nico finding me, our first kiss.

The steady stream of models and stylists slows, and I wonder if Nico found an alternate exit. Then, suddenly he's standing in front of me, a bewildered look on his face.

But happy bewildered, right? Like, he's surprised but also excited to see me?

"Lydia?" he says.

"Nico. Hi."

"You cut your hair."

My hand goes to the back of my neck. "It was getting in my way."

He nods, like this makes sense, then asks, "What are you doing here? Did Marco send you?"

"What? Why would Marco send me?"

"I don't know. Scope out the competition?"

"No. Um. I just came for myself. I mean, for you. I came to see you."

Get it together St. Clair.

"Okay."

He doesn't look mad. But he hasn't scooped me into his arms and told me he loves me. And honestly, I was really hoping things would go down that way.

"Can we talk?"

"Sure." His face gives away nothing.

The space is deserted at this point, so I lead us to seats in the back row. Nico sits next to me, and I want to hold his hand, crawl into his lap, caress his face. I clench my hands in my lap to keep from touching him.

I know what I want to say, I practiced all the way here. But I'm not sure where to start.

"I miss you."

"I miss you too," he says, and my heart unclenches the tiniest bit.

"I'm sorry," I blurt. "For not hearing you out. For not responding to your calls or messages. I was furious, and my feelings were hurt." Emotions rise in my throat, and I swallow them down. "I talked to Chelsie, and she told me how things went down with Britta. I should have trusted you."

Nico nods but doesn't say anything.

"I want to try again. The last few months with you have been the best of my life. And this thing we have between us, I think it's something special."

He takes my hand, and my whole body relaxes at his touch. *This. This is how it should be.*

"I appreciate your apology. And you're right. We do have something special between us."

His words are everything I want to hear, but his face isn't right. His eyes are sad, and his dimples have gone dormant.

"But?" I prompt him.

He shakes his head. "But...I don't think we should be together."

My skin goes cold. And then hot. I nod my head to let him know I understand. But also, I don't understand.

"Why?" I don't care if my voice breaks. I don't care if I'm begging. I need to know.

He runs a hand down his face. "You left, Lydia." My eyes fix on his Adam's apple as he swallows. "I think you're amazing. You're smart and talented, gorgeous and funny."

I nod miserably, knowing this isn't going anywhere good.

"But you leave when things get hard. Whether it's college or Milan, or people. When it stops being easy, you just quit. I wanted to work things out, and you wouldn't even try." He looks down at his hands. "When my dad left, my mom told me he still loved me, he just needed other things. I believed that for a long time, because I wanted to."

Pain flashes across his face, fresh and raw, and tears pool in my eyes.

"But when you love someone, you stay. Even when it gets confusing or messy. You figure it out, you work through it." He runs a hand down his face. "I'm not sure you can do that."

I open my mouth intending to defend myself but close it when I realize I have nothing to say.

"I want to be with you, Lydia. I want to believe that you won't leave at the slightest inconvenience. But I've been through hell the last two weeks, and I'm just barely crawling out. Maybe it's not fair, but...I can't let you break my heart again."

"I'm sorry," I whisper. "I didn't mean to hurt you."

"I know," Nico says. The way he says it, he's letting me off the hook. He knows I didn't mean to hurt him, it's just something I do. I quit. I leave. I hurt people.

And he's right. Because this conversation is the hardest conversation I've ever had, and I can't do it anymore.

I stand, and Nico gets to his feet.

"I wish it could be a different way," he says. I nod mutely, afraid that if I open my mouth, it will all come spilling from my eyes.

He steps to the side so I can get out of our row, reaching out a hand like he's going to touch me, but stopping at the last minute. I try to meet his eyes and almost make it there before turning and walking out, my heels echoing on the hard floor.

The ride home is rough. The taxi driver mutters about excessive drinking, which I get because how could a sober girl cry this much? From the smell clinging to the stained upholstery, he's transported a lot of drunk people. I gather myself as we arrive at the Rossi's neighborhood. But I dissolve again in the elevator, sobs echoing off the metal walls as I grip the cold handrail like it's an emotional support animal. The scratched metal reflects my blotchy red cheeks and the mascara smudges under my eyes like bruises.

Isa, Sofia, and Marco are watching a movie in the living room, and their eyes widen in sync when I walk in.

"Lydia! Are you okay?" Sofia asks, jumping up from the couch.

"Did someone die?" Isa asks.

"Is it your family?" Marco asks, joining Sofia by my side. "Did something happen?"

My worst nightmare, crying uncontrollably in front of other people, has come true, and it's just as bad as I imagined.

"I'm fine." But tears stream down my face, negating my words. Sofia rubs my back in slow, steady circles, like I've seen her do with Isa, and Marco fidgets uncomfortably, like every man I've ever known.

Except for Nico, who found me sobbing, wrapped his arms around me and held me until I felt better.

"Is it a boy?" Sofia asks after a moment. I lift my head and make eye contact with her. Then I nod. Marco's shoulders relax in relief, and Sofia clucks reassuringly. Pity replaces the concern in their eyes. And just like that, I've hit rock bottom and started digging.

I take a breath and manage to get out, "I'll be okay. I'm just going to head to my room for a while."

"Good idea," Sofia says.

"Maybe a nice cup of tea later," Marco suggests. As though chamomile will stitch together the gaping hole in my heart.

I change out of my dress, then slip into my pajamas and crawl into bed. It's barely 9pm, but I close my eyes and cry myself to sleep.

The next morning, I have five missed calls and ten texts from the gang.

Valentina: how did it go?

Carmen: Are you covered in frosting?

Paolo: It's not too late for me to bring a marching band

Carmen: Could you pick up an extra male model for me while you're there?

Valentina: Have you seen him yet?

Carmen: If you need a pep talk before you see him, give me a call

Valentina: Are you okay? Tried to call but you didn't pick up

Paolo: Do you want me to come get you? I can be there in 20

Carmen: Hoping you're happily making out, and that's why you're not responding

Valentina: Text us with an update when you come up for air!

How do I even respond? If I were back home, I'd spin this into a story where I was amazing, and the show was a blast and Nico who?

But I have real friends now, and I simply text,

It's over.

Then I set my phone to *Do Not Disturb* because real friends or no, I can't bear any more pity. I sleep for ten hours and wake up late the next morning.

I take a shower, and by some miracle, all the Rossi's are gone when I come out, so I eat breakfast at the kitchen table, staring out the window.

Chatter and traffic drift up from the street below as I process the fact that I will never kiss Nico again. Or make him laugh. Or listen to him sing. The knowledge that no one I ever date will live up to Nico settles over me. Whoever I end up with, I will be settling, because I could not have the person my heart longs for.

Isa's voice in the hall announces the Rossi's return, and I run to my room like a coward.

My heart broke when I thought Nico cheated on me, but I pretended I was fine. It's different this time. I don't have any pretending left in me.

I spend Saturday and Sunday in my room, and Isa occasionally knocks to see if I want tea or snacks, but I tell her I'm not hungry.

When I can't sleep at 2am, I go to the kitchen and make a sandwich. I eat it in the dark and think of every special moment Nico and I shared. And how I'll never get them back.

On Monday, I bring Isa to school, I go to the studio, I pick Isa up, and we go to the park. On Tuesday and Wednesday, it's the same. Sad and cold and empty.

Wednesday evening Carmen comes over. She brings some yummy cakes and chatters about the horrible children at her school, and when I burst into tears mid-story, she doesn't even flinch, just rubs my back and lets me cry till I'm finished.

The next week is better. Mostly because Isa stops being patient with me and demands I be a fun nanny again. Everything is still cold, but that's just Milan in March.

Two weeks after my night of devastation, I'm doing okay.

Yes, I lost the only man I've ever loved. And yes, my heart is shattered into a million pieces. But at least—

Okay, turns out I don't have a silver lining for this scenario. It sucks and it will keep sucking forever.

I lay in bed staring at the ceiling, thinking of Nico's words. I never considered how our breakup would trigger his pain from his dad leaving. I only knew it was hard, and I didn't want to do it anymore. Just like when I booked a flight home. And when I stopped going to classes, because the coursework was impossible. Even quitting swimming when I was ten because it didn't come as easily as horseback riding.

But I'm not ten years old anymore. I'm a grown woman. And I'm tired of losing the things I love.

I roll over to look at the wall.

Even though my efforts to win Nico back failed, I'm proud of myself for trying. It's something I never would have done a year ago.

And while I don't have a great track record of recovering the things I've lost, I'm not giving up. Fashion is my dream. And now that I've had a taste of it, I know this is what I'm meant to do. I just need another chance.

Chapter Thirty-Eight

"Guys, I need a favor." I wipe my fingers on a paper napkin and take a sip of Coke.

I'm out for pizza with Carmen, Valentina, and Paolo, the crowded restaurant a nice change from my stale bedroom. The three of them gave me hugs when I showed up, but none of them mentioned the breakup, which I appreciate.

"I'm going to design school next year," I tell them. "But it's going to take some work to make it happen." There's sauce on my finger, and I lick it off. "I need to get in to see Professora Lanna, and I found a back stairwell up to the third floor, but when I tried to sneak past the front desk to her office yesterday, her secretary Perla caught me.

"With my new haircut, I don't think she recognizes me as the flaky American who walked out of her exam. But she did not like me trying to sneak by her. For a woman who's at least ninety years old, she's remarkably fast."

"I've got an aunt like that," Paolo contributes. "They're not to be underestimated."

"That's where you guys come in. I need you to create a distraction, something that will lure Perla away from her desk, so I can slip past."

"What did you have in mind?" Valentina asks, and the wariness in her voice makes me regret telling her about the dean's office and the chickens.

"I don't have a plan yet," I admit. "But I thought we could come up with something together."

"I know!" Carmen says. "How about a singing telegram!"

"I don't think that's a good idea..." Valentina says.

I love Carmen, but she has one of the worst singing voices I've ever heard.

"Singing telegrams are not a thing people do in real life," Paolo says. "They're a product of American movies and sadistic fiction authors. No one actually sends a singing telegram."

Valentina raises her hand. "At the risk of asking the obvious, why don't you just call and make an appointment?"

"I tried setting up an appointment with a fake name," I say. "But Perla won't let you in to see Professora Lanna unless you've applied to the school. And if I give her my real name, she'll pull up my application, see that I walked out of the last interview, and definitely won't set up an appointment." I rub my forehead. "I tried to get Professora Lanna's number so I could apologize over the phone, but Perla wouldn't give it out. She's awful."

"Have you considered going in through the ventilation system?" Paolo asks with a hopeful gleam in his eye.

"No. Nor will I," I tell him. "I just need you guys to distract her for a minute. I'll sneak up the back way beforehand and wait in the bathroom. Then you guys come to the main entrance and draw her away from her desk and into the hall. Then I'll sprint to Professora Lanna's office. Easy."

"A singing telegram will be perfect," Carmen claps her hands and her chunky bracelets clack like castanets.

"This is never going to work," Paolo says.

"What happens if we get caught?" Valentina asks.

"This is going to be so much fun!" Carmen says.

And I guess that settles it.

Friday morning finds me sweating in the girls' bathroom just outside Professora Lanna's department. I took the back stairwell and made it to the third floor undetected. But just like last time, Perla is glued to her desk, protecting the hallway to Professora Lanna's office like a dragon protecting treasure.

I wash my hands for the third time. Either the smell of the overly perfumed bathroom cleaner is making me lightheaded, or I'm more nervous than I thought.

The fluorescent light above me flickers as my mind flashes through what will happen if this goes bad.

I won't get into design school. I won't become a fashion designer. I'll end up married to a pastel-wearing tax attorney named Greg who listens to jazz for fun.

All my hopes and dreams are hanging on this thin singing telegram thread.

After what feels like an eternity, the buzzer for the door sounds, and I hold my breath.

"Admissions department, how can I assist you?" Perla says. There's silence for a moment, and I ease the door open a crack to hear her reply.

"A singing telegram? Why?" More silence, and I pray that it's Paolo on the other line and not one of the girls. He keeps a much cooler head under pressure.

"I see," she says, skepticism strong in her voice. "I'll buzz you in. We're on the third floor."

I wait in clammy silence, wondering how long it takes three people to climb four flights of stairs.

A cymbal crashes, shattering the silence, followed by the loud thump of a bass drum.

Did my friends bring an actual drum set on this mission?

Perla jumps to her feet. "What in the blazes!"

Nico would laugh so hard if he was here right now. A pang of disappointment shoots through me that I won't be able to tell him about it.

The drumming continues, and Perla looks torn between leaving her post and putting a stop to the racket. Then Carmen's voice careens through the closed door like an alley cat being flung by catapult. She hits a screeching high note, and I wince. This gets Perla moving and as soon as the coast is clear, I sprint like an Olympic athlete past her desk.

I don't dare glance toward the door, but I catch a "Happy Anniversary," from Valentina and Carmen sings Whitney Houston's "I Will Always Love You" as I race down the hall.

I've never been to Professora Lanna's office, but if things work here like they do back home, it will be the big one at the end of the hall. Sure enough, a bronze plaque by the door reads Prof. Lanna.

I give a soft knock and then slip in without waiting for a reply. At this point, I'm more scared of Perla than Professora Lanna.

She startles when I walk in, nearly dropping the ceramic mug she's holding. The faint scent of bergamot hangs in the air, blending with the dusty leather of old academic journals stacked behind her.

"I'm sorry to interrupt your morning." My voice comes out surprisingly well, considering I feel like I swallowed a handful of pinecones.

"Lydia?" I'm flattered and nervous that she remembers my name.

"Yes. I came to apologize for my behavior the other day. Leaving in the middle of the exam was unprofessional and discourteous, and I am very sorry."

Professora Lanna nods in agreement.

I take a breath. "I also came to ask for another chance."

Her eyebrows shoot up to her hairline, but she remains quiet, presumably giving me a chance to explain. I take it.

"I didn't realize an exam would be a part of the interview." Pause. "I have dyslexia. And reading, especially in high pressure situations, is difficult for me. I should have said something instead of leaving. But I was embarrassed." My voice catches on the last word, and I squeeze my hands into balls.

Please, sweet gods of fashion, do not let me cry in front of this woman.

I take a breath and continue. "While I've struggled with this my whole life, I've only recently been diagnosed, and I'm still adjusting to what this means. In all honesty, I'm not adjusting well."

This earns me the tiniest of smiles from the professor, and my heart latches onto it.

"I'm confident that if given another opportunity, and knowing beforehand about the exam, I will pass."

This is a lie. There is nothing in my history that makes me feel confident I will do well on an exam. But I'm desperate for the chance to try.

Professora Lanna nods slowly, and I let out a shaky breath.

"Based on the determination and cleverness it took to get into my office this morning..." She pauses, and we listen to the distant sound of drums, cymbals, and wailing. "I will let you sit for the exam again."

Relief floods through me, and I want to leap, yell, throw my arms around her. But I keep my composure and say, "Thank you, Professora Lanna."

I turn to leave her office, and she stops me with a raised hand. Her eyes have softened. "Some of our students who share similar struggles to yours prefer to take oral exams instead of written. Is that something you would prefer?"

And that's when I lose my composure. Hot tears leak out of my eyes blurring the edges of the professor's form like a watercolor painting. I nod mutely.

"I'll set it up and have our secretary email you the details."

"Thank you," I whisper, not trusting my full voice to hold up.

And then I'm slipping out of her office into the hallway. All is quiet now, and I tiptoe down the hall and peek around the corner. Perla has settled back at her desk, a deep furrow in her brow.

There's nothing else to do, so I walk quickly past her toward the door, keeping my face turned away from her.

"Excuse me," she calls. "Can I help you?"

"*No grazie*," I call over my shoulder and book it out of there. For a moment, I'm convinced she's going to chase after me, but apparently, she's satisfied that I'm leaving the department, because she stays in her chair.

I'm sweaty and disheveled when I find the gang at the front of the building next to a pile of percussive instruments. Hope shines in their eyes and they don't say a word as I approach.

"We did it!" I holler and leap into Carmen's arms. She laughs and hugs me, and Valentina and Paolo cheer. "I get to take the exam again."

"Hooray!" Valentina says and pulls me into a hug. Even Paolo gives me a hug, and he's not much of a hugger.

"You guys were brilliant," I say. "Where did you get the drums?"

"My neighbor plays," Paolo says. "So I know how effective they can be at making a person agree to anything to make them stop."

"Very effective. I made it in, no problem." I leave out the part where I thought I was going to puke.

Carmen loops her arm through mine, and I'm so happy to have her back I nearly start crying again. I recount my conversation with Professora Lanna, including her offer to let me take the test orally.

"I'm going to ace that test. I'm going to get into design school. And I couldn't have done it without the three of you."

Valentina nudges my shoulder. "You would've found a way, even without us."

I look at the three of them—sweaty and grinning triumphantly—and my heart does a happy dance.

"Maybe. But I like this way better."

Chapter Thirty-Nine

One week later, Perla leads me to the conference room. Maybe she's always this cold, or maybe she suspects I'm connected to the singing telegram shenanigans.

"Federica will administer the exam," she says curtly.

Federica isn't the woman who administered my last exam, and I'm grateful. I'm nervous enough without my past failure haunting the room.

"I understand we're doing an oral exam today," Federica says, smoothing her dress as we both take a seat.

The tone of her voice and the smile on her face puts me at ease immediately. I expected questions on fashion principles or history, so Isa and I spent the weekend going over famous designers and their most iconic picccs.

But this exam is different. It's more about testing the way I think about design and design problem solving. At her request, I tell her what design I might create for a nautical themed cocktail party, which fabrics I would use for styles that emphasize durability, and how I would solve the problem of sexism in fashion. She finishes by asking which designers are particularly inspiring to me and why.

By the last question, my palms are damp, but my voice is steady. I glance at the clock—thirty minutes have slipped by like silk. Either I aced it or blacked out from panic and hallucinated the whole thing.

"That wraps up the exam," Federica says, standing. "I'll share your results with Professora Lanna, and you'll hear from us soon."

The smile on her face makes me feel like I did well, but the minute I walk out I second-guess my answers. *Was I too long-winded? Should I have tried to be funny?*

According to the school's website, application decisions will be made by March thirtieth. I check my email every day for the next two weeks, panic rising with each empty inbox.

I keep myself busy in the studio, working with Marco on selecting the right fabrics for the new collection. Since the spring show is still several months away, Nico and the other models don't come in. I'm glad Nico's not here because being around him but not with him would be torture. But the space feels dimmer without his smile.

Isa and I listen to *Glitter the Mermaid* and make up a game of trying to work quotes from the book into as many conversations as possible. I don't know how Marco and Sofia tolerate us.

By March thirtieth, my nerves are as frayed as a cheap windbreaker. I check my email at breakfast, and there's nothing. I check it again before I get to the studio, still nothing. For three hours, I focus all my brain power on adjusting a dress for a model who has put on weight. The moment I hang the dress in the closet, I check my email again.

This time, an email from Professora Lanna appears, the subject line blazing like a neon sign: Congratulations on your acceptance to the Milan Institute of Design.

A ferocious "Yes!" bursts out of me.

Danilo and Clara jump, and Chelsie peeks her head out from the reception area, grinning.

"You got in?"

"I! Got! In!" I pump my fists in the air not even caring that I look like a contestant on a gameshow.

"You got in?" Bianca asks, coming out of Marco's office.

"She got in," Chelsie responds.

Bianca sticks her head back into Marco's office and calls, "Lydia got in!"

Marco comes out a moment later, champagne in hand. "Congratulations, Lydia! We knew you'd get in."

"Did you? Because you could have told me. I haven't slept in weeks!"

He laughs and leans in close so only I can hear. "I've never seen raw talent like yours. I knew they would accept you. And I can't wait to see what you do."

Chelsie comes in with glasses and the six of us celebrate, Danilo and Clara offering begrudging congratulations.

Isa and I toast my acceptance with gelato from a gelateria near the house. Isa is full of ideas for the clothes I should design for my school assignments.

"I'll help you with your homework," she offers. "Just like you helped me with mine."

Did I help her with her homework? Or did she blackmail me into doing it all?

I don't bring that part up and thank her for her kind offer.

When Sofia and Marco come home from work, I meet the gang at a restaurant downtown for a celebration dinner.

Since everyone in the group is in a lower tax bracket than me, we always stick to casual family restaurants. But tonight I'm treating the group to dinner at Acanto, a Michelin-rated restaurant I've been dying to visit.

Crystal chandeliers bathe the room in golden light, and the scent of rosemary and truffle drifts from the kitchen.

"So much silverware," Carmen murmurs as our hostess helps her into her chair. The silverware is real silver, and the white linen tablecloth is heavy against my bare legs. My toes wiggle happily at these much-missed luxuries.

"I feel like a Kardashian," Valentina says in a hushed voice.

We enjoy their six-course tasting menu, and when I take my first bite of pan-roasted sea scallops, it melts on my tongue. For dessert there's crème brûlée alla pastiera and house-made gelato.

"Thank you for an exquisite dinner," Paolo says.

"Well, the chef did his part," I acknowledge.

The meal was exceptional. And celebrating this moment with people who truly care about me was even better.

Nico pops into my head. Even though things didn't work out with us, he's one of those guys who would still want me to be happy. *And I am. Mostly.*

"So, you're staying in Milan?" Paolo says.

"I am."

Carmen bursts out laughing, and I give her an elbow. "What?"

"Oh, just thinking about how you tried to go back home as soon as you got here. And how you nearly flew home a month ago. And now here you are, ready to stay in Milan for the next four years."

"I need to stop telling you things," I say.

"No! It's great. It shows you've changed. You used to be the kind of person that would take off as soon as things got hard. And now you've scraped and clawed your way into design school. You should feel proud."

I do. And she's right, I have changed. The last month has been excruciating, but I didn't quit. Unfortunately, my newfound tenacity came too late for me and Nico.

"So where are you going to live?" Valentina asks. "Are you going to keep nannying for the Rossi family?"

"No! I'll stay in touch of course, but they'll get a new nanny, and I'll find a place of my own."

"On your own, or with roommates?" Carmen asks.

"On my own. I hate roommates."

Paolo smirks and Carmen and Valentina share a look.

"What?"

"It's nothing," Valentina says. "Just—our roommate Giana is getting married this summer, and we were wondering if maybe you'd like to take her room and move in with us."

Wait—there's a third roommate? That apartment barely fits two!

I had pictured myself in a downtown luxury loft, not a shabby apartment that's smaller than my bedroom back home.

Then I think of sharing clothes with Carmen, watching cheesy movies with Valentina. Living with my two best friends.

"I would love to be your third roommate."

Carmen's mouth drops open. "Really?"

"Really. It will be fun. And maybe we could update some of the furniture. The sofa, and dining room table. And replace that falling down bookshelf in the living room."

Carmen smiles. "It's going to be so fun having a rich roommate."

I shake my head, but I'm smiling too. "Speaking of money, I need some help. My dad won't pay for design school. And I can't access my trust fund until I turn twenty-five next year."

Paolo's eyebrows dip in confusion, and Carmen and Valentina share twin expressions of panic.

"Um, Lydia? We're broke," Carmen says.

Laughter bursts out of me like champagne from a bottle.

"Sorry! You thought...? No. I know that." I squeeze Carmen's hand, grinning. "I'm going to ask my brother for a loan. But I need to make a really persuasive PowerPoint presentation." I turn to Valentina. "You've mentioned making them for school, and I was hoping—"

"Yes!" she interrupts, eyes filled with glee. "I will help you make the most amazing PowerPoint!"

She looks like such a dork I want to hug her.

"Thank you. I appreciate it. And Paolo, I was hoping you could draw up a loan contract? I can get you the tuition numbers."

"Happy to."

"So...when do you want to start working on the PowerPoint?" Valentina asks. "Tomorrow?" She leans forward. "Or right now?"

And that's how I end up squeezed onto Carmen and Valentina's ugly gray sofa at 11pm, watching Valentina's fingers fly over the keyboard. She puts in photos from the school's website, along with their career placement stats, and research on the growing need for designers and the average salaries they make.

The sofa's scratchy fabric prickles my arms as my gaze travels around the tiny apartment. My lips curl into a smile thinking of living here next year.

By the time Valentina has finished, it's a masterpiece of graphs, bullet points, and vibrant images.

"Do you want to practice the presentation?" Valentina says, eyes bright and excited.

Her energy is not contagious. It's been a great day, but I'm wiped out and have to get up early tomorrow.

"I'll practice tomorrow," I tell her, "when I have the energy this beautiful presentation deserves."

For now, I take an Uber home, watching the city drift past my window, and incredibly grateful that I found my place, my purpose, and my people.

The next day, I practice giving the presentation while Isa critiques my posture, hand movements, and body language. Even though I'm practicing in English, and she has no idea what I'm saying, she has a lot of feedback to offer.

When Isa declares I'm ready, I head to my room and take a breath.

I've gotten into school, and that wasn't easy. Now I just need to get tuition covered so I can actually go.

"Hello?" Robby says, when I call him, sounding tired as always.

"Robby, it's Lydia. Are you home?"

"Yes. Why?"

"Check your email—I just sent a Zoom link. It starts now, so log in." Then I hang up before he can tell me he's too busy.

"Well, hello, Robby!" I say thirty seconds later when his face appears on the screen. "You look great." He doesn't. There are large bags under his eyes and the hair on one side of his head is sticking up at a forty-five-degree angle.

"Egg, I've had four hours of sleep in the last twenty-four hours. What's this about?" His voice crackles through the speakers of my laptop, his movements choppy.

"It's about a brand-new future. And how you can be a part of it." I sound like I'm selling herbal supplements and take a breath to calm my nerves.

"I have exciting news," I say, and the smile on my face is genuine. "I got into the Milan Institute of Design."

"Really? Wow." Rob's bleary eyes have perked up. "Congratulations."

"Thank you." I pull up the PowerPoint and share my screen, just like Valentina showed me. Then I launch into my carefully rehearsed presentation. I tell him about the school. About career opportunities in the field of fashion. I share photos from Marco's runway show with the ensemble I designed. And I finish with my conundrum of tuition, a stubborn and close-minded father, and a trust fund that I can't access for another two years.

"I see," Robby says. The look in his eye tells me he knows where this is going.

"Would you like to invest in a rising fashion designer who will pay back the first year of tuition, including interest, as soon as she turns twenty-five?"

Robby's lips curve into a smile, and my heart leaps.

Got him.

"That sounds like a great investment opportunity."

"Really?" Relief floods through me, and I want to dance the flamenco.

"Really. I'm proud of you, Egg. Despite some obstacles, you found your passion."

"I love it so much. Is this how you feel about medicine?"

"It is. It means so much to you, you'll do whatever it takes to be great at it. Even if it means sleep deprivation." He rubs his eyes and smiles.

"Thank you, Robby."

"You're welcome. If you'll email me your school's information, I'll send them a check."

"Perfect. I'm also sending you a formal loan contract from my banker."

"You have a banker?"

"I'm a St. Clair. Of course, I have a banker."

We end the call with I love yous, and I flop back onto my bed like a starfish. An extremely happy starfish whose dreams are coming true.

Chapter Forty

The sun apparently remembered it's there for more than just looking pretty and warms my bare legs as I walk to the studio. The gray city winter is yielding to a vibrant spring, and I'm ready for it.

Just as I reach the familiar iron doors my phone buzzes with a text from Benedetta.

> Ciao Lydia, I'm sorry to ask, but I need some help. I think Cami has an ear infection, and I need to take her to the doctor, but I can't leave Julia at home. Could you come over and stay with her?

I am filled with questions. Why can't Nico stay with Julia? It's a Thursday so he doesn't have school. (It's pathetic that I still know his schedule, but here we are.) Also, why isn't Benedetta in school right now?

Instead of asking any of those questions, I reply,

> Be there in 30 minutes.

I let Bianca know I need to take care of something this morning, and she nods distractedly without looking up from her clipboard.

I hop into a musty cab, the cracked leather seats warm from the sun, and cling to the arm rest as we speed recklessly through morning traffic. Twenty minutes and two close calls later, I'm at Nico's apartment.

The smell sucker punches me as soon as Benedetta opens the door. Like unwashed laundry and dirty dishes climbed into a hot tub together.

"Oh!" she says when she sees me. "You cut your hair." Her face looks bewildered, like everything she knew about the world was wrong.

"I did," I tell her. "How are you doing?"

"Good. Mostly." She kisses me on each cheek. "Thanks for coming. I didn't know who else to call."

"I'm happy to help."

Cami comes up behind her sister, rubbing her ear and scowling. She's wearing the leather jacket I got her for Christmas.

"I'll let you get off to the doctor," I say. "Where's Julia?"

"Thanks!" Benedetta says. "Julia's in with Mom." And then she's gone, and I'm standing in their tiny living room more than a little confused. *If Gloria's here, why did Bene call me?*

"Julia?" I whisper. The door at the end of the hall is cracked, and I peek inside. Julia sits next to her mom, who is fast asleep. Gloria's face is ashen, her chest rising just enough to prove she's alive.

"*Ciao*, Lydia!" Julia says, leaping off her chair to hug me.

Gloria's eyes spring open, and she looks disoriented for a moment, then spots me by the door. "Lydia! What a surprise!"

"Yes. Um. Benedetta called me. Said she needed someone to watch Julia...Are you okay?"

"Oof. I look a mess, don't I?" She sits up in bed, gaining some color to her cheeks, and makes a halfhearted attempt to calm her wild curls. "I can't even imagine the state of the house. Although I can smell it."

She tidies up the mess of coloring books and dishes around her.

"What happened?" I ask.

She stops tidying and looks at me.

"Nico didn't mention it?"

"Nico and I haven't...We're not really...No. He didn't mention it."

Her eyes open in surprise, but she covers it with a smile. "I broke my leg last week."

"In three places!" Julia chimes in.

"Oh no! How?"

She waves a hand. "Work accident. I'm out for the next two months."

"Two months?"

"I had surgery yesterday, and I'm still taking the pain meds, which is why I look like death."

"Look at her cool cast!" Julia pulls the blanket back revealing a three-piece cast that starts midcalf and disappears under Gloria's nightgown. Small metal rods attach each piece to the next so they don't move.

I cringe in second-hand embarrassment, but Gloria laughs, unfazed by the lack of privacy.

This is what having kids does to you.

"I'm stuck in bed for a month. And then I have a month of rehab before I can go back to work."

"Nico does Mama's job now," Julia volunteers.

"Nico's working? What about school?" There's a weight in my stomach like I've eaten a bowling ball.

Gloria doesn't meet my eyes. "My boss Enzo wouldn't hold my spot for me. He said he'd have to hire someone to replace me, and then I wouldn't be able to come back in two months." Gloria's shoulders slump in defeat. "Nico volunteered to take my spot until I can go back."

"I thought he was graduating in a few months."

Tears trickle out of Gloria's eyes. "He'll have to repeat the semester. He'll still graduate, just a little later." She meets my eyes like she's begging me to understand her. "I didn't want him to do it. I know how much he loves school. But we need to pay rent and buy groceries. I need a job to go back to when I get better."

"Your employer can't do that," I say, furious.

She shrugs like all the fight's gone out of her. "We just need to get by for two months."

I nod, but my brain is churning.

This isn't right.

"How exactly did you break that leg?" I ask.

She winces as though embarrassed. "The industrial dishwasher came unlocked from its position and ran me over. I should have gotten out of the way, but my hands were full of trays, and there wasn't a lot of space."

My mouth drops open. "You've got to be kidding me. Your injury was their fault!? And they won't hold your position for you? Please tell me they're paying the medical bills?" I'm not a doctor, but I know surgery doesn't come cheap.

Gloria looks away. "Enzo said it was my fault for being in the way."

I'm speechless.

"We do *not* like that guy," Julia fills in.

My hands clench in anger, nails digging crescents into my palms. Gloria should not be in this position. And neither should Nico, having to quit school to support the family. And neither should Benedetta, having to take over as mom.

Gloria must see the fury burning in my eyes because she reaches for my hand. "It's okay. Sometimes things just go that way. We'll be fine. I promise."

I nod, but I'm not agreeing with her. I'm making plans.

"You hungry, Julia?" I ask, and she nods.

"Let's get a snack and let your mom rest."

Gloria smiles gratefully, and I close the door behind us on our way out. In the kitchen, I navigate around an overflowing trash can and a pile of shoes to get to the fridge. There's not much in it. I slice a mealy apple, then cut some rubbery cheese and crusty bread that flakes onto the counter.

Julia eats while I pull out my phone. "Julia, do you know your mom's phone number?"

She gives me a funny look. "Why don't you go in her room if you want to talk to her?"

"I don't want to bother her."

Julia recites the phone number, and I add Gloria to my contacts. Then I use the last four digits of her number to verify the correct Venmo. Once I'm sure it's the right Gloria Moretti, I send $4,000 to her account. That should cover rent and groceries until I can get this situation fixed.

The sink is overflowing with dishes, and piles of laundry have accumulated on the couch. The next thing we need is a cleaning service. I scroll through the ones nearby, and find one with great reviews, but before I can call, my phone rings.

"Hello," I say, pushing a pile of papers toward the trash can with my toe.

"Hello, Lydia St. Clair." I recognize the voice of Richard Stevens, our family accountant. He's the only person I know who insists on calling me by my full name.

"Hello, Richard Stevens."

"I'm calling about the $4,000 you just pulled from your account."

Wow. I knew my spending was being monitored, but this is fast.

"Yes, I pulled $4,000 from my account." I'm not giving away additional information for free.

"May I ask why?"

"You may ask."

A sigh of exasperation comes through the phone. "Must we play these games?"

"I needed it for a friend," I say.

"I see."

I truly doubt that, but I don't care if he understands or not. It's my account. When he doesn't say anything else I say, "It's been nice catching up, Richard, but I'm in the middle of something, so I'm going to let you go."

"I'm afraid I need to suspend access to your account."

"What?"

Richard has never done anything like that. Even when I flunked out of college nobody suspended access to my bank account.

"I've just spoken to your father, and he feels you're spending a little too freely at the moment."

"Too freely? I'm—"

"He's asked that I amend the account to allow monthly withdrawals of no more than one hundred dollars."

"A hundred dollars? For the month?!"

That's less than I spend on Ubers for the month.

"You are working, are you not?"

"Yes, but the pay isn't—"

"I'm sure you'll find a way to make it work." Richard has the extremely annoying habit of interrupting me, and I'm ready to throw my phone against a wall. Since I have no money to replace it, I just kick a pile of blankets instead.

"It's been a pleasure speaking with you, Lydia St. Clair." And then he hangs up.

I sink down on a chair piled with laundry and drop my head into my hands.

Am I going to have to take the bus to work? What about my monthly pedicures? And how am I going to pay the cleaners?

A quick check of my Venmo account shows that the money I sent Gloria made it through, and I breathe a sigh of relief.

Then I look at the sink overflowing with dishes.

"Julia, does Benedetta have an old T-shirt I could borrow?"

I may wreck my manicure, but I refuse to sacrifice my vintage Valentino blouse to whatever is lurking in that sink.

An hour later, after the dishes are clean, I take a breather to regroup. Under the sink I find a bottle of green liquid. The label shows a mop and a smiling woman; two things that do not go together. I pour a generous amount on the cheap linoleum floor, releasing a piney chemical scent that almost overpowers the lingering stink of sour milk and old socks.

By the time Benedetta comes back with Cami, I've finished the floor and wiped the counters. My nails are shot, and I do *not* smell good.

"How did the doctor go?" I ask.

"The worst," Cami says.

"She has an ear infection," Benedetta says. "But we got some antibiotics, and it should clear up in eight days." She glances around the kitchen in awe. "Did you do all this?" She examines me closer. "And is that my T-shirt?"

"Yes and yes," I say.

"I helped!" Julia pipes up next to me.

The shock on Benedetta's face is clear. Honestly, I'm as surprised as she is. I've never cleaned a kitchen in my life. And I may have used oven cleaner to clean the counters, but they look better than they did before.

With Benedetta's help, we do a load of laundry and clean the living room. The smell is mostly gone, but I find a scented candle under the bathroom sink and light it anyway.

I need to leave to pick up Isa, but I need information first.

"What is the name of the restaurant where Gloria works? And her boss's last name?"

"We hate that guy," Cami says with a scowl.

"It's Tavola Grande," Benedetta says. "And Enzo's last name is Malfatto."

Despite Gloria's claims, they are not fine. Nico dropping out of school to work breaks my already broken heart.

"I thought you and Nico were still together," Benedetta says, sounding flustered, "I wouldn't have called you."

"I'm glad you did." I give her a hug.

"I can't believe you cleaned our whole house when you're not even dating my brother anymore," Cami says.

"Yeah, what's Nico going to think?" Benedetta's forehead creases with worry.

That I've lost my mind. That I'm helping his family in an attempt to get back together with him. That I can't tell oven cleaner from floor cleaner.

Honestly, I have no idea.

"For now, let's just not tell Nico," I say, grabbing my purse to go.

"What aren't we telling Nico?" says a deep voice behind me. I freeze.

"We're not telling you that Lydia came over today and babysat Julia and cleaned our house," Cami says. "We thought you might think it was weird because you two aren't dating anymore."

Nico opens his mouth, closes it, then opens it again. "You came over to watch Julia?"

"Benedetta had to take Cami to the doctor," I say defensively. "And your mom needed to rest."

"Ear infection," Cami adds helpfully. She's perked up in the last two minutes. I think she feeds off other people's drama.

"I see. And you..." His eyebrows drag together as he takes in the clean house. "Cleaned the house?"

"Yes."

"She looked up how to wash dishes on YouTube," Julia says from the couch.

Isn't everyone in a sharing information mood?

"I figured it out," I say, cheeks heating.

"After you watched it three times," Julia says with a giggle.

Traitor.

"Anyway. I'm leaving." I turn to Nico. "But I'm coming back tomorrow because I told Benedetta I'd pick Julia up from school."

Benedetta shoots Nico a sheepish look. "I got in trouble on Friday for leaving early."

"I can pick her up," Nico says.

Benedetta shakes her head. "You're on lunch shift tomorrow. You won't be done until after 5pm."

Nico rubs a hand down his face. It's obviously killing him to accept help from me. Which I get. It's super awkward to break someone's heart and then have them show up unexpectedly in your living room.

"It's not a big deal," I say. "Her school isn't that far from Isa's, and I'll take her to the park with us. I'll drop her off after five."

"Thanks." He doesn't quite meet my eyes.

"*Di niente*," I respond. And then I get out of there as quickly as I can.

Chapter Forty-One

The next night is slightly less awkward. Isa and Julia spend a happy afternoon at the park, leaping around the jungle gym like flying squirrels, and I drop Julia off at 5:15pm.

Nico's already home when I get there, and Benedetta's in the kitchen cooking something that fills the apartment with the tantalizing aroma of sauteed onions and spicy sausage.

"Do you want to stay for dinner?" she asks.

"It smells delicious, but I need to get Isa back home."

And I don't want to make things weirder than they already are.

Before leaving, I peek into Gloria's room. She's reclined on the bed, talking on the phone, and waves at me with a tired smile.

"She looks better today than she did yesterday," I tell Nico in the hall.

"Yeah," Nico says absentmindedly.

"How are you?" My chest flutters nervously, like I'm breaking the rules by asking. I'm supposed to pretend I don't care about him anymore.

He nods, as though that answers my question.

"How's work?" I ask. This time he meets my eyes, and I can see the fear and uncertainty consuming him.

"I'll figure it out." Apparently, his days of confiding in me are over.

"While you're figuring it out, I Venmo-ed your mom money for rent and groceries for the month."

"I said I'll figure it out." His voice is ragged with worry.

"I'm sure you will. This is to make it easier while you do."

He runs a hand through his hair, the frustrated motion matching the helpless flicker in his eyes. "I don't want you paying our bills."

"And your mom doesn't want to be stuck in bed. Call it a loan if it makes you feel better. You can pay me back by building me a bridge sometime."

I grab Isa and leave before he can argue any more.

Isa and I pick up Julia every day that week. Sometimes we play at the park. Other times, we return to the Moretti's apartment, and I clean while the girls entertain Gloria, their voices high and sweet as they belt out Disney songs.

I'm getting better at the cleaning, figuring out which sprays are used for what. I won't say I enjoy it, but there is something oddly satisfying about scrubbing peanut butter off the counter. I haven't ventured into the bathroom yet, nor do I intend to. But I'm doing a decent job maintaining the kitchen and living room.

"You don't have to clean our house," Nico says this evening when he gets home. His eyes are tired and there's marinara sauce down one pant leg.

"Who's going to do it?" I respond. "The girls have homework, and you're too exhausted from working full-time, taking care of Gloria, and being a single parent."

Julia and Isa are putting on a puppet show for Gloria, and Cami and Benedetta are studying in their bedroom, so it's just me and Nico in the living room.

"Listen, I want to talk to you about something," I say.

A dozen emotions flit across his face.

He thinks I mean us.

My skin prickles in embarrassment and I rush to clarify. "It's about your mom."

"Is she okay?" Nico asks, glancing at her closed door.

"She's great. I've never met anyone as tough as your mom. But what happened to her isn't fair."

"Yeah, well, life's not fair. Not a lot you can do about it." The bitterness in his voice surprises me. I've never heard him like this.

"There *is* something you can do about it," I insist. "I talked to a family friend who's a personal injury lawyer. He says your mom's injury was a result of negligence on the part of her employer. Enzo should be paying her medical bills, as well as compensating her for lost wages."

"This isn't America," Nico says. "We don't just sue people."

"Well maybe you should! You have a strong case." I grab a folded slip of paper from my purse. "The lawyer's name is Brandon Dayley. Here's his number."

Nico doesn't say anything, but he takes the paper, and I collect Isa and go.

A week later, Julia and Isa are on the couch watching *Moana*, while I fold a pile of laundry. I don't actually know how to fold laundry, so I mostly sort it into uneven piles of worn polyester and wrinkly rayon.

As soon as I get access to my bank account, I am buying these girls some quality clothing.

Nico walks through the door and throws his arms around me, sending my nervous system into overdrive.

What is happening? How does he smell so good? Can I stay in his arms forever?

His usual citrus scent is mixed with tomato sauce, and my body relaxes into him, not knowing or caring why he's hugging me.

"I'm sorry." He steps away abruptly, and I miss him so much my body aches. "I just—" His eyes are shiny, but he's smiling. "I just got off the phone with Brandon Dayley. His office reached out to Enzo and when I went into work today, there was a check waiting for me." He lowers his voice. "It's more than my mom makes in a year." Joy and disbelief dance in his eyes.

A huge smile spreads across my face. "Wow. It usually takes months for everything to get filed and move through the legal system."

Nico shakes his head. "I don't think anything was filed. It sounded a lot more like blackmail. Brandon told Enzo that if Gloria wasn't fairly compensated, they'd go after him for health code violations, old sexual harassment cases, discrimination. Enough to put him out of business."

"So, he did the smart thing and wrote a check," I guess.

"Brandon said it took some convincing. Your dad got on the phone and let Enzo know it would not be wise to invoke the wrath of an American senator."

Wow.

I'm surprised my dad got involved. It reminds me of before the election when he cared more about righting wrongs than campaigning.

"Does that mean you're going back to school?"

Nico's smile grows brighter. "I called my advisor on the way home. I've only missed two weeks, so he's going to explain the situation to my professors. He thinks with some hard work, I'll be able to catch up and graduate on time."

I want to throw my arms around him, but I'm not sure if I'm allowed to, so I wrap them around my own waist.

"That's amazing news, Nico, I'm so glad."

"Me too." He looks at me and reaches out a hand but drops it at his side. "Thank you. I'm going to tell my mom the good news."

I tear Isa away from her movie, and we head to the door, just catching Gloria's whoop of joy bouncing through the apartment.

The weather warms up, and my days fall into the same routine: drop Isa at school, go to the studio, pick up Isa and Julia and take them to the park, then go to the Moretti's apartment.

Since Nico isn't working at the restaurant anymore, he could technically pick up Julia from school. But I know he's frantically trying to catch up on all the schoolwork he missed. I told him I could pick up Julia for the next two weeks so he could stay on campus and study.

Gloria is going crazy stuck in bed, so sometimes if I get the house cleaned quickly, I hang out with her in her bedroom until Nico gets home. She asks questions about fashion and listens while I talk about the designs we're working on in the studio.

I ask her if she'd consider going back to school before rejoining the workforce, and she lights up talking about how she always wanted to be a teacher. A year ago, I wouldn't have understood her enthusiasm, but now I get it. When there's something you're passionate about, it doesn't feel like work.

This afternoon was Gloria's last doctor's appointment, and she and Nico arrive home with good news. All three fractures have healed, and she's cleared to resume normal activities, with physical therapy twice a week.

Which means I'm cleared to go back to my regular life.

Benedetta and Cami cooked a special dinner to celebrate and invite me to stay.

I shake my head. "Isa and I need to get back."

Gloria limps across the room, right hand gripping a cane and pulls me into a one-armed hug. She's shaky on her feet but squeezes me with unexpected strength. "I cannot thank you enough for everything you've done for my family." She kisses my cheeks, her tears wet on my face.

"I'm so glad you're doing better," I say.

"You're going to keep coming over, right?" Cami asks.

"It's time for me to get out of your hair." I smile, but it doesn't feel right. "You guys don't need me anymore." My throat tightens, and my eyelids get hot.

"I need you." Nico stands by the door staring at me with a gaze so intense I'm pinned to the spot.

"Nico, I—" I shake my head. "As much as I'd like to stay friends, I can't. It's too hard for me." The admission costs me, and tears fill my eyes, threatening to spill.

"I don't want to just be friends," Nico says, taking a step toward me.

My eyes don't leave his, but in my peripheral vision, I see Gloria shepherding the four girls into the kitchen and limping in after them.

"I couldn't have made it through the last month without you," Nico says. He takes my hand. "I can never repay you for what you did for my family."

I pull my hand back. "I didn't help your family to win you back. You don't owe it to me to date me."

Hurt flashes across his features. "I know that. I want to be with you, Lydia." His eyes lock on mine, open and vulnerable. "I never stopped loving you."

My heart leaps in a dizzying rush of joy, but my stomach twists, uncertain.

"What about all the stuff you said before? About me leaving?" It hurts remembering his words. Feeling their truth.

"I was wrong," he says, taking my hand again. "You showed up, Lydia. Caring for my mom and sisters and doing all our dishes? That was hard. And you didn't leave. You showed up for the people you love."

I want this. I want this so bad it hurts, but I've spent months telling my heart this wasn't going to happen, and now it's confused.

"What if you change your mind?" There's a tremble in my voice, and I hate it, but I have to know.

Nico shakes his head, a smile tugging at his lips. "I fell in love with you the moment I met you. And that never changed. I'm sorry I didn't trust you before. I know I have issues when it comes to people leaving. And I didn't want to get my heart crushed when you left again. But seeing you come to this apartment every day for a month...I'm not worried anymore. I know that if you want to make this work, you have it in you to make it work."

He licks his lips nervously and squeezes my hand. "So, I guess I just need to know, is this what you want?"

Every cell in my body screams, "YES!"

I look into his eyes, remembering his goofy sense of humor when he pinned tassels to our elbows, his patient encouragement helping me with my application, the way my whole body pulses with excitement every time he touches me. Somehow, in this city I never wanted to come to, I found the man for me.

"This is what I want," I tell him, throat tight.

A smile grows on his face, his dimples greeting me like old friends, and he pulls me into his arms.

"Me too."

"Kiss her!" Julia calls from the kitchen, and any illusion we had of privacy is shattered. Nico looks at me, and I tip my face to his. Our lips meet —soft, certain, electric—and time slows. The steady thrum of our heartbeats drowns out the rest of the world. Warmth spreads through me, carrying with it the certain knowledge that no matter what it takes to be with Nico, I am all in.

There's hooting and hollering from Nico's mother and sisters, and I'm pretty sure that wolf whistle was from Isa. I break away and smile at him.

"Can I take you out for a real date later tonight?" he asks.

"Yes, please," I say.

And then I kiss him one more time, long and deep. A sweet certainty fills me up from my toes to my scalp—my running days are over, because I've finally arrived.

Epilogue

Six Months Later

"You're squishing me," Carmen says, shifting noisily in her seat. Her arm sticks uncomfortably to mine and the air in the car is thick with warm bodies. I roll down my window, letting in a cool October breeze along with the honking horns and squealing tires of Milan traffic.

"Why didn't we take our own Uber?" Nico fake whispers.

Paolo glances at Nico in the rearview mirror. "Because you love our company."

Valentina taps her phone's map. "We're almost there."

Street parking offers few options, but Paolo aims the car into a spot meant for a Vespa. I brace for the sound of metal against metal, but somehow, miraculously, he fits us in without a scratch.

Cool night air hits my arms as we tumble out like clowns from a clown car. Carmen rubs her ribs dramatically, and I give her an extra poke. "You're fine."

"That was an excellent parking job, *amore*." Valentina kisses Paolo's cheek.

Nico snakes an arm around my waist, tugging me closer.

Carmen groans, exasperated. "I'm going to kill Luca."

She's been dating a guy from Paolo's work for the last four months, but he's out of town, and Carmen may never forgive him for making her a fifth wheel tonight.

"If he'd come, we wouldn't have all fit in Paolo's car," Valentina says.

Carmen nods. "Exactly."

"Let's go. I want a good seat." I grab Nico's hand and pull him toward Isa's school.

My phone rings just as we get to the doors, and I motion my friends to go in without me. Nico glances at the name on my screen.

"Want me to stay?" he asks.

"That's okay, I'll meet you inside."

He darts in and kisses my cheek, then holds the door for Carmen and follows her inside. I punch the green button on my phone.

"Hi, Dad."

Our relationship has grown a lot over the last six months. He was furious when he found out I enrolled in the Milan Institute of Design. But I think deep down, he's proud of me for forging my own path. He reinstated my allowance and calls every couple of weeks to check in.

"How's my famous fashion designer?" he asks, voice booming over the line.

That may be the other reason for the thaw in our relationship. Three of the designs I submitted for school went viral on Instagram and garnered some international press. My father respects success, no matter the field.

"I'm doing great, Dad. How are you and Mom?"

Right after Nico and I got back together, I had a candid conversation with my mother about my father's cheating. She got angry and then sad, but a month later, she said they'd started couples counseling once a week. I'm hopeful for them.

"We're doing pretty good. Talking about heading to Italy this Christmas."

"Oh yeah?" I try to keep the surprise out of my voice. Chatting every few weeks is one thing, but doing Christmas together is an entirely different outfit.

"I know we usually do Tuscany in the spring, but we thought we'd try Milan in winter." He clears his throat. "Your mom misses you."

Maybe I could even get Robby to come out. He could definitely use the break.

"I'd love to spend Christmas with you guys." Thinking about my family squishing into the Moretti's tiny apartment makes me smile. I'm sure we'll end up in whatever penthouse apartment my father rents. And honestly, I wouldn't mind a little luxury for the holidays.

"Perfect, if you'll send your school calendar to Karen, she'll book the flights around your break."

"Sounds good, Dad."

"Talk to you soon."

I hang up, excitement and anxiety creeping up from my toes. Christmas could very well be a disaster. But...it might also be okay. I'm weirdly excited to introduce Nico to my parents.

I push my way through the heavy school doors. The auditorium crackles with conversation and crinkling candy wrappers. The lights are bright overhead and even though we're twenty minutes early it's packed. Nico waves from the third row, where the four of them are sitting with Marco and Sofia.

"How is she doing?" I ask Marco, settling into a seat between him and Nico.

"Nervous."

"And the dress?"

"It's perfect."

"You don't think I should have—"

"It's perfect," Marco repeats with an exasperated smile.

Isa spots us and leaps off the stage. Her red velvet cape swirls behind her, silk trim catching the light like rippling water. I want to look at the ruffled hem, but it's hard when she's running.

"You came!" she says.

"Of course I came!" I answer.

Nico nudges me. "I think she was talking to me." Isa gazes at him with adoring eyes, and I shake my head. She's almost as in love with him as I am.

"You look great," Nico says, and she beams.

"Now get back up there," I tell her. "Or they'll start without you."

"They can't start without me. I'm the lead."

"So glad that didn't go to her head," Nico whispers as she scampers away.

Carmen leans over Paolo and Valentina to call down to me, "The outfit looks amazing!"

"*Grazie*!" Pride flares in my chest. Even if it is for a second-grade play, it's some of my best work.

The lights dim, and we watch a bunch of eight-year-olds perform *Little Red Riding Hood*. Isa is hilarious and dramatic, nailing her lines and garnering a standing ovation at the end.

When the lights come up, we gather our things and Isa barrels into me, arms flung wide, smelling like stage makeup and biscotti. I hug her tight and kiss her forehead and tell her how great she did. She graciously acknowledges that the costume I sewed was part of her success.

I lean in to kiss Marco and Sofia goodbye, and notice a young redhead, half-hidden behind Sofia. Her hands hang stiffly at her sides, and her freckled cheeks are flushed.

"You must be the new nanny," I say to her in English.

"I am." She offers a shy smile.

"My name is Lydia."

"Emma."

"Great to meet you, Emma." I tip my head back to acknowledge Nico, Valentina, Paolo, and Carmen. "We're going out dancing this Wednesday. Want to come?"

She answers, "Yes," before the words are even out of my mouth.

"Great answer. I'll come by and pick you up." I plant two kisses on her cheeks. "Welcome to Italy. You're going to love it here."

Thank you for reading! Did you enjoy? Please add your review because nothing helps an author more and encourages readers to take a chance on a book than a review.

And don't miss more in the *Ciao Bella* series by Libby Tanner coming soon, and sign-up for the newsletter at www.libbytannerauthor.com

Until then read THE ONLY CATCH by City Owl Author, Jess Turner. Turn the page for a sneak peek!

Also be sure to sign up for the City Owl Press newsletter to receive notice of all book releases!

Sneak Peek of The Only Catch

BY JESS TURNER

For Chloe Foster, life both ended and began with the broken lock on the office door.

Earlier in the evening on that particular Friday, dinner service at Redbud was a meticulously controlled chaos. Chloe had been the executive chef for almost three years, and as *Food & Wine* had recently declared, the Chicago restaurant was having a moment. Reservations were booked for six months straight, the hostess phone ringing nonstop with hopeful pleas of anniversaries and date nights, marriage proposals and 50th birthdays.

Chloe was unaffected by the hype, the clamor for tables. She was unmoved by the fact that every Chicago magazine had declared her the "chef to watch" based on her vibrant, modern plates and almost religious devotion to local, seasonal ingredients. For her, it was always about getting food from the kitchen to the table with efficiency and flawlessness. She was a technician.

"One swordfish, two pork bellies, one ribeye mid-rare, one ribeye medium!"

Her expediting voice had taken practice. Too soft, and the sous chef and line cooks would think she was asking. Too loud, and it sounded like she was competing with other sounds in the kitchen. She'd made it very clear that in her kitchen, her voice was the only sound that mattered.

"One citrus and fennel, two arugula, one chard!" Medium volume and always unwaveringly steady.

Servers were in and out, picking up plates at the pass. A flame raged a little too high, and a grill cook barely blinked while he used one hand to smother it with a pot lid, while the other hand sautéed tiny cubes of celeriac for the winter root hash. The kitchen was full of the sounds that Chloe loved most—the hiss of a steak hitting a cast-iron pan, the rhythmic chopping of tarragon and sage, bourbon being added to a reduction, and the *fwwwwoooomp* of the flame as it caught.

A server presented a steak to her. "Too rare."

The chef gently poked the top of the perfectly cooked meat with her middle finger, declaring it medium, just as it had been ordered.

"Re-fire steak!"

The diners were always right, even when they were wrong.

She used the corner of her towel to wipe a speck of clementine reduction from a plate of seared scallops, paper-thin slices of beets, and smoked pistachios. She pinched her tweezers to place a tiny tangle of baby pea shoots atop the dish. She sourced the greens from a grower who produced them in a rooftop greenhouse right here in the city.

Out of the corner of her eye, she saw David Newhouse enter the kitchen. With his coiffed hair and Prada suit, shirt slightly open at the neck, he always looked like he was headlining as "rich man" in a play and had been playing the part of the restaurant's owner since its inception. His wealth flowed from his wife, Lila Harris, but he carried himself as if it had always been his own. He had a clichéd obsession with luxury, which translated into pressure for Chloe to add more black truffles to the menu, more foie, more matsutake mushrooms. Recently, he'd tried to coax her to edit her scotch quail egg, the dish that had put both Chloe and Redbud on the map, and gild it with gold leaf. *Gold leaf!* She generally met these suggestions with a flash in her green eyes as she demanded that David concentrate on writing the checks and leave the cooking to her. He was trim, fit, and arrogant, way too tan for winter, almost trite in his sex appeal, and moved through the world with the confidence of someone who had never been asked to wait for anything.

They had been sleeping together for two years.

"Chef," David greeted her with a wide smile. Even his teeth were too white.

"Why is this plate still sitting here?" Chloe demanded, choosing to ignore him. "I sauced this two minutes ago. It should have hit the tablecloth three minutes ago, max!"

"Table eight keeps changing their mind about entrees after they've been ordered," a food runner replied.

"Well, congratulations to table eight! Get this damn plate off the pass then!" Chloe snapped.

David calmly cleared his throat and placed his hand lightly in the center of the chef's back.

"Can you take a minute to come out and meet someone?"

Chloe used the point of her tweezers to reposition a flake of Maldon salt atop a carefully formed oval of beef carpaccio. Her kitchen sometimes felt more like a lab—precise and sterile. This is what people wanted out of fine dining: tweezer food.

"David, we're really in the weeds in here. Can it wait?"

He responded by cocking his head to one side, his manicured brow arched.

"Fine." She sighed, smoothing the front of her chef coat. She tucked a strand of her short brown hair behind her ear, noting that it had grown too shaggy for her liking. When did people find time to get haircuts?

She followed David through the kitchen's swinging doors and out into the dimly lit dining room. She was always struck by how gorgeous it was, how perfect the temperature was, how the acoustics of the space were so thoughtfully designed that certain sounds were muted while others—like the clink of a champagne toast or the gentle peal of a woman's laughter—rang out softly. A young couple sat side-by-side, their backs to the exposed brick wall, their heads bent low over a shared dessert. The woman closed her eyes and tipped her head back at the first taste of raspberry elderflower panna cotta, a dish that Chloe had finally declared "right" only that morning. Another duo spoke softly to each other over flickering votives, ignoring their entrees completely as the man reached across the table and ran his fingertips across the woman's knuckles.

I don't care if you're on a first date or if he's about to propose. The raviolo needs to be eaten when it's hot! Chloe wanted to scold.

There were only fifteen tables in the small restaurant, all topped with pressed white linens and surrounded by modern, black, ladder-back chairs. Fifteen tables meant long wait lists, constantly filled reservations, and exclusivity—the basis of every restaurant The Harris Group owned.

David adjusted his pocket square and led her to the best table in the house, a two-top positioned against a floor-to-ceiling window, the perfect place to enjoy optimal people watching on Randolph Street. An actress whom Chloe recognized was seated across from a young politician who'd recently achieved notoriety for her fiercely outspoken behavior on the Senate floor. This is what restaurants like Redbud were great at—bringing together seemingly random combinations of people who met to discuss "projects" over their shared love of tweezer food. It was all designed for people who wanted to see and be seen, who would inspire other diners to tell their rich friends, "You'll never guess who I saw sharing a blood orange tart at Redbud!"

"I'd like you to meet the chef, Chloe Foster," David said, his hand still resting on her lower back.

David loved parading Chloe to the tables of VIPs, showing her off to them, showing them off to her. It was his very favorite thing, throwing open the doors to his manor like Gatsby and opening his arms as if to say, "This is mine, all mine, and aren't you lucky to be invited inside!"

When Chloe swiftly and gracefully excused herself, David exchanged air kisses with his guests and followed her through the swinging doors.

Everything on the line was running like the well-oiled machine Chloe had designed herself. Tickets were in order, Chloe's sous chef, Steph, was expediting with confidence, and the plates looked flawless as they left the kitchen, one after another.

"Can I talk to you in the back for a minute?"

This time, David followed her, past the walk-in, through the dry storage, and into the tiny back office. Chloe locked the door with a brittle-sounding snap, and in less than a second, their mouths were on each other. David was an absolutely ravenous kisser. It was the thing that had surprised her the most the first time this had happened two years ago. He looked so proper, so refined, not a hair out of place, but when they were alone, his desire was almost desperate.

"We can't keep doing this," Chloe breathed, David's lips on her neck.

"Why not?" he replied, making quick work of unbuttoning her chef coat and groaning when she drew his lower lip between her teeth.

"Your wife," she offered as an image of icy, beautiful Lila flashed through her mind.

As they kissed, his hands in her hair, under her bra, his fingers sliding down the front of her pants, she wondered for a moment what David and Lila had been like when they'd first met, if they'd shared first dates over candlelight, moony-eyed as the food grew cold between them. Was their passion undeniable? Had they ever discussed children? Had either of them ever given up anything for the other?

"Hmmmm?" David responded, his mouth full of her.

"Your wife," she said again, her half-hearted resolve weakening when she felt his breath, hot in her ear.

"I promise you, the last thing she would notice is what I'm doing."

Chloe backed up against the desk, resisting the urge to sweep the papers onto the floor in cinematic fashion, and sat atop the stack of invoices that she would attend to in the morning. His mouth was everywhere—on her collarbone, her hip, her belly—until finally he was on the floor in front of her, her hands entwined in his hair.

And that's exactly how his wife found them when that lock on the door announced its failure with a sad little click. When Chloe would replay the scene over and over in the coming days, she would blame that broken lock for delivering the most humiliating moment of her life— the moment when she was looking directly into Lila's face for three full seconds while David's head was still buried between her thighs.

Chloe wasn't sure if the "no, no, no, no," that sounded in her ears had actually been spoken aloud or if it was simply a silent, echoed refrain in her own mind. She was, however, sure of what had flashed in Lila's eyes for the briefest of moments. She had seen a tiny flicker of what had looked like hurt, a barely-there twitch at the corner of her lipsticked mouth, before her tight frown had returned.

"Get up, David," Lila said in a voice so calm that Chloe shivered.

David flinched like someone had attacked him from behind, and in that second before he rose from the floor, he looked up to meet Chloe's eyes and she just knew that it—all of it—was over.

Somehow, she finished dinner service. When the final tickets came in, she excused herself from expediting and locked the staff washroom, where she avoided looking at her flushed cheeks and slightly swollen lips in the mottled mirror. She ran her hands under the water and clenched and unclenched her fists, trying to get some feeling back into her trembling fingers.

WHY? she screamed to herself.

David wasn't at all her type. And what was her type anymore? Her sixteen-hour workdays hardly left time for a dating life. But why on earth would she risk it all on *him*, a married man whom she didn't even like that much?

She wondered if Lila was still in the back room, if they had been negotiating, if David had begged, if he'd thought to defend Chloe in any way.

She exhaled slowly and clutched the sides of the small sink. She thought for a moment that if she could just squeeze her shoulders through the tiny window, she could roll out into the alleyway and start sprinting. She could leave the whole mess behind and open a burger shack on a beach somewhere.

"You OK?" Steph asked when the chef eventually returned to the kitchen. Her sous chef was looking at her with deep concern and something else, maybe pity, with a tinge of embarrassment.

"I'm fine," she responded too brightly, faking a half smile for Steph's benefit and summoning every ounce of energy to push her shoulders back. "I'll be fine."

Lila marched through the kitchen and out the side door, David trailing behind her, his head bowed. No one said a word. Whatever agreement the owners had reached about her future, it was painfully clear: this would be Chef Chloe Foster's last night at Redbud.

There was nothing more to do but collect her bag and jacket from the staff coatroom and pause to look around her kitchen one last time. She cleared her throat amidst the din of the breakdown routine, willing her voice to carry over the sound of the flat top being scraped, the counters being scrubbed, the racks of glasses being loaded into the sanitizer.

"Thank you, everyone," Chloe called out. The kitchen fell quiet immediately. "Thank you for...everything."

"Good night, chef!"

"Have a good one, chef!"

"See you tomorrow!"

Chloe held her breath as she walked through the chorus of farewells and see-you-laters from her unknowing team. She squared her shoulders again and willed her neck to support her head as she pushed through the side door to the alleyway. She didn't wait around to hear the words, "pack your knives and leave." She already knew.

It was only when she reached the sidewalk and the frigid Chicago air slapped her across the face with all the cruelty of February that she allowed herself to break down sobbing.

Don't stop now. Keep reading with your copy of THE ONLY CATCH

Don't miss more in the *Ciao Bella* series by Libby Tanner coming soon, and sign-up for the newsletter at www.libbytannerauthor.com

Until then read THE ONLY CATCH by City Owl Author, Jess Turner.

She came to cook. Love was never on the menu.

After a public meltdown torpedoes her culinary career, chef Chloe Foster reluctantly agrees to a hush-hush job as private chef to Hollywood's clean-eating heartthrob, Charlie Davis. But instead of sunny L.A., she's shipped off to a remote island off the coast of Maine. In the dead of winter.

Stuck in a sprawling mansion with a moody A-lister who barely eats, Chloe's hoping to keep her head down, cook her heart out, and regroup. But Charlie turns out to be more complicated—and more tempting—than the tabloids suggest. Then there's the rugged local lobsterman with a quiet strength and a wicked smile, who offers a different kind of heat.

With her career hanging in the balance and her heart pulled in two very different directions, Chloe must figure out what she really wants: the dream job that once defined her, or the messy, mouthwatering life that's taking shape on the edge of the Atlantic.

The Only Catch is a delicious love story with a recipe for heartbreak, healing, and second chances—served with butter and a side of steam.

Please sign up for the City Owl Press newsletter for chances to win special subscriber-only contests and giveaways as well as receiving information on upcoming releases and special excerpts.

All reviews are **welcome** and **appreciated**. Please consider leaving one on your favorite social media and book buying sites.

Escape Your World. Get Lost in Ours! City Owl Press at www.cityowlpress.com.

Acknowledgments

Well team, we did it again. Book number two is out in the world, and the second time around I *almost* felt like I knew what I was doing.

The last year has been a debut author's dream-- book conventions, panels, signing events, podcasts, *checking my book out from the public library.* I feel like a rock star.

Of course, between marketing the first book and writing the second and third, my life is being held together by dry shampoo and granola bars.

Thank goodness I'm married to the greatest human on earth. Thank you, Hubs, for the million ways you love and support me. You are a unicorn, and I'm grateful I get to do life with you.

I had no idea my four children would turn into an undercover marketing team. Thank you Eila, Annabelle, Xander and Gabriella for talking up my books wherever you go. (And to the lady in the hot tub at Myrtle Beach- sorry my children interrogated you about your reading preferences.)

Thank you to my parents, Parkes and Christie Tanner, who make publishing a book feel like being awarded a Nobel Prize. You are exceptional cheerleaders, and my very favorite parents.

Thank you to my siblings for listening, brainstorming, and buying copies of my book for your friends for Christmas. I'm so glad we ended up in the same crazy family together.

To Jamie Fieldsted and Mariah Reid-You are my people. Thank you for making every part of this process- and life in general- better because of your friendship. The heap measure men are exhausted trying to measure all my heaps of love for you.

A big thank you to Tina Moss and Tee Tate and the whole team at City Owl Press for bringing this book into the world.

Thank you to the person at Versace who read this manuscript and gave us permission to use Versace in the title. If you'd like to use the design Lydia creates in chapter 15 for your next runway show, feel free. You're welcome.

To Timothee Chalamet- if you're reading this, I'm surprised and flattered. Thank you for your support. I loved you in Wonka.

A huge thank you to all my author friends who have given me good counsel, celebrated my successes and reassured me that everyone Googles "is my book terrible?" at 2 a.m.

Thank you, Rita Potter and Shalon Atwood, for making this story better and making me a better writer. I am lucky to have you both as critique partners.

An extra loud shout out to the Tanner Tribe for spreading your excitement for my books. You guys are the best. Should we get t-shirts?

To my readers- Thank you for reading, recommending, reviewing, and cheering on my first book. You deserve green lights, the last cookie, and extra fuzzy socks. Writing stories for readers like you is one of the great joys of my life. I can't wait to share the next one with you.

As always, the biggest thank you to my Heavenly Father who has given me so much. I'm doing my best to use those gifts well.

About the Author

LIBBY TANNER grew up in a small town in Northern California that would be charming in a novel but felt suffocating as a teenager. Yes, she left as fast as she could, and yes, she misses it very much.

In college Libby earned a degree in Communications. She wishes she would have studied creative writing instead of playing it safe, but also remembers she had student loans to pay off.

She is the mother of four sweet hooligans and is married to the world's sexiest accountant (the world's only sexy accountant?).

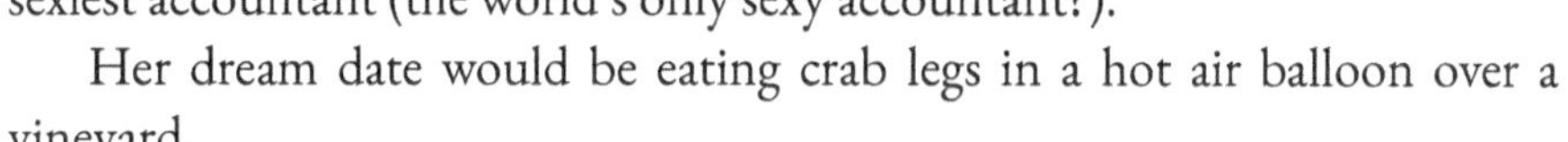

Her dream date would be eating crab legs in a hot air balloon over a vineyard.

www.libbytannerauthor.com

instagram.com/libbytannerauthor

About the Publisher

City Owl Press is a cutting edge indie publishing company, bringing the world of romance and speculative fiction to discerning readers.

Escape Your World. Get Lost in Ours!

www.cityowlpress.com

facebook.com/CityOwlPress

x.com/cityowlpress

instagram.com/cityowlbooks

 pinterest.com/cityowlpress

 tiktok.com/@cityowlpress

www.ingramcontent.com/pod-product-compliance
Lightning Source LLC
LaVergne TN
LVHW091024080826
845145LV00002B/354

* 9 7 8 1 6 4 8 9 8 5 4 8 5 *